A WEDDING AT CAFÉ LOMPAR

A WEDDING AT CAFÉ LOMPAR

Anna and Jacqui Burns

HONNO MODERN FICTION

First published in Great Britain in 2022 by Honno Press
'Ailsa Craig', Heol y Cawl, Dinas Powys, Vale of Glamorgan,
Wales, CF64 4AH

1 2 3 4 5 6 7 8 9 10

A catalogue record for this book is available from the British Library.

Published with the financial support of the Books Council of Wales.

ISBN: 9781912905607 (paperback)
ISBN: 9781912905614 (ebook)

Cover design by Anne Glenn

Cover heading illustrations: shutterstock.com

Text design: Elaine Sharples

Printed in Great Britain by 4edge Ltd

You must do the things you think you cannot do.
Eleanor Roosevelt

To all women everywhere – you're stronger than you think.

CHAPTER ONE

❧ Kat ❧

I caught my reflection in the stainless-steel frying pan and noticed the sheen on my forehead. The lights were so bright and hot, no amount of powder caked on by the make-up artist could stop the beads of sweat showing. I could barely see the audience; they'd dimmed to black shapes behind the glare. I exhaled, trying to keep calm, but I could hear the rush of blood in my ears.

No matter how many times I'd been on TV, it always filled me with nerves.

A cameraman swung the heavy black machine in my direction, paused to look at his screen, then gave me a thumbs up. My segment was next.

'By now you'd have to be living under a rock not to have heard of Café Lompar. The seaside restaurant in Tivat has been making waves in the food scene since they reopened last year, and I'm very lucky to have head chef Kat Lompar here to talk more about it and give us a demonstration.' Lena Simovic strolled confidently across the studio, microphone poised in hand. She was such a skilled presenter, host of Montenegrin's prime-time breakfast show at the age of twenty-five. Her blonde highlights shimmered in the studio lighting, perfectly coifed curls settling at her shoulders. There was no hint of a nervous, shiny forehead on Lena.

1

Behind her, I saw the studio team rush to clear away the last item, an interview with a politician. The man was shaking hands as he was ushered off set. I hadn't listened much, my nerves getting the better of me. I'd done a few interviews by now, but it didn't get easier. I never knew what the interviewer was really interested in: if they'd want to celebrate the food or stick the knife into our family scandals.

We had a moment to get in position while the introduction played. Lena joined my station, a makeshift stand of kitchen units on wheels. She extended a hand in greeting. 'Hi Kat, nice to meet you.'

'Nice to meet you too,' I said, my voice wavering. I shook her hand and noticed she held on a beat longer than necessary. I'd never greeted TV royalty like Lena before. Was I expected to curtsey?

The monitor behind me showed a few pictures of our restaurant, including my favourite shot of our family of four laughing outside on the beach. I smiled, remembering my engagement party last spring.

The cameras panned back to us as Lena said, 'Welcome, Kat, it's a pleasure to have you here.'

'Thank you for having me.' I hoped I'd absorbed some of her confidence in that hand shake. I tried to keep my shoulders back and just ignore the camera, as Mum had told me a hundred times.

'You've had such great success in the last year. Why don't you tell us a bit about Café Lompar and how you came to be there?'

'Well, I used to work as a chef in London, before coming to Montenegro after the death of my father. My mum and I discovered he had another family living here.' I had told this story before and I started to relax, waiting for the familiar gasp of shock from the audience and their pitying expressions. 'Call us crazy or not, but we knew we had to meet them, and so we came to visit my half-brother, Luka, and his mother, Rosa. They owned Café Lompar, they needed a chef, and I started cooking at the restaurant. The rest as they say is history. Now, we're proud of our story and our background; all families are complicated, but love is the most important thing.'

'And good food, of course.' Lena gestured to the screen behind us, where photographs of our food were being shown.

'Of course. I absolutely fell in love with traditional Montenegrin cooking, but wanted to put my own stamp on it. That's my favourite dish.' I saw the orada sea bass with a lemon and wild garlic reduction magnified on screen. 'The flavours are so simple but together they really showcase the amazing fish we have on the Montenegrin coast.'

'Yes, I've heard the fish at Café Lompar is caught locally by a very handsome man.' Lena gave the camera an over-exaggerated wink.

'That would be my fiancé, Milo,' I said, sounding coyer than I'd intended. 'Our restaurant's secret ingredient.'

'From what I hear, *you* are the secret ingredient to the Café's success,' Lena laughed, little dimples appearing in her cheeks.

I was quick to say, 'That's not true. We're a real family-run business. We all listen to each other's ideas and have our own areas of expertise. I'm in the kitchen, Rosa manages the front of house, and my mother Grace works here half the year and runs the marketing from home in Bath in the UK the other half.'

Lena cocked her head to the side. 'So, your mother actually works with your father's mistress? Isn't that awkward?'

I felt my insides churn, that familiar stab. Would we ever get past these digs at our family structure? Sometimes it seemed to be all people wanted to talk about. I wondered if this was another interview where I'd end up talking more about my dad's affair than the food I was so passionate about.

'Not at all. We work very well together, despite our shaky foundations.' I kept my answer clipped, hoping to convey that this was no longer up for discussion.

'And how have you found working with a different cuisine to your home country? Was it a difficult adjustment?' Lena asked.

'My British training and the traditional Montenegrin cuisine blend together more easily than you'd expect,' I said, giving my practised answer about the shared focus in both countries on using supreme local produce and keeping flavours simple. 'Montenegro obviously benefits from the sunshine, though, with beautiful citrus fruit and wine here, and from its location, with the best of both the coast and the mountains.'

Lena was nodding along. I was beginning to feel more relaxed. I'd been on a handful of cooking shows since our restaurant gained popularity, and my cookbook, released over Christmas, had sold really well in Montenegro and across Europe. I still had to pinch myself to believe this was all happening. How much life had changed. I'd gone from being under the thumb of a head chef in London who made Gordon Ramsey look like a kitten, to being head chef myself in a foreign country. I'd also swapped a boyfriend who took me for granted, and was now soon-to-be Mrs. Martinovic.

Would Dad recognise me if he could see me now? It was an unsettling thought.

'You're going to be giving us a demonstration today, aren't you?' Lena asked. 'What are you making for us?'

'My favourite food in the whole country, but with a Café Lompar twist.' I gave a dramatic pause. 'Bureks.'

'I *looove* bureks,' Lena laughed, although looking at her toned physique I guessed she didn't eat them as often as I did. The buttery savoury pastries with meat and smoky paprika had become something of a snacking obsession since I'd moved to Montenegro.

'Well, I'm going to make sweet versions with white chocolate and pistachio. Utterly beautiful.' I smiled. The camera zoomed in on my assembled ingredients. 'I'm going to show you a few shortcuts so that you can make these easily at home, perfect for a lazy Saturday breakfast.'

As I began, I couldn't help thinking about last Saturday, when I'd sat next to Milo on our balcony with a pot of coffee and two steaming bureks between us. We'd started planning our wedding, and I was in my element flipping through a bridal magazine with my feet up on the railings, the palm trees rustling in the breeze and traffic noise mixing with the gentle lap of the sea. Of course, I'd flipped straight to the food section of the magazine, tutting as the menu ideas looked too simple, like a child's birthday party.

I knew the whole family would chastise me for it, but I wanted to cook my own menu. I couldn't have someone else making food for my wedding. We didn't want a big event, just family and friends, so I knew me and Lovro, my trusty sous-chef, could handle it. I was envisaging arancini appetisers, beef in red wine

5

jus, maybe a chocolate fondant. But I was keeping my plans to myself for now. I wasn't ready for Milo's protestations. He'd say I was pushing myself too hard.

Sometimes I was frightened it was true. Recently, being head chef seemed to get harder, not easier, as if I was losing my focus. I was always worried this would slip through my fingers, that it couldn't be real.

I shook myself and got to work rolling out the shop-bought filo pastry for the bureks. Making my own pastry would taste better, but I'd been told by the breakfast show's producers to keep it simple for the viewers. I brushed warm butter along the edge of the dough, before adding my filling and curling it into a snail shape.

'Here's one I made earlier.' I took the tray out of the oven, the smell of pastry and warm nuts filling the studio. I hoped my microphone wouldn't catch the grumble of hunger from my stomach.

'While we tuck in to these, I just want to know,' Lena asked, picking up the tiniest sliver of pastry, 'what's next for Café Lompar?'

'Good question,' I stalled, having never been asked that before. 'This last year has been such a whirlwind, I think we need to keep doing what we're doing. As long as we're making people happy, then we're one happy family.'

In all honesty, we hadn't really thought about what was next. We'd been carried along by the popularity of the restaurant, without much room or time for planning.

'You're not hoping to move on somewhere else?' Lena probed, head tilted to the side. 'A popular and successful chef like you can't be staying in little Tivat forever?'

I wondered what her game was; whether she was hoping I'd stumble and spill some exclusive story. I scratched my ear nervously, and tried to think of something diplomatic to say.

'Café Lompar is my heart and soul. I love working there, we all do. We have big things planned in the future, but my lips are sealed for now.' My stomach flipped. The cookbook and tv appearances were beyond my wildest dreams, but I knew we had no other plans. The success had taken us all by surprise, and I didn't want to run before I could walk.

'You heard it here first, guys, big things planned!' Lena turned to camera. 'Join us after the break when we'll be speaking to a local hero who turned redundancy into triumph when she started a new business selling jewellery.'

I marvelled at how quickly the television presenter façade was lost when the cameras were off. Lena turned to sip water through a straw and simultaneously scrolled through her phone. The mega-watt smile had vanished.

I sighed, glad the heat was off me. I wondered what Mum and Rosa would say about the end of the interview.

As I collected my equipment, a shape emerged from the audience. I grinned, able to make out Luka's face.

'So? What did you think?' I asked my half-brother.

'Do you think Lena's single?' He strode to my side. 'I'm sure I saw her look my way a few times.'

'Luka, we can't see anything from up here.' I gestured out at the studio audience. A few figures had stood up to stretch their legs.

'I know what I saw,' he shrugged, then casually grabbed a burek. 'You'd better introduce me before we leave, the handsome brother.'

'I thought you were here in pure support?'

'Please, I'm just here to ferry you back to work before the lunch time rush begins,' he grinned. It was true, Luka was helping me out while home from uni for the weekend. He leaned against the counter and coughed, angling his body towards Lena.

'You're sickening.' I grinned, as he ran a hand through his hair, quite possibly the cheesiest move I'd ever seen. 'Do you have anything to say about my interview at all?'

'It was good. Very mysterious, though. I'm wondering what these big plans are?'

'Come on, I'm getting you out of here before you start humping the set.' I swung my bag over my shoulder, grabbed his arm and dragged him to the door.

'But Lena? We have time,' Luka protested, clearly loving the limelight on set.

I groaned. 'You know we've got to get back. It's a special night tonight.'

CHAPTER TWO

 Grace

It was only nine thirty and I could already feel the sun burning my shoulders. I was trying to hold the cobra position when a fly landed on my nose.

'Inhale for a count of seven. Feel your shoulders expand as the air fills your lungs. Hold it, hold it.' Milena, the yoga instructor, was incredibly bendy, swapping positions and holding poses as if it were the easiest thing in the world. I had all the grace of a grey seal on a particularly slippery rock. She frowned as she saw me wrinkle my nose. 'And *rel-eeease*.'

I sneezed. Oh, dear Lord, I'd leaked again. I crossed my legs quickly. Milena darted me a disapproving look.

At last, my favourite bit, lying on my fuchsia rubber mat as we wound down and meditated. God bless corpse pose. I could hear the swishing of the Adriatic to my right. Not bad for a Monday morning. No fighting the traffic in Bath, no exhaust fumes. Just me – well, and twelve others – on a beach in Tivat, Montenegro. A place I'd only really become familiar with about a year and a half ago, when Dan died and Kat and I came out here to find his 'secret' family. It still seemed unreal that I had a home out here, a business too.

I picked up my towel, rolled the mat under my arm and headed along the promenade. A few of the locals nodded and greeted me as I passed. A fifty-metre stroll brought me to Café Lompar. I paused. Mine and Kat's restaurant. And Rosa's too.

Most of the time I didn't think about it, but hearing Kat's interview earlier, everyone's fascination with how Rosa and me could work together, had reminded me how I felt when I saw this place for the first time. The business owned by Dan's mistress. When Dan died and I saw those photos... It still had the power to take my breath away. I'm not sure you ever get over a betrayal like that.

It had been more café than restaurant in those days, rustic and rough around the edges. Popular, though, with the locals and passing tourists. Now it was a destination place.

It was already open, and I allowed myself a minute to take it in. Stylish. Classy. The huge bifold windows at the front, offering uninterrupted views of the shimmering Adriatic, were the star of the show. Inside, the thick, maple-wood tables, locally sourced, kept things relaxed in the day and elegant at night, with ivory candelabras and white gardenias on each table. The pale grey granite flooring had cost us a fortune, but had been worth it. We all agreed the impression we wanted to make: a place to enjoy amazing cuisine in laid-back surroundings. My heart skipped a beat. I was proud of it and what we had achieved.

Inside, our staff were working hard. Davor was polishing glasses at the bar, Ana was serving early breakfasters, and Lovro was holding the fort in the kitchen while Kat was away for the morning. Ticking over like a well-oiled machine. Rosa would be in soon, front of house. I wasn't sure how many women would work with their husband's mistress, leave alone invest in her business, as my sister Claire kept reminding me.

'I'd want to throttle her,' she told me only last night when I'd moaned about Rosa changing table decorations again.

'It's water under the bridge now,' I said, which was how I wanted to feel, though it wasn't always easy. I thought about her brush with breast cancer last year. 'She's okay,' I said. 'The restaurant means a lot to her.'

'Ah, yoga,' Mila said, sidling next to me and making me jump out of my skin. She pointed to the mat under my arm. 'It is good for you, no? Help you relax. You are so busy busy busy.' She made a scurrying movement with her hands.

Mila owned Boutique Borozan, a few doors down from Café Lompar. She stocked expensive brands, Emilio Pucci, Cividini and Alberta Ferretti. The clothes she sold were all silk and linen in whites, beiges, ivories and fawns, the palest end of the Dulux Colour Chart. I'd gone in a few weeks ago and the prices were eye-watering. They were all in sizes for minuscule women with microscopic waists, who existed on poppy seeds and celery. I couldn't get a pair of linen trousers past my knees.

I turned to look at Mila, and she smiled. Although in her late sixties, she was effortlessly chic, with bobbed grey hair and ice-blue eyes. 'Yes, I am trying to relax a bit more,' I conceded. 'Difficult with travelling back and fore to the UK.' I suddenly felt quite tired.

'You must keep on top of your game, no? Especially with the new restaurant opening.'

'Yes,' I nodded. 'Wait, what new restaurant?'

'There,' she said, pointing her perfectly French manicured beige nail at the building between Boutique Borozan and Café Lompar.

I shook my head. 'I heard that it's going to be a perfumery. A small artisanal fragrance store.'

She flashed a mischievous smile. 'Those are tables, no? I spoke to one of the builders yesterday. It is going to be a restaurant. A British couple have bought it. I wonder if they will serve a fusion menu.' She was enjoying this a bit too much. I felt sick.

Minutes later, I stood in Café Lompar's kitchen. Kat's sous-chef, Lovro, was serving his minced beef bureks and tiny, delicate *mantije* with yoghurt. It seemed an odd breakfast when I first moved here but the Montenegrins were obsessed with bureks and ate them at all times of the day.

'Lovro,' I said, a bit breathlessly, 'that perfume shop they're opening is not a perfume shop. It's a restaurant. A British restaurant.'

'I know,' he said, placing two plates on the pass.

'And you didn't think to tell us?' I was exasperated.

'My cousin Pajo sold the place. I did not think it would be a problem.' Lovro seemed to have cousins everywhere. 'Don't worry,' he grinned. 'They know nothing. Very inexperienced.'

'I hope you're right. I just wish you'd given us a heads up.'

'Heads up?' He looked puzzled.

'Never mind. How is lunch looking?'

'Busy.'

Hmm, good. This was what success looked like. It might still be early May, with tourists a bit thin on the ground, but locals and people across Montenegro were coming here throughout the year. That's why I could only afford a week or two in the UK before returning for the hectic summer season.

For me, the UK was Willow Cottage in Meadow Ponsbury,

with its gorgeous walled garden. Willow Cottage and the even more gorgeous Neil Hadley nearby. For some inexplicable reason Neil, the golf pro, fancied by all the women at the golf club, fancied me, Grace Lompar. I couldn't imagine myself with anyone after I lost Dan, but Neil had his own pain, having lost his son, and seemed to know exactly when I needed him and when to back off. This time tomorrow I would be on a plane back to the UK and into his arms. Tonight, we had a celebratory night in Café Lompar planned. I just needed to get through lunch service and then I could relax later with friends and family.

That evening, at exactly seven thirty, the sun was setting and Kat was at my door. She looked fantastic in a tomato red jumpsuit and leopard-skin, skyscraper heels.

'Wow, you look amazing.'

'Did you see it?' she asked, kissing my cheek.

'Of course, I saw it. You were wonderful. Confident but not arrogant.'

Milo, Kat's handsome fiancé, stood behind her in the doorway.

'Come on in, Milo,' I urged. 'I'm almost ready.'

Kat reapplied her bright red lipstick in the mirror in the lounge. 'It's so nice not to be the one cooking tonight,' she said. 'Are you sure you don't mind having a meal at Café Lompar?'

'Why would I? It's the best restaurant in Tivat.'

'Montenegro,' Milo grinned.

Bojan and Ivan were cooking tonight, and it would be nice to have Kat's company for a change, if she could resist popping into the kitchen. Rosa and Luka would be there, Lovro and some of Luka's friends. I was only going home for a couple of weeks to sort things out before the summer season started in earnest. Then it would be all hands on deck, as I would be needed front of house with Rosa.

I reached for my handbag from the coffee table and glanced outside, before closing the patio doors to the balcony. I loved this view of Tivat. Fishing trawlers, leisure boats and opulent, gleaming yachts sat cheek by jowl, rising and falling rhythmically in the swell. The Adriatic dazzled as the pink sun slipped behind the Volujak Mountains.

It was only a short stroll to the restaurant. Milo and Kat held hands and I walked beside them. Palm trees along the promenade waved gently in the breeze. You needed a cardigan in the spring evenings, but Kat was oblivious to the cold as she chattered away happily.

Rosa arrived first, joining us at the long table nearest the window. She had an elegant black dress on, and long, silver earrings. She wore her hair short now through choice and it suited her.

'Well done, Kat. You were wonderful this morning. Just perfect and we have had lots of bookings this week already.' She nodded 'hello' and smiled at me.

As I went over to the bar to choose a bottle of wine, I glanced at the gallery of photographs on the wall. We'd covered the wall in family photographs: Dan, Kat and I; Kat's first day in primary school; holiday photographs of the three of us, in Kos, Jersey, the Isle of Wight; Dan with Rosa and Luka, most in Montenegro but then there was Dan with Luka in Berlin. His other family.

The Montenegrins were very traditional in their thinking. Family was everything. It was a real risk displaying these photographs, telling the world that this was us, our messed-up, complicated lives. But it worked and many came to see the restaurant where the wife and mistress worked together, where the half-siblings got along. We were almost as famous for our family as for our food.

Later, I sipped my chilled rosé among the jetsam and flotsam of our discarded plates and empty wine bottles. I loved it here, felt I really belonged. I was going to miss it, but at the same time I couldn't wait to see Neil again. He'd be coming out later in the summer, but just for a short holiday.

Outside, it was dark and the harbour lights cast pools along the promenade. The Adriatic was inky black, and the mountains brooded beyond. I yawned, thinking of my early start. Kat had disappeared, back in the kitchen, no doubt.

'I think I'll make tracks,' I told no one in particular.

But just as I was getting up, Kat pushed through the kitchen doors, her face ashen. In her hand she clutched a colourful flyer.

'What the hell is this?' she asked. '*Ensambla!*' She slapped the flyer on the table, making the plates clatter. 'A restaurant next door. A British restaurant!'

CHAPTER THREE

❦ Kat ❦

'Let me see that!' Rosa got to her feet and took the flyer from my hand. I looked at the calm faces around me: Mum, Milo and Lovro, all sipping serenely from their drinks. I couldn't believe it.

'You knew about this?' I demanded.

Mum shrugged. 'I didn't want to say anything, but it's been on my mind since I saw them decorating earlier.'

'Earlier! Didn't you think it was important to mention?'

'Well, Lovro's cousin sold it.' She sent him a look. 'But he told me not to worry...'

Milo pulled my chair out, ushering me to sit down. I didn't want to and paced to Rosa's side of the table, reading the words again over her shoulder.

'"New British-Montenegrin fusion restaurant coming soon to Tivat. Michelin-starred-standard cooking."' I stopped. 'Michelin starred?'

'It's such an obvious copy.' Luka stood at Rosa's other shoulder, frowning. 'What the hell do they think they're doing?'

'It is pretty damn cheeky,' Mum said. 'A bit desperate, if you ask me.'

'They're next door to us!' Luka was practically spitting. I could feel my heart pounding. I didn't think I'd felt such rage since our last chef, Ivan, threw my recipes in the bin last year.

Perhaps it was the Montenegrin blood in me, but I'd definitely become more fiery since moving out here.

'We need to do something,' Luka said, nodding at me. 'Send them a message. Let them know they have to put a stop to this, or else we will.'

I found myself agreeing, before Milo's voice broke the spell. 'Luka, this isn't the Mafia! No one's sending any kind of message. Can everyone just calm down?'

Perhaps we were over-reacting. Next thing, I'd be following Luka to the restaurant to start a fight.

'What do you think, Rosa?' I asked. This place was her baby. She started it all. Surely, she must hate the thought of direct competition opening up. Next bloody door to us of all places.

'If they want to compete with us, let them try,' she said. 'You'll be better than them, Kat. *Pfft*, we have nothing to worry about.'

'Rosa's right,' Mum said. The two shared a nod. 'Notice it says "Michelin starred *standard*". Not actually Michelin starred. Sounds to me like they're all talk and no game.'

'I hope to God you're right,' I said, finally taking my seat next to Milo. He placed a reassuring hand on my knee.

'It's a compliment more than anything,' he said.

'Milo's right,' Mum agreed. 'We've made such a name here that others are copying us.'

'But we're the originals.' Rosa grinned in triumph.

'What kind of name is *Ensambla* anyway?' Luka was still reading from the flyer, curling his lip.

Lovro asked, 'When are they opening?'

Rosa read from the leaflet, 'One month.' Her expression wavered. 'The same night we're planning our summer launch party.'

I felt a new swell of heat in my chest. We'd been advertising our party on chalkboards outside. It was meant to kickstart the summer season, get the tourist trade flocking in. Ensambla must have seen this.

I caught Mum's eye; she looked a little more nervous now.

I shook my head. 'I don't like this one bit.'

The day after Mum left Montenegro was always a difficult one for me. I loved being able to pop across my courtyard to visit her cosy flat. It was reassuring knowing she was there, knowing she was okay. She was in good hands with Neil, though.

'Are you ready?' I called out to Milo. We'd planned a good distraction for the day, something exciting.

'What time's our appointment?' he asked, grabbing his keys.

'Twelve o'clock.'

He locked the door behind me while I checked my appearance in the porch mirror. I loved having an early season tan, before the real heat kicked in and I had to either stay inside, hermit-style, or apply so much sun cream I looked like a Moomin.

We headed to the sea. Milo's boat bobbed about in the middle of the bustling harbour. Fishermen unloaded early morning stock, the salty scent from their catches making my stomach rumble. Milo clutched my arm as I swung my leg over the edge of the boat and flopped into a seat. How some people managed to do that gracefully I had no idea. I'd been in Montenegro over a year, been out on the boat with Milo countless times, and still

I looked like a baby deer learning to walk. I assumed a relaxed position, hoping no one had seen the flash of knickers under my black maxi skirt.

Milo hopped on with ease, and moved towards the controls. His muscular forearms peeked out from under his blue shirt. He looked like a Dolce and Gabbana advert sometimes, and it took my breath away. I noticed a group of women standing at the edge of the harbour, their eyes drawn by my fiancé. I didn't want to be the jealous type. I wasn't usually, but long hours as a head chef meant I didn't exactly have much time to spend on my appearance. I often wondered if people questioned what Milo was doing with me.

Still, I looked better now than when I worked in a London kitchen. I lacked so much vitamin D there, people often asked if I was feeling ill. I sometimes hated seeing old friends from school, knowing years in the kitchen had done nothing for my complexion or my figure. I clocked their worried glances and fake 'you look good' greetings. Things were different out here; the tan helped, and I didn't have that awful commute. I could cycle everywhere here, when the weather wasn't so hot, which helped counteract my constant baklava and bureks.

But did I measure up to gorgeous Milo? Montenegro's answer to Jamie Dornan?

He smiled down at me. 'Are you ready?'

I nodded.

'Let's go to our wedding venue!'

The journey to Ostrvo Cvijeća took no more than a few minutes in Milo's speedboat. It still gave me a thrill when he went full throttle, the smack of the boat against the waves spraying sea-water up onto my face. I shrieked and ducked and Milo laughed good-naturedly.

The small island sat like a jewel in the heart of the bay of Kotor, peeking out of the blue Adriatic just opposite Tivat. The 'Island of Flowers' was no more than three hundred metres wide, and housed a few stone villas and an old monastery. We could see the tear-drop-shaped island from our bedroom window, and I loved the thought of us getting married among the cypress trees, looking back across the bay to the magical place I'd called home for the last year. Tivat held Café Lompar, our villa, my Montenegrin family.

As we pulled up to the pebbly shore, I felt a tingle on the back of my shoulders and neck. I knew instantly it was the right place for our wedding. Milo met my eyes, a small smile on his face.

'What do you think?' he asked.

'It's beautiful!'

There were potted flowers in rainbow-coloured displays lining the small road on the sea front. I'd never given a thought to the small community of less than a hundred people who lived here and kept it so well maintained. Although they were connected to the mainland by a narrow isthmus, it still felt so cut-off, a world away from busy Tivat with its designer shops and tourist traps; an idyll. It was silent as well – no need for traffic or roadworks here. My eye was drawn to the monastery that had stood in place since the thirteenth century.

Everything seemed so ancient and unspoilt that I laughed in surprise when a pot-bellied man on a stand-up paddle board glided serenely past us. He gave a little wave, before moving on unhurriedly. Milo waved back before shouting, 'Morning, Akso!'

'Are you serious?' I asked him. 'Do you know everyone in this country?'

'There are only...' He pretended to count on his hand. '...six hundred thousand of us. So pretty much, yes. But I don't know him.' He had a wicked glint in his eye.

I hit Milo on the arm. 'Come on, we're going to be late.'

We wandered along the small lane to a dusty building with a flowered archway covering the door. The sign said 'Villa Anika'. I recognised it immediately, having spent countless nights researching venues. Villa Anika had stood out: an old stone villa with a charming reception hall and beautiful garden. But now I was here I could see the pictures online really didn't do it justice.

'Oh my God,' I breathed as we pushed open the door to the welcoming hall.

'Hello!' An older woman with black hair pulled back in a bun rushed over to greet us. She found our names on the list on her clipboard. 'Milo and Kat? Ah, yes. Welcome to paradise!' She swept a hand in an arc. 'I'm Nina, and I will show you round today. We hope you'll choose our beautiful venue for your special day. The perfect place to start a forever together.'

I wondered if the people in the wedding business ever got bored of the sales patter and commercialisation of romance and marriage. I'd already been shocked by the additional money businesses would charge for things when it was for a wedding: cakes that cost five times what any other cake would be, and flower arrangements with astronomical price tags just because they had the word 'bridal' in front of them. Everything was either 'special' or 'precious' or 'romantic'. The insincerity churned my stomach at times.

No amount of commercial nonsense could dull the shine of Villa Anika though. The old stone building was lit by tiny lanterns dotted around the room. Pale pink curtains lined the route as Nina led us down to the reception hall, which was a gorgeous space. Milo squeezed my hand, pulling me close to him. He whispered in my ear, 'I think I want to marry you here.'

I leaned into him, feeling his breath against my cheek. 'I can imagine you standing there, waiting for me to walk down the aisle.'

He grinned, holding my hand to his chest.

Nina had clocked it all of course, her eyes lighting up at the money coming her way. I coughed, trying to regain my composure.

'I like it,' I said coolly, although inside I wanted to dance. It was like something out of a fairytale.

Nina guided us through the doorway to the outside, where a stone path led to a platform on the edge of the island. Standing on it, the expanse of blue and rising mountains wrapped around us in every direction.

'Some people choose to get married out here, of course. We can set up an altar and chairs however you'd like.'

'I think I'd like that very much,' I said to Milo, taking it all in.

'It's even more beautiful in the evening,' Nina added. 'Especially in September when you want to get married. You'll have that dusky pink sunset and the lights along the bay. How romantic!'

I didn't want to be carried away by the sales pitch, but I couldn't help it. I was picturing our first dance here, a band playing traditional Montenegrin music while our close family and friends clinked glasses.

'I'll give you a moment to explore together,' Nina murmured, walking back into the hall. I bet she was going to rub her hands together once she was out of sight, knowing she'd made the sale.

'Look, you can see Café Lompar,' Milo smiled, pointing along the shore to Tivat, a line of buildings like gleaming white beads on a necklace.

'And look, there you can see Luka getting a telling off from Rosa,' I joked.

'I know I'm meant to be all macho about this,' Milo said, leaning against the wall that lined the platform, 'but I have a very good feeling about this place.'

'I guess it's all right, but just to be sure, I think we should practise.' I held out my hand and Milo took it. We swayed from side to side.

'You may now kiss the bride,' he mock-announced, then placed both his hands on my face and pulled me in to him. I melted against his lips, excitement building, knowing that one day we'd be doing this for real. I'd actually be kissing my husband here, in this very spot.

I moved away, gazing into Milo's chocolate eyes.

'I think we'll take it,' I said.

He shrugged. 'I'd better start saving.'

23

CHAPTER FOUR

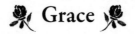 Grace

The hectic departure lounge at Bristol Airport and the mad drive through rush hour traffic stressed me out, as always. So different to Tivat's laid-back lifestyle. But driving into Meadow Ponsbury instantly made me relax again. It was only ten thirty when I pulled into the village and the hawthorn hedges were in full bloom. Willow Cottage was at the end of a row of little terraced houses that looked a cross between *The Vicar of Dibley* and *Midsomer Murders*. I'd only moved in about a year ago and it marked a turning point for me. It was something that I had chosen for myself, a new stage in my life.

I loved this time of year, with optimism filling the air. Burgundy and white, feathery astilbes lined the path to the front door, with delicate potted pink peonies flanking the porch. When I ran my small gardening business, before Kat started school all those years ago, I was obsessive about flowers and plants, and going back to the garden had kept me sane in the early days after Dan died.

Stepping inside, I swept up the flyers and letters that had accumulated in the hallway. The house smelt a bit musty after two weeks away, and I wouldn't be here for long before I'd be flying out to Tivat again. It was hard getting used to flitting back and fore. It wasn't half as glamorous as it sounded. For now, I was grateful to be back and couldn't wait to see Neil later. My stomach did a little flip just thinking of him.

He'd called on the drive home, promised to bring a takeaway. He was thoughtful like that, worlds away from Dan, who always seemed so self-absorbed and distracted. It all made sense when I found out about Rosa and Luka: why he was away so much and why he never felt very present even when he was with me.

The second anniversary of his death was in a few days. When I first learned about Rosa, about six months after his heart attack, I used to have these angry conversations with him. Like a mad woman, I'd say the words out loud in my kitchen in our old house in Bath.

'How could you, Dan?' I would demand, fighting back tears of frustration. 'I thought you loved me.'

I'd imagine him answering me back, making excuses, telling me he cared about me and didn't want to hurt me.

'Bullshit.'

One day, I was shouting at him. 'You humiliated me!' I really got going. 'You spineless, gutless bastard!' I didn't realise my neighbour, Steve, was creosoting his shed until I saw him look over the hedge and rush into his house, dripping paintbrush in hand. His wife, Louise, came over after that on the pretext of borrowing a cake stand and asked if I was okay. It was so frustrating that Dan had gone before I could have it out with him.

I was just filling the washing machine when my sister Claire walked through the door.

'Hi, hon. Welcome home,' she said, giving me a quick peck on the cheek.

'What are you doing here?'

'Charming!' She grinned. 'Shall I leave and come in again?'

'You know what I mean. It's Tuesday morning and you're not in school.'

'I'll get the kettle on, shall I?' Her back was turned to me as she reached for mugs. 'I haven't been sleeping well and I'm shattered. I can afford a day or two.'

'But you're never off school.'

'Did you have a nice time?' Claire asked, in a deft change of subject.

'It was great to see Kat. I miss her so much when she's away. I know she left home years ago, but it's different now. We're closer than we've ever been.' I switched on the washing machine and we both sat down. 'She was on that morning show yesterday. She told me she was nervous, but she didn't show it. I'd be a quivering wreck.'

'I'd love to have seen it.' Claire handed me a coffee. 'Did you get much work done?'

'Not as much as I'd have liked. I was going over the menus with Kat and the other chefs, making orders, looking at some advertising ideas. The cookbook's selling well, too, but we have to keep promoting it. It's hard to fit it all in.'

'Well, you've got quite a nice tan from all that work you've been doing,' Claire teased. 'I might even come out there myself in the half term.'

'You and Stu are always welcome,' I said, almost in reflex. 'What about the twins?'

Claire laughed. 'You must be joking. Laura is crazy about her latest boyfriend and Liam has some project he's working on. He's really enjoying college.' She sipped her coffee. 'It might just be me coming out, actually.'

'Oh?' I started. Claire and Stuart weren't the type to holiday alone. Claire had the odd spa day with friends, and we'd had weekends away together. 'Is everything OK?'

'Course, why shouldn't it be?' Claire answered. 'It's no biggie. I've got a lot of stress on in school and sometimes it's just nice to please yourself. Only for a few days.'

'I'd love you to come out. It's hectic, though. Just getting into the crazy summer season. We're busy now, but it'll be off the scale soon.'

'I can help out,' Claire offered.

'No, you need a break. We'll manage, but I might not be able to spend too much time with you.'

'Reading a novel on the beach, lazy lunches, cocktails in the evening... God, how will I cope?' She laughed. 'Are there any biscuits in this house of yours? Or are you abstaining to keep your figure for the Gorgeous One?'

'There might be some chocolate fingers in the cupboard. I am trying to be good, though. There's nothing like the thought of a new, well, newish, man around to keep you on your toes.' I grinned.

'Well, enjoy it while you can. I think I could walk around the house starkers and Stu wouldn't bat an eyelid.' She rolled her eyes. 'We went out on Saturday night and I bought new underwear, but when we came home, he fell asleep watching *Mrs. Brown's Boys*. I don't know why I bother. I know all his *moves*,' she said, making air quotes. 'A hurried bonk, a fart, roll over and go to sleep.'

'All relationships are like that,' I reassured her. I tried to imagine feeling like that about Neil. I knew I would at some point. I wasn't some love-sick teenager, but I felt that we connected; were friends as well as lovers. 'Why don't you and Stu come over for dinner on Saturday? It'll be a chance for the men to really get to know each other.'

'That would be nice,' Claire said. 'Are you sure, though? I know that you won't have long before you're going back to Montenegro. You must want to spend time together on your own.'

'Come over at eight on Saturday and I'll think of something impressive to cook.' That meant I'd be asking Kat for advice. 'Look, Claire, we all feel like this sometimes. Dan treated me like I was invisible...'

'Well, you can hardly use Dan as a measure. Most husbands don't have other families on the side.' Claire stopped. 'Sorry, I didn't mean that to sound as harsh as it did. I'm just in a bit of a funk, that's all.'

'Funk?'

'Another of Laura's words,' Claire laughed, seeming like her old self again.

When she left, I finished unpacking and had a long bath, with candles and a glass of wine, thinking of the evening ahead and pondering over what to wear. I decided on a green wrap dress that showed off my tan. I was just spritzing on perfume when I heard Neil's key in the lock. I'd given him a key before I left for Montenegro so he could keep an eye on the place. It felt like a big step.

I dashed down the stairs and was swept up in his arms.

'Hello, you,' I said.

'Hmm, hello, gorgeous. You look great.' He kissed me hard on the lips. When we came up for air, he handed me a bouquet of flowers: roses, freesias and gypsophila. He knew I couldn't bear lilies since Dan's funeral. Just a whiff of them and I was transported back to that awful time, those horrible memories.

'I suppose we'd better eat first.' He grinned. 'I've brought Thai.'

'I've missed you.' I said, as he pulled me to him again. I breathed in his sexy, masculine smell. Each time I saw him after I'd been away, I was struck by how good-looking he was: his athletic body; his blue shirt tight over his forearms; his peppered hair and grey-blue eyes; and how totally unaware he was of his effect on women.

We dished out the noodles, chicken larb and an aubergine curry. We ate at the kitchen island, enjoying the informality, drinking Prosecco and catching up on each other's news.

'Cass called last week,' he said, not looking up.

'You didn't mention it.' Cass, his ex-wife, rarely called him.

'It wasn't important. She just wanted to tell me that she and Mike are getting married in September.'

'How do you feel about that?'

I felt the atmosphere shift. 'Fine. Why wouldn't I be?'

'It's just that you were married over twenty years, had two sons. Losing Max – you've been through a lot. It must be a bit strange.' I tried to keep my voice light.

'I guess.' He sipped his wine. 'She and Mike have been together for over three years though.' He smiled. 'And I've got you.'

'I've invited Claire and Stu over for dinner Saturday,' I told him. 'Is that OK?'

'Have you asked Kat what you'll make for us?'

'You know me too well.'

As we filled the dishwasher, Neil said, 'I know it was only two weeks, but it seemed a long time.' He sighed. 'And then you'll be off again.'

I bit my lip. 'You'll come out after the senior series ends.' The summer was a busy time for Neil at the golf club with tournaments, different classes and competitions.

'Course I will. I've booked the time off. I never see enough of you. Perhaps we ought to think about something more permanent?'

'Let's see after the summer. There's so much to think about at the moment.' I wasn't ready for this conversation now. Did he want us to move in together?

Lying next to him in bed later, I couldn't sleep. I didn't know how I felt about Neil moving in. I loved him and we had told each other how we felt. But I was scared. Was I ready to commit?

Part of me wondered whether Cass getting married had pushed him to this. He wanted something more permanent to show her that he had moved on, too. It seemed a long time before I fell into a fitful sleep.

CHAPTER FIVE

🌿 Kat 🌿

Since our visit to the Island of Flowers, I'd thought of nothing but the wedding. I found my thumb scrolling through Pinterest images of wedding dresses, up-dos and flower arrangements when we were sitting in front of the television at night. I couldn't believe I had to wait over five months; it was consuming my life and we'd only just started planning it.

'Shouldn't you be in work?' Milo asked, getting home from a day of tourist trips on the boat. I was jotting down cake ideas, wondering how I could construct a White Forest gateau, a combination Lovro had dreamed up for Café Lompar. We served it in ice cream form, but I was convinced it would work as a wedding cake. White chocolate sponge, cherry compote and caramel buttercream... superb for a fancy centrepiece.

'I'm leaving soon,' I said, putting my pen down. 'I have to be there in ... shit, twenty minutes.'

The afternoon sun was warm on my face as I cycled to the restaurant, feeling the shifting grit of sand in my trainers, left over from the last time I'd had a picnic on the beach with Mum. How different a commute this was to London! I waved at the owner of the little corner shop at the end of our street, and laughed as I caught the strains of a telling-off drifting through the open window of poor Mrs. Jankovic's flat, as she struggled to keep those children under control. I was starting to feel a part of the community here. Although Tivat was often crowded with tourists in the height of summer, it was the locals who kept it pulsating, with – I liked to think – Café Lompar at its beating heart.

I checked the time on my phone as I arrived, happy I could pedal fast enough to make up for leaving late. I could see Dav inside, polishing glasses at the bar. I tied my bike to the little posts along the shore front, taking a moment to glance over my shoulder at Ensambla next door.

The sign had gone up in the last few days, and I was not happy to see how fancy it looked. They'd chosen matt black for the front of the restaurant, with the name in gold leaf font. *Ensambla!* with an exclamation mark. It would make a stark contrast to Café Lompar, with our big windows, rustic tables on the pavement, our wall of photographs. Admittedly, our renovations in the last year had added a bit more elegance, but Ensambla were clearly going full-on upmarket. I scoffed, thinking they'd misjudged Tivat. It was all about sea views, candlelight dinners, fine dining with a more relaxed feel. Their stark, white tablecloths and black-painted wood looked cold, uninviting.

I reassured myself that Café Lompar was beloved – we had a weekly roster of regular customers; 'a real family gem', our most recent review had said. Our beauty was in the casual, cosy feel we created before we wowed customers with our food.

A woman came out of the door to Ensambla, wearing paint-spattered dungarees and carrying a chalk board. I turned away quickly, realising I had been blatantly staring at the restaurant frontage. I busied myself with twisting the numbers on my bike lock.

'It's Kat, right? Kat Lompar?'

Damn it. I'd been spotted.

I turned to see the woman walking towards me, hand extended.

'Hi,' I smiled. 'Are you the new owner?'

'Lizzie.' She took my hand, pumping excitedly. 'Well, yes, me and my husband.'

She had blonde curly hair, cascading from a bouncy ponytail at the crown of her head, and freckles covering her nose. With her nose piercing and leather bracelet, Lizzie seemed a bit too hippy to be opening up that fancy restaurant.

'Here he is now. David!' she shouted.

A man in a white shirt and corduroy trousers came to join us. He shook my hand, his smile a little less wide than Lizzie's.

'So, this is the famous Kat Lompar,' he said.

'I don't know about famous!' I pulled back. 'The place looks great.' I nodded to the newly painted sign.

'I didn't know if the black was a bit stark,' Lizzie said. 'Didn't know if it would look a bit cold. We must have tried about a hundred pots of paint. We had Farrow and Ball shipped over from the UK in the end. David said the street needed something classy, though. I think it looks good, don't you?'

David winced at his wife's chatter, but there was something else in his expression, something I didn't like.

'It looks great,' I repeated. 'What brought you out to Tivat then?'

'I've got some family here and used to visit every year as a kid.

It was my dream to start some kind of business out here. David's the chef though and he's been dying to open his own restaurant abroad, haven't you?'

David barely had time to nod before Lizzie continued, 'He's had such success in the UK, three restaurants in Manchester, but it doesn't compete with this scenery, does it?'

'What kind of cuisine?' I asked him directly.

'In Manchester? We experimented with European-British fusion. Thought it's time fusion was brought to the next level, especially out here.'

'Snap,' I said.

There was that expression again, as if he was looking down his nose at me. Lizzie started chatting about how some of their family would be joining them to help decorate but they'd been delayed at the airport.

'Well, it'll be lovely to have more of a British contingent out here. We'll have to get to know each other. I just hope our fusion cuisine won't be too similar,' I said, laying my cards on the line, and wanting reassurance.

'Oh, it won't be. We wouldn't want to step on the toes of the famous Café Lompar.' David's tone was dismissive.

'We'll make sure of it.' Lizzie's smile was more genuine. 'You've done such incredible things here, Kat.'

'Thanks. I'm looking forward to seeing inside the place,' I said. 'Anyway, I'd better head in for service.' I shifted my weight. I had the distinct impression that David didn't like me, and the feeling was mutual.

'You're welcome anytime.' Lizzie grinned, waving me off.

I had a strong sense of foreboding as I made the short walk to

Café Lompar, looking back to see David still watching me. What exactly did he mean, *bringing fusion to another level*? There was definitely some malice in his tone. Maybe he was ashamed at how closely they were copying our concept? He ought to be.

I practically slammed the door behind me as I entered the kitchen. I tried to let this place I loved, the cooking smells, the stainless steel gleaming under the restaurant lighting, comfort me.

'What's up with you?' Lovro asked.

I grabbed a spoon to taste the herby marinade he was stirring. 'Mmm, delicious.'

'I added a secret ingredient.' He winked.

I dipped my spoon in again. 'Paprika?'

'You know me too well.' Lovro smiled. 'Anyway, you ignored my question.'

I lowered my voice, even though they were nowhere near earshot. 'I just met our new neighbours.'

'What are they like?' Bojan, one of our newer chefs, came over, intrigued.

'Nice. Well, a bit weird. The woman, Lizzie, seems lovely, but David, the chef, is...'

'A bit arrogant?' Bojan asked.

'Yes,' I agreed. 'And snooty.'

'I thought they were okay.' Lovro shrugged.

'You would, you're too nice.' I buttoned my chef's whites and started to chop some tomato for our salsa-stuffed salmon. 'They're a weird pairing. I'd never put them together,' I mused aloud.

'What do you mean?'

35

'Lizzie looks like she's just got back from a gap year in Thailand, and David looks like a school headmaster. There's got to be some story there,' I said, and then realised I was being a bitch. They'd been perfectly nice, especially Lizzie, and I was brooding over nothing.

'Well, you know what they say, keep your friends close and your enemies...'

'Closer,' I finished Bojan's sentence for him, realising he was right. If Ensambla were going to be our direct competition, it was better we kept them on side.

'Table five want one bowl of calamari, one Buzara, and one Ipsod saca,' Rosa called out a little later, passing the order slip over to Lovro.

'Ooh, are the Buricos here again?' I shouted over my shoulder.

'Every week, the same order,' Rosa sighed. 'I try and get them to taste the specials but no, Buzara and Ipsod saca every Saturday.'

'I'll get the calamari,' I called to Lovro and Bojan. 'Oh no, what's happened here?'

I noticed the smell of burning just before I found my deep-fried squid singed to a crisp. Black and crumbling, they'd lost any discernible shape. This was the third item I'd overcooked tonight. I was not on my game. I kept replaying the conversation with the neighbours in my mind, seeing that sly look of David's as I walked away.

Saturdays were always busy and sweaty. We had a full house and I needed to concentrate. Orders were coming in thick and fast. I went to the fridge, hoping to find more squid, but we'd run out.

'Sorry, Rosa. We're all out of calamari. Can you offer the Buricos free Cevapi?'

'Leave it with me,' she said.

'Plan B, I'll make the Ipsod saca,' I told Lovro. I took the lamb out of the oven, leaving it to rest while I assembled the accompanying potato gratin, glazed carrot pearls and bone marrow broth.

Lovro and Bojan were like gold dust, at my side with a conveyor belt of fine dining dishes, each more innovative and stylish than the last. I often thought we were like a synchronised swimming team, each in tune with each other, dancing around the kitchen. If Ensambla wanted to take us on, then good luck to them, bring it on. I squeezed both Lovro and Bojan on the shoulders. 'What would I do without you?'

Rosa appeared, her curly black hair bobbing over the top of the kitchen pass. 'It's a firm no to the Cevapi. They've said they will just take the Buzara and Ipsod saca. I offered free desserts and everything,' she shrugged.

'Typical,' I muttered, although I loved our regular customers. The Buricos were a lovely older Montenegrin couple who lived just up the road in Kotor. I passed the finished two dishes across to Rosa. 'Let's hope these make up for it.'

We carried on, with Bojan starting to prepare the panacottas as the first few dessert orders of the evening came in. The kitchen filled with the thick smell of chocolate and dark, glorious caramel. I took a morsel of baklava as I passed the fridge. The orange water and hazelnut combination I'd created last week was heavenly.

Suddenly there was a huge crash from the dining room. Lovro

peeked over the pass, then grimaced at me. 'It's the Buricos. They don't look happy. It looks liked they're leaving.'

'What happened?' I asked as Rosa came in to the kitchen.

'Ana took them the wrong order. I don't know how since I could serve theirs in my sleep. Then the table they were sitting next to had children and one of them knocked over the wine. It smashed on Mrs. Burico's dress.'

'Oh no!' I grimaced. 'Still, it's an accident. It seems silly to leave over that.'

Rosa hovered near the pass. She looked nervous, all of a sudden.

'What?'

'It's nothing, honestly... Well, they complained about the Ipsod saca.'

'What about it?'

Rosa looked even more sheepish, fiddling with her earring. 'It's the lamb. They said it's undercooked.'

'Undercooked?'

Ana arrived, carrying a tray with their leftover food and smashed glass. I took the lamb, noticing the pink flesh. The Buricos were right.

I felt sick. Not since my training days had I undercooked lamb. It was such a rookie mistake. I'd served three other Ipsod sacas already – were they all undercooked? How could I do this?

I checked the temperature on the oven, keen to hide my face from my colleagues. It was stupid but I could feel the tears welling. I'd always had high standards, a perfectionist, as my ex-boyfriend Adam used to call me. Mistakes were bound to happen, but I'd had so many tonight I felt incompetent. And it was always worse when regular customers were on the receiving end.

The oven temperature was fine. Maybe I'd put the lamb in too late? Not rested it enough?

I had to focus. I was letting all this wedding and Ensambla stuff distract me. Café Lompar had to be the priority. No more stressing about book promotion or rival restaurants or table settings.

I just hoped the Buricos would forgive us.

CHAPTER SIX

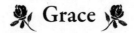 Grace

'I hate to see you so upset like this,' I soothed.

'But, Mum, it's such a rotten review. Listen to it: 'We were given the wrong order and no apology was made. When our food did eventually arrive, the ispod sacas were tasteless and undercooked. Kat Lompar seems to be losing her touch.' *Losing her touch*,' Kat repeated. 'Perhaps only a true native can appreciate the fine balance of flavours of Montenegrin cuisine. It's the last time we will ever go to Café Lompar!'

That was the third time Kat had read the review to me over Facetime. It obviously touched a nerve. 'One bad review is not the end of the world.'

'It's like dominoes, though, and this could start something, a downward trend. It could really damage us.' Kat sighed. 'It's the Buricos, I know it. And they were our best customers.'

'Don't be so dramatic, Kat. You need to develop a thicker skin.'

'I know. It just seems so unfair. We work so hard...'

'Yes, I know how much the restaurant means to you. To me, too. And Rosa and Luka. We'll have a conflab when I'm back and think about that evening to launch the summer season.'

'Well, we'll have to up our game with Ensambla opening soon,'

Kat said, injecting as much venom as she could muster into the name. She sighed. 'Anyway, what are you making tonight when Auntie Claire and Uncle Stu are over?'

'I've gone for the pork fillet with mushroom sauce and lemon potatoes, as you suggested. It seems straightforward enough so even I can manage it,' I laughed. 'And then kiwi...'

'And lime cheesecake,' Kat finished.

'Am I that predicable?'

'Let's just say it's your go-to dessert.'

'Ah, well, we can't all be head chefs!'

'Even head chefs losing their touch?'

Gosh, she was on a downer. I sometimes wished she'd chosen another career. Working in a professional kitchen was so tough and she was too hard on herself. I didn't like the sound of this new restaurant opening up right next door to Café Lompar but Tivat was such a lively, bustling town, it could probably sustain two similar restaurants.

Neil arrived early to help me prepare the meal.

'You didn't need to help,' I told him when he kissed me in the hallway.

'I know.' He grinned. 'But it was a good excuse to see more of you.' I couldn't help thinking how handsome he looked in his black shirt and beige chinos.

'Come on, let's open some wine while we cook,' I said, holding his hand as we walked into the kitchen.

As Neil chopped onions and trimmed asparagus, he told me about his day on the golf course. 'I had back-to-back lessons today. And that crazy woman – Cherry – had another lesson. She's the one I was telling you about with the older husband. I've

41

never known such a rubbish golfer. I don't know why she keeps turning up because she doesn't seem to get any better.'

I knew why Cherry kept turning up, but I didn't share it with Neil. I told him all about Kat's worries in the restaurant. Neil topped up my wine and pulled me to him.

'Hey, I'm feeling a bit tipsy already,' I protested. 'They'll be here soon.'

When he let me go, he looked suddenly serious. 'Cass phoned again today. She's invited us to the wedding.'

'That's nice of her,' I said, not really knowing what to think. I'd only seen Cass in photographs, in golf events, in the newspaper articles when they lost their son Max. Once from a distance in a restaurant with Neil. In a way, she wasn't a real person in my head, but an impossibly glamorous, skinny goddess with flawless skin and layered blonde hair.

'It's not for a while yet,' Neil said, 'and Ollie will be there.'

'*Coo-eee*!' Claire said, popping her head into the kitchen. 'Are you decent?'

'Come in,' I told her. 'You're incorrigible!'

'I come bearing gifts.' She handed me two bottles of Prosecco. 'I can see you two have already started.'

Stu stood awkwardly behind her. 'Alright, mate.' He nodded to Neil. 'She's got you cooking, has she?'

'Ignore him,' Claire said. 'He needs GPS to find his way to our kitchen. Although he can find his beer in the fridge, no problem.'

Stu rolled his eyes. You could cut the tension with a knife. This was going to be a fun night.

I turned to Neil. 'You and Stu go into the lounge. Claire and I will finish off here.'

As they sauntered off, I couldn't help comparing the two of them. Stu was like the stouter sidekick in a cop show, the one who's killed off in the second episode. He always wore that checked shirt, with the missing button at the belly, and his dark jeans rested below his paunch. But Stu was a good man, and Claire wasn't the easiest to live with. I could think of several times Claire completely lost it about the kids or work and Stu had borne the brunt of it and understood.

'Gosh, what's up with you two?' I asked her, as soon as they left the kitchen.

'Nothing,' Claire said. 'Just the usual. I had an endless pile of history essays to mark this afternoon and I asked him to mow the lawn. That's all, just mow the lawn, and then the lazy bugger fell asleep on the sofa. I ended up doing it myself.'

'Typical,' I laughed.

'God, sometimes just the way he breathes sets my teeth on edge.'

'Everyone feels like that, don't they? That passionate, rip-each-other's-clothes-off stage doesn't last long.'

'I know,' she sighed, 'but I wouldn't mind a kiss that was more heartfelt than a peck you give your elderly aunt. The twins have their own lives now and I can't help wondering what we'll have in common when they leave home and there's just the two of us left.'

'You'll have time for yourselves again, without running after Liam and Laura.'

'I look at these couples on *Escape to the Country* and they're walking hand in hand, planning crafting activities, or painting stained-glass windows. I think Stu and I would kill each other. All he likes is fishing or building computers.'

'Relax tonight. A few glasses of wine might get you and Stu in the mood.'

'I'm driving,' Claire said, 'and I'd need more than a few glasses of wine to make me feel sexy. Stu will be snoring like a pneumatic drill by the time I've got into bed.'

At the dinner table, Neil and Stu were talking animatedly about fishing. 'I'm at Fairwood Lakes most weekends in the spring and summer,' Stu said. 'I caught a 7lb bream there last year.'

'Ollie and I go there,' said Neil. 'He's into every kind of sport. Skiing, golf, football, you name it.'

'You sound really close,' Claire said.

'We are. He's my best mate.'

'Does he miss his brother?' Claire asked. I went cold, surprised how direct Claire was. Even I didn't like to probe too much.

Neil paused, sipped his wine. 'I think he probably does. There were just three years between Max and Ollie. I know in those first few years, we all went through a horrible patch. Cass and I neglected Ollie when we should have comforted him. I never ask if he misses him. I probably should.'

I touched his leg under the table.

'I'll have to leave the mushrooms, Gracie,' Stu said, rubbing his stomach. 'They make me really gassy.' Claire gave him a withering look.

'What does Ollie do?' Claire asked.

'He works in London in finance, as an actuary. Statistics. He assesses probability and risks. I'm aware that sounds like a LinkedIn profile.' Neil laughed. 'He gets his brain from his mother. He's an adrenaline junkie, though. Max was quieter, more sensitive. I always wonder what he'd be doing now, what kind of man he'd have made.'

'Do you mind talking about him?' Claire asked.

'Not at all. People avoid the subject all the time, tiptoe around it, but it's refreshing. I want to talk about Max. It's a relief in many ways.'

I glanced across at the photograph I kept on the sideboard of Dan, Kat and me on the beach in Newquay, Cornwall. Kat was about twelve and Dan had taken her surfing for the first time. It was the only one of him I'd left on display. It had rained for most of our week there, but I remembered the board games we played in the nights and that fish restaurant we went back to three times because we liked it so much. Kat was obsessed with lobster, not the usual junk food most kids her age liked. Despite all his secrets, he was still Kat's father and there were happy times.

'I know what you mean,' I said. 'People's tolerance around grief is quite low. I don't like to talk about Dan too much, but it's only been two years. It makes everyone feel a bit uncomfortable.'

Neil gave me a sideways glance. 'It's a bit different, perhaps, to losing a son.'

I felt as if I'd been slapped in the face and I could see Claire looked a bit shocked.

'We were together nearly thirty years, Neil. I know he cheated but it was still a lot to come to terms with. Still a tragedy.'

'Sorry, I didn't mean it like that,' he said.

There was an awkward silence. I sipped my wine without looking at him.

By the time we were on dessert, we'd deliberately moved onto lighter topics.

'This is the best lime and kiwi cheesecake you've ever made,' Claire announced, 'and you've made, like, a lot!'

'Thanks,' I mouthed at her. 'So you approve of this new boyfriend of Laura's then?

'He's lovely. Dylan. Very polite. Spotty and very earnest. He wants to become a chemical engineer. Has his shit together and will probably be very successful.'

'You don't think it'll last then?'

'God, no,' Claire said. 'He's far too nice. Laura likes the bad boys, unfortunately. Just like her mother ... until I grew all sensible.'

'Hey, I can be bad,' Stu protested.

'Like falling asleep when you're meant to be mowing the lawn.'

'Haven't you let that go yet?'

I made another attempt to change the subject and soften the mood, but it was obvious the evening had done nothing to dissipate the frostiness between them and as they were leaving, I could see Claire's irritation as Stu stumbled into the car, visibly worse for wear.

Neil kissed my neck as we waved them off. 'There was a bit of tension there,' he said. 'Stu was telling me that he feels he can't do anything right these days.'

I shrugged, but I thought about how new relationships could be fraught too, navigating the areas between the sore spots, seeing how far you could go before you offended each other. Grief still caught me out sometimes and Neil would have to get used to that.

CHAPTER SEVEN

🌿 Kat 🌿

'God, it's hot,' I sighed, feeling the flare in my cheeks. 'I've forgotten how sweltering this country gets.' I looked across to see Lovro rolling out pastry with a force I couldn't seem to muster today. It wasn't fair: he'd barely cracked a sweat.

'Hmm,' he agreed half-heartedly.

'It must be the English in me talking,' I said. As much as I loved the Montenegrin weather, the heat was sometimes unbearable. And it was only May. I knew it would get much hotter. Today was only twenty-nine degrees. Kitchens tended to be fire pits anyway, with all the ovens and steam and rushing around. I remember returning home from Truffles frazzled and singed, and that was in London temperatures. When would my Montenegrin DNA kick in, I wondered?

'Refreshments!' Rosa's voice called out, and I turned to see her carrying a tray of drinks.

'Ooh, you read my mind.' I rushed over to take a tall glass with slivers of cucumber and mint swimming in a generous serving of crushed ice. I pressed it to my forehead, feeling the cool condensation on my face. 'It's like a furnace in here.'

'Davor said he's used cucumber vodka – made it himself.' Rosa winked. 'Lime soda, vodka and mint syrup. Thought you might need it. It's going down well with the lunch crowd, anyway.'

'Your boyfriend's a genius,' I called to Lovro, as I felt the ice-cold bubbles trickle down my throat.

'He's been talking about this for the last two weeks. How do you say...? Non-stop!' Lovro rolled his eyes at me, taking his own glass.

It was hard to believe Davor had become such an enthusiastic barman. Last year, he'd been a waiter, and a lazy one at that – always slipping off for a cigarette, taking twice as many breaks as the other staff. Mum had cooked up the idea of training him to run the bar. We'd paid for a wine-tasting course for him and he'd never looked back. He dreamt up new cocktails faster than Lovro and I changed the food menu.

'The amount of money we spend on alcohol for his creations,' Lovro grumbled. 'I can feel the supermarket lady judging us every week.'

'You love it really.' I prodded him. 'How Montenegrins put it away, I'll never know.'

'I didn't see you complaining at our flat last weekend,' Lovro joked.

'Milo had to carry me home afterwards!' I shuddered. It had been the evening after that awful review from the Buricos, and I'd definitely been drowning my sorrows. The juicy cocktails washed away every last insult and complaint they gave, at least for one night.

'That's not as bad as me. Dav said I was dancing to the Spice Girls on the balcony after you left.' Lovro hid his eyes behind his hand.

'We hadn't all left by then,' I teased, pulling his hand away. 'But it's okay, Milo was dancing with you like an idiot. Anyway, when I got home, I cried at an episode of *Say Yes to the Dress* from 2010. I've barely seen Milo since then. I hope I haven't scared him off!'

'You are quite scary!'

I heard a familiar voice behind me, then I felt hands on my waist.

'Speak of the devil.' I planted a kiss on Milo's cheek.

Milo greeted Lovro. 'We're going to stop coming round to you and Dav's place,' he said. 'I think I'm still feeling the hangover.' He held his stomach. 'It has not been easy running boat trips the last few days.'

'What are you doing here?' I asked, offering him a sip of my drink.

'I had a break for lunch and thought I'd drop by. If I go home, I'll only collapse on the sofa,' he shrugged. 'Plus, you look like you need a rest.'

'Well, things are winding up here.' I glanced over the pass to see Rosa clearing tables, the last few customers scanning dessert menus. 'Do you mind if I take a quick break?' I shouted to Lovro, who was back at the other side of the worktop now, engrossed in cutting pastry for our pecan tartlets.

He waved me off. 'Don't worry, I know you're a terrible boss!'

'And you're an even worse assistant,' I joked, being led out by Milo.

'I wish we had more time to see each other,' I moaned as I realised we didn't have long before I'd have to head back to the kitchen.

We were sitting on the stone steps leading down to the beach. 'It's feels like we're only together when we're in bed.'

'Like passing ships,' Milo agreed. It was true, he was usually up so early to prepare for the day's sailing, and I was home late after evening shifts. Weekends were usually our busiest times in work. Tuesdays were the only days we had off together when Café Lompar closed for the day.

'Still, those nights are the best times.' He kissed my palm, and I remembered him rolling over when I got in bed last night, pressing against me, his breath hot as he kissed my neck.

'Maybe we'll do the same tonight,' I murmured.

I waved him goodbye as he made his way back to the harbour. I sighed, getting up from the steps and shaking the sand from my skirt. Back to the grind.

Lizzie waved from atop a ladder outside Ensambla. I gave my best fake smile. They were hanging some kind of advert and I made a mental note to sneak out later on to read it.

I paused at the back of Café Lompar to put my apron on, when I caught Rosa out of the corner of my eye a little way down the street. She was walking towards the restaurant with a man by her side. I squinted, trying to make out who it was. I didn't think I recognised him.

I was about to step out of the shade of the door and wave at her, when I saw the man snake an arm around her waist. She laid her head against his shoulder. Rosa was completely oblivious to anyone else in the street, and I watched from fifty feet away as they stopped and he pulled Rosa in for what can only be described as a full-on snog. Like teenagers at a school dance. I wanted to look away but felt glued to the spot.

I had no idea Rosa was seeing someone. She had never mentioned it. She was always the picture of hard work and determination at Café Lompar.

I smiled. It was great she had a new man on the go. She was always on my mind, a worry after the breast cancer scare last year. Good for her. They were clearly in to each other; his hands roamed around her body, settling on the small of her back. Rosa pulled back, then looked around furtively.

I didn't want her to know I'd been watching. Could I stay hidden out here and then catch her on her way back into the restaurant? I wanted to find out everything about him. Who he was. How they'd met. How long this had been going on. Why it had been kept a secret.

They moved apart and Rosa hung back whilst her new guy got on a moped. She scanned the street, probably looking for people she knew, then kissed him again, before he revved the engine.

He was coming this way.

I ducked back against the doorway, losing my flip flop in the process, my heel grating against the step. But I couldn't resist looking back as he got closer.

He was young.

Really young.

He looked about Luka's age. Olive-skin, long lashes, his face unlined. Cropped jeans and a leather jacket.

I stood in disbelief, the happy buzz I'd felt fading away.

Surely my eyes were deceiving me? He stopped at a traffic light and I noted the mole on his left cheek, his muscular jaw, not a hint of stubble. This guy was without a doubt in his twenties, if not younger. Much younger than Rosa. Younger than me, even.

Did Luka know about this? What would he say? Did he know this guy? They could have been in school together. I stared dumbfounded at the man's retreating back.

'Hi Kat.' Rosa had caught up, shocking me out of my stupor.

'Hi...' I said, shakily. She smiled, her lipstick perfectly in position, a rosy shade glittering in the afternoon sun. Not a wisp of hair out of place. Did I really just see her snogging the face off a twenty-something hunk?

'Good break?' she asked me.

'Uh huh ... uh, yeah.' I sounded like a blithering fool. I couldn't get over the shock. And how she was acting now. Like nothing had happened. Clearly this had been going on some time. She knew how to carry on like nothing was wrong in the world.

And nothing was wrong, was it? Rosa was entitled to date who she wanted, wasn't she? Regardless of age? I didn't know why I felt so unsure.

'You?' I asked in return.

'Just did a bit of shopping. It's amazing how quickly I get through the chocolates at home. I thought it was Luka that ate them all but with him away at uni I find I'm running out just as quickly. Seems I've got in to a bit of a bad habit.'

I wondered which habit she was referring to, the chocolates or the man, and gave a nervous laugh. Rosa shot me a quizzical look, then pushed open the door to the kitchen.

I watched her go, realising I didn't know everything about my new Montenegrin family. Could I bring it up? The last thing this family needed was more secrets.

I kissed Lovro goodbye as he swapped with Bojan, and we carried on prepping for the evening. My feet weren't the only things aching. I was absolutely dying to tell someone what I'd witnessed earlier. Maybe I could tell Milo later tonight? Mum, when she came out to Tivat next week? I needed advice on whether to let Luka know or to confront Rosa first.

'Are you all right, Kat?' Bojan asked. I bumped in to him as I manoeuvred round to the sink. 'You seem a bit distracted tonight?'

'Yes, it's just the heat,' I said. 'And this bloody deep fat fryer is on fritz again. I'm so glad we ordered a new one. I'm having a nightmare with these tempura prawns. They're not crisping up at all. I don't think it's even hot.'

Deep fat fryers sounded like the stuff of greasy caffs and chippies, but in reality, they were a chef's best friend. There was no end to the delights we made in them, from sweet doughnuts, to arancini bites. It didn't have to be oily and fattening. Our coconut tempura prawns served with tacos and salsa were a summer favourite in the Café. I didn't know what I'd do if I couldn't get it to work again tonight.

'Ana?' I stopped the waitress as she walked through the kitchen. 'Any news on the fryer we ordered last week?'

'It's not here yet? They told me it would come on the weekend.' She shrugged. 'Let me check and get back to you.' She headed off into the restaurant.

It was no use, the oil wasn't even hot. 'Shit,' I swore, taking out the batter. It was far too pale. Not the golden-brown, crispy deliciousness it should be. I'd have to think on my feet and cook the prawns another way, maybe shallow fry them on the hob, although it would take longer.

I needed this fryer for nearly every dish on the menu. Bojan frowned, catching on to my concern. It would mean a major menu shift for the night.

'Was it working earlier?' he asked.

'Barely. I think Ana's on the phone to the company now.'

I walked over to find her. She had become somewhat of a guru with our stock and equipment. Everyone in Café Lompar had their own place and area of expertise, like a well-oiled machine.

'Nooo!' I heard her howl down the phone. 'And when did you say it was delivered?' She furrowed her brow even more when she saw me, indicating it wasn't good news. She mouthed something at me but I didn't catch it.

'On Saturday? Well, it's not here.' I heard the Montenegrin fire in her voice, glad I wasn't on the end of a European rant. Ana and Rosa could be scary when they wanted to be and yet they were always the picture of loveliness with customers.

'It's signed for? Well, no one here signed for it.' She followed up with a stream of angry Montenegrin. I rocked back and forth, panicking at the dramatic change of plan needed for tonight. Things did not sound hopeful for my menu. I could already picture the bad reviews pouring in, chaos in the kitchen, more echoes of 'Kat Lompar, losing her touch'. I couldn't stand thinking of that line, how hurtful it was.

Ana was shaking her head. 'No, no, that can't be right. There has to be a mistake.'

'What is it?' I asked.

She held the phone to her neck, eyes wide. 'They're saying a waitress at Café Lompar signed for it. They definitely said they worked for Café Lompar.' She spoke into the phone again then looked up at me. 'Someone called ... Lizzie.'

Well, it was game on now.

CHAPTER EIGHT

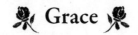 Grace

'She's a dark horse, that Rosa,' I mused. 'But then, she's had plenty of practice.' I couldn't resist sniping sometimes. I kept my residual resentment deep inside, but it was there. Rosa and Dan had been so adept at lying about their affair for so many years.

'I swear to God, he looked younger than me,' Kat said.

'And she didn't say anything?'

'Not a thing about the man. She said she'd been shopping but she didn't have any bags with her.'

'You're a right Sherlock Holmes!' I laughed. 'Well, it's good she's having a bit of fun. She had an absolutely shit year last year and she's only ever been with your dad. Much like me.'

'Do you think I should tell Luka?'

'God, no. Leave her be. It's her place to tell him, not you.'

'I feel bad, though, especially if he finds out I knew.' She sighed. 'It's probably just a bit of fun, as you say, and she has seemed more like her old self lately. Happier somehow. How's Neil, by the way?'

'He's good. I haven't mentioned it's the two-year anniversary tomorrow of Dad's death to him. It's not that long, is it?'

'I'm sorry I can't be with you tomorrow. What are you going to do?'

'Don't worry. I'm meeting Claire for lunch and will just go to the grave later. Neil's coming over in the night. He's putting a bit of pressure on me to move in here.'

'How do you feel about that?' Kat asked, sensitive as always to my moods.

'I don't know.' I paused. 'Maybe it's a bit soon. He's wonderful, don't get me wrong. It's the first time in my life that I've lived alone, though. I kind of like it.'

I looked around at the bright sunshine spilling into the kitchen. The Cath Kidston oven gloves on the stove, the matching apron on the back of the kitchen door, the polka-dotted kettle. 'I wasn't in a hurry to meet someone else, as you know, but Neil came along and, well, you can't plan these things.'

'Tell him, Mum. He'll understand.'

'Yes,' I said, biting my lip, not quite as sure he would. 'How're the wedding plans?'

'I was working on the seating plan last night and I asked Milo about his dad again. He still insists he doesn't want him to be there. Natalija, his sister, is coming over soon. I've been dying to meet her and I'm hoping to find out more about Milo's father.'

'It's funny you haven't met her yet. I know you've met on FaceTime calls but it's not the same.'

'She lives in Milan. She's studying fashion design, which sounds impossibly glamorous. Milo is so protective of her. You know what he's like.' She suddenly gasped. 'Is that the time? I'll have to go. I promised Lovro I'd get in early.'

I finished checking the dates for Kat's book tour in late September, after she was back from honeymoon. After that, I planned to pop into town to do a bit of shopping. I wanted to get flowers for tomorrow and something nice for dinner.

My feet were killing me as I trundled around the shops. I'd been distracted in Monsoon and had tried on a few dresses to take back to Montenegro. I'd be in Tivat until after the wedding and wanted to add to my summer wardrobe. I'd already bought my outfit for the wedding. It was a dusky pink dress with a lacy, three-quarter sleeve top and chiffon skirt. Modern and classy, I hoped. I hated those staid, sorbet-coloured, mother-of-the bride dresses.

I stopped off in Café Nero for a well-deserved latte. I was glad I wasn't seeing Neil tonight. A tv-dinner watching *Line of Duty* after a long bath was what I needed.

'Grace? It is Grace, isn't it?' A blonde woman in the queue in front of me turned around.

I didn't have a clue who she was for a moment and felt a bit wrong-footed. Then the penny dropped. I felt my face drain of colour.

'Sorry to accost you like this. It's Cass,' she said, her hand taking mine, not just a polite handshake, but both hands covering mine. Seeing my puzzled expression, she said, 'I feel like I know you. I have to confess when Neil told me about you, I looked you up on Facebook.'

'It's l-lovely to meet you at last,' I stammered.

'I've just been shopping for nighties. Not for me, my mother. She's in a care home.' She shuddered. 'Do you fancy a coffee with me?'

'I'd love to,' I said, my mind racing. It was the strangest

situation. Meeting and having a coffee with Neil's ex-wife. Had she engineered this? And if so, why? She looked lovely, as I expected, with her smooth, blonde hair and over-sized sunglasses perched on her head. Being tall, she carried off her floral maxi dress with aplomb.

'Let me get these,' she insisted, ordering a latte for me and an espresso for herself. 'Let's be naughty and have some coffee and walnut cake.' Looking at her svelte figure, I doubted she was 'naughty' that often.

We sat at a table in the window, looking onto the busy street. Opposite, a busker was singing *Wonderwall* and a small crowd had gathered.

'Ooh, he's good,' Cass said. She twisted the end of a sachet of brown sugar and poured it into her coffee. 'I'm terrible. No wonder I'm so hyper. I take two of these and drink so much espresso.' She looked the opposite to 'hyper,' seeming very serene and collected. 'Michael's always trying to get me to cut down. And now with the wedding...' She rolled her eyes. 'Well, it's all so stressful.'

'Yes, my daughter Kat is getting married in September, too,' I said.

'Neil has told me. Is that the daughter living in Montenegro?'

I wondered how much Neil had told her about Kat and me and the whole Rosa and Dan situation. 'It's only one daughter I have. Yes, she's a chef in a restaurant in a coastal town there, Tivat.'

'That's your restaurant, isn't it? Wow, that must be stressful. Neil says you run it from here and spend part of the year abroad.' She stopped, cutting a corner of her cake with a fork, nibbling a minuscule piece.

'Our wedding's on the 28th,' Cass said. 'I'm not sure I'd bother myself. With the wedding, I mean. I'd be quite happy carrying on as we are. Michael is keen. I'm so busy with work, though.'

Neil had told me she worked as an estate agent three days a week. How stressful could that be? I wondered why Neil had let this gorgeous creature go.

She fixed me with her hazel eyes. 'It's always men that want the commitment, despite what people believe. Neil says that he's moving into your place this summer. How exciting is that!'

'What?' I jumped and a big piece of coffee and walnut cake slid onto my lap. I started scooping it off with my fork, dabbing myself down with a serviette.

Catching my surprised expression, Cass said, 'Oh, sorry. Have I said something wrong? Was I not supposed to know?'

I recovered as quickly as I could, still dabbing at the stain, not looking her in the eye. 'No, that's fine. We hadn't intended to tell anyone just yet. I haven't even told my sister or Kat.'

What was Neil thinking? Nothing had been agreed. We would eventually move in together, no doubt. But to tell Cass, his ex-wife?

'Don't worry,' Cass said, 'my lips are sealed.' She made a motion with a finger across her lips. 'I hardly see Neil these days and we don't even have the same circle of friends. You know what it's like when you divorce? Oh, sorry, your husband has passed away, hasn't he? I'm such a klutz sometimes.'

'Yes, two years tomorrow,' I said tightly.

'Gosh, that's so hard. It's still fresh for you.' Her expression was solemn. 'I'm sure Neil has told you about Max. He was such a sweet boy. God, I miss him. He's forever frozen at eight years old.'

She gazed out of the window. 'It's nearly sixteen years ago now and I can remember in perfect detail everything I did that day. What I did beforehand. When my neighbour came to tell us.' She shivered. 'Those months afterwards, years after, passed in a blur.' She picked up her coffee. 'Sorry, I didn't mean to put a dampener on everything.'

'It must have been a terrible time.'

'It was,' she agreed. 'And Neil, well, we just couldn't reach each other. We both went a bit mad. He was on antidepressants for years afterwards. Poor Ollie, what he must have gone through. There's some horrible statistic out there about divorce rates being higher after the loss of a child. God, the strain it puts on a marriage.'

I remembered Neil saying something similar when we first met. He'd never told me about the antidepressants, though. He should have. It was important. I didn't like that he filtered what I knew about him. Of course, didn't we all do that? Yet, he'd shared this piece of news with Cass and we hadn't even agreed upon it.

As we finished our coffees, Cass got up to leave. 'Michael's home from work soon and I promised to pop into Sainsbury's.' She kissed me on the cheek. 'I'm so glad to have met you, Grace. Neil's a lucky man.'

'He's got good taste,' I joked.

When she left, I watched the busker pack up his guitar and collect his coins from the case. What the hell was Neil playing at? Sometimes I felt I didn't know him at all.

CHAPTER NINE

❧ Kat ❧

A week had passed since the Grand Theft of the Deep Fat Fryer, as I'd come to think of it. I didn't know what I was waiting for, maybe hoping Lizzie would realise her mistake and bring it over. What if it was no mistake, though? Ana's conversation with the delivery company niggled in my mind: 'They said they worked for Café Lompar.' Lizzie had seemed so nice when I first met her. This had to be David's doing; he struck me as the kind of chef that did whatever he could to get to the top, much like my old boss, Marc Douvall. Marc's name still brought shivers to my spine, remembering the way he used to talk about other restaurants, stealing their ideas. I'm sure this was a move he would have made, given half a chance.

I huffed, seeing the patchy crumb on the arancini I was working on. This starter was a favourite at Café Lompar. They should have been sun-kissed bites of pea and mint risotto with melting mozzarella in the middle. The breadcrumbs round the outside turned golden and crispy in the fryer, but doing them in the pan would never achieve the same result – I'd spent the last week trying.

'Not again,' I groaned.

'Arancini?' Lovro guessed. 'I don't see why you don't just go over there and call them out on the fryer?'

'You know confrontation's not my style. I don't want to start things on a bad note with the Ensambla team. We have to work next door to them!'

I carried on determinedly with my next batch. The arancini rolled to one side of the pan, spraying a shower of burning oil droplets over me. 'Ow,' I shrieked.

'Everything all right?' Rosa appeared at the door, carrying a tray of dishes. 'Table five are disappointed we're not serving Priganice tonight. They said it's the thing they look forward to all week. Are you sure you can't make them another way? Do you really need the fryer?'

That was it. The last straw. I had to do something about this.

I threw down the towel I'd used to wipe the spitting oil off me. 'I'm going over there.'

'Can I come?' Lovro pleaded, enjoying the drama of it all.

'I could do with back-up,' I admitted. 'A bit of muscle.'

He flexed his non-existent biceps and followed me out across the road. We peered through the door to Ensambla, still clearly unfinished, one wall unpainted and the tables crowded in one corner of the room. I knocked on the door, then pushed it open, not willing to wait. I knew if I waited, I'd only chicken out.

Lizzie bounded out of the kitchen, still in her denim dungarees, this time with a headscarf woven through her braid and stretching down her back.

'Kat! To what do I owe this surprise?' She smiled, looking genuinely pleased to see me. I hesitated, regretting my crossed arms and Lovro's stance at my side.

I started speaking but Lizzie interrupted. 'We were actually planning to come for a meal in Café Lompar tomorrow night.

63

David and I walked past earlier and the smells coming out of that kitchen were divine. I can see why you have so many regulars.' She ushered us over to a table and plonked herself down on the surface, like a makeshift bench. 'I'm Lizzie, by the way,' she introduced herself to Lovro. 'I heard you make the best ice cream in town. David made some of the recipes on your website before we moved out here. The tonka bean and vanilla cream – to die for!'

'Thank you so much.' I could feel Lovro blushing, with a beaming smile.

I couldn't let my resolve slip now. David came down the stairs, behind Lizzie, and placed a hand on her shoulder. The movement was protective, like he was her father. 'Hi, Kat,' he said, with a thin smile.

'We were just talking about you,' Lizzie said, although the atmosphere had definitely changed when he'd come in the room.

'Anyway, the reason we're here,' I cut in, 'is that we ordered a deep fat fryer a couple of weeks ago and it hasn't arrived. Our team spoke to the company this morning and it sounds like it might have been delivered to the wrong place...' I wavered, not wanting to accuse them so blatantly.

'Shit,' Lizzie said, her hand flying up to her face. 'Oh God, I'm so sorry, Kat!'

David frowned. Lizzie continued, 'I thought that had turned up quickly. We only ordered it the day before. Was that your fryer?' She looked mortified.

David leaned uncomfortably against the table. 'Why didn't you say anything before? That arrived last week. I've used it a good few times to try out recipes for the menu,' David said, turning the heat on me. Now it was my turn to look embarrassed.

'Well, we didn't want to say anything. I know it must be chaos setting up a new restaurant.'

David shrugged, but Lizzie was full of apologies. 'David, go and get the machine now. They can take it back with them, or we can bring it over. Or you could have our new one when it finally arrives?'

'I'd have to clean it first.' He scratched his head, obviously reluctant.

'It's okay,' I mumbled.

'I'm so sorry, Kat and Lovro, honestly. You must think we're nightmare neighbours. How embarrassing! You must take our new one,' Lizzie said, and we eventually agreed, although inside I wanted the exact one I'd picked out. I'd spent hours poring over the kitchen equipment website. Why had I rolled over so easily?

'We look forward to seeing you tomorrow,' Lovro said, as we got to the door, then left, no deep fat fryer in hand. He turned to me once we were out of earshot. 'They were nice.'

'They were not nice.' I shook my head. 'Lizzie makes you think she's nice but we know she pretended to work for Café Lompar. They did not mix up the orders. They wanted our expensive machine.'

'You don't know that,' Lovro said. 'Their machine will probably turn up now and be even nicer.'

'Mark my words, we won't be seeing any machine for a long time. They'll be busy ordering a crappy one online as we speak.'

Lovro stopped, looking incredulous. 'When did you get to be so cynical?'

I thought about his question all afternoon, wondering if my fingers had been burned by Dad's betrayal, or whether it was working with horrible chefs like Marc and Ivan in the past. All I knew was, I didn't like David and Lizzie one bit.

The doorbell rang. I squeezed Milo's hand, nerves bubbling inside me.

'She's here.' Milo sprang to his feet. He hadn't seen Natalija, his twenty-one-year-old sister, in over a year, and I was meeting her for the first time today. Milo had slotted in perfectly amongst my assorted family, and it was hard to believe I hadn't met any of his yet. I was dying to see where Milo came from.

As I followed his six-foot frame to the front door, I wondered for the umpteenth time what Natalija would be like. Whether we'd get on or not. She was studying fashion design at Milan University, which sounded like a pretend life, too glossy to be real. Would she think I was really dowdy? I'd seen pictures of her, but from years ago when she was a young teenager, tall and gangly like Milo.

'I hope she likes me,' I said as Milo paused at the door.

'Of course, she will,' he soothed. 'Here goes!'

Light filled the hallway as Milo opened the door and plenty of shrieking ensued.

'It's my sister, *cectpa*!'

I stood on tiptoes, trying to get a glimpse. Milo enveloped her in a hug, and I caught my first eyeful of long brown hair.

'Milo! I've missed you.' I could hear the smiles in their voices. 'Let me see Kat!'

He stepped out of the way, revealing a girl who could have been a supermodel. Natalija was tall, just a shade below Milo's height, with dark poker-straight hair reaching all the way to her bottom.

'So nice to meet you,' I grinned, as Natalija fixed her blue eyes on me, so mesmerising they were almost turquoise. She pulled me in for a hug and I was enclosed in a fog of perfume.

'Milo said you were a looker but I didn't imagine this.' Natalija pulled away, turning to her brother. 'She's stunning!'

'You're one to talk,' I said. 'Did you Martinovics have to take all the good genes in life? It's not fair.'

'Are we going to stand in the hallway all day?' she said, good-naturedly.

'Come on in, it's about time we opened the wine.'

I realised I was letting her lead me through to our open plan kitchen-diner. Natalija was one of those people who commanded attention. I bet she fitted right in in Milan. She looked every bit the budding fashion designer in a fur gilet that had a lived-in, chic feel, and a nude-coloured dress so short you could see every inch of skin possible without actually being indecent. I'd never be brave enough to wear that.

'What are you wearing?' Milo asked, following behind and reading my mind.

'What do you mean?'

'Wouldn't it be easier just to be naked?'

I laughed, but when I turned back he was frowning.

'She looks amazing,' I said, wanting to make a good impression.

'Don't worry, Kat. Milo's always thought I dressed a bit, how you say, "out there".' She rolled her eyes. I moved away from them both to open the chilled bottle of rosé I'd bought for today.

'It's not "out there",' Milo said, still staring, 'it literally is ... *out there*. Everything. Men can see everything. You need to be careful in Italy.'

'I know, I know.' She rolled her eyes again then turned to me. 'I thought having a protective older brother was meant to be a good thing.'

'He is protective.' I nodded, watching Milo sulk as he took a beer from the fridge. I followed Natalija out to the terrace, sitting down next to her. Milo came to join us.

'Well, I can see the family resemblance,' I said to them. 'The same dimples, cheekbones.'

'We got them from Mum,' Natalija said, flipping a lock of hair over her shoulder. I noticed her long nails, painted a deep red, as she expertly poured the wine. 'But I got Dad's eyes, lucky me.'

Squinting, she covered her eyes with sunglasses that would look more in place on the Cote D'Azur.

She definitely had that diva persona, and there was something about Natalija you couldn't take your eyes off. But I liked her instantly. She had such an energy.

'Tell me everything about you, Kat. You know what Milo's like, he's given me no gossip. I want to know where you're from, what you think of Montenegro, how you met. And how on earth did my brother get someone as hot as you?!'

As I chatted to Natalija, she demanded to see pictures of Mum and Bath. I enjoyed showing her. I said, 'I can't believe it's taken us so long to meet.'

'I know.' She smiled. 'I wanted to come but it's hard being a student and Milan's so expensive.'

'Your turn. Please, I want to know everything about Milan.'

'Ah, you know what it's like.' She waved her hand. 'So much good food there but no one eats anything. You have to be skinny skinny to fit in, otherwise you're in exile.' She shrugged, then popped an olive into her mouth. 'This would be dinner for most of the girls I know.'

'I wouldn't fit in at all then,' I laughed.

'Kat makes the most amazing food,' Milo said, relaxing a little now and rubbing my arm.

'I am desperate to try something of yours. I've been following the Café Lompar meals on Instagram and salivating. It's been ages since I've had good food.'

I felt like I was giggling with a school friend.

'Natalija,' Milo warned, 'I hope you are looking after yourself. Cooking, eating properly?'

She ignored him and sipped her wine, popping her sunglasses to the top of her head again, pushing back her hair and revealing those gorgeous eyes. 'You should see the men in Milan, Kat. They are so hot, oh my God. Every night you can have a date with a different supermodel.'

'I don't want to know this,' Milo said. I laughed, but again I could hear the serious edge to his voice. 'This is not like you, Natalija.'

'*Pshhht*. You haven't seen me grown up. He still thinks of me as a little teenager,' she explained.

'I'm just saying you can't go off with different men. I hope you're joking. It's not ... decent.' Milo shook his head.

I turned to him in shock. I hadn't seen this side of him before. I knew he adored his sister – it was obvious in the way he spoke about her – and I knew he'd be protective. This was another level though; he'd turned into some fuddy-duddy traditionalist.

'You're not her grandfather,' I said to him.

'Don't worry, Kat,' Natalija said, but I noticed her pull one side of her dress down. The further she pulled the hem, though, the more cleavage peeked out the top.

'That dress!' Milo muttered to himself. Silence fell on the table for an uncomfortable second, before he got up. 'Excuse me.' He left the room.

I felt a little affronted, surprised at this glimpse to a new Milo. I tried to lighten the tone.

'Well, I'm jealous. Life sounds so glamorous there compared to me in my chef's whites every day.'

'It is not so glamorous. I'm still a student, after all.' She shrugged.

'When I was a catering student, I'd spend all day learning how to cook something amazing like venison or lobster, then come home to beans on toast because that's all I could afford.'

'Money is tight. It's hard on my course, especially. Fashion design is a lot of networking. I can't turn up to these events looking like shit.'

I laughed. 'How do you manage it?'

'I do a bit of extra work on the side. Some modelling, party dresses, underwear, that sort of thing. All tasteful, of course. Milo would kill me if it was any worse ... actually he'd probably kill me anyway.'

I giggled along but knew she was right. I doubted he'd like the thought of his sister modelling underwear.

'I see some guys as well, you know,' she said. 'Just go on dates to the theatre, restaurants. It's fun. Nothing further. The money's great and you get presents. Like this.' Natalija showed me her watch. I'd already clocked it. The level of bling was unmissable. I was surprised it didn't dazzle planes out of the sky.

'Wow,' I said, suddenly wishing she wasn't telling me this. When was Milo coming back from the bathroom?

'I couldn't get through uni without the money,' Natalija confessed. 'Here's my brother now. Please don't say anything,' she whispered.

I gave a small smile, feeling stuck between a woman I was trying to impress and my fiancé. I still had the dilemma of whether to say anything to Rosa on my mind. Why did I have all this information I couldn't talk about? I hadn't asked for any of this!

'I've set your suitcase up in the spare room.' Milo rejoined the table. 'Do you want a tour of the villa?'

The two of them walked inside. I sat, drinking my wine, pleased to see our beautiful cat Bella sidling up to me. She let out a gentle miaow, looking up to beg for some food.

'Oh, Bella. What am I going to do?'

CHAPTER TEN

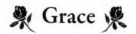 Grace

'So, what was she like?' Claire asked. 'Ouch!'

'Sorry,' the nail technician apologised. 'If you're not used to having your cuticles done, it can hurt a bit.'

Claire turned to me. 'Since when did cuticles become a thing? I've never noticed someone with untidy cuticles before. Have you?'

The young girl had turned to the sink, and I could see her shoulders droop, thinking, *We've got a right pair here.*

It was Claire's idea to get our nails done at 'Get Nailed!' in town. 'Seriously, though, you won't get a chance when you're back in Tivat.'

My technician had such long acrylic nails she was having trouble opening the nail varnish.

'Cass was lovely. Very glamorous. Charming.'

'You didn't like her?'

'I did,' I protested. 'She just said a few things I wasn't quite sure how to take. She told me Neil was on antidepressants for years after Max was killed.'

'That's understandable,' Claire said, as the technician started filing her nails. 'It must have been hellish for him. It was good he was able to be so open the other night. He didn't tell you, I take it?'

'No. I suppose it's not something men like to talk about. The other thing she said was that Neil told her he was moving in with me soon.'

'What?' Claire was aghast. The nail technician shifted in her seat. 'Surely Neil wouldn't have said that without checking with you first?'

'You'd think. I didn't show Cass my surprise, though, I hope. But he's over tonight and I'll have it out with him then.' My hand was shoved unceremoniously under the LED light contraption.

'It'll take about five minutes for the gel to harden,' the technician explained and stood up to eat her prawn cocktail crisps.

'Perhaps she got the wrong end of the stick,' Claire said. 'I can't imagine Neil would tell her that. It's not like him.'

'You never know. I never thought Dan would do what he did.'

'Yeah, but this isn't the same as shagging other women and having a family on the side in another country.'

Claire's technician took an intake of breath. Her eyebrows were micro-bladed to within an inch of their lives, the high arch giving her a quizzical look.

'Neil's a good sort,' Claire said as an afterthought.

'I hope so,' I said.

My technician wiped the crisp crumbs from her hand and inspected my nails.

'Let's go for some tapas for lunch,' Claire offered. She always decided where we'd eat. 'I haven't booked but we should be early enough to get a table. Go on, you might as well get your toenails done. It'll be a while before I finish here.'

At lunch at El Toro, we shared tapas for two: deep-fried calamari, patatas bravas and meatballs.

'I love tapas.' Claire beamed. 'Stu is so fussy about his food and his dodgy stomach. Honestly, he's so boring sometimes.'

'Things seemed really strained between you the other night,' I ventured.

'You noticed? Well, not more than usual. It's not that he's changed, it's me. Sometimes he really gets me down. We've been together so long, there's no surprises anymore. I know exactly what he'll order in a restaurant, what he wants to watch on telly, what his views are on anything and everything.'

'It's inevitable,' I told her. 'All relationships get like that.'

Claire pierced a meatball with her fork. 'Perhaps I'm going through a midlife crisis. I'm forty-seven this year. It kind of makes you reflect. Then there's you and Neil and the way you look at each other, the way he undresses you with his eyes. I'd like a bit of that, too. If I remember how it all works.'

I blushed. 'Yes, but we're in that new phase.'

'I'm being silly, I know,' Claire said. 'I can't help thinking: *Is this it?* Liam and Laura will leave home and it will just be Stu and me, with his hairy toes, his morning nasal evacuation and *Match of the Day.*' She shuddered.

'Have you spoken to Stu about it?'

'God, no,' Claire snorted. 'He hates talking about his feelings and I don't want to hurt him. I'll work it out.'

As we left El Toro, Claire paused at the doorway. 'I'm a selfish cow. I've been talking about my problems and it's two years today since Dan died. I can come to the cemetery with you, if you want.'

I kissed her on the cheek, 'Don't be daft. I'll be fine. Anniversaries are never the easiest. And it's just so odd – I'm torn between grief and bitterness. What a combination, eh? And now

I run a business with his mistress. Jerry Springer would have a field day with our family.'

'For what it's worth, I think you have held things together marvellously and I am proud of you.'

I didn't stay long at the graveside. I threw away the flowers I'd placed there two weeks ago and replaced them with chrysanthemums and azaleas. I took out some wet wipes and scrubbed at the rain spots on the headstone and read the inscription for the hundredth time, despite knowing the words off by heart: *In Loving Memory of Danilo Lompar. Born 20th September, 1965. Died 8th May, 2018. Devoted husband to Grace and doting father to Kat.* Simple but Dan would have hated anything showy and he wasn't religious.

I sat on a bench adjacent to the grave. When Dan died, I had no idea about Rosa and Luka. The words 'devoted husband' had seemed a mockery when I found out. He was a good father to Kat and Luka, though, despite all the deceit. One day, I would think of him and the good times we had and the memories would not be tainted by his betrayal. It was too soon yet. He hurt me too much.

More than that, I'd become distrustful, cynical. There was good in the world. In my heart, I knew that. But when you had lived and slept next to someone for years, let them know parts of you others never saw, to then find out the person you trusted lied to you for years – dreamt of another woman when he made love to you; held another woman's hand as she gave birth to their son – while you waited at home and missed him, it changed you. Tears streamed down my face.

This distress happened less often now. I was stronger and Neil was in my life. Neil, who said he loved me. But now, I knew, I kept part of myself back. A nugget of myself that belonged only to me.

When I got home, I did a bit of weeding and pruning in the garden. It was lovely in spring and I'd added my own touches since I'd moved in. The magnolia I'd planted at the bottom of the garden was blooming in a glory of blushing pink. I'd found a wooden wheelbarrow on eBay and filled it with dahlias and a rustic arch mirror added a quirky feel. I loved being creative in the garden. It was my thinking space and I'd lose myself in tending to the plants and herbs. Years ago I'd run my own garden nursery and it had taught me so much, but it was stressful when Kat was small. Now all my imagination and passion were caught up in Café Lompar and how to improve our marketing and keep the customers coming through the doors when there were so many other restaurants around. I got up from my knees and my back ached. A nice ache, though.

I was staying with Neil tonight. Usually, he liked coming out to Meadow Ponsbury, but it was a nice change for Neil to cook and I enjoyed going back into Bath once in a while, now that I'd escaped the buzz of the city. I had a quick shower and spent time over my hair and make-up. Claire was right. This stage of a relationship was exciting. I had bought new underwear, a sky-blue lacy bra and knickers. I felt excited butterflies in my stomach as I put them on, thinking of the night ahead and Neil's electric touch on my skin. I opted for a navy-spotted, jersey dress. Not too over the top and easy to take off.

I knew I had to talk to him about what Cass had said and it made me a bit nervous. It was important we got this straight. I would have to tell him I wasn't quite at that stage yet. But how would he take it? My dress might be staying firmly on!

When I arrived, Neil took the bottle of Prosecco from me, placing it on the hall table and pulling me in for a kiss. His tongue slid inside my mouth, sending me almost crazy with desire for him. But I pulled back and he gave me a puzzled look.

'Hmm, that smells nice. I had lunch with Claire in town but I'm ravenous.'

'I've made paprika chicken, with new potatoes and asparagus. I've even made us a panna cotta.'

'Talented as well as handsome. I can't believe you made dessert.'

He laughed, 'Okay, I lied. The panna cotta is from M&S.'

I sat at the kitchen island as Neil laid the table in the open-plan dining room. The decor was as opposite to my cottage as a place could be. His kitchen was all stainless steel and pewter units, high spec and contemporary. Black shelving held white crockery and an array of fluted and cocktail glasses. He handed me a chilled glass of Prosecco and we chatted about our day. I felt suddenly apprehensive, not quite sure how to broach seeing Cass, knowing it would dampen the mood when we only had a few days left before I was on a flight to Montenegro again.

We sat at the table and Neil lit the candle. 'I've been looking forward to seeing you all day,' he said, his eyes holding mine.

'I saw Cass yesterday.'

'Yes, she told me. You had a coffee.'

I was taken off guard. I stopped, with no idea what to say.

'She told me that she thinks she's upset you. And I have an apology to make. I lied to her. I said we were moving in together.'

'Why, Neil?' I put down my fork. I felt sick.

'Because I'm an asshole, that's why. It was when she told me she and Mike were getting married. I feel nothing for her, you've got to believe me. It was stupid male pride. I wanted to make it seem that I was moving on, too. Which I have, of course.'

'I was surprised,' was all I managed.

'It was utterly stupid. I know what we have is great, I don't want to spoil it. I really don't.'

'I do think we'll move in together. I do, Neil, but I can't be forced into anything yet.'

'I know, darling,' he said, reaching over to hold my hand. 'It's just that I miss you so much when you're away. It would be great to make this more permanent.'

'We know what we feel about each other. There's no rush,' I said. 'Let's see where we stand at the end of the summer.'

Neil smiled, 'Okay. I won't put pressure on you.'

We ate and the atmosphere was easier. I thought of Claire and Stu. She envied what I had with Neil. It was stupid to risk it. I did think of asking about the antidepressants, but decided we'd had enough drama for the night. Afterwards, we watched an episode of *Would I Lie to You*, giggling on the sofa.

When it finished, Neil took my hand and the bottle in the other and we went to bed. Our love-making was tender and gentle. I felt safe in his arms afterwards, listening to his soft snores and some late-night revellers laugh on the pavement outside, the taxis revving in the street. It was chilly and I pulled the sheet over my shoulders.

In a few days, my life would be frantic again. I'd feel the Montenegrin sun on my skin, squint at the glittering Adriatic. Café Lompar would consume my waking hours. It was an odd existence, but I liked having my feet in both worlds. I wasn't sure I was ready to change things quite yet.

CHAPTER ELEVEN

🌿 Kat 🌿

'Have you seen what she's wearing today?' Milo folded a t-shirt. 'That skirt.' He shook his head.

I couldn't really argue. Natalija's skirt was nothing I would dare to wear. Although it was long, there were two thigh-high splits, Natalija's almond-coloured legs flashing through them. Milo nearly choked on his espresso when she'd come down for breakfast wearing it. He was taking her to visit their father in Cetinje today, and I could tell he was stressed. He'd made disapproving comments all through breakfast.

'My dad will have a heart attack,' he said, sorting through a pile of laundry that was toppling out of the basket. 'She doesn't understand these things. I think she's doing it to wind me up.'

I lifted my head, knowing I couldn't carry on working through recipe notes while Milo was having a rant like this. His face was red and crumpled with frustration.

'I don't what the big deal is. Isn't everyone like this in their early twenties?' I hoped to calm him down. 'You should have seen some of the stuff I wore in uni.'

'I don't want to know,' Milo huffed. I'd never seen anyone fold a t-shirt with such force. The sunlight was burning through our slanted window, kicking up a stream of dust that glimmered in the bedroom air. Just as I was about to pick my pen back up, Milo had another outburst.

'That thing she said yesterday. About dating different men. Terrible.' He was fiddling with his watch strap now.

'That's ridiculous,' I said. 'She's young and living in a vibrant city. She's allowed to date who she wants.' It sounded as if it was a lot more than dating, though. Milo would have a fit if he knew the truth about the modelling and gifts. Why had I been forced into keeping a secret from him?

'It's,' he wrinkled his nose, 'unseemly.'

'Come on, Milo, you've been through your fair share of women.'

He glared at me. 'Things are different for men.'

'Things are different for men!' I repeated with derision. 'You sound as if you're from the 1950s.'

'Don't start,' Milo said, slamming his watch down on the bedside table. He muttered something in Montenegrin I didn't understand, which I thought was deliberate.

His anger hurt me. I'd never seen Milo this irate. I liked having Natalija in the house, she was a ball of energy, but I couldn't believe how it affected Milo. And he didn't know the half of it. An uncomfortable feeling crept in to my stomach and I didn't like it. I let out a sigh.

'I'm sorry.' He turned round, more gentle now.

'It's fine.' I wasn't ready to be consoled yet.

'I just want what's best for my sister.' He stood behind me and planted a kiss on the back of my neck. I hated that it made my skin tingle, even though I was mad at him.

'Do you ever think that she might be the best person to decide that?'

Milo grunted in answer. I watched him move across to open his wardrobe. He took his t-shirt off, revealing his smooth, taut back.

'I wish you were coming with us today.' He selected a shirt and slid it round his shoulders.

'I wish I was coming too,' I said. 'I can't believe I'm busy the first time you're seeing your dad in years. Maybe it's for the best. I want to meet him before the wedding, though.'

This brought a new tension to the conversation. Milo was reluctant to invite him. 'I don't want a drunk to spoil our day. A man I don't even recognise as my father,' he'd said when we discussed the guest list.

'Trust me, today's nothing special,' he said now. 'But still, I wish you were by my side.'

Milo knew I was needed at the restaurant. Preparations for the summer launch party had reached fever pitch, and we hadn't even printed the menus yet. We had a flurry of bookings, and were planning to expand our tables out onto the beach. I'd heard whispers a few journalists were coming, as well as a reviewer for *Lonely Planet*. It was going to be a big night, and there were less than forty-eight hours to go.

Today Mum and Luka were arriving and I was playing taxi driver to pick them both up from the airport.

After Milo and Natalija left and the house was quiet again, I continued finalising the menu for tomorrow night. We'd be starting with a crab ceviche, fancy lime pearls and a tomato salsa. Then Bojan was cooking our main: Montenegrin rack of lamb with sautéed samphire, the salty vegetable complementing the succulent meat in an unexpected twist. I had charge of the dessert, and was cooking my white forest gateau. It was going to have four tiers, and a brandy glaze, with individual *petit four* truffles served alongside. I had never been much of a baker but was trying to expand my skill set.

I had the idea to name each plate after a Montenegrin island. Vranjina would be the starter, named after the location where the crab was caught. Sveti Nikola for the main, as our samphire supplier was a native to the tiny island. I'd been planning to pick the island of flowers for the dessert, after our wedding venue, but I wasn't feeling so charitable towards Milo now, so I chose Sveti Marko instead.

After confirming the names, I uploaded the menu to our Café Lompar staff WhatsApp group and immediately had replies of 'I love it!' and 'Can't wait' from Lovro and Ana. Mum wouldn't be able to reply as she was currently airborne.

I stood up to adjust my blue and white Grecian sundress, and felt a little dizzy. I still wasn't used to the heat here. My back felt sticky. The lightheadedness passed quickly and I skipped out to my car.

The drive to the airport was one I'd done many times. I thought back to the first time Mum and I had travelled on this road, a year after Dad had died. Such a short time ago, really. No wonder I wasn't used to the sun. I was still a Montenegrin newbie.

I parked between two tour buses, their drivers smoking cigarettes and chatting animatedly, leaning against their vehicles, as busy tour reps herded passengers onboard. One held a clipboard aloft, clearly enjoying the authority.

It was a good sign. The summer season was beginning, and

soon trade at Café Lompar would be at its peak. I just hoped tomorrow night would go well.

After a brief wait in arrivals, I saw Luka's brown mop of hair in the approaching crowd. Sometimes seeing him from afar took my breath away. The likeness between him and my dad could catch me off guard. He spotted me at the same time.

'Kat!'

We hugged. Luka's skin felt cold against mine from the air conditioning on the plane.

'I thought you'd at least be carrying a sign,' he said, looking me up and down.

'Lompar entourage?' I joked. 'Give over.'

'Where's the lovely Grace?'

'Looks like the Bristol flight's been delayed. I think we've got time for a coffee.' I pointed towards the arrivals board. As we sat and ordered two frappucinos, ice cold but sugary, we caught up on each other's gossip. It sounded like Luka was doing well on his law course, despite his protestations and his chilled demeanour. I still couldn't imagine him as a stoney-faced lawyer.

'How's the love life?' I asked.

'Non-existent after those exams.' Luka took a noisy sip. 'Anyway, I couldn't go for uni girls knowing Natalija is at home.'

'She wouldn't be interested in you,' I laughed, although I could see her appeal to any red-blooded male.

'Please, I think she has a thing for me.'

'In your own mind, maybe.'

'Maybe. Although after what I've seen of her online...' He took another sip. It took me a while to register what he had said.

'Oh no. What do you mean?'

'You know she does some modelling, right?' he said.

I lowered my voice even though I knew Milo and Natalija were miles away. 'She told me that she does some underwear and bikini modelling?'

Luka was silent a moment, weighing up this information. 'Well, she does a little bit more than that.'

'Oh God, oh God,' I said. I had suspected as much, but didn't want it to be true.

'Yes. Full frontal,' Luka said. I couldn't tell if he was enjoying the conversation, but he definitely found this more amusing than I did. I didn't want to be told this.

'I don't even want to ask how you found out?' I grimaced.

'Let's just say I use certain sites.' Luka shrugged.

'Gross.' I didn't want to finish my frappuccino now, but kept drinking despite myself. My mind was whirring. What would Milo say?

'There's even a video,' Luka started.

'Stop. Just stop!' I put my hand in front of his face. 'Look, Natalija's an adult. She can do what she wants. And you shouldn't be watching her. Milo would freak out if he knew. You should see how protective he is of her.'

'I know what he's like. He was even worse as a teenager. Milo expects her to be a saint.' Luka mimed praying and drew a cross on his chest. I had to laugh.

'I don't know whether to tell him about Natalija or not,' I said. I would have to ask Mum tonight. I realised I was chipping the varnish off my nails with anguish.

Luka said, 'I'm not going to tell him. But you are engaged, so maybe you should? If it was me I'd want to know.'

'Thanks for throwing me under the bus,' I said, although now I was thinking about the implications of telling him about Rosa. 'If anyone tells him, it should be Natalija.'

We both sat quietly. I was wondering what to do, when Luka said, 'How's my mum doing?'

'Don't you know? You speak to her every day.'

He scratched his head. 'Usually yes, but she's been quiet lately. Sometimes when I call home, she doesn't answer, then afterwards when I ask what she was doing, she says nothing.'

I felt my cheeks flare and worried Luka would notice. I fanned myself down, hoping the heat would explain the redness.

I mumbled, 'She seems ... fine to me.'

'I don't know. I get the impression something's going on with her. It's like, weird, because we never have secrets. She'd kill me if I was keeping a secret from her.'

'Mmm, weird.' I tried to sound non-committal.

Luka was digging his thumbnail into the side of his empty frappuccino cup, peeling off the sticker in tiny fragments. 'I just hope it's nothing to do with her health. Would she tell me if the ... cancer came back?'

Of course that was his worry. It would be mine too. I felt instantly guilty. I could put him out of his misery if I told him the truth, but that was another secret I had to awkwardly hold on to. 'She looks healthier than ever to me.'

'Really?'

'Honestly.' I nodded.

'Ok, that's good. Will you do me a favour and keep an eye on her? Let me know if anything is different? Let me know if you see anything unusual?'

I gulped, wondering if not telling him the truth was the same thing as lying.

'Hi, you two!'

'Mum!' I shrieked, relieved to have the interruption. I flung my arms around her, breathing in her beautiful perfume and squeezing her close to me.

We whispered our love yous before she gave Luka a squeeze too. It still caught in my chest when I saw the two of them getting along. She used to feel awkward around him, but now I think he was becoming the son she never had.

'Bloody hell, you've packed light.' I pointed to the suitcase behind her, so big you could fit a thirty-piece orchestra inside. We laughed at the difference between her bags and Luka's neat rucksack, before heading for the car. We knew we were needed at Café Lompar.

'Let me help with that,' Luka said, skipping off to fetch a trolley.

As soon as he was out of earshot, I grabbed Mum's hand. 'Boy, do I need your advice tonight.'

CHAPTER TWELVE

🌹 Grace 🌹

The heat seemed to radiate from the concreted walkway leading away from the airport. Dear Lord, I'd forgotten how blisteringly hot Montenegrin days could be. It was still only May and it would get hotter as the weeks went on. Could I really survive until the end of September? And without Neil for most of it.

Kat had seemed so relieved to see me, enveloping me in a tight hug in the arrivals' hall. She was all of a-fluster and obviously rattled by Natalija staying and the tension with Milo. Luka was his usual cheery self as he folded himself into the back of Kat's battered white Skoda, his legs far too long to fit comfortably behind the driver's seat.

'Let me go in the back seat,' I pleaded.

'No way, José,' he said, and Kat and I burst out laughing.

'You need some more English phrases, Luka,' Kat said.

'*Pfft*!' Luka laughed.

'So, are you ready for tomorrow night?' I asked her as we hugged the coastal road back to Tivat. The glittering Adriatic was so bright, it made my eyes water.

'The menu's all in place, but, as you know, Ensambla has chosen to open on the night of our summer launch.' She shrugged. 'I don't think it's a coincidence. It's bloody annoying!'

'It's certainly brave of them to take you on. You've built a real reputation for yourself in Montenegro. I don't think you have anything to worry about.' I thought it wise to change the subject. 'How's uni going, Luka? Kat told me you did well in your exams.'

He coughed awkwardly, 'Law is hard, but I am determined. I want to do my mother proud!'

Kat sniggered. 'I don't know how proud of you she'd be if she saw your pics on Instagram in that toga party, sandwiched between two busty blondes.'

'It's not my fault. Girls are drawn to me like bees to a honeypot.'

'In your dreams!' Kat teased.

The talk continued in the same vein all the way to Tivat. I wondered if Kat and Luka would have got on so well if they'd been brought up together.

As we drove along the promenade where Café Lompar looked out onto the harbour, I felt that familiar tingle of excitement at my first glance of the restaurant where my daughter was Head Chef.

'What the hell?' Kat burst out, slamming on the brakes so abruptly, my sun hat flew from the back ledge.

'Oh. My. God!' Luka said at the same time.

Kat had stopped the car in the middle of the road outside Ensambla. I craned my neck to see a huge banner draped across the front of the other restaurant: 'Ensambla's Grand Opening: Leon Lazovic Singing Live!'

'Who's Leon Lazovic?' I asked, wide-eyed.

Luka spluttered, 'He's the most popular singer in Montenegro. A sex god. All the girls love him. Even my mother!'

'This is war!' Kat muttered darkly.

'It does seem rather unfortunate,' I agreed, trying to keep a lid on the rising panic in the car.

'Unfortunate!' Kat repeated. 'All the crowds will be at Ensambla, all the newspapers will be there.' She took a sharp intake of breath. 'Look, look...' she stuttered, unable to get her words out. She pointed at the blackboard menu outside. 'They're doing lamb and samphire and white forest gateau! It's almost the same as ours. Okay, so there's no crab ceviche, but this is NOT a coincidence. How on earth do they know this?'

I could see Kat's eyes fill with tears. I patted her leg, 'Come on, Kat, let's go to my apartment and we can talk this through. They can copy all they like but they won't have the famous Kat Lompar cooking the food.'

By the next evening, Kat had calmed down. She'd made a few changes to the menu for the launch that night; the lamb dish was now transformed to ipsod saca, roasted under a metal lid covered with hot coals, served with homemade crispy bread and Kačamak, a polenta-based dish mixed with potato, and cheese. It was quite dramatic as the dish was 'revealed' at the table. Her white forest gateau was replaced with a sheep's milk mousse with coconut curd and caramelised puffed rice. The dishes looked spectacular but Kat had been at the restaurant since five in the morning and she had huge, dark rings under her eyes. Still, she had changed into a beautiful dress and was greeting guests, seeming calm and happy with each of them. She was the star of Café Lompar and she stood with the four of us, myself, Rosa and Luka under the now iconic photograph of our crazy, mixed-up family. We were all wearing black, as we'd planned, and we gave out free glasses of Montenegro's finest wines, white Krstač and red Vranac. Kat's cookbooks were displayed on the bar and on the lectern at the entrance.

Milo was helping Davor at the bar and I was so glad he was there. He knew how to calm Kat down. But every time I caught her on her own, she was frowning. I nudged her. 'Come on, cheer up. This is your night.'

'Did you see the crowds outside Ensambla?' she asked for the hundredth time. 'Oh, what am I thinking? Of course you did. We had to fight through them to get to Café Lompar!'

When I arrived back, after going home to change, I had been startled to see three sleek, black Limousines parked outside Ensambla, taking up most of the street. All for Leon Lazovic and his entourage, no doubt. There seemed to be dozens of excited teenage girls squealing outside the restaurant and I caught the briefest glimpse of the much lusted-after Leon, chatting to a very animated Lizzie, her blonde ponytail bouncing with every word. He was clad in black leather, the tightest trousers I had ever seen, glossy as liquorice. He wore mirrored sunglasses like some throwback to a seventies' porn star.

'Is that him?' I'd asked though it was pretty obvious. Then I'd come to my senses and grabbed Kat's elbow, steering her inside Café Lompar. 'Come on, we've got our own night to think about.'

As we passed the window, the Buricos, sitting inside Ensambla, gave us an extravagant wave. They had defected and I hoped Kat hadn't seen them. It didn't help that inside Café Lompar, Ana and one of the new waitresses, Masha, kept giggling and drifting towards the windows in the hope of catching a glimpse of the pop star. They kept singing Hej *Seksi*, Leon's breakthrough single. The chorus was horribly catchy and I even found myself humming along. I stopped abruptly when Kat came into earshot. Lovro was in terrible trouble in the kitchen, too.

'He's like a bloody meerkat,' Kat muttered. 'He's watching that back window all the time. Apparently, Leon was his teenage crush and he had posters of him all over his bedroom.' Kat shuddered.

Rosa was full of nerves, I noticed, and it was clear that Ensambla's aggressive tactics were getting to her. She looked stunning in her simple black shift dress, her elfin hairstyle and bright, brick-red lipstick. She was the consummate professional front of house, making each customer feel they were the most important person in the restaurant.

As the night wore on, Café Lompar was full, but the atmosphere was a bit flat compared to the buzz of next door. At nine, there was a sudden earthquake of noise as the electric guitar and drums leapt into life.

'What the fuc..!' Luka said, rolling his eyes.

'That is taking the piss!' Kat growled.

Hej Seksi could be heard in decibels loud enough to make the floor tremble.

'This is ruining the night for our customers,' Kat moaned.

'Don't worry. We've had lots of compliments on the food tonight. Don't let it get to you, Kat,' Rosa said.

We were busy and my feet burned in pain. I still wasn't fully recovered from the journey yesterday. Even my cheeks ached from the constant smile I had plastered on my face.

I saw Kat gaze at two young men who'd just entered. Rosa rushed over to them. They were in their mid-twenties, and one was extremely good-looking, with wavy black hair, piercing blue eyes and even, white teeth.

Kat's face blanched. 'That's him,' she hissed. 'Gosh, she's got a nerve.'

'What? Ooh,' I said, as it suddenly dawned on me that this was Rosa's new beau.

I could see what Kat meant. If a part of me hadn't believed how young he was, I was firmly convinced now. Rosa was the ultimate professional, but her body language was obvious. She blushed and giggled, leaning over to point at something on the menu. She twisted her hair behind her ears and threw her head back and laughed again. It certainly wasn't subtle. *Good for her,* I thought, but it was probably wise for Luka not to see her.

'Luka, can you help Dav with the wine?' I asked.

'That couple just said they didn't want dessert,' said Masha, joining Kat and me. 'They complained the music is too loud.'

'That's it!' Kat announced. 'I'm going over there. It's ruining everything.'

'I'll go,' I sighed. 'You stay here and hold the fort. We can't let this become a full-scale war.'

Kat nodded. 'Just tell them how unfair this is. That all our customers are complaining. That we'll seek legal action.'

'Let's not go that far yet. It's their first night. They were bound to try something attention-grabbing.'

I hated confrontations and this needed careful handling. Blowing up tonight wouldn't help anything and frosty relations might be very damaging in the future. But Kat had a point. This had to be at least a hundred decibels, and I could feel my ears popping.

I marched out of the restaurant. By Kat's reckoning, Lizzie was more reasonable than her husband. I would appeal to her, perhaps negotiate a time it would finish or ask them to turn it down. Could you do that with a famous pop star? I had seen Lizzie a handful of times scurrying around Ensambla, but never spoken to her.

When I reached the entrance, crowds were spilling onto the pavements and it didn't look as if anyone was eating. What a daft idea for the opening night of a restaurant, I thought. Leon Lazovic was thrusting his hips. It didn't really go with fine dining.

As I reached the door, I was dragged in by a very excitable Lizzie. 'You're Kat's mother, Grace. I saw you with her yesterday. Oh, do come in.' She thrust a glass of Prosecco in my hand.

'Uh no, I just came over...'

'What?' she asked, puzzled. 'What did you say?'

It was bloody impossible. My teeth were rattling with the noise of the bass guitar.

'It's great, isn't it?' Lizzie said. 'We've been fully booked. Dave's shattered.' She pointed to the kitchen. 'We've stopped cooking now, though,' she bellowed. 'Everyone's just enjoying the music.' I thought 'enjoying' was rather euphemistic. 'How's it going at the Café?'

Hmm, I didn't like her calling it 'the Café'.

'Well, if you must know...' I started. Lizzie turned to look at the stage. How rude! But she couldn't even hear me if I did give her a piece of my mind. I gulped my Prosecco, feeling immediately guilty in case Kat caught me. God, how would it look?

94

Leon Lazovic's face was dripping with sweat under the bright lights of the makeshift stage. The music had stopped as the band prepared for the next number. Leon gulped his inky-black drink, looking a bit worse for wear, no doubt living up to his presumably bad boy image. He was pointing at a blonde girl, drinking with her boyfriend at a table in the middle, and wiggled his finger in a gesture meant to entice her up with him.

'Hej seksi,' he said. The girl giggled and shook her head. 'Come on,' Leon insisted. I admired his cheek. Perhaps being a pop star made him think he had the right to pull anyone, even if it was in front of her boyfriend.

Suddenly, there was a loud scream as a table was overturned. I saw the girl's boyfriend pounce on the stage and grab Leon by the scruff, his sunglasses flying off. Customers moved quickly to the sides of the restaurant as camera phones flashed around the room.

I put my drink down and sidled out of the restaurant to give Kat the first good news of the night.

CHAPTER THIRTEEN

❦ Kat ❦

The music kept on playing but the singing had stopped. Lovro filled in the words, humming just loud enough to hear, 'The way your body moves, mmm so *seksei*,' before his ears perked up, sensing drama.

I continued my task, passing the coconut curd through a sieve to ensure it was as silky smooth as it should be. Lovro moved behind my back, racing to the window for the thousandth time to spy on Ensambla. Vague shouts and the noise of cheering could be heard.

'Oh my God,' he shrieked, high-pitched.

'Stop perving on Leon,' I said, feeling my irritation level rising.

'No, Kat, I think something's happening...'

The shouts were getting louder but I carried on working with the curd, a martyr.

'I'll tell you what's happening: the desert course,' I huffed. Lovro didn't turn as he usually did. I felt irrationally angry, but knew my anger was all directed at bloody Ensambla. Ensambla and the prick that was David.

'Little bit of help here?' I said to Lovro.

Lovro glanced back, before turning to the window again.

At least there wasn't a big demand on dessert. A number of diners had drifted out of Café Lompar before the final course.

I'd spotted one couple swaying on the street outside Ensambla in time to the music. They'd completely overtaken us tonight, stolen our thunder. As soon as I'd seen the sign for Leon Lazovic I knew what they were doing.

Numbers in Café Lompar were dwindling, whereas Ensambla looked like they held the headline act at Glastonbury.

'Kat.' Mum burst through the kitchen doors, her black, polka-dot skirt trailing in the wind behind her.

'You took your time,' I snapped.

'It's all kicking off over there,' she told me, excited. 'Leon called some woman up to the stage to dance and her boyfriend decked him!'

I had to admit, it made me smile, before the gloom of the night set in again.

'Well, I'm sure they'll get lots of publicity for that,' I said. 'Remember when we had that article in the *Pobjeda*? What you said? All publicity is good publicity?'

Mum frowned for a fraction of a second before her smile returned. 'I'm sure this is just opening night hype.'

'The fight's already on snapchat,' Lovro said unhelpfully, waving his phone in the air.

'Did you get to speak to Lizzie?' I asked Mum.

'Barely. The music was too loud to make myself heard. You're right, I think she's a fake.'

'She's not that bad,' Lovro said from the window, still watching like a hawk for any sightings of Leon.

'How can you say that?'

I felt a reassuring hand on my shoulder. 'Calm down,' Mum told me. 'It'll all be fine.'

'Café Lompar's doomed.' I crossed my arms. I knew I was being childish now, but I cared so much about the restaurant. It was my whole world, held everyone I loved, and was what I poured my passion into. Tears stung the back of my eyes, a familiar feeling.

I was annoyed. Rosa was busy flirting with her new guy and Mum had gone AWOL when I needed her here. Why did no one else care as much as I did?

'Come on, that's a bit dramatic,' Mum said. 'A bit Marc Douvall?'

The reminder of my old boss helped to shake me from my sulk. I carried on working, preparing the dessert plates. Seeing the flecks of black vanilla seeds speckled throughout the mousse calmed me, and the artful pattern we created with puffed rice and praline crumb looked chic and inviting. Café Lompar would never need gimmicks to sell our food, although it was a shame the crowds at Ensambla wouldn't taste this food tonight. I mentally scoured any celebrity contacts we had, before telling myself off.

The last of the dessert plates went out. It sounded like Ensambla had transitioned to a DJ now, the techno music thumping through Café Lompar so loudly, wine glasses were vibrating in the cupboard. Would it be like this every night? Were they a restaurant or a nightclub?

It was game on tomorrow. I planned to march in to Ensambla and complain. I wouldn't pander to Lizzie's niceties or David's understated snipes. They needed to know they couldn't pull a stunt like this again. I'd complain to the council if I had to.

I heard laughter coming from the restaurant, a familiar cackle.

Natalija had arrived. I checked the time. Ten o'clock was a bit late for her to turn up for dinner. She'd promised to come earlier. We'd even saved her a table for the launch.

I went over to see her. She was standing at the bar, looking Amazonian in a white crocheted dress that only emphasised her neon underwear beneath. All eyes turned to her wherever she went.

'Hey, Kat!' Her eyes lit up when she saw me. 'This is my friend, Lejla.'

I greeted them both with air kisses. I wanted to make a comment about their lateness but hadn't quite reached that level of comfort with Natalija yet. Luka materialised at my side, wanting in on the action.

'Luka!' Natalija looked pleased to see him, giving him a tight hug. 'I haven't seen you in ages.'

I could practically feel the smugness radiating from him. 'I know, it's been, like, five years.'

'Cool party next door, right?' Natalija said, turning to me. 'They're making some insane cocktail with glitter!'

'Is that Ensambla?' Luka asked. 'You don't want to go there. Café Lompar is much better.' I was pleased to have at least one person on my side.

'Yes, but the vibe...' Natalija started.

'And Leon Lazovic,' Lejla reminded her. 'He is hot.'

'Swoon,' Natalija said. The smile on Luka's face drooped slightly.

'Excuse me a moment.' I backed off. I didn't care if it was rude, I just couldn't take any more talk of Ensambla and Leon fucking Lazovic. I went to the bathroom for a break, relishing the cool feel of the air-conditioning on my skin.

I caught my reflection in the mirror. I looked stressed and hot. My mascara smudged the bottom of my eyelids. I rubbed at it but it only made it worse.

The staff bathroom at Café Lompar was next to the courtyard at the back of the restaurant. As I stood there, I could hear voices coming through the wall, giggling, then a long silence.

'Awww, when are you going to tell him?' a man's voice said.

Rosa's familiar voice now. 'Soon, I promise. Soon.'

'I want us to be public.' The kissing was audible. 'Come on, Rosita.'

I smiled at the name Rosita. I knew I shouldn't be snooping, but if they were going to talk so close to the restaurant, I reasoned it was fair game.

'I hate all this sneaking around,' Rosa said. She was taking a risk, fawning over him so blatantly at the restaurant, and kissing so close to Luka.

There was more heavy petting and then he said, 'I can't wait to come home with you tonight.'

'We can't. Luka is at home.'

'But my roommates are in tonight.' He really did sound young. I half-expected to find out his roommates were his parents.

I didn't want to be caught spying, and turned the hand drier on loudly.

As I came out of the bathroom, Luka was milling around. I glanced at the outside door, worried if he had heard anything.

'Listen, Kat.' He came over. 'I know Natalija and Lejla are too late to have food here so we're going to go over to...'

'Ensambla, you don't need to say it.'

He'd changed his tune now he was being included in their

100

plans. I couldn't keep quiet. 'Do you really have to be so fickle?'

Luka looked winded, shocked. There was an awkward pause before he responded, 'Don't be like this, Kat.'

'I'm serious.' I was riled now. This tension was new territory for us. Luka gave a nervous laugh. 'I thought you were meant to be loyal to Café Lompar.'

'This isn't Shakespeare, Kat. "Two households." I don't need to be loyal here.'

'I just wish you didn't ditch me every time a mildly attractive girl walked past.'

'Where the hell is this coming from?'

'On the talk show with Lena? Anywhere we go? You always think of yourself first.' My fists were clenched. I had the uncomfortable sensation I was saying something I would regret, but I couldn't stop now.

Luka looked wounded, and I hated to see it, but I kept going.

'God, Luka, will anything get in the way of you and your ego? Except maybe your penis?'

'Don't be so childish, Kat. Just because Ensambla are doing better than us tonight. Talk about an ego – you can't handle anyone else's success.'

My anger flared. 'Don't.'

'It's true. It's the reason you're being such a bitch tonight.'

Now he'd bitten, I felt I could really let loose. 'At least I'm not following Natalija around like a puppy dog. It's pathetic.'

Luka ran an exasperated hand through his hair. 'I think you should go home, Kat. It's clearly been a stressful night for you. Have a rest.' His calmness only irked me more. He was being patronising.

'I'm fine,' I spat. 'But I think you might be a bit more stressed if you knew what was going on closer to home.'

'What's that supposed to mean?' A look of confusion crossed his face.

'I just think you'd be a bit less calm if you knew what was really happening.' I was on the verge of blurting out the truth about Rosa. It was awful but I wanted to hurt Luka. I needed a reaction from him. It wasn't a nice side of me, but my buttons had been pushed.

We stood across the hall from each other, a no man's land of unspoken words between us.

At that moment Rosa's laughter got louder, and the door to the courtyard swung open. The guy stepped inside, looking dishevelled, every bit the naughty schoolboy, and Rosa followed behind him with her hand linked through his arm, her hair ruffled and her usually pristine lipstick wiped off. It was obvious what they had been doing.

Luka looked at them, then back at me, then at Rosa. Realisation and accusation dawned on his face.

'Oh,' Rosa said, guilty now.

Luka's mouth was open but he didn't speak. He looked vulnerable.

I couldn't breathe. A wave of nausea came over me. Oh God, I'd hinted at this and now it was happening. I immediately regretted what I'd said. He was right, I was being a bitch tonight and taking it all out on him, just because he'd been in the wrong place at the wrong time.

My heart wanted to grow legs and climb out of my chest, just to get to Luka and protect him. I wanted to reach out and pull him away.

Rosa's boyfriend was still looking at her with hunger in his eyes, taking a second to catch on to what was happening.

'Is this Luka?' he said after a moment. I thought I was going to be sick.

'I don't...' Luka started, eyeing Rosa. Then he turned and pushed through the door.

Panic flashed in Rosa's expression as she looked to me.

I immediately took off after him. 'Luka!' I shouted. He was already a few paces ahead. He ignored me. 'Luka, please.' I couldn't run too fast, the nausea was growing. 'Luka, please talk to me.'

Chattering came from Ensambla, but it sounded as though the crowds were dispersing now.

Luka stopped all of a sudden and turned to me. 'Well, I hope you're happy now.'

'I...'

It was too late. He walked away from me.

PART TWO

CHAPTER FOURTEEN

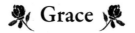 Grace

It was Sunday morning and I could hear the bells of St Mary's ring out heartily from the mountain above Tivat, disturbing the early morning remnants of my dream. It was eight o'clock and I stretched in bed, enjoying the luxury of a lie-in after a busy Saturday service. There seemed enough customers going around at this time of year not to worry too much about Ensambla. Anyway, the fight between Leon Lazovic and the jealous fiancé was all over social media and had clipped their wings.

I had to be in by lunchtime, but later this afternoon I was picking up Claire and Laura from the airport. They'd booked an Airbnb a few streets away from my apartment. I was looking forward to seeing them both, but it was strange to think of them coming without Stu and Liam.

'Liam's staying home with his mates and Stu's too busy at work. Anyway, we're hardly joined at the hip,' Claire said, with an unfamiliar, hard edge to her voice. 'Laura can't wait to come out now she's between boyfriends.' Claire's predictions that the kindly Dylan was not going to be long-term had proved true. Claire continued, 'How I'll be able to rein in a horny teen, I'll never know. She's got the wardrobe of a Miami hooker, all teeny-weeny shorts and tight body-con dresses. Stu nearly had kittens when he saw what she was wearing to go out the other night.'

'It'll be lovely to see you both,' I laughed. 'You deserve this break, Claire.'

'Well, I won't have a chance to take such a long summer again. I was glad to hand my notice in at Hillview. Now Liam and Laura have left, I don't have to put up with that arsehole of a head.'

'East Bridge is much smaller. I'm sure you'll be happier there.'

'I don't even want to think about school. This time tomorrow, I'll have a cocktail in my hand and the tight buttocks of some hot Montenegrin waiter in my eyeline!'

'God, and you wonder where Laura gets it from?' Although I kept it light, I felt a bit awkward when Claire made jokes like this. She never used to.

I grabbed a glass of juice from the fridge and took it outside to soak up the gorgeous views from my balcony. This was my favourite time of day. It wasn't baking hot and I could see the harbour yawning and stretching to life. Tourists strolled by, grabbing a pastry for breakfast before pausing to gaze at the sparkling Adriatic, and the majestic, opulent yachts anchored next to the humble little fishing skiffs. Above, the cacophonous squawks of seagulls, lured by the fishing trawl, resounded through the skies. It was early but already the heat was making its presence felt and the wrought iron seats warmed my thighs as I sipped my juice.

Only three weeks until Neil and Ollie came out to stay. I smiled thinking of my handsome boyfriend. I still felt a little awkward as a woman in my fifties referring to him as my 'boyfriend,' but 'partner' threw up all sorts of ambiguities;

business people had 'partners.' I missed him when I was out here. He made me feel loved and cared for in that old-fashioned way, opening car doors and putting his jacket over my shoulders when we walked back to his place from a restaurant and I felt a bit chilly. And the sex was great. It was wonderful just to feel desired again.

Dan never made me feel like that. I just thought it was the way with married couples, like Stu and Claire. You become part of the furniture, a rather lumpy but familiar armchair to sink into. But Neil looked at me the way Milo looked at Kat and it felt good.

Though there was a bit of tension between Kat and Milo lately. Milo was so protective of his sister. It was a side we hadn't seen of him. And don't get me started with Rosa and Luka. You could cut the air with a knife when they were together. Luka just couldn't get used to the idea of his mother dating a younger man. It turned out he'd been a few years above Luka in school. Matija was now studying architecture in the University of Montenegro in Podgorica, she told me yesterday when we were sorting orders for the week ahead.

'So, how are things with Luka at the moment?'

'Hmm, frosty, you say?'

I nodded.

'He is angry that I am dating and Matija is a lot younger than me.' She shrugged.

'Good for you,' I told her. 'Luka will get used to it. You have your own life to lead.'

'He is a good boy,' she went on, always the protective lioness. 'It has always been just him and me, with Danilo often away.'

I couldn't help but wince at my husband's name used so freely.

'How did you meet Matija?' I asked, moving onto safer territory.

'Last year, November. When we were having that work done on the restaurant. He was one of the designers. He is very creative.' Her eyes lit up. 'He was the one to come up with the recycled church pews as seating for us. He's into all this sustainability, like young people are.'

'Gosh, you're a dark horse,' I teased.

'A dark horse?' She raised her eyebrows. 'At first I wasn't interested. I was exhausted after the treatment and did not feel attractive. He was very insistent.' She smiled.

Anyone looking at Rosa would have thought she was bursting with confidence. Cancer had knocked the stuffing out of her, but she had come out the other side. She was a beautiful woman, fragile yet strong, her eyes inky dark and her hair growing back, not as thick as it had been but stunningly glossy.

'After Danilo, I didn't ever believe I could trust a man again, but Mat makes me feel young. He's the more mature one sometimes.'

I felt angry that Luka was making her feel bad for wanting another man. She was ten years younger than me and had given too much of herself to Dan. As had I.

'Danilo was a wanker,' I said, and we both laughed.

As we drove from the airport, each new vista drew gasps of appreciation from Claire and Laura. They'd been to Montenegro before, of course, last year to celebrate Kat's twenty-fifth birthday and engagement, but the scenery had the same effect on me every time I came back.

110

'Wow, look down there, Mum,' Laura said, pointing at a promontory falling into the cobalt sea. Tiny, picturesque villas clung like lichen to the cliffs and above them, stood luxury apartments with wall-to-ceiling windows to maximise the views. 'Imagine living there,' Laura sighed.

'I could get used to this,' Claire said. 'I can imagine a Daniel Craig lookalike handing me a gin as we gaze at the sunset.'

'Mu-um, for God's sake. Daniel Craig wouldn't look at you.'

Claire rolled her eyes. 'So, what are the plans for today?'

'Well, I thought you two could check into the Airbnb and settle for a while. Kat says she's going to come over. We've both got the night off. Perhaps we'll just go to Café Lompar, eat and have a couple of cocktails.'

'Hmm, now you're talking my language,' Claire said.

'What are the beaches like here, Auntie Grace?' Laura asked, leaning forward. The strong smell of her jasmine perfume made me feel a bit sick. 'I want to go back with a nice tan.'

'Not great in Tivat. It's more about the harbour here. But Mogren and Budva have glorious beaches. You're here long enough this time to make a few trips.'

We soon arrived at their villa, *Vue Mer,* or Sea View. Very original. It had a small, private pool and before Claire and Laura's luggage could be placed inside the hallway, Laura had stripped down to her tiny, lime green bikini, her clothes discarded at the door.

'Come on in, you two!' she squealed.

'You're alright,' Claire said, as we turned to explore the villa. It was ultra-modern, with fossil-grey kitchen units and white leather sofas in a living room looking onto a small terrace and swimming pool. As we looked around, Laura ensconced herself on the sun-bed after her dip, scrolling through her phone, her sunglasses pushed to the back of her head.

'Very nice,' was Claire's verdict. 'I can't tell you how much I need this break. She placed her suitcase beside the double bed in the biggest bedroom. 'Two weeks with the bed to myself, no snoring carcass next to me. I can stretch out and just think about myself for a change.'

I laughed, 'You make Stuart sound like some oafish clown. He's not that bad, surely?'

Claire flopped onto the bed, ignoring my question. 'I'm knackered after that flight. A quick nap and I'll be ready to party tonight.'

I shuddered. Claire was determined to enjoy her freedom, yet I had a summer of work ahead of me.

'Cooee! I hope I haven't come too early.' We could hear Kat's voice in the hallway. Milo and Natalija followed her.

Milo kissed my cheek and Claire's. 'This is my sister, Natalija.'

'Lovely to meet you,' Claire said, and her eyes widened at Natalija's outfit, a pale pink body-con dress – slashed at the back – and gold gladiator sandals snaking up her tanned and flawless calves.

Natalija threw her arms around Claire. 'It's so nice to meet you.'

Laura appeared, hovering behind Milo and Natalija. She'd hurriedly pulled a t-shirt over her wet bikini and looked coy, standing on one foot.

'This is my daughter, Laura,' Claire said.

Natalija wrapped Laura in an equally effusive hug.

'Two of my bridesmaids finally meet!' Kat said, laughing. Milo frowned. 'You'll see the third, Maria tonight. Although she'll be working. We'll all meet up in Café Lompar and you two can get to know each other.'

Laura was delighted. I could see Natalija was everything she longed to be, older by a few years, a sophisticated fashion student, a passing relationship with clothes... They were going to get along like a house on fire. I was relieved I hadn't told Claire about Natalija's modelling.

Claire rummaged in the cupboard for coffee or tea. 'Hmm, I'll have to pop out. Where's the nearest supermarket?'

'I'll get a few things in,' Milo volunteered.

We sat in the living room as he left and Laura and Natalija drifted to the pool, catching up on wedding news.

We arrived about eight at Café Lompar and Rosa had reserved the best table for us, looking out to sea. It was Claire, Laura, Natalija, Kat and I. Milo had agreed to help with front of house as I was having the night off. Natalija and Laura sat next to each other, Laura squealing as Natalija scrolled through her phone showing her photographs of Milan. They both drew stares from the passing tourists with their short dresses and striking looks.

'That's from last year's Milan Fashion Week. All the top designers were there – Prada, Fendi, Max Mara... Fendi had this romantic collection, dreamy linen and crocheted pieces, all naturals and sepia-toned.'

Laura looked agog.

Natalia cried, 'Oh my God, you should so come along to the next one. It's the end of June.'

Laura's eyes darted to Claire's. 'Mum?'

'We'll see,' Claire said enigmatically, sipping her Mojito, which was her stock response when she didn't want to say no immediately.

'How you'll keep these two under rein, I'll never know,' I said quietly to Kat. 'Remember it's your choice for the bridesmaids' dresses. Don't be dictated to by them.'

'I know.' Kat nodded. 'Natalija has these fixed ideas on what she wants and it's a bit intimidating as she's a fashion student.'

'Any luck with Milo and his father?' I whispered. 'Is he still determined his dad shouldn't be at the wedding?'

Kat shook her head. 'Milo clams up when I ask him about it. I don't really know what went on. I mean his father brought the two of them up. You think they'd be really close.'

She glanced over at Milo, who was serving wine at a table. I looked at him too – he really was good-looking with his chiselled features, dark hair and olive skin. He and Natalija were very alike.

Kat went on, 'His father was a heavy drinker.' Her voice dropped, as she glanced over at Natalija and Laura, still engrossed in the images on her phone. 'His dad hurt him and he's finding it hard to forgive. I just wish he'd open up to me.'

I thought for the millionth time how families were so bloody complicated.

'Natalija told me her father wants to be there at the wedding. She still sees him a lot. I'm tempted to just invite him. I'm sure Milo somewhere deep down wants his father there at such an important day. He just needs a push.'

'I'm not sure that's such a good idea,' I said, but the conversation was cut off as Ana brought the food to our table.

As everyone complimented the food, Kat's face glowed with pride.

I didn't have the opportunity to chat to Kat alone later. The dress fitting was tomorrow and we all went back to our own places for an early night. Not before Laura tried to escape for a night on the town first.

'Can I go with Natalija to this club, Mum? I won't be long.'

'No, you cannot,' said Claire in her bad-ass voice that would contemplate no arguments.

I did wonder, though, how long it would take for Claire to be ground down by Laura's persistence. I had a real sense of foreboding as we strolled back home, the drone of cicadas accompanying our weary steps.

CHAPTER FIFTEEN

❦ Kat ❦

We got home late. I looked in the mirror of our dimly-lit bathroom. My lipstick had smudged off, leaving a ghostly trace of pink on my lips. My hair looked thin and frazzled, and my eyeliner was in dark pools under my eyes.

I sighed. I didn't normally wear much make-up but the thought of sitting across from Natalija and Laura, who were both always done up to perfection, had got me putting on a shade of lipstick called 'The Cat That Got the Pink'. Whatever that was supposed to mean.

I hoped this wasn't a premonition for my wedding day. I could just imagine myself looking as crumpled and limp as a bedsheet, while Natalija dazzled in some skimpy number. Surely it didn't matter as long as Milo's eyes were on me? But he'd seemed distant recently, not himself. I didn't know if it was the stress about his father.

Every time I tried to bring it up, he just grunted or evaded my questions. It was exhausting. I wanted to be there for him. Milo had told me a lot about his father, and although he was an alcoholic, I knew he wasn't a monster. It was important for me to get close to Milo's only family. God knows, family had taken on a new meaning for me over the last two years.

What I really wanted to tell him was that he would regret it if his father didn't come to the wedding. It was important to tell people you loved them while you still had them. I knew that better than anyone after losing Dad.

I could hear Milo pottering about in the bedroom, but didn't want to broach the subject with him again tonight. He'd had a long day on his feet, plus I was going dress shopping tomorrow in Podgorica and needed my energy. I didn't want an argument with Milo to put a dampener on such a special day tomorrow.

I checked my phone as I brushed my teeth. Still nothing from Luka.

I'd texted him every day since he went back to university, straight after the night of the summer launch. I'd only received one word replies here and there. My message from earlier glowed blue, unread: '*Saw a kid with bad highlights at the harbour today and it made me think of those pics of you at your school dance. I think you should get them again. The 90s is back in fashion. Call me, you idiot!*'

I had tried to keep the tone lighthearted but the desperation was so pungent you could smell it through the screen.

I still felt so guilty for making hints about his mother and her younger man. Luka must think I orchestrated it all.

I couldn't stand another night of agonising over it. I pressed *call*.

Luka didn't pick up on the first ring. Or the tenth. It was a lost cause. I hung up. Then I saw my message had now been read.

My phone started ringing. He was calling back.

'Hello, Kat speaking.' I felt strangely nervous, my voice coming over all formal.

'What do you mean, "Kat speaking"? I know it's you, loser,' Luka said. The relief I felt was immense.

'Well, excuse me. I feel nervous talking to you. You've gone quiet on me and it's weird,' I said.

'I know, I know,' he replied. 'I didn't know how to answer your desperate messages.'

'You've got me there,' I said, because he had. Luka went quiet, and I couldn't tell what he was thinking.

'Are you still mad at me?' I asked, unable to think of anything else.

'Honestly? I don't know.'

I exhaled. I felt so sorry for him after everything that had happened. I wanted to make it better, but the conversation was delicate, as if we were doing a dance and only Luka knew the choreography.

'It's so weird, Kat. My mum and Matija. He didn't know who I was, but I used to worship him in school. He's only a few years older than me. He used to wear his hair slicked back like he spent all day in the sea. He was cool.'

'He doesn't sound cool,' I laughed. 'It must be strange, though.' I sat on the side of the bath, folding my legs up to balance on the edge.

'Super strange. I'm sure I talked about him a few times to Mum. Did she know who he was?' He paused. 'Even though I have no right to say this, I don't like them being together.'

'I know,' I said. I had to be cautious here. 'But she seems happy.'

'I want her to be happy,' he said forcefully. 'Just not with him.' He laughed. 'It's a ridiculous thing to say, I know.'

I felt a bit more confident of his feelings now. 'Luka, you know

I didn't mean for you to find out like that. Your Mum wasn't even aware I knew they were together.'

'That's another thing that hurts,' Luka grumbled, his tone darkening. 'All the secrecy. Why didn't you tell me, Kat?'

My words got stuck. I didn't know what to say. So I said the truth. 'I wanted to tell you. I agonised over it, went back and forth. Milo said it would be best coming from Rosa...'

'Wait, Milo knew about it too?' he interrupted, incredulous now. I felt him slipping away from me again. Why did I have to open my big mouth?

'I made him promise not to tell you. Please, Luka, don't blame him.'

He paused, then said, 'Okay.'

God, I was making a mess of this.

'Luka, I'm always on your side. I'm your sister.'

'Half-sister,' he reminded me, but I could hear the smile in his voice.

'I saw Rosa with Matija a few weeks ago but I didn't know what was going on. I really didn't want to gossip and, honestly, I thought it was your mum's place to tell you. I'm guessing it didn't exactly go the way she wanted it to, either.'

Luka grunted. He sounded as sullen as Milo. Why did I seem to be in everyone's bad books at the moment?

'I'm sorry I didn't tell you. And I'm sorry I was a bitch on Friday night.'

'A big bitch,' he laughed.

'What can I say? The stress got to me! Have I done enough grovelling now?'

'We'll see,' Luka said. 'Anyway, I must go, there are many

attractive girls here and I have no time to speak to you anymore.'

I grinned. I deserved it. 'Did I ever teach you the word "dickhead"?'

'Bye, Kat.'

'Bye.' I hung up, feeling immediately lighter. Now if I could just get through to my brooding fiancé.

'Well, I never thought I'd see the day.' Mum reached in her handbag for a hankie.

'You're not blubbing already?' I said. 'I haven't even tried anything on yet.'

Mum laughed. 'It's a big deal though.' She ran her hand along the rails of white material, netting, lace, satin. 'I remember my wedding day to Dad.'

I looked up. Rosa was on the other side of the shop, out of earshot. Laura had been taken along quite willingly by Natalija to look at the bridesmaids' section.

'I thought you wore a suit?' I asked, remembering the dusty pictures of her in a white skirt and jacket next to Dad with a moustache he soon outgrew.

'She did. Your mum looked chic in that skirt,' Auntie Claire said, overhearing. 'Not like me: I wore a big meringue on mine. It was the only thing that covered my growing stomach. You know what they say, the bigger the dress, the duller the marriage.' She moved off.

Mum and I eyed each other with mutual wariness.

I turned to the rail. 'I don't know what I want.' I'd dreamed of getting married, but in my dreams the dress was a vague blur.

True, Milo had surpassed my childhood expectations of marrying Justin Timberlake, and sunny Montenegro was a more glamorous location than the church in Bath I'd always imagined for the big day. But the dress was where I drew a blank.

'I'd be more comfortable in chef whites than this,' I said, plucking out a giant taffeta number that looked like something a podgy five-year old would wear to a beauty pageant.

'We'll find something perfect.' Mum squeezed my arm. 'Your dad would be so proud today.'

I eyed a short dress with cut-outs, and wondered if Milo's prudishness over his sister would extend to what I was wearing. I knew I wanted something simple and elegant but the question was what.

'How about this?' Mum asked, holding up a cake-topper layered dress, a grin spreading on her face.

'I'll take the skirt suit,' I said. At this rate Milo would be standing at the end of the aisle, looking like an Instagram model, and I'd be coming down in a dressing gown.

'Hey, Kat? How do you feel about giant zips for the bridesmaids' dresses?' Natalija's came in from the next room. Mum gave me a sympathetic look. The dress Natalija was holding up wouldn't look amiss in an eighties' dance video. It was fuchsia with multiple zips, creating a zig-zag pattern across the front. Laura was standing by Natalija's side looking delighted, probably imaging her long legs and slender waist on full display in her matching one.

I opened my mouth to speak but Claire did the work for me. 'Laura Jones, you are not wearing that in public.'

Laura gawped at Claire, then pulled at Natalija's elbow to retreat. 'I'm sorry about her,' I heard her muttering.

'It's not that revealing?' Natalija sounded puzzled. I mouthed 'thank you' to Claire.

My frustration rose with each rail I went through. No dress even came close to being 'the one'. I felt like I was on an episode of *Say Yes to the Dress*, only without expert personal styling help. When was my time to say 'yes' coming? Each monstrosity so far was a 'hell no'.

'Don't worry, we'll find something,' Mum soothed, aware of my building tension. 'We can always look somewhere else, just you and me.'

'That would be great,' I said, although I knew this was one of the best dress shops in Montenegro. Maybe the problem was me, not the dresses. Maybe I just wasn't the wedding type. At the moment I was more interested in the food than the flowers, place settings or dress. When would I get my bridezilla moment?

'I think we've found the one,' Laura came in, excited. The bridesmaid dress she held up was a bit more modest than the last: the asymmetric hemline was only crotch-grazing on one side.

'Uhh, maybe,' I stumbled.

'Gio's going to love you in that,' Natalija giggled.

'Who the fuck is Gio?' I heard Claire say to Mum. This day was turning in to a nightmare.

'I think you would look good in this, Kat, no?' Rosa had joined in the fun now, displaying a strapless satin dress.

'Are you struggling, Kat?' Natalija came over. 'Don't worry, I see this all the time. You just haven't found your personal style yet.' She said it pityingly like I was missing a limb.

I was really flailing.

'Natalija found this as well.' Laura was showcasing a long skirt and crop top. 'It's really modern. I like it. Maybe not for the wedding but Natalija's setting us up on a photoshoot together!'

I wondered if this would be one of Natalija's less tame photoshoots. God, I should have known Natalija and Laura would be a bad combination. Natalija was all Laura's teenage fantasy on steroids.

'Your dad will have kittens if you wear that in public.' Claire grabbed it from Laura's hands.

'I think we should hold off on bridesmaid dress shopping altogether until Maria gets here,' I said. I knew Maria would be less extreme in her choices. She was my best friend in Montenegro, an ex-Café Lompar waitress turned student. 'Why don't we go for coffee until she meets us?'

Mum looked confused.

'I need a break,' I explained quietly.

I led the pack out of the fancy shop, waving our apologies at the shop assistant who would be tasked with clearing up Laura and Natalija's detritus. No doubt they wouldn't be welcoming us back with open arms and their signature bottle of champagne.

I stepped into the street, my eyes squinting in the midday sun. My vision adjusted as I looked past the shoppers and tourists milling around, and I spotted a vintage shop across the street. In the window was a long, flowing, sleeveless, white dress, figure-hugging and classic, purely silk. Like Monica Geller's in *Friends*. I knew it was the one.

I couldn't help the tears. I'd found my bridezilla moment.

CHAPTER SIXTEEN

 Grace

'What do you fancy? A bit of culture? A museum or art gallery? A wildlife park?' I had asked Claire the night before, half-serious.

'Get me to the nearest beach. I want to spend the day soaking up the sun and having a nice lunch.'

'Mogren is a lovely, sandy beach,' I said, 'and there are a few nice bars and restaurants nearby.'

So it was agreed. We'd have a day lazing on the beach at Mogren in Budva, a welcome rest after the frantic day of wedding dress shopping the day before. Poor Kat had to work at lunch, but I'd promised to be at Café Lompar for evening service.

I'd had such a lump in my throat yesterday when she tried that dress on in the vintage store. The owner of the charity shop, a large woman with greying, curly hair, had been keen to shut the shop for the day, but when Kat told her she wanted to try on the wedding dress, the woman nodded, turning the sign around from 'Zatvoreno' (closed) to 'Otvoreno'. And when Kat came out of the changing room, she was simply beautiful. It was very Kat, classy and stylish. The way she immediately started describing how she would wear it, with flowers in her hair and silver sandals – she would look sensational. I thought about Dan and how he would have loved to give her away at her wedding.

'You look stunning,' I told her, taking both her hands, not trusting myself to say anything else, as I choked back the tears. I knew Kat was thinking about her father too. They were so close.

'I know, Mum. I wish he was here too.' She gave a small smile. 'Isn't it perfect, though?'

'Perfect!'

Natalija gave her approval. 'It's very on trend. Very now. I love it.' She gave a dramatic wave of her hand. Laura squealed.

The sound of the taxi pulling up outside made me hurriedly shove my book and sunglasses in my beach bag. Claire was sitting in the front seat with Natalija and Laura in the back, both in tiny, frayed denim shorts and vest tops. Budva was only half an hour's drive and I sat back, enjoying the coastal villages we passed on the way, some tiny hamlets with the familiar terracotta roofs of grey stone cottages. Natalija and Laura were going to do some shopping in TQ Plaza, the popular shopping mall in Budva, and would join us later on the beach.

'I allowed Laura to go out with Natalija last night. A little test, shall we say,' Claire had told me on the phone earlier this morning as we made final arrangements for the day. 'But they were back by eleven and Laura was on her best behaviour. She'd obviously had a bit to drink but she managed to walk in a straight line and could string a few sentences together before she went to bed. She's dying to go clubbing with Natalija.'

'Remember what we were like? I do believe Strongbow was our tipple of choice.'

Claire nodded, 'We were so much more sophisticated than the youth of today. Remember when we went to Odyssey and you borrowed my pink cardi, then threw up over it.' I was usually the sensible older sister, but Claire had rescued me from some scrapes.

'Yes, you didn't speak to me for a month.'

I bit my lip wondering if it was the right time to tell her about Natalija's modelling, but decided it was probably best to leave it. Natalija was hardly going to try to get Laura into the same. She wasn't that stupid, surely?

It was so hot in the taxi and I had to peel my legs from the plastic seats as we drew into Budva. The girls were dropped off first and then Claire and I headed for the beach. Mogren has a beautiful, horse-shoe beach bordered by pine trees and oleander, almost Caribbean with its crystal, turquoise waters and powdery sand. The beach was split in two and Claire and I walked through a cave to the other side where it was quieter.

'Very quirky,' Claire said, dropping her bag onto the sand. 'Shall we hire an umbrella and sun-beds? Then we can have a day of bliss.'

Just as I was settling onto my sun-bed and spraying my arms with suntan oil, my phone buzzed in my bag and Neil's face lit up the screen.

'Oh, it's Neil,' I told Claire. 'Perhaps I'll ring him later.'

'You carry on,' she said. 'I've got my book and I'll be nodding off in a few minutes.'

'Hi, Neil,' I said, smiling.

'Well, hello, gorgeous.' I heard Claire sigh next to me. 'Ooh, are you on the beach? I wish I was there to rub some suntan oil on you. I'm sure you missed a bit on your front.'

I squirmed. Claire stared fixedly at her book, just raising her eyebrow slightly. 'How come you're not in work?'

He turned the phone around, giving me sweeping views of the golf course. 'My last client cancelled. And I thought I have some time on my hands and I'd call my lovely girlfriend. How's it going there? How did wedding dress shopping go?'

'Brilliant. Well, it was a long day and Kat didn't see anything she fancied at first, until she spotted this dress in a vintage shop. She looked beautiful.'

'Takes after her mother.' He smiled.

I felt self-conscious again, aware that Claire was listening, and other sunbathers close by.

I swivelled the phone around before Neil could say anything else that might embarrass me. 'Claire's here.'

Claire waved. 'Hi Neil. It looks like it's a bit drizzly there. Shame. It's twenty-five degrees here and it's ... what ... only eleven thirty in the morning? Might have a glass of Prosecco or a cocktail at lunch.'

'Okay, okay, I'm green with envy,' Neil said.

'I am working tonight,' I insisted. 'You'll be out in a couple of weeks, anyway.'

'I know and I can't wait. Look, I'll leave you two to enjoy your hectic day of sunbathing and boozing. I'll ring you later.' He blew a kiss.

I lay back, listening to the gentle lapping of the waves.

After a minute, Claire propped herself on her elbow and let her book slip off her lap. 'I want that.'

'What?' I wondered, looking out to sea.

'What you and Neil have. That sweetness, that tenderness. And bloody hot sex!'

'What about St...?'

'Really? Stu? Is that what you were going to say? Have you not listened to a word I've been saying lately?'

I was quite taken aback. She sounded so angry. This was unusual for Claire. She always came back with a joke even at the most serious moments.

'Look, it's not your fault,' she said, 'and I shouldn't take it out on you. But I am SO bored with him, so fed up with my marriage. I really don't think I can stand it anymore.'

I sat up. 'I didn't realise things were that bad.'

'Well, they are.' Claire reached for a tissue from her bag. 'It's not that I haven't tried. God almighty, I've tried.'

'How long have you been feeling like this?'

'Three, four years maybe.' She looked me in the eye. 'Yes, that long.'

'Does Stu realise?'

'Yes. How could he not? I try to hide it, but we know each other so well.' Claire grabbed her water bottle from her bag and took a small sip. 'He wants to try. He even suggested we go to therapy. Stu! Can you imagine? He hates talking about his emotions.'

'Perhaps you should give it a go.'

Claire shook her head. 'No, the relationship is dead in the water. No amount of emotional CPR is going to revive it. I've asked for a divorce.'

I tried not to look shocked. She needed to talk, but it was like hearing – my brain scrambled for examples of rock-solid celebrity marriages you could never imagine breaking up. Tom Hanks and Rita Wilson. Was that the best I could do? I kept quiet.

'Remember Mum and Dad? That undercurrent of bitterness between them. Married for forty-odd years. They might have been happier with other people. Then Dad got Parkinson's and it was too late. There was no question Mum wouldn't look after him. And what was her reward? Dementia. God, it was so sad, Gracie. I don't want that for me. I want a bit of a life, some happiness. And I know it sounds selfish, but I can't help it.'

Right on cue, a young couple strolled past, hand-in-hand. The girl rested her head on his shoulder.

'What Neil and I have, it's so new. I'm not so unrealistic to expect that the passionate stage will last forever,' I told her.

'It's not about you and Neil. Yes, I am envious that you have someone who clearly adores you. And, God, you deserve that after Danilo, the absolute shit! But Stu and I, we have nothing in common anymore. We don't like doing the same things, eating the same food, watching the same things on telly. He physically turns me off. And I know that sounds terrible, but it's the truth. We haven't had sex for over a year. He probably doesn't fancy me either!'

'Perhaps you need to work through it.'

'Bit of Elastoplast and it'll all be fine,' she said, bitterness in her voice. She twisted the leather strap of her beach bag. 'Laura and Liam will be eighteen this year and they'll be going off to university and I can see nothing but a wasteland in front of me.'

'Do they know?'

'Well, they live in the same house,' Claire said, looping the strap around her finger. 'But teenagers, I don't know. They're so wrapped up in their own lives.'

I touched her arm. 'You should have talked to me sooner.'

'I know, but you were dealing with Dan's death. It didn't seem fair to lumber you with my problems. It seemed kind of petty to say I was bored with my marriage. It goes deeper than that, of course.'

'So, is it divorce?'

She nodded. 'I think so, Gracie. I want what you have with Neil. Is it too much to ask?'

I gave her a hug. 'Course not.'

We were subdued after that. We cheered up at lunch with a few Peroni inside us and a Sopska salad, with copious amounts of sirene cheese on top.

'I'm going to be half a stone heavier going back,' Claire laughed, 'with all these cocktails and rich food.'

'On that note, let's have an ice cream and go back to the beach.'

At four, I was becoming anxious. Natalija and Laura were supposed to join us and the taxi home had been booked for four thirty. I had to make time for a quick shower before I was due at Café Lompar for the evening service.

'Where the bloody hell is she?' Claire snapped, after ringing for the third time. 'She knows the taxi is due in half an hour.'

Five minutes later, emerging from the tunnel separating the two beaches, we saw Natalija and Laura, strutting their stuff in their bikinis, carrying shopping bags and giggling and nudging each other.

'Here they come. At last,' I said, with relief.

'Where the bloody hell have you two been?' Claire called.

'Sorry, Mum. We took a bit longer shopping,' Laura giggled, not reading the atmosphere very well. 'You've got to see what I've bought. Natalija is so great at picking out stuff.'

'Sorry, Claire,' Natalija said, sheepishly.

'You've been shopping all this time?' Claire asked.

'No. We did go to the beach,' Laura said, catching Natalija's eye, before sniggering. 'We went to Jaz, the other side of Budva.'

'I thought you were coming here.' Claire rolled her eyes.

'Oh, Mum. We had to go just for a look. Natalija said there's a nudist part. Oh my God, it was the funniest thing. There was this really old couple there. The woman was so hairy and the man, his willy was all red and wrinkled like a chorizo! Ugh!'

Natalija smiled awkwardly, probably preferring Laura to keep quiet about what they'd seen.

'They were so old,' Laura continued. 'Women with boobs like udders.'

'Well, that's what they all look like when you get to a certain age,' Claire said briskly. 'Even yours will. Come on, let's grab a few bottles of water before we get into that sauna of a taxi again.'

CHAPTER SEVENTEEN

❧ Kat ❧

I listened carefully for the sound of footsteps in the hallway, but the coast was clear. I unzipped the navy-blue clothes carrier and saw the familiar, tight-fitting, silk bodice of my beautiful wedding dress, hanging up neatly in my wardrobe. It brought a smile to my face every time. I couldn't wait for the day I'd get to wear it, standing opposite Milo, no doubt looking all handsome in his suit. I just needed a way to stop myself eating too many baklava and bureks, Lovro's exquisite desserts, if I wanted to still fit in to the dress come September.

It was all coming together now: I had the venue, the dress, the guest list. The next big thing would be the food, but I didn't want to broach that with Milo given the mood he'd been in for the last few days. It was probably best to wait until Natalija had left for Milan, although that day seemed to stretch further and further away. She was such a force, she'd taken over the house. But I didn't care when I had my beautiful dress to gaze at.

The click of keys in the lock interrupted my thoughts. It was time to zip up and stop daydreaming.

'*Ciao*!' I heard Natalija shout up the stairs.

'Hi,' I called and padded out of the bedroom, picking up a pair of heels she'd kicked off in our room yesterday. Tall, strappy and neon yellow, they definitely weren't mine.

'How was Café Lompar?' she asked as I came down to greet her.

'Exhausting.'

Trade was really starting to pick up for the summer, and to my relief we hadn't seemed to lose many customers since Ensambla opened. Their little stunt on opening night may have pulled in quite the crowd, but I'd noticed Lizzie standing in the open doorway twiddling her thumbs a few times as tourists queued at our door. I could have sworn I'd heard her shouting to a few of them earlier, calling them in for free starters at Ensambla, but Rosa told me I was imagining things. I just hoped our luck wouldn't change.

'How about I make you a cocktail?' Natalija shrugged off the leather jacket she'd been wearing over a frilly summer dress, with her long caramel hair tied up in a high ponytail. My eyes followed her as she slipped the garment over the banister, adding to the pile of three jackets she already kept there. I hoped she didn't clock me looking. Milo was already enough of a stern sibling to her. I didn't want to be another.

'No thanks, I feel a bit off, to be honest,' I said, letting her guide me to my own kitchen.

'You know I'll never give in to making you a tea. You're an honorary Montenegrin now – it's espresso or cocktails, always.'

I laughed as Natalija clicked across the floor in her heels, flinging the door open to our fridge and pulling out a tub of Greek yoghurt. She grabbed a spoon from the drawer – she knew where we kept everything now – and dug right in to the pot. I was forced to scream internally, not wanting to let my inner clean freak out over her double dipping. It came from working in the kitchen. I wasn't so obsessive elsewhere but I liked hygiene standards to be the same with food at home as they were in the professional kitchen of Café Lompar.

'What have you been up to today?' I asked, unable to watch as Natalija put the yoghurt pot down, half eaten and open on the counter, as she went searching through the cupboards for another snack. Maybe if I distracted her and sidled over, she wouldn't notice the yoghurt heading for the bin.

'My friend Gio has a spare moped,' she started, 'so we ran the bikes to Budva for sunbathing. I found the best beach there yesterday with Laura. I can't believe I didn't know about it before. Maybe I'm losing my touch.'

With one swift movement, I knocked the pot into the bin and the spoon into the sink.

'I think I should introduce Gio to Laura. They'd be perfect together. I showed him her picture and he said she was hot. It'll have to be soon though, before he goes back to Italy for football training.'

'How you know all these glamorous people I'll never know,' I said, wondering what Auntie Clare would make of Laura with a semi-professional footballer.

She waved a hand as she opened a bag of crisps. 'Photoshoots, fashion shows for college, that sort of thing. Believe me, no one's that glamorous when they are sweating on the back of a moped.'

I had to laugh. She ploughed through the crisps, and I started to make two mojitos from a base recipe Dav had given me. They were delicious even without the rum, although I gave a hearty splash to Natalija's. I followed her out to the terrace, feeling dowdy and short next to her in my cropped jeans and vest top. We sat opposite each other at the wrought iron table and clinked glasses.

'So, Kat, I'm thinking of going back to Milan for a few weeks after the meal this weekend.'

'What?' I hoped the relief didn't show on my face.

'Well, I don't want to get under your feet.' She paused to sip her cocktail. I looked away quickly, not wanting to meet her eye. Maybe my poker face at the yoghurt earlier wasn't as good as I'd hoped. 'And I need to do an assignment for university. I thought I could do it here but I need to be in the design studio.'

'That's a shame,' I said quickly. 'I'll miss having you here. The house will be quiet without you.' It was true, I realised. 'You're welcome anytime.'

'I don't know if Milo would be so kind.' Natalija shook her head.

'Oh, he's just been grumpy lately,' I said.

Natalija gave a world-weary sigh. 'I don't know why, but it seems harder and harder for us to get along.'

'Go on,' I prompted, sensing I was coming closer to what was really happening.

'Well, we were close as children. But I think he blames me.'

This was unexpected. 'What do you mean?'

'I'm sure he's told you about our mother. Milo was so close to her. The two of them were like a little team. I was always a daddy's girl.'

'Me too,' I smiled, thinking of my own dad and the way I used to cling to him, using his legs like a tree to climb when he'd get home from work.

'We were so young when she died. It was impossibly difficult for both of us.' Natalija stirred her drink with the sprig of mint I'd put in, pensive. 'I think Milo thought it was more okay for me because, you know, I had Dad. He thought he had it worse. He just didn't realise that a girl losing her mother at that age is a different thing entirely. I needed that chance to have her guide me through life, my role model. I was lost.'

I reached out to put my hand on hers. 'It must have been so hard.'

Natalija pushed her sunglasses further up her nose, but not before I spotted the glisten in her eyes.

'I loved her just the same as him and I needed her more.' She was quiet for a while before she spoke again. 'Milo was always, how you say, the martyr. He thought me and Dad had no room for him, blamed me for keeping them apart, but it wasn't true.'

'I'm sure he knew that,' I said. Milo was a lot more sensitive than his tall frame and rugged looks would suggest.

'Maybe, but then Dad started drinking. He wasn't fit to raise us alone, really. We went from having two parents to no one. He used to walk out, sometimes leave us alone for weeks at a time, then when he was home, he was quiet and angry, really angry.' This time Natalija couldn't hide her sniff. 'Milo really resented that, but I knew Dad was hurting.'

'Why do you think he blames you?'

'I was more ... lenient on our father. I always tried to get them to make up. I still do. He's our dad, even though he drinks so much that he forgets that. He should be at the wedding, if only Milo would give him a chance. What do you think?'

'I...' This was awkward. My loyalty for Milo was at odds with Natalija's story. 'You two need to talk it out.'

'Well, I think if you met him, you would get along. He would love you, Kat. And Milo would see that he should be involved in your lives, and that Dad isn't a monster. He couldn't help it.' She pushed her sunglasses back on the top of her head, taking a few tendrils with them, and looked right at me. 'That's why I think he should come to your meal this weekend.'

Now I was uncomfortable. I didn't want to invite him if Milo didn't want to. But Milo wouldn't talk to me about it, no matter how much I tried. Maybe it wasn't the worst idea ever.

'You should tell Milo beforehand.'

'He'll just say no,' she said, sounding like a pleading child now. 'And Dad has agreed to come.'

'Oh.' The decision was out of my hands already. It might be my cynicism but I wondered if this was the reason for Natalija's departure after the weekend. She didn't want to deal with an angry Milo. And neither did I. This was a family thing, not for me to sort out. She'd put me in a really difficult position. My stomach churned, not for the first time in the last few weeks.

'Oh, Natalija, I really think you should tell Milo.' Now I was pleading.

'I don't know.' She shook her head.

'You should.'

'Tell me what?'

Like a soap opera, we both turned to the dramatic figure in the doorframe. Milo stood with his arms crossed, watching us. His white shirt was unbuttoned just that perfect amount, and he looked good enough to eat, but his expression was steely.

'Come on.' I beckoned him, hoping to break the ice and offered him my cocktail. Even Natalija had the decency to look uncomfortable. Her confidence had all but gone now, and the sunglasses were firmly back on the bridge of her nose.

'What were you talking about?' Milo took a few steps forward. I tried to catch his eye and smile, but he was fixed on Natalija.

She took a deep breath, readying herself. 'I invited Dad to the meal on the weekend. It's time, Milo.'

He didn't react, didn't flinch, but I noticed his fingers gripping his elbow tight. My heart went out to him but I stayed motionless. 'Why did you do that?' he asked coolly.

'You know why. He's our dad. And you're getting married. Don't you want him to meet the love of your life?'

I couldn't breathe now. Milo looked to me but I couldn't read his expression.

'Natalija, you know that's not fair, of course I do. But that man is not my father, and you're not going to bring us together into one happy family. It's just not going to happen, however much you want it.'

'He's changed, Milo. He's not as bad as he used to be,' she huffed, exasperated.

I was a very unwilling spectator to this conversation. The tension simmered in the air between them like static electricity.

He let out a laugh, which sounded cold and cruel. 'Is that what he's told you? The fact you believe that means you're even more childish than I thought.'

'Milo!' Natalija and I started at the same time.

'You can't make this right,' he said to Natalija, 'with one big happy meal out together. It's pathetic. Not going to happen.'

'I know that, but it's a start.' Her arms were crossed now. 'You always wrote him off, but he's our dad.'

'Do you ever think maybe there's more to this than you know?' Milo said. This seemed to shut Natalija up. I didn't recognise the anger in his voice. 'You were young when I was at home. There were things I hid from you, just so your whole idea of your precious papa wouldn't be spoilt.'

This made me realise just how hard things must have been for Milo. I wished he'd told me more. It hurt that he hadn't. I looked at Milo and wondered if the man I was going to marry was near enough a stranger.

'What kind of things?' Natalija sounded furious now.

'Just drop it, Nat. You never should have done this and invited him. Now I have to clean up your mess, just like I did for him.'

'Here you go again, playing the martyr card.' Natalija said something in Montenegrin that I couldn't understand.

Milo's eyes lit up with anger, his face full of fire.

'Get out of my house.' He said the words quickly, then paused, almost as if they surprised him. 'We've both agreed that you've already outstayed your welcome. Think about Kat here.'

'Milo, don't be ridiculous,' I said. He held a hand up to stop me, and I felt a rush of my own anger. I shouldn't be dragged to the middle of this. I turned to Natalija. 'I never said that.'

'I know, Kat,' she said to me. 'It's just my brother, wanting to hurt me.'

He ran a hand through his hair. 'I don't mean that,' he finally relented. 'Of course, you can stay, I just...'

'No, it's fine, I'll leave.' Natalija pushed herself up from the chair, almost eye to eye with Milo now.

'Please don't...' I started.

'I will stay with Laura until my flight back.' And with that, she turned and walked away.

I felt glued to the spot, unsure how I felt or where I stood.

'Kat...' Milo reached across the table to me. I felt sick again.

'I don't want to hear it.' I turned to follow Natalija.

CHAPTER EIGHTEEN

🥀 Grace 🥀

'You look like shit. What's happened?' I asked as Claire stood at the door to my apartment.

'Thanks for that.' Claire winced. 'Well, I haven't had a wink of sleep for a start. That girl is such a cliché!' she sighed as I let her in.

As we sipped orange juice on the balcony, Claire filled me in.

'I let Laura go to a club with Natalija last night. Since Natalija left Kat's, I've had the two of them getting at me. Anyway, it was a big mistake!'

'Zivjeli?' I asked.

Claire nodded. 'Yes, that sounds like it. The one in the centre of town. She is seventeen, after all. She'll be off to uni next year. I gave her strict instructions to be back at one, which meant of course that she staggered in at three.'

'Hmm, predictable,' I murmured.

'Natalija was carrying Laura's shoes and bag. She told me that she tried to stop Laura drinking, but she was chatting to some guy at the bar.'

'Natalija's not a bad kid,' I said.

'Yes, but she's twenty-one and there is a big difference in ages. Anyway, I'm sure you can guess the rest. I undressed her, got her in bed and then about four in the morning I could hear a little cry, "Help me." I found her kneeling on the bathroom floor, head in the toilet bowl.'

'We've all been there,' I laughed.

'She thought she was going to die, vowed she was never going to drink again. I didn't have much sympathy in the early hours, I must admit. With Laura throwing up in the bathroom and Natalija snoring on the sofa, I couldn't get back to sleep. It smelled like a brewery, too. I just had to get out.'

'Let's have some breakfast. I've got some bureks that Kat made yesterday. Sweet ones with honey and pistachio.'

'The Montenegrins do love their bureks!'

We sat on the balcony watching the world go by. It was only nine in the morning and the clatter of crockery drifted over from a café about fifty metres away.

'Gosh, there's some serious money here,' Claire said, looking at the opulent yachts moored in the harbour. Bicycles whizzed by on the palm-lined promenade. The glittering water rippled as a fishing boat chugged from the harbour, its engine coughing into life. 'Not a bad life this. No wonder Kat has decided to make her home here.'

'Yep,' I agreed. 'It's stunning. She feels it's part of her, I guess.'

Claire nibbled her burek. 'I'm going to see a solicitor when I get back,' she said, keeping her eyes fixed on the harbour.

'When will you tell Laura and Liam?'

'Not yet. Soon. But not until I have to.'

'Will you be okay today?' I asked guiltily, knowing I was on duty at Café Lompar for lunch and dinner.

Claire laughed. 'Hmm, what on earth will I do with myself? Sunbathe? Sleep? Have a nice lunch out?'

'Okay, okay. Pop in for a coffee if you've got time.'

'I was thinking of going to Ensambla tonight. Do you think Kat will mind? I might just check out the competition.'

'Perhaps best not to mention it. You know how touchy she is about Ensambla. It's a good idea, though, you can let us know what it's like. Tell us if we need to be worried.'

Claire kissed me on the cheek. 'Well, I'd better check on the drunken duo!'

I was tidying the living room and getting ready to go into Café Lompar when my phone rang and Stuart's face popped up on the screen. Shit! Stu never rang me. I couldn't ignore him. I braced myself.

'Hi, Gracie,' he said, his voice in a monotone.

God, he looked like he'd been crying. 'How are you, Stu?'

'I'm not going to lie, I've been better. I suppose Claire has told you all about the trouble we're going through?'

'Uh, yes, she has mentioned it.'

'Can you knock some sense into her, Gracie? We've been together forever.'

'I think that's the point, Stu. It's a lifetime and sometimes people grow up and grow apart.' God, this was excruciating.

'We're meant to be together, me and Claire. It would be like separating rhubarb and custard, or cheese and onion crisps.' Had he been drinking? It was only half ten in the morning at home.

'Do you think it's a midlife crisis? Perhaps she's menopausal and going through some sort of manic depression or a psychotic episode,' he went on. I didn't think he was helping his case if he was saying things like this to Claire, as if it was all her fault and she was going a bit mad.

'Do you know what she said to me? She said that she wouldn't mind if I had someone else or if we had an "open" arrangement. For fuck's sake, Gracie.' Ouch, Claire really had had enough.

'She didn't mean that, I'm sure.'

'I've even suggested we have counselling, but she wasn't having any of it. I just don't know what to do, how to fix it. Tell me what to do,' he wailed.

Oh no, I thought he was going to cry. 'Look, Stuart, I'm sure she just needs some space. Give her time. This break now might do her good.' I kept my fingers crossed as I said it; Claire had just told me she was going ahead with divorce proceedings. 'How is Liam? Are you two coping and not having takeaways every night.'

'Liam's round his friend's all the time. I don't usually get up until late and by then he's left. He comes back in the evening. I can't say I blame him.' Poor Liam, I thought.

'What's the weather like there, Stu?' This was desperate. Anything rather than talk about Claire. He seemed to manage to bring every topic around to her, though.

'It's crap,' he said, his eyes glancing towards the window. 'Not that I care. I bet she's on the beach all the time topping up her tan. Does she talk about me much?'

'Course she does. She's thinking about you all the ... quite a bit.'

He seemed to perk up. 'Perhaps she will feel better when she comes home and this strange turn of hers will have passed.' He made it sound like she had shingles or something.

'Are you working, Stu?'

'I've taken some sick leave. I can't face it. The boss is okay, quite supportive.' His face looked haggard and he obviously hadn't shaved for days.

'Look, Stu, I've got to go into work now. You hang in there, okay.'

He nodded miserably, his bloodshot eyes filling the screen. 'Just don't tell her I called.'

Maria was opening the bifold doors as I arrived at Café Lompar and Ana was putting out the A-board with today's lunchtime specials: Skadar Lake Carp with Kuvana Krtola, a potato dish; Corbast Pasulj, which was a bean stew with smoked ribs and Kat's chorizo-style sausage; and a chicken risotto with blitva or spinach. All, of course, with Café Lompar's special twist. I glanced across at Ensambla and Lizzie was writing on her chalk board outside, her blonde curls loose for once and falling about her shoulders. I was dying to see what she was writing but couldn't make it obvious.

Rosa was putting flowers on the tables when I walked in. She had the night off tonight, appearing much keener to take time off since Matija came on the scene.

'He plays the guitar,' Luka had told Kat the night before. 'I just hate to picture him singing to my mother, like some love sick puppy. She'd better not invite him around when I'm here. I'm not having it.'

'Come on, Luka, you're not ten. She's entitled to have a life.' Kat had told me he got quite testy when she'd told him this and they had to avoid the subject as much as possible.

'Morning,' Rosa smiled. She definitely had a sparkle since she met Matija. Luka would have to get over it.

'Have we got many bookings for lunch?' I asked.

'Some, but you know most will just drift in.' She saw the doubt on my face. 'Do you think we need to do more to find customers?' she asked.

'Well, I heard Ensambla has a Ladies' Night tomorrow and all the drinks are half price up until eight o'clock for women.'

'Maybe we should do something, too,' she said, biting her lip. 'I know I have been a little distracted lately.'

Lovro strolled in, looking casual in his shorts and vest top, the helmet for his moped hanging from one arm.

'Morning.' He smiled. 'Where's Kat? I see that Ensambla is running cooking classes on Thursday mornings.'

'That's a good idea,' I said, wondering why we hadn't thought of that. 'You'd better see what mood Kat is in before you deliver that piece of good news.'

'We must up our game,' he said, as he went to join Bojan in the kitchen.

'Should we be worried?' I asked Rosa.

'No, I don't think so. Kat is a top-class chef. We've had lots of publicity, not all of it good, of course, but the food speaks for itself.'

'You're right,' I agreed, 'but we can't be complacent.'

Kat had her cookbook out and she had made several television appearances, but you were only as good as your last review, the last night's takings. Ensambla was definitely using aggressive tactics to promote the place. When we went through the orders and bookings for the day, I was mentally thinking of ideas to promote Café Lompar. Perhaps loyalty promotions – free courses or discounts for second and third visits – or themed nights. I wondered how much an advert on the television would cost and made a mental note to check it out. I could picture shots of the kitchen, Kat and the other chefs at work, zooming in on the meals we cooked – they really were a work of art – and then panning round the crowded restaurant and ending with a sunset.

When I eased off my shoes at the end of the night, I did wonder why we worried about getting in more customers. We'd been rushed off our feet all day. Cleaning my teeth, I wandered to the balcony and gazed absent-mindedly at the silvery moon suspended in the inky-black sky. The television was blaring in the background. Feeling chilly, I went back into the apartment when something on the local news channel caught my eye.

It took a few moments to realise I was looking at the interior of Ensambla. I'd recognise that tacky, faux leather seating anywhere. A news reporter was positioned outside the restaurant smiling broadly whilst speaking nineteen to the dozen in Montenegrin. Then there were shots of the inside: a man was kneeling before his girlfriend at a table, some strange tableaux playing out as the reporter laughed into the camera. The girl was obviously saying 'yes' to his proposal as she jumped from her seat and they hugged and he swung her around.

Wait a minute, I recognised that couple. When the face of Leon Lazovic appeared on the screen, it all clicked into place. This was the man who punched lechy Leon on opening night. This was all a set up. A clever one, and what a great way to get a bit of publicity! I couldn't make out what the reporter was saying but Ensambla was mentioned several times. When the couple were being interviewed by the reporter outside Ensambla, the girl flashed her ring in the camera. In the background, you could see people drift out from the restaurant, Claire being one of them. I prayed Kat wasn't watching this.

Suddenly the phone buzzed on the coffee table.

'Mum, have you seen the news?' Kat asked with no preamble.

'Uh, yes.'

'The sneaky bastards. Milo told me Leon Lazovic has agreed to play at their wedding. It's all a bloody set up. And do you know their lunch menu was almost identical to ours today?'

I made sympathetic noises, mentally relieved she hadn't seen Claire leave Ensambla.

'And Auntie Claire was there! Natalija had told me, thankfully, or I would have had a hell of a shock to see her leave the restaurant.'

'She was just checking out the competition, Kat, honestly. Now, don't over-react. It's not worth getting upset about.'

Kat drew in an exasperated breath. 'Well, if they can play dirty, so can I. I don't know what their problem is with us, but Café Lompar is not taking this lying down. If they want a fight, that's what they're going to get.'

CHAPTER NINETEEN

🌿 Kat 🌿

It was an overcast day in Tivat, one of the few Montenegrin days that weren't filled with beaming sunshine and scorching heat. I didn't mind, I was glad for the respite, especially as I cycled to Café Lompar for my lunch shift. The tourists were still milling around the high street in their sandals and expensive kaftans, not perturbed by the change in the weather. This would register as a heatwave in Britain.

I waved at Rosa as I spotted her outside, before going to tie my bike up. Lizzie and David were outside Ensambla, pinning an enormous poster to the restaurant frontage. 'Fusion Cooking Class, Montenegrin's first of its kind! 25th June, please register inside.'

It irked me that we hadn't thought of it. Cooking classes were undoubtedly a good idea and a surefire way to draw in the crowds. People loved learning to cook dishes that would remind them of their holiday at home. My cookbook had that role before now, but the cooking class was creating a real stir. The *Pobjeda* had done a whole feature on it, a double-page spread next to my sad little column on how to make limoncello sorbet in last week's issue.

I'd felt so much frustration the last few days with Luka's

silence, Milo and Natalija at each other's throats, wedding planning. I'd almost forgotten the feud with Ensambla and their OTT opening night. And to think it was all planned, all staged with Leon Lazovic to create a talking point! I knew something was off about them. It was just nice that Mum and everyone else could see it now.

Lizzie stood back to admire the poster, before turning and giving me a smile. It was so smug, I felt my skin crawl.

'Morning!' I waved. Kill them with kindness.

'Kat!' They both waved.

'Great minds think alike,' I pointed at their sandwich board, the menu nearly identical to ours.

Lizzie laughed in that contrived, high-pitched cackle of hers.

David sneered, 'Yes, I thought it was time we introduced Kaymak into the fine dining scene.'

'We did it in an ice cream last month,' I said, remembering the soured milk dessert we experimented with. I knew I shouldn't bite, but David's smarmy comments really got my back up, as I'm sure was his intention.

'Yes, I think the flavours really blend themselves with the risotto. You should try it in a savoury dish.'

'Maybe I will.' I hoped my facial expression conveyed that I wouldn't.

'If you wanted to try ours, you should come over. It might give you some good ideas.' How David could say it so brazenly I would never know. What was his problem?

'I could come to the cooking class,' I said. There was an awkward pause before Lizzie started cackling again.

'You are funny, Kat,' she said.

David pulled a face, as though I was something unpleasant he wanted to wipe off his shoe. 'Anyway, I'd better get on with the lunch service.' He pulled Lizzie inside, turning to give me one final glare.

What was that man's problem? To copy our menu so blatantly in front of us, and then pass his dishes off as innovative? The man still made foams, for God's sake. Foams were so 2018. To get revenge would be so sweet. I looked at the poster for the cooking class in front of me, an idea forming. It would be naughty...

'Kat, are you coming in?' Rosa called from across the street.

'I'll be there now,' I shouted, stalling for time.

I couldn't do it, could I? I knew there was a marker pen in my bag, and Lizzie and David had gone into the back of the restaurant. The feeling was building that I *should* take action. Yes, we'd been lying down too long in Café Lompar, letting them steal our menu and walk all over us. And now the cooking class. I was only playing as fair as they did.

Before I knew what I was doing, my hand was moving, adding the thin black line that changed the date on the poster from the 25th to the 26th.

It looked convincing. Okay, so maybe they'd notice and correct it. Or maybe they wouldn't, and have some very angry customers that missed the course.

I hurried away before anyone could see me, surprised at my own mischievousness. Butterflies of excitement and disbelief flew in my stomach. After all, I'd told Mum that I could play dirty. This was just the start.

The shift at Café Lompar was a busy one; we did a last-minute price drop on the set menu for lunch that drew in a lot of customers while the weather was cloudy. All through it, I couldn't stop thinking of the potential shit-storm I'd caused in Ensambla. It was what they deserved. But I didn't want to tell Lovro, even after he asked me multiple times what I was smiling about. I didn't know why he was friendly with Lizzie and David. I had the distinct feeling Lovro wouldn't approve of my hi-jinks, and so I kept *schtum*.

I really needed a few quiet nights in, not the tense family meal with Milo's father tomorrow. As I drew up to the house, I felt I was going to the lion's den. Milo had been sulking over his argument with Natalija for the past week.

'Anyone home?' I called tentatively as I came through the door.

'Katty!' Milo came up, enveloping me in his arms. He could still take my breath away. He pressed his lips hard to mine, his hands on either side of my face, pulling me close. It was hot but very unexpected.

'This seems ... maybe not what I was expecting,' I said, eyeing him as we pulled apart.

'I think I need the kiss for strength,' he smiled, squeezing my hands.

'Have you thought of Dutch courage?' I asked, half-joking. It was certainly going to be my tactic to deal with the coming Martinovic family drama. I needed at least a bottle of wine.

'Well, my father will already be drunk so why not join him?'

I realised my suggestion had been in bad taste and turned to gauge Milo's reaction. He was smiling but it seemed a little thin.

He really was stressed for tomorrow, and his anxiety was contagious.

'I'm nervous,' I said to him. 'I want your dad to like me.'

'You shouldn't worry,' Milo followed me upstairs. 'He will, and anyway, I don't care what he thinks. You've met Natalija, she's the most important person in my family, and she loves you. More than she loves me, I think.'

'Well, there's good reason for that after your argument,' I said, hoping to make light of what had been a very tense conversation.

'I just...' He huffed, sinking back onto the bed whilst I opened the wardrobe door. I'd already chosen my outfit, a green t-shirt-style maxi dress that was figure-hugging but still casual. 'I just wish she hadn't gone behind my back. She should never have invited him before I was ready.'

'I know that...'

'Natalija's selfish, though,' Milo interrupted me. 'She always has been. She doesn't know the full extent of our father's problems, what he did to me.'

I was fiddling with a pair of earrings, but this made me stop. 'Milo, do you mind if I ask something?'

I moved over to sit on the end of the bed, by his side, so we were eye-to-eye.

'I wasn't going to ask this tonight, but I feel I have to. What did happen with you and your father?' He sighed but I kept talking. 'You've told me his drinking was bad, and it sounds like you were more of a father to Natalija than he was for a while, but is there more to it than that?'

He was quiet, staring at me, and I didn't know if he was going to speak or cry or shout.

I said, 'You may as well tell me, seeing as I'm going to be sitting across the table from the man in under twenty-four hours.'

'It might take that long,' Milo muttered, but I could tell he was relenting. 'Look, it's a long story, a long unpleasant one. After Mum died, he held it together for a while, but when I was a teenager the problems really started. He would go away for weeks sometimes, and we didn't know where he was. It was worse when he was back. He would break things, urinate in the cupboard, that sort of bullshit. I cleaned it all up. I didn't want Natalija to see – she was just a child.'

I listened intently to his story. It was so much worse now I knew the details. I knew alcoholism was a disease, but Milo had had to put up with so much from his father.

Milo relaxed back against the pillows of our bed. 'One time, when Natalija was small, she made this rocket ship for a school project. This thing was a masterpiece. She's always been creative, but she spent weeks on it, made it out of egg cartons moulded and painted white. I swear this thing could have been a NASA replica or something. My dad came in, as you say "pissed" one night and fell over, crushing it to pieces. I didn't know why, but he was laughing like it was all some kind of joke.' Milo's face held so much anger. 'I tried to remake it overnight. It looked nothing like Natalija's but she never said anything. She must have known. God, I could have killed him.'

I rubbed Milo's knee. I had the feeling this was the tip of the iceberg.

'He used to embarrass me, flirt with my friends, be inappropriate in public. I stopped inviting him to school events after he passed out during a summer carnival.'

'God, Milo, I had no idea. I wish you'd told me this before,' I said, understanding so much more now.

'I don't like to talk about it. It sounds like I want sympathy. I don't want anything except to have as little contact with him as possible.'

'I get it,' I said. 'Did things change as you grew up?'

'Only that he stayed away more and more. Obviously, he lost his job so I had to work after school, in a newsagent, then the petrol station on the weekends. If I didn't, we wouldn't have been able to eat. Dad never ate much, and he never cared if we did.' Milo was on a roll now. 'I needed something to give a better life for us, make sure Natalija could go to university. There was no way I could go. Who would protect her from this monster? You know, one time I bought a car, something really old and cheap, and do you know what he did? He got in it one night and crashed into an old woman's car outside, then ran away.'

I gasped. 'Oh my God.'

'She was okay, thank goodness. I had to clean up that mess too, pay for her insurance. My car was ruined.'

I didn't know what to say. Milo had shouldered this burden for most of his adult life, and I knew he'd had very little contact with his father since moving away. I could see why he was in no hurry to form one happy family again. 'Did you ever try and get him support?'

'All the fucking time. I made appointments for him, bunked off school so I could escort him personally to the doctor, but he was never home. It was like he didn't want to try. You know me, I never wanted to give up on him, but he made it impossible. He didn't care how much it was breaking me and Natalija.'

I gave Milo a hug, hoping something would comfort him. It broke my heart to hear this. He was stiff at first but then relaxed and held me tight.

'I can see why you're so upset at him being invited tomorrow, and to the wedding,' I said.

'It's not just that,' Milo spoke into my hair.

I pulled back, wondering what was coming.

'I haven't seen him since I left Centinje, since... Okay, I worked really hard to get the boat. I wanted to start the business and needed to make some real money, not just stay in the petrol station for the rest of my life. I started with another boating company, was working my way up, learning about sailing and the business side of things. I told you I left the company when I bought the boat?'

'Yes...' I heard the dread in my voice.

'I left the company because I was forced to. My dad kept turning up drunk at the harbour, being loud and obnoxious. Almost as if he was deliberately sabotaging my chances of making something of myself.'

'Why would he do that?' It sounded unfathomable.

'I've no idea. Perhaps he wanted me there, stuck, like him.'

'Milo, that's awful.'

He went on, 'In the end, they said I wasn't needed anymore. But I knew the truth. I was an embarrassment. Well, my father was.' He shook his head, as if he were reliving that awful time. 'I haven't spoken to him since then.'

I sat in stunned silence, thinking about what he'd told me. 'Natalija never knew about it?'

'I never told her,' he confirmed. 'But honestly, Kat, this man

156

tried to ruin my life. How can I sit there and look at him tomorrow?'

I'd almost forgotten we were meant to meet them. I didn't know what to do, and as we sat holding each other in our bedroom, I willed time to slow down.

'What am I going to do?' Milo said. His eyes bore into mine, willing answers.

'I have no idea.'

CHAPTER TWENTY

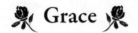 Grace

After a day of respite from the sun, the heat returned with a vengeance. My face was constantly red, my hair stuck to the back of my neck and the creases under my boobs left damp patches on my t-shirt. I had tried to freshen up before Neil called, but at the end of a long shift at Café Lompar, I was hot and bothered, positioning myself as close to the air conditioner as possible. Facetime was a great invention but not when you felt like a sweaty heffalump!

'Hi, darling,' he said, smiling. 'Are you okay to chat? I hope you're not too tired.'

I shook my head. 'How's your day been?' I eased off my sandals as he told me about the clients he'd seen and how he'd been trudging around the sodden golf course.

'I can't wait for a bit of sun. Only two days now and we'll be together at last.'

I had to pinch myself sometimes to believe how keen Neil was. Would the novelty wear off? Would I one day feel like Claire did? Was it inevitable that relationships sink into boring monotony when even the noise they make when they sip their tea annoys you? The things you found endearing and quite cute at first morphing into something that set your teeth on edge?

God, I hoped not. There were many happy couples out there who'd been together for eons. There was Mr. and Mrs. Peters who lived next door to us when we were growing up. He died just two months after his wife; couldn't cope without her. Perhaps I was spending too much time with Claire.

'How's Claire?' Neil asked, almost reading my thoughts.

'Well, she's going ahead with a divorce,' I said quietly.

'Poor bastard.'

'It's not Claire's fault,' I said defensively. 'Sometimes marriages fall apart. It's not anyone's fault.'

'I know, I know,' Neil countered. 'It's just that you told me how cut up he was over Claire. It always seems like one partner is more relieved and happier for the split than the other.'

'Hmm, I suppose,' I agreed, wondering if it was Neil or Cassandra who'd wanted out of their marriage. There was an awkward silence.

'I hate being apart,' Neil said. 'It's not the same like this, on the phone. These snatched moments when we say things that can be misinterpreted. I miss you.'

I nodded, an ache of longing in my stomach. 'I can't wait to see you. Is Ollie looking forward to it?'

'Course he is. He wants to hit the golf course. Kat won't mind him staying there, will she?'

'No,' I said unconvincingly, shaking my head. 'I wish I had more room here but it's so cramped. Kat's place has three bedrooms. Things are still strained, though, and tomorrow they're having dinner with Milo's father. Very much against Milo's will. Goodness knows how that will turn out.'

'You're off tomorrow, too?'

'Yep, but I'm not going to the dinner with Kat. I will be recovering from tonight: I promised Claire we'd have the night together and go out for a few drinks.'

'Two girls on the town, hey?' Neil smiled, but it didn't quite reach his eyes.

I laughed. 'There's no need to come over all jealous. I'd rather an early night with a book and a long sleep.'

'We're so well suited,' Neil said. 'That definitely sounds more appealing.'

By the time Claire arrived at mine, I was even more reluctant to go out. I'd just had a shower but my linen dress stuck to me like damp cardboard and was already creased. Claire had a red floral dress with a shorter skirt than she usually wore. Her hair was darker than mine, but she'd had layers put in and some blonde highlights. With her scarlet lipstick, she looked years younger. Different.

'Wow, I love your hair,' I gushed.

'I had it done in the salon in town. Salon Femija. It sounds like somewhere you'd go for a smear test! They hardly spoke English but she convinced me to have a few layers and highlights. Laura loves it. She kept saying Dad will go crazy when he sees it.' Claire bit her lip. 'I feel so guilty.'

'They'll cope,' I said. 'It's your time now.'

Claire grinned, pulling a bottle of Prosecco from a carrier bag. 'It certainly is. Now this is what Laura and her mates call pre-drinks.'

'I am going to have to pace myself. Hangovers last three days at our age.'

'Speak for yourself. I intend to enjoy myself tonight and just be Claire. Exciting Claire, without the boring husband, without the boring job and certainly without the two stroppy teenagers!'

I swallowed my foreboding along with my first glass of Prosecco, the bubbles fizzing up my nose.

We hit a champagne bar in town. I was already feeling woozy.

'Is it me or are Montenegrin men all hot?' Claire asked, smiling at the security man at the door, a burly, six-footer looking like an extra from *Men in Black*.

'Really?' I asked. 'You've already had too much.'

Claire ordered a bottle of champagne before I could stop her. 'Come on, let's celebrate being mature, confident and sexy women.' She winked at the barman as the ice bucket was handed to her across the counter.

It was going to be a long night. I turned around. Oh no!

Positioned at the window were Rosa and Matija, her new man.

Rosa saw us and waved us over. Matija gave a wide smile, revealing white, even teeth. He was wearing a white vest top and jeans with a shirt open, casual and effortlessly stylish as young Mediterranean men often are.

'Fancy seeing you two here.' Rosa kissed me then Claire on the cheek. 'Who on earth is holding the fort tonight?'

'Bojan, Ivan and Lovro are there,' I said. 'It's nice to have a night off.' I mounted the high barstool in a most unladylike fashion.

'When are you going back, Claire?' Rosa asked.

'I've got another week.'

Rosa smiled, 'Well, the sun obviously suits you. You look lovely tonight. Is your husband joining you?'

Claire shifted in her seat. 'Uh, he can't get the time off work.'

Rosa gazed at her closely, and nodded as if she understood the situation exactly. She looked stunning as always in her sky-blue maxi dress and hoop earrings. She had lines on her face but she was still a beautiful woman, a head-turner. I tried hard not to picture her and Dan together, but it caught me sometimes. Not yet water under the bridge, no matter how hard I tried and how much time had passed.

'So how did you two meet?' Claire asked.

'Mat did some work on the restaurant,' Rosa began, and her hand slipped into his. 'He's an architect.'

'I was training then,' he told us. 'My supervisor took me there. I am glad he did.' He looked at Rosa and smiled. Draining his Corona, he said, 'Shall I get us another? Strawberry Daiquiri, Rosa?'

When he left, Claire turned to Rosa. 'Wow, he's gorgeous. How old is he?'

I nudged her. 'Claire!'

'No, it's okay. He's twenty-four. I'm twenty years older than him. I have no idea what he sees in me.' She batted our protests away. 'I am a middle-aged woman who's had breast cancer. I've seen life and he is just a baby. But you know what? I don't care. My illness has taught me one thing. I don't give a damn what people think of me. None of us knows what's round the corner.'

'Here, here!' Claire and I said in unison, clinking our glasses.

There was a difference in Rosa since she had been ill. I had seen her at her most vulnerable. I'd been scared she wasn't going to make it when she got that infection last year and we'd had that dash to the hospital. It was a godawful time but she had come out the other side. Now she was radiant. She had a strength I envied.

Claire asked, 'What's the sex like?'

'You are shameless!' I said.

Rosa laughed. 'Amazing! Amazing! Young men are so desperate to please you. And as you get older you learn to ask for what you want.' Her hand brushed her hips. 'My body is not what it was, but I don't care. Who knows how long it will last, but I am enjoying myself.'

'I hear you, girl!' Claire said, draining her drink. 'I want some of that.'

'She's had a bit too much,' I told Rosa as Matija came back to the table with the drinks.

'What are you ladies laughing at?'

And there it was: ladies. Not girls. That age gap was not getting smaller, but Rosa was happy for now.

'You know Milo's father, Nikola, I think?' I asked Rosa.

'Nik, yes. Not very well. I have met him a few times but most of what I know about him is what Luka has told me.'

'What is he like?'

'Stubborn. A traditional Montenegrin man. They like to think they are kings of the house and women are put on earth to look after them, serve them. After his wife died, he took to drink. God, it aged him. He looked seventy at forty-five.'

'Milo hasn't spoken to him for a long time. He can't forgive him, Kat says.'

'He tried his best but wasn't really a father to them in those last few years. I think Milo brought Natalija up, tried to give her some stability. She's a wild one, too.'

Hmm, none of this boded well for the dinner tomorrow. I worried about Kat and how she was going to handle it.

There was a small dance floor at the back of the bar. Matija pulled Rosa over to it by her hand and they danced slowly to the music in the now smoky, cavern-like darkness.

'Shall we grab a late-night snack somewhere?' I asked Claire.

'I'm ready for a cocktail now. Come on, let's not go yet.' She paused. 'Rosa and her man seem smitten with each other.'

'She seems realistic about him, though. Okay, one cocktail and then let's head back.'

Claire came back with two Mojitos each. 'And before you complain, it's two for one after ten.'

I rolled my eyes. 'I can't have two. I'm in work in the morning.'

'You need to let your hair down, Gracie.' Her words were slurred. 'Live a bit. You were married to Dan all those years and have quickly got into another relationship. Neil's great and all that, but don't you want to try what's out there sometimes?'

I shrugged. 'I am very happy with Neil, but perhaps he's trying to rush things a bit. I want to enjoy my own space for a while.' I hadn't admitted this to myself.

'Well, I intend to enjoy every bit of my freedom,' she giggled, dragging me onto the dance floor.

As we danced, or should I say moved awkwardly to some music we'd never heard before, I caught myself in the floor-length mirrors opposite, and shuddered. Claire was well into it and started throwing her arms in the air. A man in his thirties with a cigarette dangling from his lips and very dodgy sideburns like some seventies' porn star was watching Claire intently. She ignored me when I begged her to sit down.

'Well, I'm off for a drink,' I told her. 'Non-alcoholic!'

I was grateful to get to the barstool as I ordered a diet Coke.

When I next turned around, Claire was dancing with Mr. Sideburns, her arms draped around his neck as he held her hips. His cigarette still dangled precariously from his lips. I dreaded to think what would happen if Laura walked in here now. I sipped my Coke, wondering if I should step outside for some fresh air. I'd have to have some toast when I got back. I was starving.

Glancing over my shoulder, I looked at the mirror opposite the dance floor. Claire was snogging Mr. Sideburns with great alacrity, his arms encircling her waist, the ash falling from his cigarette onto Claire's dress.

I marched over, seized her by the arm and dragged her away. 'Come on,' I ordered in my best older sister voice, 'we're going home!'

'What do you think you're playing at?' she snarled, removing her arm from my grip.

I was quite taken aback by the vehemence in her voice. 'You've had too much to drink. We need to get back.'

'No, *you* need to get back. *I'm* having fun. Remember that, Gracie? The trouble with you is, you never let yourself go.' Mr. Sideburns stood behind Claire, grinning, but clueless as to what we were arguing about.

'Well, I'm not leaving you here. It's not safe.'

'You can and you *will*,' Claire said. 'I'm not twelve anymore. You can't tell me what to do, so why don't you just go!'

It was ridiculous how quickly we resorted to the teenage sisters we were when we used to argue about make up or whose turn it was to put the dishes away. There was no reasoning with her when she was in this state. Tivat was a safe town, but I felt worried as I walked out of there. Rosa and Matija were still there, so she wouldn't be on her own. I hoped to God she'd come to her senses. I didn't like this side of Claire. It was new and unfamiliar. But what I could I do?

CHAPTER TWENTY-ONE

❧ Kat ❧

I used tweezers to place the final micro basil leaf on top of the panna cotta, trying not to focus on how much my hand was shaking. I stood back to admire my handy-work. Not bad. The gold spray gave it a fine dusting, like sun-kissed sand on a beach.

'How do you do it?' Rosa shook her head, walking past with a tray of empty plates.

'I think I was a surgeon in another life,' I said, proud of my precision plating. Beautiful presentation was a real trademark of Café Lompar, and the panna cotta was a most decadent pudding, strawberry and tonka bean blending with the creamy texture of the dessert.

'If I'm honest, I think the desserts are helping to take my mind off tonight,' I said to Lovro, who was using a blowtorch on a leg of lamb.

'Still stressing about the big family meal?'

I went over and rested my forehead against his shoulder. 'I've never been so stressed, not even for meeting Natalija,' I sighed.

Lovro laughed, easing away from me to plate up the main courses.

I sighed. 'You know, it's odd, normally when you meet a boyfriend's parents you're worried about them liking you. But tonight I'm worried about World War Three breaking out.'

'I thought World War Three was already going on between you and Ensambla,' Lovro said.

I turned away quickly, hoping my face didn't give away my guilt. I still couldn't believe I'd changed the date on the poster for the cooking course. No one had noticed yet. It was still standing proudly outside the restaurant when I passed this morning. Lizzie would have kittens when she found out. I hadn't told anyone what I'd done. I was tempted to tell Luka. Surely, he would be the most receptive to my menacing streak, after all we shared the same genes, but I felt this would be crossing the line even for him.

'Very funny,' I said, sarcasm covering my fretting.

'You'll be fine,' Lovro reassured me. 'Where are you going for food?'

'Kuhinja in Centinje. His dad, Nik, invited us for food in his house, but we suggested the restaurant. I thought neutral ground might be better. Milo's edgy enough as it is without introducing his childhood home into the mix.'

'Kuhinja, is that the restaurant where the whole menu has flavoured foams?'

'I think so.' I wrinkled my nose.

'Ugh, foams.' Lovro swatted a hand. 'So last year.' And despite myself, I had to laugh. He was so much like me.

The car journey to Cetinje was tense to say the least. I kept pulling at a frayed edge on my handbag every few minutes. I was going to dissemble the whole thing before we got to the restaurant at this rate.

'Is that the car whistling again?' Milo asked, frowning as he hit the brakes.

168

'I don't think so.' I strained to listen. 'I can't hear anything.' He gave a world-weary sigh.

'I knew I shouldn't have trusted that mechanic. He didn't do a good enough job.' He shook his head.

'Milo, I can't hear anything.' He didn't respond.

We were silent as the car climbed into the mountains, the forestry verdant and lush in the cooler air of the higher ground.

'My ears just popped then,' I said to Milo with amusement. He barely cracked a smile.

He was doing nothing to ease my tension. I didn't know what to expect from tonight. We were meeting Nik and Natalija in the restaurant. She'd been staying with him for the last few nights. I knew Claire was pleased to get her away from Laura. Although, I think Natalija's wild side had rubbed off on more than just Laura, from what Mum told me about Claire's wild night out. Poor Uncle Stu. I couldn't believe things were on the rocks between them. They were my aunt and uncle, married forever, 'Claire and Stu'. Marriage was their identity, but I supposed that was part of the problem: they needed their own lives too.

I looked across at the silent man beside me. I hoped things wouldn't change when we were married, the pressure of obligation and formality spoiling what was precious between us. I reached out a hand to rub his knee, and was pleasantly surprised when he took it and lifted it to his lips. He could still make my world turn upside down.

'Milo, I love you,' I said.

'I love you too.' He smiled. 'I'm glad you're by my side tonight.'

Cetinje was a beautiful city, nestled in amongst the Lovcen

mountains, with colourful, historic buildings. Kuhinja was in the centre of town, and Milo managed to park across the road. The relaxed Montenegrin way of life still amazed me; a prime space like this in the centre of London was unheard of.

I wiped my hands on my green Grecian-style maxi dress and checked my reflection in the car window. Milo offered his hand and squeezed mine as we crossed the street towards the glass-fronted Kuhinja. I didn't know who was encouraging whom.

Natalija was waiting inside on a sofa near the entrance, stirring a cocktail. The man next to her was clearly Milo's father; he was the spit of Milo, even though his face was more lined. He wore a blue shirt, unbuttoned just a little more than British culture permitted, and his hair was greying at the temples. His tanned skin was elegant and eye-catching. If this was the vision of my future husband, then I was fully on board and signed up. I didn't know what I'd expected, but he looked nothing like the unwell alcoholic I'd been told was waiting for us.

He glanced towards us, nervously, his hands clasped together, and rose to his feet as Natalija did. As we approached, a warm smile crossed his face, the same that endeared me to Milo.

'You must be Kat.' He held out a hand. We shook formally and awkwardly. 'I was expecting a beauty and you really are.' I warmed to him at the compliment, and leant in for a much more relaxed kiss on the cheek. I saw Milo being hugged by Natalija at the corner of my eye.

'I've heard so much about you,' Nik said.

'Likewise.' I smiled. 'From Natalija and Milo.'

'I'm sure not all of it is good.' He rubbed his jaw and I saw in the gesture how nervous he was.

'I've been looking forward to getting to know you.' I tried to be diplomatic. 'Especially with our wedding coming up.'

'Ah yes, the wedding. I must offer my congratulations to you both. In fact, I have a gift for you but I've left it at home,' I didn't know if I imagined the glisten in his eye. I saw immediately how important it was that we had him at the wedding; he couldn't be excluded.

'You didn't need to.' I smiled.

'Please, it's nothing.' He waved a hand. 'I so wish Lucija was able to meet you. She would say you are perfect for our Milo.'

'I am so sorry I can't.' It was lovely how openly he spoke of his late wife. It must have been difficult. Nik's accent was harder to understand than Milo's, who was used to speaking to tourists, but his warmth and approachability came through easily. It was difficult to marry up this man to the monster I'd been warned about. Was this really the man that destroyed Natalija's school projects and made Milo's teenage life so miserable?

As if on cue, Milo and his father turned to each other for the first time.

'Milo, Milo,' Nik said, gazing at him fondly. 'How sorry I am it has been so long.'

'I know.' Milo slow-blinked. It was a strangely sombre moment and I shifted towards Natalija uncomfortably to give her a hug.

'Looking fantastic as always,' I said to her, as the waiter came over to usher us towards the table.

We followed in single file to our small table of four at the back of the restaurant. Natalija's halter-neck dress exposed full side-boob and drew the eye of everyone we passed. They clearly didn't care much about personal space in Kuhinja. We had large tables on either side of us, practically sitting with us, and a raucous laugh went up from the family to the left as we sat down. The different emotions in our party were clear. I sat next to Milo, opposite Natalija, to leave the two men facing each other.

'So, Kat, I want to hear all about you. I hear you are half-Montenegrin? And a chef? Café Lompar looks so amazing. Always a favourite place of mine and now even better. I can't wait to visit.' Nik was effusive and likeable.

'Thank you so much, we'd welcome you any time.' I smiled. Milo was studying his menu with forensic concentration. 'Yes, my father was from Montenegro. Perast, if you know it?'

'Know it? My first girlfriend was from Perast! I used to beg my Papa to drive me to see her, and cry when he dragged me away.' He laughed at the memory. 'One time I hid in the boot of her family's car just so I could spend another hour with Elena.'

'What happened?' I asked.

'I didn't do a very good job of hiding. My shirt was sticking out from the boot and they caught me. I had to spend a very uncomfortable night waiting for the first bus in the morning.' I laughed with him.

'Tell Kat about the...' Natalija started, but the waiter came back to take our drinks' order. 'Ooh, yes please, Kat and I will split the Pinot Grigio. Is that okay?'

'You know I'm always up for that.' I needed the wine to calm my nerves.

'Soda and lime,' Milo said.

'Coca Cola,' his dad said to the waiter.

I spotted the flicker of muscle in Milo's jaw. Nik caught it too. 'There was a day when I would have had vodka,' he said, when the waiter had moved away. I smiled politely as if this was news.

'It was more than a day,' Milo said, under his breath. I frowned at him.

'But that time is behind me now,' Nik told him.

'I could never give up wine.' Natalija didn't read the room. 'Too nice with an aperitivo.'

Nik patted her hand. 'It has been hard to quit,' he said.

'You've had a difficult time.' I tried to ease the tension around the table.

'When Lucija passed, it was a very dark time for me,' he began.

'It wasn't great for us either,' Milo snapped.

'I know, and I wasn't there for you,' Nik said gravely. 'I was young, I have two children, I did not know what to do. And the grief...' He trailed off. 'Drink was a crutch for me.'

I nodded, not daring to speak.

'I tell Natalija and Milo all the time how sorry I am, for everything.'

There was silence around the table, although Natalija reached across and rubbed his arm. I couldn't believe how quickly we'd got to this subject. I expected it to be brushed under the table. The Montenegrins weren't like the British, though.

'I am a terrible father, yes, it is true.' He waved off Natalija's protestations. Milo regarded him with a cold stare. 'But I want to make it right now.'

Milo scoffed. The drinks were brought and we ordered food.

'Tell me all about this wedding then,' Nik invited.

I told him about the venue we'd chosen, the view from the

173

ceremony. 'You can see Tivat and Café Lompar. It felt like the perfect setting.'

'It is beautiful,' Milo conceded and I wondered if he was warming.

'My boy is getting married.' Nik shook his head with wonder. 'I wish Lucija could see you.'

'What do you do now, Nikola?' I asked.

'I used to work as a mechanic, in a car garage,' he said, then looked down at his plate. 'Now, I can't. Too difficult to remember. It is like the drink has made a huge part of my brain just blank. Destroyed my past. Destroyed me, really.' He gave a small humble laugh, although he knew it wasn't funny.

'That's not true,' Natalija said.

'I would like to do it again, maybe I ask in the garage one day.' He rubbed the back of his neck, weary. 'Now I take deliveries. I like it. I get to see this beautiful country every day.'

'It is beautiful. When I came here for the first time, I fell in love with it,' I told him.

'How are the boats, the business?' he asked Milo now.

'Fine,' Milo said, arms crossed. We all watched him expectantly. He took a sip of his drink, then placed his glass back on the table slowly. As he set it down, the table next to us let out another roar of laughter, and Milo jumped and knocked Nik's glass towards him. The brown liquid exploded in a spray that went straight over Nik.

'Oh!' we all gasped as it soaked his top and pale trousers, the dark stain expanding in the worst possible way. Milo's eyes widened as though he couldn't believe it had happened. Nik looked up at him.

'Well, I know you aren't a fan of mine, but did you have to do this?' He smiled and we all laughed, slowly, unsure at first until it gained momentum, rivalling the table next to us. The tension seemed so absurd when Nik was covered in coke. Milo shrugged, this time with a smile on his face.

'I think I deserved that,' Nik laughed.

'You deserve a lot worse,' Milo said, although I could tell this time he was joking. I squeezed his hand under the table, pleased.

The evening seemed to relax from there, with Natalija telling stories of Milan and Milo talking about the first time we met. Milo seemed to have softened a little, laughing about a trip they made with their mother, camping on the Italian coast, where they'd had to check into a hotel due to unprecedented rain. I could sense he wasn't quite himself, though. Nik mentioned Milo being naughty as a school boy and he jumped in to reply, 'Things have changed a lot since then – you do not know,' a little harshly over what had been a lighthearted story.

'I know. I have been out of your life for years now,' Nik said. 'Not my fault entirely though...'

'Who wants dessert?' Natalija asked, cutting across deliberately.

Later, as we got up to leave, Nik said, 'Kat, it has been a pleasure to meet you.'

'You too. I'm so glad I finally got to see you.'

He leaned in to give me an air kiss.

'Are you sure you'll be alright tonight?' Natalija asked him as we moved to the door. She was coming back to stay with us, ready to get an early train to Milan in the morning.

'I will be fine.' He gave her a kiss and then turned to Milo.

'When will you two come and visit? I have your gift at home. You could come tonight?' He looked expectantly at us.

'I have work in the morning,' Milo said, although I knew he wouldn't start until lunchtime. Things hadn't thawed entirely then.

'Go on, I won't keep you long, a coffee and some gelato?'

'That sounds lovely,' I started but Milo interrupted.

'No.'

'Okay.' If Nik was hurt, he didn't show it and waved us off as we headed for our car.

Back at the house, I could ask Milo why he was so desperate to get away. Natalija had gone to bed in the spare room, and I heard her unzipping one of her giant suitcases.

'Well, what do you expect?' he asked me as he undressed. I was wiping my make-up off.

'I thought it went really well,' I said. 'Your dad seems lovely.'

Milo shook his head. 'He always seems lovely, but you do not know him.'

I'd hit a nerve. After a pleasant evening, I was disappointed we were back here again, with Milo sulking in the bedroom.

'True,' I conceded. 'But it felt like a start.' He crossed the room to hang his shirt up in the wardrobe. 'And he's important to us.'

Milo paused, and I found it hard to read his emotions. I hoped he didn't think I was overstepping the mark.

He came to sit on the bed. 'Kat, I just find it hard to get past what happened. We can't play happy families at the wedding.' He ran a hand through his hair, pulling the skin on his forehead taut. If it was possible, he looked even more attractive, boyish. It really was quite distracting at times.

'I know,' I soothed. 'I will never understand how hard it is for you. But, Milo, he's your father. I know what it's like not to have a father.'

'I forget that sometimes.' Milo softened, reaching out to touch my foot. His skin felt silky soft as he rubbed my sole.

'I'd do anything to still have my father around. But then maybe I wouldn't have found out about my other family, and maybe I would never have met you. Still, I miss him. I'd love him to be at my wedding. I know Mum would too. But it can't happen.'

'There will be two very important people missing that day, Lucija and Danilo,' Milo said.

'Don't make it three. Your dad needs to be a part of it,' I said.

'I know, I know,' Milo conceded. I saw a smile grow on his face. His eyes were dark under those lashes as he looked up. I knew that smile.

'What do you want?' I acted innocent.

'Some stress relief.' Milo moved closer to me.

'Milo Martinovic, if you weren't so handsome...' I kissed him, deciding stress relief was exactly what we both needed.

CHAPTER TWENTY-TWO

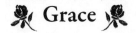 Grace

'*Bokeljska Noc*?' I asked.

Ana laughed. 'We call it Boka Night. They have boat parades, fireworks, food. It's at the end of August. Herceg is in the Bay of Kotor. Very beautiful. The mountains behind and the sea.' She was very expressive, her hands flying around, painting the image for me.

'Well, Kat's been asked to do a cookery demonstration there. She has a lot of these requests, but the wedding won't be too long after that. I don't know if she has time.'

'Lots of TV cameras. Thousands go,' Ana said. 'It will be good publicity.'

'OK, I'll mention it to Kat. What is Statehood Day?'

Ana laughed again. 'It celebrates the time Montenegro became independent. July 13th. Basically, an excuse to get drunk.'

'Sounds just like the UK. We'll have to think of something special for that night. Some traditional Montenegrin dishes with Kat's twist.' I chewed the end of my pen. 'Perhaps Davor can come up with some special cocktails.'

I glanced over at our barman. Davor was chatting to a girl wearing a denim dress and dark hair that fell almost to her waist. He was showing off and spinning a spirit bottle. I couldn't look.

Lovro and Dav had been a couple for a while, but the way he was chatting to this girl made me wonder whether he was just stringing Lovro along. Who knows, I thought ruefully.

I was finding it hard to concentrate. Neil was arriving this evening and he and Ollie were hiring a car. They were due to get to my apartment at eightish. Then Ollie was staying with Kat. Natalija was returning to Milan, so poor Kat and Milo had barely any time to themselves.

I heard a bottle smash and the chatter in the restaurant paused for a moment. Dav mouthed 'Sorry' to me and the noise resumed. It was absolutely heaving and I barely had a chance to say the briefest hello to Kat. Still, I wasn't complaining. I didn't know why Kat worried so much about Ensambla; we were packed to the rafters most days. The stress with the wedding and Milo being awkward about his father was obviously getting to her.

As lunch service drew to an end, I saw Claire sidle in, taking a seat in a quiet corner. She hadn't taken her sunglasses off.

'Well, she's surfaced at last! Sore head?' I teased loudly, walking over. I sat down opposite her. 'What time did you get back last night?'

'Late,' she winced.

'Or was it early? You were a real party animal last night. I couldn't peel you from that creepy guy.'

Claire took off her sunglasses and her eyes were red-rimmed. 'I should have gone home with you.'

'Yes, you should have, but we've all done it. It's just that you're old enough to know better.' I smiled.

Claire's eyes brimmed with tears.

'Are you okay? I'm only teasing.' I reached out and touched her hand. 'You'll feel better once the hangover wears off.'

'I've been a fool, Gracie. A real fool.' She put her head in her hands. 'I went back to Anto's last night. The guy in the bar. I didn't even fancy him. What was I thinking?' she wailed.

Ana approached our table. 'Can I get you something?' she asked but I waved her away.

I had a horrible sense of foreboding. 'What happened? You didn't stay with him?' I paused, dreading what she'd say. 'Sleep with him?'

She nodded.

'Oh, Claire,' was all I could manage.

She closed her eyes. 'I couldn't wait to get out of there this morning. I'm such a bitch.'

I didn't trust myself to speak.

'All I can think about is Stu and how hurt he'd be,' Claire went on. 'I feel an absolute shit!'

'Are you going to tell him?' What could I say to her? I knew what it felt like to be on the receiving end of betrayal.

'I don't know. I don't know.' She closed her eyes again. 'I think I'm having some sort of mid-life crisis. I'm not excusing myself or anything, but I've been a bit mad lately.'

'I'm not going to argue with that,' I said, ruefully.

'I want to go home,' she said. 'I can't think straight. I need to see Stu.'

At the apartment later, I waited for Neil and Ollie to arrive. I couldn't stop my thoughts returning to the conversation with

Claire at lunchtime. I wasn't sure whether I'd tell Neil about it. It was too personal. I didn't want him to think badly of Claire. I wasn't sure what I thought about it myself.

I would have picked Neil and Ollie up, of course, but they wanted a car for their stay and, as I would be working most days, if they rented their own, the two of them could play golf when they got a chance. I liked Ollie. He seemed chatty and uncomplicated and he looked so much like his father. Those were good genes, I thought, smiling. What you saw was what you got with Ollie, or so Neil told me. As I got ready, the butterflies in my stomach were more insistent. I loved this excited feeling before we were reunited. I slipped into a loose yellow t-shirt dress, which showed off my tan. I'd never have dared wear it at home.

Home. Where was home exactly? It was a strange existence this, spending long summers here, a completely different life to my cosy cottage in Meadow Ponsbury. Now Neil was putting pressure on me, wanting to move in together, was I going to have to choose? He was jaded with life in the city, he said. I had been non-committal, but knew I couldn't hold him off forever.

After all the times Dan and I had been apart, I thought because of his job, and knowing now what a lie that was, could I really choose another long distance relationship? Would I be able to trust him and would he trust me? Was it stupid to try?

Spritzing on some perfume, the doorbell rang. I raced to open it.

'Well, hello, you two. My favourite men!' I smiled.

Neil grabbed me for a hug, but it was fleeting, with Ollie standing behind him. He gave me a kiss on the check.

'How was the flight?' I asked. 'Tea, coffee? Or something stronger?'

'Going from Gatwick was a bit of a pain, but at least we could fly straight into Tivat,' Neil said. 'It seemed quite a long flight. Four hours. Coffee for me. I don't think I could drink alcohol at the moment.'

'Dad slept through most of it,' Ollie laughed. 'I'll have a beer if you've got one.'

'Sure. You two make yourselves at home. Kat has invited us over. She's finished early at the restaurant, so she asked us to call in around nine.'

I could see the disappointment in Neil's face. Like me, he had probably been hoping for this first night to ourselves.

'I could have booked into a hotel,' Ollie said. 'I don't want to put Kat and Milo out.'

'Don't be daft,' I said, handing Ollie his beer and the bottle opener.

'I forget how hot it is out here,' Neil said, taking off his jacket. His blue shirt stretched over his arms and I couldn't wait until we were alone.

We caught up with all the news and I talked about Kat and Milo's wedding plans.

'She's such a perfectionist and the planning has got to her lately, especially with Ensambla opening.'

Ollie rolled his eyes, 'That's all I hear lately is weddings. It's all Mum talks about.'

'Cass has asked Ollie to give her away. Her father passed away a few years ago and so she's asked my man here to step in.' Neil patted his son's knee.

Ollie raked his fingers through his hair nervously. 'I'm honoured and all that, but I've got to make a speech and I'm useless at speeches.'

'True,' Neil said solemnly, before grinning.

'Thanks, Dad. That's really supportive! I just don't know what to say. I'm sure I'll make a complete hash of it.'

'I'll help if you like, if it's not too awkward, I mean,' I said. 'Sylvie and I had to make lots of speeches for the charity. I know a wedding speech is different.'

'Thanks, Grace.' Ollie drained his beer.

'That went down quickly,' I laughed. 'I'd offer you another but we'd better make tracks to Kat's.'

'Are you sure they don't mind me being there? I don't really know Milo that well.'

'Stop worrying,' I told him. 'They're really happy for you to stay.'

As we approached Kat's villa, the smell of roast lamb greeted us. The villa was whitewashed with the ubiquitous cerise bougainvillea framing the windows. Clouds of white mimosa flanked the garden path and Kat and Milo waved at us from their first-floor balcony. Although further from the harbour than my apartment, they still had glimpses of the glittering Adriatic between the villas in front of them and tonight the sky was aflame, casting blood red strokes on the still water in the harbour.

'Hey, you two!' Neil waved cheerily. 'Nice life for some!'

Kat and Milo disappeared inside to meet us, and after greetings were exchanged, Milo got some beers from the fridge.

'I'll put the dinner out,' Kat called.

'Thank God.' Milo handed bottles out, Neil unresisting this time. 'I am hungry.'

'You didn't have to wait for us. I could have cooked something,' I said.

'It's fine,' Kat reassured me. 'Milo's always hungry. It's only something simple. We're starting with japraci, rastan leaves stuffed with minced pork and spices – a bit like the stuffed vine leaves you have in Greece.'

The smell was heavenly and we tucked in with joy, food filling the gaps in the conversation of people who hadn't been together for a long time. Ollie had only really got to know Kat last year, when he came over with Neil for Kat's engagement party. He made appreciative noises. 'You're a genius, Kat!'

'Well, I hope you like the main and dessert as much.'

I followed Kat into the kitchen to help serve the lamb stew. She'd cooked it in milk with bay leaves and vegetables. I'd had it many times with her and the lamb was usually so tender, it fell away from the bone.

'You know what I'm like,' she said. 'Anyway, it's only sugared *Priganice* for dessert with ice cream.'

'Homemade?' I asked. Kat laughed in response. 'Do you ever give yourself a break and consider serving a frozen cheesecake or some chocolate brownies?'

'Sacrilege!'

'It wouldn't do us any harm, you know. You're working far too hard and worrying too much. We've been so busy lately and I honestly think all this fretting over Ensambla is not worth it.'

Kat paused as she ladled out the stew. 'It's funny you should say that but I did something I shouldn't have. I...'

Milo appeared in the kitchen. 'Do we have lemonade? That boyfriend of yours is a lightweight,' he said, meaning Neil.

Kat and I laughed at the awkwardness of the English colloquialism spoken in his heavy Montenegrin accent.

'He's getting old,' I joked.

Kat focussed on putting the final flourish of parsley to the stew.

'What were you saying?'

'Nothing. Come on, it's almost quarter to ten. We'd better eat up or none of us will sleep tonight.'

'Do you think Milo minds having Ollie to stay?' I asked.

'God, no. It'll take his mind off all this upset with his father.'

'He's still brooding over it, then? I wanted to ask about the meal...'

Kat nodded. 'Nik seems determined to make amends but Milo is stubborn. I can understand. He wasn't there for him when he needed him most. But sometimes you have to forgive.'

We fell silent for a moment. I thought about Dan and the way he had hurt me. He wasn't there for me to forgive and if he had been, would I have been able to?

'God, families are complicated,' I said.

Kat picked up a tray. 'You can say that again. Luka is home on the weekend. He finished a couple of weeks ago and Rosa is convinced he's avoiding her because of Matija.'

'He needs to grow up.'

'It's not easy for him, though,' Kat said, immediately jumping to her brother's defence. 'It's always been just the two of them.'

As we sat around the table littered with empty plates, the atmosphere was light-hearted. Neil held my hand under the table, and I knew he was as desperate for us to be alone as I was. I was hungry for him.

Ollie was in full flow, telling Milo about his job in the city as an actuary. 'It assesses risks and probability of accidents. It sounds boring but we've got some huge clients and the company is expanding all the time.'

'He's just had a promotion,' Neil said proudly. 'He was always so good at maths in school.'

'Dad needs to listen to my advice sometimes. It's a good time to invest if you know where. He's just had his flat in Bath valued and if he sold that, he could free up some money. It would make sound economic sense.'

'And move in with me?' I asked. I sensed the mood shift at the table.

'I just wanted to see what I'd get for it. It wasn't serious,' Neil explained, not meeting my eyes. Kat coughed.

Ollie didn't read the atmosphere well and continued. 'Dad would make a decent profit on it and then rather than just leave it lying in the bank now that interest rates are pretty crap, I know ways where he could make a sizeable profit.'

'My job couldn't be more different,' Milo said, changing the subject.

'Kat told me you have three tourist boats,' Ollie said, 'so you must be doing well. I wouldn't mind coming out with you one day. Tomorrow, though, I'll just be chilling on the beach. We are going to get some golf in, too. You'll have to come with us, Milo.'

Kat snorted, 'Milo playing golf? He's got two left feet and is totally uncoordinated.'

As everyone laughed, Neil tried to reach for my hand under the table, but I sipped my water and avoided eye-contact. I'd been so looking forward to tonight, but now my spirits had been dampened. Couldn't Neil just wait? Couldn't he understand I needed time? The night had soured quickly.

As we walked back to the apartment soon after, Neil grabbed my hand firmly. 'I seem to be making a habit of this. Putting my foot in it. I honestly just wanted to see what I'd get for the apartment. I wasn't even going to tell you. Ollie has a big mouth sometimes.'

'I won't be pushed, Neil. You know I love you, but let's take our time. You said even Cass and Mike have been together three years and it's only now they're getting married. Why rush things?'

'They moved in after six months.' Neil sighed. 'Look, that's irrelevant, anyway. Do I have to make excuses because I want to be with the woman I love? Why must I feel guilty for that?'

'I thought you understood.' I felt exasperated. 'Dan cheated on me for years. Do you know what that does to you?'

Neil stopped walking and pulled me towards him. He kissed me on the lips, gently. 'You have to trust me, Gracie. I am not Dan and never will be like him.'

We walked on and both of us flopped into bed, too tired to make love. He held me until he fell asleep and I watched the curtain billow in the breeze, wondering if I could ever trust anyone again.

CHAPTER TWENTY-THREE

🌿 Kat 🌿

I felt groggy and nauseous when I woke up, and thought the last few nights of rich meals and drinking until late – first with Milo's family and then Mum and Neil – had caught up with me. Was I getting old? I used to be able to handle nights out on the trot in catering college and still get up for classes in the morning, but now the room was sliding from side to side as I lay in bed.

Milo had been up and out before seven this morning. Now the height of summer had arrived, his business was in full swing. He was going to a fancy hotel in Budva this morning to pick up guests for a private tour around the Balkans on a catamaran he'd hired. Milo was thinking of getting a yacht and expanding into more luxury tours; today was a trial run. I should have wished him luck before he left but I barely stirred. I wondered if he felt woozy at all or was the Montenegrin heat shrivelling my liver?

I rolled over in bed, pleased to have the space to myself and nothing to do this morning. Breakfast and a film in bed maybe? Something easy on the stomach, and a gallon of coffee.

I heard footsteps coming from the spare room, and could follow their path around the house. The sound of the fridge door opening. A cupboard. I guessed Ollie was up and not feeling the effects of the wine like I was.

I sighed. With Natalija having only just left, Milo and I were desperate to have the place to ourselves again. Ollie was nice but was little more than a stranger at the moment, and our house didn't afford a lot of space for guests.

I sat up and saw my reflection in the mirrored wardrobe. Ghastly. Ruffled hair, pale cheeks, and ogre-like puffy eyes. Shit, I'd have to make an effort with my appearance and small talk if I wanted that coffee. It wasn't worth it. I lay back down, the small sliver of sunlight through the curtains falling across my chest, the heat palpable. It was going to be a scorcher.

I heard the fridge open again. More footsteps. The sound of a voice. Maybe Ollie was on the phone to Neil, complaining about my lack of breakfast provisions.

I had to face the day. I ran a brush through my hair, and took a few shaky steps towards my dressing gown. It was just about decent despite the tea stain on the front. It would have to do. I caught sight of the clock on the bedroom wall; it was quarter to eleven. I hadn't slept in this late for a long time. No wonder Ollie was getting impatient.

'I'm up, I'm up,' I started as I came down the stairs. 'Don't call me a lightweight but I've got the hangover from...'

'Hello.' Luka stood across the kitchen from Ollie, stirring a cup. The smell of toast hung in the air.

'Luka!' I raced the last few steps and flung my arms around my brother. 'I didn't think you were home until next weekend.'

'You look like shit,' he said, pulling back. 'God, are we really related?' He turned to Ollie, smirking.

'At least I can make toast,' I said, flicking the toaster off and pulling out a blackened slice of bread. 'Haven't you learnt anything in uni?'

'Pfft, I am too busy.' He waved away my insult.

'Well, come on, who's the girl then?'

Luka frowned but moved to the fridge to take out a carton of orange juice. 'What girl?'

'You've stayed on two weeks longer in uni. Me and Milo said there must be a girl.' I poked him in the ribs to stop him swigging straight from the bottle, garnering a satisfying yelp. He treated this home like it was his own, which was actually how he treated most places.

'Well, you know me, Kat,' he said. 'Many, many girls.'

'I'll get it out of you later,' I joked. 'Tea or coffee?' I offered to Ollie. He was looking from me to Luka and seemed a little out of place, standing with his weight on one foot and rubbing one elbow. I sympathised, having been an only child myself until a year ago.

'Coffee please, milk, no sugar.' He smiled.

'You've met Luka before, haven't you?'

'Last year at your engagement party,' Ollie said.

'How long are you staying for?' Luka asked him. I knew they would get along, Luka being easy company.

'Two weeks, then I have to be back at work. I'm coming back out for your wedding, Kat, and then home again for Mum's.'

'Urgh, too many people getting married.' Luka grimaced. 'Me, I don't think I will ever get married.' I wondered if he was worried his mother and Matija would go down that route. I wanted to ask Luka how he felt about it, but with Ollie present it wasn't the time.

'Bollocks!' I laughed. 'You were telling me last month you were going to marry that TV host Lena Simovic.'

Luka clutched his heart. 'Don't talk to me about Lena Simovic.'

'And I'm pretty sure you'd marry Natalija in a heartbeat if she gave you the time of day.'

'How's your love life, man?' Luka turned to Ollie, who told him about his single status. I smiled, knowing I could rely on Luka to include him in the conversation.

'What are you grinning about?' Luka turned back to me.

'I've missed you,' I said, honestly.

'I've missed you too,' Luka said, and an oddly serious look crossed his face. I was convinced his extended uni stay was for a girl. I wondered if I could get Ollie to prize the story out of him.

'Give over. Right, this toast is so burned, it's well … toast. Who wants pancakes?'

'Me!' Ollie and Luka both perked up, and I wondered if I was more sister or mother in this situation.

I headed out of the Café Lompar kitchen for a break and a stroll along the harbour with Lovro, but our paths were blocked by a delivery van. Its open end was facing towards Ensambla, and as we rounded the corner, we saw Lizzie signing a clipboard. She waved to us, before lifting two boxes.

'Hi,' Lovro called out, his wave more enthusiastic than my guilty one.

'Some aprons.' She motioned with the boxes. 'For the cooking course. I wasn't sure they'd come in time. What a relief!'

My cheeks flared. Shit.

'How many have booked?' Lovro paused to chat. I ignored the urge to keep walking. I would definitely look guilty if I did what I wanted to and ran away.

'Twenty, the full course. We've had so many enquiries, we're thinking of starting a regular thing,' she said, her blonde ponytail bouncing.

'Wow,' I said, half-heartedly.

'Sounds great. What are you making with them? Pasta?' Lovro asked, listening intently as Lizzie spoke.

I couldn't concentrate, my eyes drifting to that poster and the mark I'd made. I had to stop or she'd notice. Was it too late to change it back? I still couldn't believe I'd done something so bold. It wasn't like me.

'Classic dessert, tiramisu, nothing complicated for the first lesson,' Lizzie finished.

'Well, good luck for today,' I smiled, hoping I sounded genuine. I hoped Lizzie and David would have a full class. I'd only changed the date on the poster, after all. The real date of the 25th was still all over their website and on leaflets. I hoped the damage wouldn't be so great.

'We'll let you know how it goes in ... eek, one hour!' Lizzie checked her watch.

'See you.' Lovro waved.

'By the way, Lovro, I wanted to come and see how you make those ice cream truffles. The sample I had was wonderful!' Lizzie called after us.

I rolled my eyes. Could she be any further up his arse? I constantly batted back and forth between guilt and glee at my actions, sometimes thinking that they deserved it.

'Ice-cream truffles? Why haven't I seen those?' I cocked my head quizzically when we were out of earshot.

'Just a little something I tried out for Dav on the dinner shift last night. We had some left and offered Lizzie and David coffee after work.'

'Traitor!' I said as a half-joke, although I did feel a stab of betrayal.

'They're nice people.' Lovro linked his arm through mine as we walked, dodging a street vendor selling beach towels as he unrolled one violently on the pavement. 'And you know what they say, keep your friends close and your enemies...'

'I didn't know Montenegrins say that too,' I laughed.

'That and love thy bed as you love thyself,' he said.

'You're speaking to my hangover there, babe.'

It was nice to splash our feet in the sea as we sat on the harbour wall, dangling our toes towards the impossibly cold water after walking along the shore. The heat outside was so suffocating, it was always a surprise that the sea wasn't the same balmy temperature. Lovro and I both shared a tub of strawberry ice cream we'd bought from a stall on the sea front. It was nice to just kick back and be a tourist for once, mingling with the crowds of people enjoying the scenery and bustle of Tivat. Montenegro held my entire life, my home, my fiancé, my work. It was hard to believe that I was just a tourist here little over a year ago. How much had changed since then.

'You shouldn't be eating this, with the wedding prep coming up,' Lovro teased, stealing the plastic spoon from my hand.

'I know,' I groaned. 'It's killing me. I've had some lovely salads in the last week, but when I see you with those *priganice* doughnuts every night, a little part of me dies inside.'

'I was thinking of trying honeycomb and cranberry next week,' Lovro said, chuckling.

'Don't do this to me. Must fit in to the dress. Must fit in to the dress,' I reminded myself, but still reached for the spoon after him.

'This is nice,' Lovro said, 'but it needs a splash of balsamic or some mint. It's a bit flat.' He had a look of such disgust it made me laugh.

'I don't think the average tourist minds,' I said. 'Actually, people love their classic ice creams.'

Lovro's eyes lit up at the same time as mine.

'We could do desserts inspired by classic flavours!'

'Raspberry ripple soufflé. Rum and raisin brownies.'

'Mint chocolate chip ... as a meringue pie with chocolate kisses.' I loved that Lovro got as excited as I did with new food ideas.

'Yes! Let's try some for tonight's service,' I said.

'I think sometimes we're telepathic.' Lovro reached in for the last scoop of ice cream.

'What would I do without you?' I sighed. 'Maybe we're the ones that should be getting married.'

Lovro looked at me in surprise. 'Come on. I know I'm handsome but I thought Milo was more your type. More, you know, straight?'

'That's true. We're both so stressed at the moment though, and we've had so many house guests. We've barely had time to kiss, let alone do anything else. Plus, Milo's been so grumpy over his father. Every time I bring up the wedding he just huffs and walks away.' I sighed, my feelings tumbling from my chest. 'And

194

yesterday, I suggested doing the catering myself for the wedding. I thought he was going to have a heart attack!'

'Montenegrins are fiery like that. And you're fiery too. Remember when Ensambla opened? I thought you were going to kill David!' Lovro said. 'You got over it, and Milo will get over this.'

I thought Lovro was over-estimating how 'over it' I was when it came to Ensambla. I didn't want another reminder of my sabotage.

'All I'm saying is I could do with the honeymoon right now, not in bloody September,' I said. 'Come on, we'd better get back to work if we're going to pull off this ice cream idea.'

My stomach twisted as we reached the frontage of Café Lompar. Lizzie was outside wearing dark sunglasses and pulling the poster down. She didn't look happy. Did she know?

My pace quickened. I wanted to get inside without any drama. My pulse was suddenly racing. She wouldn't know it was me, I told myself. Maybe they'd had a full class and I'd misread the situation.

When we were nearly in safety, my heart sank as I heard Lovro call out, 'How's it going?'

Shit. We should have gone in the back entrance.

Lizzie looked up, surprised to see us. 'An absolute disaster!'

'Oh?' I tried to show shock. This was a nightmare.

'We've only had four people arrive. Two couples! No one else has turned up,' Lizzie said. I couldn't see her expression beneath the sunglasses but she was clearly hurt. My pulse was deafening now. I wondered if Lovro and Lizzie could hear it.

'Oh, Lizzie,' Lovro said in sympathy. 'Have you tried calling the other bookings?'

'I spoke to one of them. They said they thought it was tomorrow. I don't know why, it's clearly the 25th.'

'Easily done though, isn't it? People on holiday lose track of days,' I tried to explain. I felt bad that I was acting innocent when I was anything but. What was I meant to do?

'Weird that sixteen people all got the wrong date, though.' Lizzie's voice sounded both upset and furious at the same time. 'When I think of the money we've spent to set this up...'

'There must be a mistake,' Lovro said. 'Have you checked the date on the website?'

'No, maybe I'll do that.' She pushed her sunglasses up to her forehead. It was worse now I could see her eyes, blue and teary.

'David's had to go ahead and run the course today for the four people, but we can't afford to put it on again and miss out on another lunch service. We'll be at a big loss.'

Lovro and I both murmured how awful it was and offered to help in any way possible. As we walked back in to Café Lompar, I felt like the worst human being ever.

CHAPTER TWENTY-FOUR

🌹 Grace 🌹

'Morning, gorgeous.' Neil kissed me. 'It's so lovely to wake up next to you.'

'Hmm,' I murmured, kissing him, aware that my mouth must taste sour from the late dinner and alcohol last night. Neil lay on top of the bedding, his tanned skin looking darker against the white cotton sheets.

The bedroom had a Juliet balcony and the doors were ajar, letting in the buttery morning sunlight and the sounds of the harbour: the shouts of the fishermen bringing in their catch, the chatter of tourists and the clattering plates from the cafés and bars preparing for the day.

'I'm grateful for a lie-in,' I said, stretching. 'Thank God I'm not in until this evening.'

Neil got up from the bed, just in his boxer shorts, and opened the curtains, looking out at the scenery.

'God, what a breathtaking view,' he gasped. 'What's that mountain called over there?'

'Mount Volujak. Kat and Milo have been hiking there. The views of the Bay of Kotor are fantastic, apparently.'

'Everyone seems to head for Croatia but I think Montenegro is even more beautiful.'

I joined him at the window and pointed over to the island opposite. 'That's the island where Kat and Milo are getting married. It's perfect, quite secluded, and so green with olive and cypress trees.'

'No wonder I'm finding it hard to drag you away from here. Do you think you could move out here permanently?'

Last night's revelation that Neil had had his apartment in Bath valued still hung in the air. Why did he have to pick at this scab?

'I don't think I could, Neil. I admit I love it and Kat's here, of course. I feel closer to her now than I ever did when Dan was alive. But you're in Bath and I have Claire and the kids there. Friends.'

'It might be harder when Kat has children.'

'I know, but let's cross that bridge when we come to it. At the moment, I have the best of both worlds. I get to come out here in the summer and have the rest of the year at home with you.'

'I'm sorry I make things difficult for you,' Neil said. 'You must be torn sometimes, and I try to imagine how I'd feel if Ollie was abroad. I promise I'll try to be more understanding.'

'Come on, let's have coffee on the balcony and I've got some pastries from the restaurant, honey and pecan.'

'I didn't think I'd feel hungry after last night's meal, but I'm just about ready to have something now.' He grinned.

Taking our cups and plates through the living room onto the bigger balcony, we sat and watched the world go by.

'I thought we'd all take a trip to Herceg Novi today. It's not far and it's so beautiful. You'll love the historic buildings and there's the beach at Boka Bay where Laura can top up her tan.' I sipped my coffee and gazed at the marina, the water glittering in the morning sunlight. 'Claire and Laura only have a couple of days left and Laura's at a real loose end since Natalija left. Claire says she spent most of the day yesterday mooching by the pool and watching Tik Tok videos.'

Neil shrugged. 'I can think of nothing worse.'

'Yeah, but you're not seventeen,' I laughed. 'There's eons between us and teenagers. Even Kat says she feels the age gap and she's only twenty-five.'

'Do you think Claire's dreading going home?'

I paused. Before her revelation yesterday, I would have agreed. Now, I wasn't so sure. 'I think she's actually missing Stu. Absence makes the heart grow fonder and all that.'

Neil raised an eyebrow as if he didn't believe a word of it.

'No, really, I think the break has done them good, made them realise what they mean to each other.' I wasn't ready to share what happened the other night. It was a bit raw and I didn't know what Neil would think of Claire.

I pushed my plate away from me. I'd barely eaten the pastry.

'I'll have that.' Neil grinned. Then his face became serious. 'With me and Cass, there wasn't anyone else, but after Max was killed, we just stopped communicating. You'd think we'd have turned to each other for comfort, but neither of us did. The pain is so agonising, so awful, it's as if you can't cope with someone else's grief.' He touched his chest. 'It felt like a physical pain.'

'I'm glad you can talk about it now. It's important.' I reached for him and he kissed my hand.

'Well, it's not something you can talk about freely, especially when you first meet someone and you're trying to impress them.' He smiled sadly. 'You were the first one who really seemed to understand, perhaps because you had been through grief yourself.'

I nodded. 'I felt I always brought the mood of a room down. People tiptoed around me, even Claire. I could see they felt guilty if they laughed, as if being happy was a betrayal.'

'Grief is like a madness, I think. I saw a counsellor for a while. I had to do it for Ollie, though. He was only ten. He deserved to have parents who weren't sad all the time. Cass and I both came to the same conclusion.' He sipped his coffee, 'As tough as it was, we would put on a brave face for Ollie and carry on with life. And it gets easier with time. It never goes away, but you learn to live with it.'

'I guess it puts things in perspective. With Claire and Stu it's just a blip, I think. I hope.' I trailed off.

'I'm sure,' Neil agreed. 'At least Cass and I have moved on. Although she's going through a terrible time with her mother at the moment. I think the wedding is giving her something to focus on.'

I wasn't looking forward to Cass's wedding. I didn't tell Neil this. I knew there was nothing between them, but it would still feel awkward. A wedding where you only knew the person you came with and that person was once married to the bride.

Neil scrolled through photos of Herceg Novi and looked up golf courses while I showered. I slipped a floral t-shirt dress over my bathing costume and stuffed a towel and sunglasses into my beach bag.

'I'll drive us,' Neil called from the bathroom.

'No, it's okay. You've only just got here and I'm more used to the roads. Claire should be here soon and we can go around and pick Ollie up.'

Neil pulled me to him, a towel wrapped carelessly around his hips after his shower. 'Hmm, so what are you saying about my driving?' He kissed me hard on the lips.

'Claire will be here any second,' I warned, laughing and feeling a bit giddy.

On cue, the doorbell rang. I left the bedroom as Claire popped her head around the front door. 'You two dressed and up and about?' she said, shielding her eyes.

I nudged her. 'Come on, that's getting so old,' I said.

Laura rolled her eyes. 'Oh, for God's sake, Mum. I'm going to sit on the balcony.'

'What's up with Laura?' I asked as soon as she was out of earshot.

'Well, since Natalija has gone, she's been climbing the walls, saying Montenegro is full of old people. Plus, she's started messaging some guy at college and they're arranging to meet up.' Claire sank on the sofa. 'Teenagers, don't you just love 'em!'

'I'm sure we were as bad. How do you feel about going home?'

Claire shrugged. 'It's been nice to have a break. At home, even when you're on holiday, you find things to do about the house. I've had a real rest, but I'll be glad to get back. Although I'm sure the house will look like a bomb site!' She rolled her eyes.

Her voice sounded strained. 'It'll be lovely when you're all out in September for Kat's wedding.' I said.

'Well, I'm going to enjoy these last two days. I intend to have a nice boozy lunch and sleep it off on the beach. At least Ollie is with us and Laura will be happy at that. Anything other than the oldies.'

'Less of the old,' Neil said, kissing Claire on the cheek.

'How disappointing!' Claire replied, looking at Neil's outfit of white t-shirt and dark green shorts. 'You really are letting the side down. I thought you'd at least keep your socks on with your sandals, German-tourist style. This isn't what Laura was expecting of us middle-aged folk.'

Laura came in from the balcony, rolling her eyes again.

When we went to pick Ollie up, Luka was at Kat's. He came out to the car, and wrapped me in a warm hug. He and Ollie were obviously getting on like a house on fire and had been lying on the terrace drinking beer.

'Kat's sleeping off her hangover.' Luka grinned.

Ollie stood behind Luka. 'I'm gonna stay here if that's okay, Dad?' he said. 'Me and Luka are going to this private pool of a friend of his and there's a party later.'

'Uh, but...' Neil started.

I touched Neil's arm. 'Course it is. You two go and enjoy.'

I tried not to catch Laura's eye. She looked crestfallen, but Luka and Ollie obviously had no plans to 'babysit' for the day. 'Right, let's go,' I said, briskly. 'Luka, are you going over to the restaurant tonight?'

'Yeah, see you later.' He waved.

The journey to Herceg Novi took nearly an hour, along hairpin bends and sheer cliffs. It was breathtakingly beautiful. Montenegro was a riot of colour, sage green mountains with cypress trees and olive groves, the pink oleander and crimson bougainvillea and the omnipresent and beguiling, indigo-blue Adriatic. It was as if we lived with a veil over our eyes in Britain and this is what the world really looked like in all its glorious technicolor.

'It's so beautiful,' Neil gasped as we turned another corner. The traffic was busier than usual but this was the summer season and Montenegrins themselves were drawn like magnets to the gloriously sandy beaches.

We parked in one of the side streets that meandered through the town. Grand hotels stood cheek by jowl with antique limestone buildings with terracotta roofs. We wandered the labyrinthine streets and shops, selling leather goods and souvenirs, postcards of the Bay of Kotor and Perast, *Kapas*, or quaint folklore hats and embroidered waistcoats, and the ubiquitous prosciutto hams.

'I'm after something for Liam,' Claire said, picking up a scarlet Montenegrin flag with its golden eagle in the centre.

'He'll love this.' Laura balanced one of the folk hats on her head and took a selfie.

Claire laughed. 'God, what the heck can I get him? It hardly screams gifts for seventeen-year-old boys, does it? I'll probably end up just giving him what I always do – money!'

In the end, Neil helped her choose a watch for Liam. 'It's more than I wanted to pay, but Laura has had a holiday and I bought her loads of new clothes before we came out here.'

I thanked Neil for being so patient, trudging around the shops with three women, and we settled on one of the smart hotels looking onto the beach for lunch. Laura had perked up no end after a bit of retail therapy and was ladened with carrier bags as we walked over to a table on the terrace.

'I'll pay you back once I start work in the salon,' she promised, referring to her holiday job at a hairdresser in the centre of Bath. Claire said nothing, having no doubt heard this vow a million times before.

'I'm going to pop to the loo quickly,' I told Neil. 'I'll order in a minute or two. Ana told me the food is fabulous here.'

I liked the silver heart coasters they had on the tables and the cute glass holders for candles. I made a mental note to look these up later. I could never switch off from Café Lompar.

As I made my way back to the table, something had changed and it took my brain a while to catch up with what I was seeing. Laura was sobbing loudly and unselfconsciously, her hands covering her eyes. Claire was staring into space, her face as white as a sheet. Neil was looking very solemn as he handed a serviette to Laura.

He stood up as I approached the table. 'It's Stuart,' he said. 'He's had a terrible car accident.'

CHAPTER TWENTY-FIVE

🌿 Kat 🌿

'Uncle Stu! Oh no, what's happened?' I listened to my mum's voice at the other end of the phone, gripping the stainless-steel kitchen worktop. I'd come to work early to prepare for dinner service and to check our ice creams had set ready for the menu shake-up.

'A car accident. We don't know much yet. A police officer phoned from the scene.' I was on loudspeaker and I heard a choking cry in the background; I couldn't tell if it was Claire or Laura. My heart went out to them. It brought back the utter panic I'd felt when I was told Dad had been taken ill. I hoped this wouldn't end the same way for my poor Uncle Stu.

'Oh God, is he alright?' I asked, keen for details.

'We don't know.' Mum sounded frustrated. 'He's been taken to hospital. The officer found his wallet in the car and called Claire as his next of kin. Liam's not answering his phone.'

'Where are you now?'

'Driving to the airport. Claire and Laura have managed to book us on a flight to Gatwick. We've had to pack as best we can.'

'Do you want me to meet you there? I could try and get a flight?' I offered.

'No, don't worry,' Mum said. I heard Claire protesting in the background too. 'There's no point. You need to hold the fort.'

I felt useless and frustrated, but knew Mum was right. 'Will you let me know? Keep me updated, with everything,' I demanded. I felt lost without my family.

'Of course we will, darling.' Mum's voice sounded hard with worry. 'I'll let you know what flight we're on when we get there.'

'Oh God, what about Neil? And Ollie?' It dawned on me that they'd only just flown out to Montenegro. Would they go home as well? They wouldn't want to stay, surely?

'I don't know. I think he's going to try and get a flight too. The Gatwick one is full now so they're going to see what's available.'

The whole thing was a mess.

We hung up after vowing to keep in touch.

I felt sick to my stomach. I loved Uncle Stu. He'd been in my life since I was born and was a goofy, fun-loving kindred spirit when I was a child. Even though he was only related through marriage, he'd always treated me like blood, always given me hugs when he was babysitting, bought me toys and spun me round in a fireman's lift that made me shriek but that I secretly loved. We didn't speak as much now, but I adored Stu. Why do you always appreciate people more when you're losing them? I wanted to be there with him, needed to know he was okay.

I called Milo, needing comfort. He expressed equal concern, but I could tell he was busy at work.

'Can you call in sick?' he asked. 'You should be with family.'

'I can't. We're thin on the ground with Bojan and Ivan away on leave. It's just me and Lovro and we're fully booked tonight. Plus I'm already here.'

'Rosa would understand. You could close for the night?'

'You know as well as I do that I would never do that,' I said.

'There's nothing I can do. I may as well work to take my mind off it.' My words were true but they didn't stop the horrible twisting feeling in my gut.

'Only if you're sure,' Milo said. 'I love you.'

I smiled despite my worry. 'I love you too. See you tonight. I can't wait to be in your arms.'

'I'm going to hold you tight,' he soothed. I imagined his arms around me and felt a keen ache. As I came off the phone, I wondered how it was possible to feel like I'd known Milo forever when in reality it was just over a year.

'Is everything alright?' Lovro asked, shrugging off a denim jacket as he came into the kitchen and caught the end of my conversation.

'A family emergency. But it's alright,' I said, sounding braver than I felt inside. Cooking would take my mind off it and Lovro and I had a lot of work to do today if we were going to trial the new menu. Lovro read my mind, taking his place at my side in his chef's whites.

It seemed counter-intuitive but in Café Lompar we tended to start back-to-front with dessert prep first, as these often took longest to set or bake. Lovro and I were a well-oiled machine, working side by side in harmony.

'How did Dav's wine course go?' I asked him.

'Sounded great to me,' Lovro said as he whisked egg whites, ready to add sugar. 'Wine tasting at some fancy vineyard. I wish he hadn't shown me a photo of him with the owner. He looks like an older Noah Centineo. Now I worry he was flirting all day while I cook and clean at home.'

'You're safe with Dav,' I reassured him, although I'd noticed

207

Dav's wandering eyes on Milo before. I didn't like being jealous, but I knew Milo was a looker, and when he came back from a day on the boat, hair ruffled from the sea spray and shirt unbuttoned, he was definitely eye-catching. Kitchen grease and sweat didn't make me quite so irresistible, unfortunately.

'He got back last night and Lizzie invited us over for food at theirs. David made Montenegrin tacos with sea bass and salsa verde, yum!'

'I'm sorry?' My head whipped up. I felt like I'd been slapped in the face.

Lovro continued whisking, pouring sugar that he didn't have to weigh. He knew instinctively how much was needed for the perfect Italian meringue.

'Those two have a nice house, near Kotor, a beautiful view of the bay. You'd like it.' Lovro's words were innocent, and he spoke them oblivious to my terror.

What was Lizzie's game inviting Lovro and Dav for dinner with them? I knew Lovro got on with them better than I did, I wasn't blind, but inviting them for dinner?

Was I just being cynical? I found myself unable to control my spiteful thoughts as I moved about the kitchen, keeping an eye on the *dulce de leche* pudding mixture to check it wasn't over-whisked. Did David and Lizzy have an ulterior motive?

'What did you guys talk about?' I asked faux-casually, unable to drop the topic.

'Mainly the restaurant and the business in general. David was very keen to hear my experiences. He thinks it's incredible I'm doing so well at twenty-one.' Lovro beamed.

I softened, despite myself, and squeezed Lovro's shoulder.

'He's right there.' Maybe I needed to show my appreciation more.

'David even offered me a job.' Lovro was laughing. 'He said if I ever get bored of Café Lompar or want a change of scenery, I'd be welcome to take head chef, no interview! He knows I wouldn't leave here, though.' Lovro didn't meet my eyes. I wondered if he could sense how I felt.

'I thought *he* was head chef?'

'I think he wants more of a role in the business, overseeing front of house and kitchen, branding, menu development. He said he wants someone to take care of the kitchen for him.'

'And he's asked my best chef?' I asked, unable to hold back now. That David made my blood boil. The whole Ensambla team did. Any goodwill was well and truly gone now. What were they playing at?

'Don't worry, Kat,' Lovro said. The smile in his eyes was genuine. 'I would never leave here. I love it too much. Cut me open and my insides say "Café Lompar",' he mimed, pulling his chef's whites apart at the chest.

'That's a bit dramatic,' I laughed. 'But I don't like him asking you ... although you do deserve it.'

'Mainly we talked about the cooking course.' Lovro changed the subject, sensing my anger. 'They are both, how do you say, devastated, at what happened. Such a shame.'

'Mmm.' I had to tread carefully here. 'Have they found out what caused the confusion over the dates?'

'I think one of their posters had the wrong date on it. The one outside the restaurant.' Lovro poured his mixture into a tray. If he knew anything, he didn't let on.

'Oh.' I swallowed, guilt rising again. 'It's an easy mistake I suppose...'

'Well, no, Lizzie thinks someone deliberately changed it. All the posters were printed with the same information.'

Oh God. If they knew that, it was only a matter of time before they found the culprit. I should never have done this. I felt suddenly hot, sticky. I didn't say anything, hoping the conversation would go no further.

'They've reported it to the police, I think.'

I froze.

Lovro pottered around and carried on talking, not at all suspicious. 'The good thing is, there's a street security camera outside the restaurant. David's sent off a request to watch the tapes. They should get it today. Hopefully it will have caught the person. Thank goodness, right?'

'Lovro, it was me.' The words blurted from my mouth, a train I couldn't stop, leaving wreckage in its wake. 'I changed the poster. I did it on an impulse. I'd spoken to Lizzie outside and she was so smug, so condescending about Café Lompar. I was so angry and I changed the date.'

He stopped stirring. He looked at me, eyes wide.

'I know I shouldn't have but I didn't think it would matter. I didn't change anything else. I feel so guilty, so, so guilty. Especially after it all went wrong for them, it was awful. I wish I could take it back but I can't.' I faced him, palms up. I sounded so self-pitying I hated myself, although a part of me was relieved to say the words out loud. 'It was me.'

Lovro was still, not breathing. Not even blinking.

'I'm sorry. I know you like Lizzie and David, and they've been

210

lovely to you. I never meant for anyone to find out, and shit, what am I going to do? I'm in so much trouble.' The truth of this was dawning on me now. 'They're going to find out when they watch it.'

'And if there was no film, would you have told anyone?' Lovro asked. It was the first time he'd spoken and his voice sounded cold.

'Yes ... I was just waiting for things to die down.' I knew it was awful as soon as I said it.

'For things to die down? This is their livelihood, Kat.'

'I know. I've never done anything like this before. I feel such an awful person.'

'You do?' Lovro was suddenly in action, putting down his spoon and bowl. 'Well, I'm not going to argue with you there.' He moved to the door.

'Where are you going?' I called, desperate.

He didn't answer, just left the kitchen. It felt like a punch to my stomach and my eyes filled up. I knew I had no excuse to cry – I'd put myself in this mess – but I couldn't help it.

The truth was all going to come out now. Rosa and the other staff members would soon come into work and what would I tell them about Lovro? I'd screwed everything up. I'd wanted us to be better than Ensambla but I'd only made things worse.

I heard footsteps coming through the door to the kitchen. I turned to see if it was Lovro, but my heart jolted at the sight of Lizzie.

'Hi, Kat,' she said, and I could read the anger pouring out of her. I was just glad she was on her own.

'Lizzie,' I said.

She gave a cruel laugh. 'So, it was you. Your fault no one turned up last week.' She said it as a statement, but I nodded anyway. I couldn't deny things now.

'I'm sorry, Lizzie.' It was all I could say.

'I just want to know why, Kat? Surely no one would do this out of pure jealousy? Spite? You wanted to ruin our business?'

I looked heavenward. 'If I'm honest, probably a combination of both. It was stupid and pathetic and if I could take it back, I would. It was a one second decision that I regretted instantly and couldn't do anything about.'

'And what – do you want us to feel sorry for you?' Lizzie asked, outraged. 'You know if you'd told us before, we could have changed it?'

'I know ... but...' I was at a loss. 'I just never thought it would actually ruin the course. I thought people would see the right date.'

Lizzie laughed again.

'I want you to know that it was a mistake and I'm just as disappointed in myself as you are.' I leant against the kitchen work surface, needing it to support my weight.

'Disappointed doesn't even begin to cover it,' Lizzie said. 'We thought Ensambla was struggling because we'd never built up a reputation or a regular crowd visiting the restaurant. We thought it was because Café Lompar was so successful, we couldn't even try to compete. But it was more than that. You sabotaged us. David was always suspicious of you, but I defended you. I never thought you'd do this.'

'I...' My heart had sunk too far to speak. Guilt seared through me.

Lizzie turned to leave, then spun around again. 'You know we're going to take this further, don't you? This is vandalism!'

I knew it was but the word vandalism made me wince. 'You have every right to.'

'Well, if you thought this was going to end the competition between Café Lompar and Ensambla, then you have no idea what's coming,' Lizzie said.

This time she walked out, leaving the door to slam in her wake. The threat hung in the air behind her.

What had I done?

PART THREE

CHAPTER TWENTY-SIX

🌹 Grace 🌹

'This is Captain Conway speaking. The crew and I would like to thank you for flying with EasyJet this evening. In about ten minutes, we'll be landing at Gatwick Airport. The temperature is a rather cool eleven degrees and it's raining in London. Remember to put your clocks back one hour as the time in the UK is 11.30pm. Please keep your seatbelts fastened until the light goes out.'

The sky outside was an opaque black. Laura had fallen at last into a feverish sleep after crying for most of the three-hour flight. Her blonde hair tickled my nose as she rested her head on my shoulder. Claire stared into space, across the aisle from us, and I felt rattled by her silence. She hadn't eaten or had a drink since she found out about Stu at lunch. We had spoken to an emergency doctor at A&E in Bristol Royal Infirmary, his solemn voice filling the apartment as Claire and Laura hurriedly packed their suitcases and I rang around for last minute flights.

'He was crossing a road and didn't see the car, apparently,' the doctor said matter-of-factly. 'He is bleeding internally, which is a cause for concern, and at the moment we think he has a ruptured spleen. It is possible that he has broken his pelvis, which can cause dramatic bleeding. His left leg is badly broken. We'll know more when he has surgery, which will be in the next hour or so.'

Claire's voice sounded shaky. 'Will he be okay, do you think? Is he conscious?'

'He's asleep now, but we'll know more after his surgery.'

'Thank you, doctor. We're on our way and should be there later tonight.' She looked to me for confirmation, before ending the call.

I shook my head. 'We're not going to get a flight directly to Bristol. It'll be Gatwick, I think. Neil will take us to the airport and I'll hire a car. We'll go straight to the hospital.'

Neil waited with us at the airport for as long as he could, and he hugged me tightly before we went through security and the departure lounge. He kissed my head. 'We'll be together soon. I hope Stuart is okay. Let me know as soon as you hear something.'

'Of course, I will. I'm so sorry... Just as you and Ollie came out here.'

'Hey, stop worrying. It can't be helped and it's only for a short while. Ollie and I will play golf.' He grinned. 'We'll be able to take care of ourselves.'

As I felt the plane descending and my stomach flipped a little, I couldn't help but feel torn. It was as if Neil and I were fated not to be together.

Poor Stuart. Was he going to be okay? I wondered. And if he was badly injured, I knew Claire would never forgive herself for this holiday and what they'd been through in the last few weeks.

At the hospital, we waited outside ICU. Claire, Laura and Liam had been in to see him for about fifteen minutes, but he was asleep. I spoke to Kat on the phone while I sat outside. She didn't sound her usual self and I knew she was upset about Stu. She loved her uncle and anything that reminded her of her father and that awful day over two years ago when he died sent her into a terrible spin.

'Try not to worry, sweetheart. It sounds as if he'll be okay. The doctors have had to remove his spleen because it was too badly damaged. His pelvis is okay but he's badly broken his leg.'

'God, what does that mean? Can he survive without a spleen?'

'Apparently so. There's a greater risk of infection afterwards, but he'll be able to go home in a few days.'

'How did it happen?'

'He stepped into the road. He was with his colleague, Dave, and he didn't look where he was going. The driver felt awful, but there was nothing he could do. Claire blames herself for it all.'

'Poor Auntie Claire. It isn't her fault.'

'I've told her that, but she says Stu hasn't been sleeping well and they've been going through a terrible patch lately.' I hadn't told Kat too much about it or about Claire and the creep the other night, but she'd have had to be blind not to know there was something going on between Claire and Stu.

'I can't believe it,' Kat said. 'It just reminded me of...'

'I know,' I said. 'Me, too.' She didn't need to finish her sentence. 'Stu will need looking after for a while. He'll be having his leg pinned and he'll be in a wheelchair and on crutches after that. It'll take months for him to recover.'

'Thank God, he's okay. How are Laura and Liam coping?'

'Well, they're really upset, as you'd expect. I'm sure they'll all pull together. I'll do what I can while I'm here.' I sighed. 'I'm worried about you at Café Lompar, though. Will you manage without me?'

'Rosa has got a friend in. She helped out a few years ago but couldn't when Rosa was ill as her daughter had just had a baby. Radmila – I haven't met her yet. Luka says she's about a hundred years old, and has a hairy chin, and will put the clients off. You know how he exaggerates.' Kat's voice sounded flat.

'Are you all right, Kat? It'll all be sorted and I'll be back in a few days.'

'Well, I didn't want to tell you this as you have enough to think about,' she hesitated, 'but you will hear sooner or later anyway.'

I braced myself, hating to think what was coming next. 'Go on.'

'Have you looked at Facebook or Instagram today?'

'I haven't had time.' Normally I'd check and update our social media posts every day. If you were running a business, it was all part and parcel of promotion. I had learned that when I worked at the charity.

'Well, there's some horrible posts on there about me.' She paused. 'And it's what I deserve.'

'What do you mean?'

Kat's voice became quiet. 'I changed the date on Ensambla's cookery course poster and hardly anyone turned up. It was a moment of madness and I'm deeply ashamed of myself. If I could turn back time...'

Kat sounded so wretched, but I was shocked. I kept my voice even. 'Don't worry. Just go over to apologise and it will be forgotten.'

'You don't understand,' Kat wailed. 'I was caught on CCTV and now Lizzie has posted it all over social media.'

'Oh no!' I tried to think. 'Well, there's nothing you can do about it now. It will come out in the wash, I'm sure.'

When Kat came off the phone, I scrolled through Instagram and Facebook and sure enough, there was Kat crouching over the board outside Ensambla, pen in hand. Underneath the caption read: *So-called 'celebrity' chef Kat Lompar is a vindictive bitch and can't stand any competition to her precious restaurant. She's been caught on CCTV altering the date of Ensambla's cookery course. We've lost a fortune and I can't believe how spiteful she is. Show your disapproval by boycotting Café Lompar. They don't deserve your custom! #revenge #spitefuldeeds #Cafélomparrestaurant*

I gulped. What on earth had come over Kat? This had the potential to really damage us. I couldn't believe it. We'd have to work out a response but at that moment I couldn't think how we'd retrieve the situation.

Claire, Laura and Liam emerged from ICU, all three looking drawn and grim-faced. Claire had dark rings under her eyes, but she hadn't cried. I knew she was internalising everything. Laura's mascara had smudged and Liam looked terribly upset.

'The surgery went well,' Claire said. 'But it's early days.'

The car journey back to Bath seemed endless. I was relieved to get my key in the door of Willow Cottage. The rain had stopped and I smelt the sweet honeysuckle from a corner of the front garden.

Dumping my suitcase in the hallway, I made myself a cup of tea with some UHT milk I had in the pantry and went straight to bed.

The next few days were spent ferrying Claire and the twins to the hospital. Stuart was on the mend and I was relieved to see he was back making jokes again about the hospital food and 'catching some x-rays'.

'It's the only rays I'll get with all this bloody rain,' he said, wincing, when Laura sat on the bed. I noticed Claire holding his hand.

'Are you feeling nervous?' I asked, referring to his surgery the next day to insert pins in his leg.

'Nah, it's got to be done and in a few days I should be back home.'

'Ray from next door helped me move the sofa bed into the study,' Claire said, 'so it's all ready for you.'

I didn't like to meet Stu's eye as she said this, knowing how difficult things had been between them. I'd barely had a chance to speak to Claire to find out how things were really going.

'I can't wait to get back home,' Stu said, pointedly.

On the way back, we dropped Laura at a friend's and Liam at Le Jardin for his shift.

'Fancy a coffee?' Claire asked as we pulled into her driveway.

She showed me the study and how she had moved the desk into the dining room to make room for the sofa bed.

As we sat at the kitchen table, alone for the first time in a few days, I asked how she felt about Stuart. Where did all this leave them?

She sighed. 'I really don't know how to feel. I was distraught when I heard about the accident. I felt it was all my fault.'

'Oh, Claire, come on, it's not anything you've done.'

She batted away my protestations. 'I know, but he's been in a real state since I left for Montenegro and I was talking about divorce. Now, I feel different about everything.' She sighed. 'He's going to think I'm staying because of the accident. And I'm really not. Since that night with that gross Neanderthal in the champagne bar, well, I feel ashamed of myself.'

'We all make mistakes.'

'I'll have to tell him, of course.'

I remained silent, not really knowing what to say.

'I can't lie. If this marriage has any chance of surviving, I have to be honest with him, no matter how much it hurts him.' She stirred her coffee without looking up. 'To be honest, I didn't think I could spend another night in the same bed as Stu. I honestly felt on some occasions that I actually hated him. I fantasised about him dying and even pictured the funeral, where everyone sympathised with me.' She stood up, pouring her coffee down the sink. 'I read once that something like a third of women picture the clothes they'd wear at their husband's funeral.' She gazed out at the garden, the overgrown patch of lawn that Stuart had neglected. 'And what would have been my excuse for divorce? Boredom?'

'Well, you won't be the first. Look at Danilo – his boredom with me led him to cheat on me for years.'

'I suppose you're right,' Claire conceded. 'But this isn't some film where the hero has an accident and the wife falls into his arms realising she's made a huge mistake. And they live happily ever after!'

'Who'd play you in the film, do you think?' I grinned, lightening the atmosphere.

'Emily Blunt, perhaps.'

'That's rather flattering,' I said. 'She's years younger than you. And Stuart?'

'Ricky Gervais, the David Brent years. Quite rotund and thinking he's far cooler than he is.'

'Ouch!' I laughed.

'So, when are you going back to Tivat?' Claire asked.

'I was thinking of looking at available flights tonight and going tomorrow or the day after. You know how busy it is at the moment.'

I managed to get a flight booked for the next day and packed my suitcase. Neil and Ollie had another week there.

I still had Kat's problem to sort out. I was monitoring our social media when I could, reading what people had said. There were dozens of messages of sympathy for Lizzie and David. No mention of their dirty tricks, stealing Kat's recipes and commandeering kitchen equipment Kat had ordered for Café Lompar. Kat had told me last night that the Pobjeda had ditched her column saying that there was a lack of interest in it. She had been foolish but she didn't deserve this. She was under a lot of strain. Releasing an apology would just remind people what Kat had done, so it was difficult to know how to react.

It hadn't hit restaurant sales. People were still visiting in droves, but they were tourists, of course. The locals felt differently. However, Café Lompar was a well-established business and Rosa still had lots of people that would be loyal to her. Kat said she had been kind to her over this. Luka had laughed, thinking it hilarious. All we could really hope was that the storm would die down and we'd be back on an even keel again. I just hoped stress wouldn't drive Kat to make any other mistakes.

CHAPTER TWENTY-SEVEN

❧ Kat ❧

'Here she is, the bandit!' I heard Luka shout as I rounded the corner towards Café Lompar.

'Don't,' I said, batting him away as he came closer. 'I feel awful as it is.'

'Look out, it's the notorious vandal, the infamous Kat Lompar. Everyone take shelter!' he continued despite my protests.

'Ha ha, how funny,' I said stoney-faced. 'I've never felt so awful in my life, honestly, Luka. Look at me, I've had to walk an extra twenty minutes to work just so I could take the route that doesn't bring me past Ensambla. I feel like everyone's looking at me, whispering.'

'Don't be such a big head. You're not that famous,' Luka laughed.

'I know, but Lizzie's made such a song and dance of it. I see those grainy photos of me, marker pen in hand, everywhere. It's still all over social media and it was over a week ago now. That's the problem with living in a tiny town like Tivat, everyone knows your business and nothing else happens around here. If it was anywhere else, they would have moved on already.'

We strolled down the street together and I fanned my neck from the blistering heat. My hair was sticking to me like a thick, sodden scarf.

'You're thinking this is a bigger deal than it is, seriously. What you did wasn't that bad. You only changed one poster. You're hardly a master criminal.'

I frowned, but I knew he was right. I regretted my actions but from Lizzie's Facebook posts you would think I'd killed their head chef. Talking to Luka was the only thing that made me feel better. His joking normalised everything.

'What do you have in store for me today then?'

'You're on starters today. Those hands are too clumsy for desserts!' We laughed.

Luka was helping out in the kitchen since I'd argued with Lovro. He wasn't skilled or fast, but we needed any extra hands we could get.

'Hey, I only smashed one plate.'

'And nearly took the top of your finger off.' I took his hand to get a look at the knife-wound from yesterday. 'In the UK, you're what we'd a call a liability.'

I really did feel better after talking about something else. My stomach flipped again, though, when we saw Lizzie and David in the distance, standing outside Ensambla. Luka saw them too and hung back, sensing my discomfort. I knew I'd have to see them and apologise, but I wasn't ready yet. I needed to think about how to do it first. I was grateful to Luka for slowing down with me.

We walked at a snail's pace as we watched Lizzie and David turn and enter the restaurant, blending in with the heads bobbing along the pavement. I almost breathed a sigh of relief, but behind them trailed Lovro, dressed in jeans and a white t-shirt. His slim frame and spiky hair were unmistakable.

'What's Lovro doing with them?' I said to Luka.

He shrugged. 'Don't know.'

'God, I can't take this anymore.'

I already knew it was going to be an awful day. I missed working with Lovro. I couldn't bear to know he was with our competition. I'd be wondering all day what he was doing with Lizzie and David.

'At least we can go inside now,' I said.

'It's going to be a busy one,' Luka nodded at the crowds of tourists already building up.

'I hope so,' I said. 'Unlike the locals, maybe they won't have seen the Facebook page.'

We busied ourselves in the kitchen, preparing for lunch service. Luka was slow and struggled to dice vegetables as finely as Lovro did for our salsa. He usually helped out front of house in the summer months between school and uni, and it was clear the cooking genes had not been passed to him.

I sighed, stopping at the window again to see if I could spot Lovro coming out of Ensambla. I needed to speak to him. What were they doing in there?

'Is this the right size fillet for the sea bass?' Luka snapped me out of my thoughts.

'A little bit smaller ... actually, don't worry, I'll do it.' I shooed him away. I was planning to serve the sea bass with a lemon butter reduction, wild garlic, on a bed of asparagus, lentils, with shards of crispy skin balanced to look like the sails on a boat. It was a simple dish but classic, the Café Lompar ethos.

I hoped our food would be enough to pull us out of the media storm. I remembered last year when the news came out about

Dad's affair and the Pobjeda had reported on our 'Sordid Set-up'. I worried what would become of the restaurant then, but at the time we did nothing, and rode the wave of gossip and intrigue in the restaurant. Would it work if we did the same again?

'You look lost in thought?' Rosa nudged her way into the kitchen, tying her apron with one hand and carrying cleaning spray in the other.

'Just thinking about Café Lompar … and what I've done,' I said, trying to focus on the fish. Rosa frowned one eyebrow.

'I think we should go for a chat,' she said, with that firm voice of hers. 'Come on, my son can hold the fort for five minutes.'

I was reminded of her determination and the drive it took for her to set up Café Lompar. She'd started the business and grown it from nothing. The breast cancer ordeal she had last year had been a real knock but Rosa still had the same boss-like mentality underneath.

Which was why I needed to speak my mind as we sat at a table laid for lunch service with stacked plates and pearly glasses. The sea glittered in the sunlight outside the window, providing the backdrop to the beautiful café.

'What's on your mind, Kat? I can tell when someone's holding something in.' She cast a discerning eye my way.

'I've brought so much shame on the restaurant. It was such a stupid thing to do, a split-second decision that's cost me so much. But there's no excuses. I did a petty and awful thing, and I can't bear to see Café Lompar lose customers as well as its reputation. I wonder if I should step down as head chef, even just for a little while?'

'Oh, *koka*,' Rosa said, a Montenegrin word meaning 'little

chicken'. I'd heard her call Luka *koka* before. 'This is the most ridiculous thing I've ever heard and I've raised your half-brother.'

'It's not, Rosa. Look at Café Lompar, look at what you've done here. This is all you. The restaurant is so well-loved and popular, and you've worked so hard on it. I will feel awful if it loses its reputation because of me and this bloody Ensambla feud.'

Rosa smiled. 'Kat, this is all you. I worked hard on it long ago but it wasn't this beloved until you arrived. The food you make is wonderful. Exciting, innovative, complex, exotic. See, all these complicated English words I've learnt since you came here! It would be nothing without you.'

'You'd find another head chef,' I said.

'Not like Kat Lompar I won't. Your soul is in your cooking. Everyone loves it. Café Lompar *is* your cooking. The only way we'll lose customers is if you leave.'

Her words brought tears to my eyes. I tried to blink them back, but it didn't work.

'If you leave, Kat, then Lizzie will have won. How awful that she has to resort to such things as bad-mouthing us online. It reflects badly on her, not us. You just need to stand proud.'

'Thank you,' I said, thinking about Lizzie.

'They need to tear us down so they can look like the better restaurant. They know their food doesn't compete. Café Lompar will come out on top here.'

'It's not a competition,' I said, although I'd thought it many times. 'Maybe I should apologise to them and just keep my head down.'

'Maybe,' Rosa said, a thoughtful look on her face. 'Or maybe you keep your head up. Apologise to them, apologise online, apologise to the Pobjeda. Tell the truth and your honesty will make people forgive you. Who looks better then, Ensambla, who make nasty comments and tell tales, or Café Lompar, who says sorry when we're wrong and stands strong?'

She was right. I could see that. I didn't need to lose my job over this. I just needed to be honest. I would run it past Mum tonight for her thoughts, but I was sure she'd agree.

'Ugh,' I sighed, 'why are you such a genius?'

'It's my business skills.' She polished a non-existent speck of dust off the table. 'Or my age. My grand old age.'

'Come on, you're not old,' I said.

'Compared to Matija, I am a dinosaur.' She didn't meet my eye. I could tell something was up.

'Now you're the one holding something back,' I prompted.

'Do people think I am a complete idiot for going out with someone his age?' she asked, looking up towards me. 'Be honest.'

'No.' I shook my head. 'It's a shock, I'll admit, not something you see every day. Traditionally men are the people who get to date someone younger and be proud of it, not women. But you and Matija work, so why worry what other people think? And he clearly adores you.'

The lines on her forehead drew deeper. 'He does, I know that.' She shrugged. It was always weird to see Rosa vulnerable, the softer side underneath that tough exterior. She looked over her shoulder to make sure Luka was out of earshot.

'This younger man thing is wearing thin, though,' she said, giving a gentle laugh. 'I knew he wasn't experienced, knew he wouldn't be like Danilo. That was part of the attraction, something different.'

I bristled, still finding it weird that she was with my father. I didn't like to think about that too often.

'But really, is it a sustainable relationship when I have to remind him to take a packed lunch to work? Or iron his shirt? Or make phone calls for him?'

I had to laugh despite her tone. 'Are you serious?'

'It's not quite that bad but, yes, there is an age gap,' she admitted. 'I am worried as time goes on it will become worse.'

'I understand.'

'I don't want to be his mother. It's been fun but I think we need to end things soon,' she said.

'He'll be heartbroken.'

'He's young, he'll find someone else,' Rosa sighed. 'I worry though what people will think when they know. What will I tell Luka?'

'Tell Luka the truth. He'll understand. It's just not working. And to hell with what people think. We're strong women and we can do what we want – hold our heads high.'

'You're using my line on me. I think you're the genius, Kat.'

'What are you two talking about?' Luka stuck his head round the door. A smear of red sauce dripped down his face.

'Not you, if that's what you're thinking.' I stood up reluctantly. 'Need any help?'

'No, it's all under control,' Luka said, although the wobble in his voice betrayed him. There was a clatter behind and the sound of a pot bubbling over.

'Shit,' he said and turned. I looked to Rosa and we rolled our eyes, before both going after him.

I took a deep breath and read the words on screen. I'd re-read the paragraph so many times now I'd lost all perspective on my words. It was important to get this right.

Milo bent down so his chin rested on top of my head and his arms covered mine.

'Let me know what you think,' I said, anxiously. 'I don't know if it's ready yet.'

He started to read aloud. 'I'm Kat Lompar, Head Chef at Café Lompar in Tivat. Last week some photos came to light that I am deeply ashamed of. I want to explain the reasons for my actions, which I bitterly regret, and to offer my most sincere apologies towards Lizzie and David of Ensambla.'

His eyes moved from side to side as he read, pausing to take a sip of my water half way through. I had explained the irrational reaction I had to our competition, the decision I wanted to take back.

'Ensambla is a wonderful restaurant with cutting-edge food and a glorious setting. I hope they accept my apology and succeed in the future. Café Lompar will be supporting them every step of the way.'

'What do you think?'

'It's very dignified,' Milo smiled.

'Kill them with kindness,' I offered.

'You make killing them with kindness an extreme sport.' Milo kissed the top of my head. 'Dinner's nearly ready.'

'Good, I'm starving. Although, you didn't add too much basil to the sauce, did you? Have you tasted it?'

'Shhh, you're at home now. Anyone would think you're a professional chef,' he said over his shoulder, leaving the room.

Between the tutting and the sarcasm, Milo could pass for British, I thought.

I started to read the statement again, ready to post on Facebook, the *Pobjeda* website, and Café Lompar, before my phone pinged.

It was Mum. Two words. 'Post it.'

Now all I had to do was find some way of getting my right-hand man, Lovro, back.

CHAPTER TWENTY-EIGHT

🌹 Grace 🌹

'You look a vision,' I told Kat, giving her a hug. She was wearing a skin-tight, red dress with a slit at the front, and killer heels.

'Wow!' gasped Milo. 'I don't think you are safe to go alone without my protection.' He slid his arms around her waist and lifted her from the ground.

'Hmm, I don't think that grooms-to-be are welcome in a hen party,' she said, kissing him back and laughing.

It was good to hear her laugh again, as the fall-out from the recent bad publicity had really affected her. The others were due to arrive in the next half an hour and there would be ten of us in all, including Kat and me – Rosa, Claire, Laura, Natalija, Maria, Ana and two other waitresses, Adelisa and Dijana. A nice crowd. Claire and Laura had flown back out for a few days now Stu was on the mend. We would have drinks and nibbles at Kat's place first and then move on to the bars in Tivat.

Kat sighed. 'I always hoped that Lovro would be here at my hen party...'

'Cheer up,' I said. 'It's your special night. He'll come round eventually.'

'I doubt it. Not after my behaviour.'

'You've been fantastic to him. He wouldn't be half the chef he is without your support. He'd still be serving *cremolatto* on the promenade. You've nurtured him and shown him how to produce high-end cuisine.'

I handed her and Milo a glass of champagne, hoping she'd throw herself into the celebrations. 'Here you are. I want to make a toast before the others arrive.' Breathing in deeply, I raised my glass. 'Kat, you are my beautiful, talented daughter and I couldn't be prouder of what you have achieved.'

'But...'

I stopped her before she could go on. 'You care passionately about everything you do. If your father were here, I know that he would feel exactly the same as I do.'

Kat's eyes shone brightly.

I turned. 'And, Milo, I am so pleased Kat found you because I know you love her as much as I do and you make each other so happy.'

We bumped glasses and took a gulp of the champagne.

The door swung open and Claire popped her head around. 'You've started without us, you buggers!'

Behind her came Laura and Natalija, laughing loudly and in high spirits. 'We've got the accessories with us!' Natalija announced, handing Kat a pink sash with 'Bride to Be' on it. I was duly handed a 'Mother of the Bride' sash.

'This is for Maria when she arrives,' Laura said, producing the 'Maid of Honour' sash, and then she and Natalija proudly spun around to show off their Bridesmaid sashes, each in the same neon pink. Both of them wore minute bodycon dresses, worthy of *Love Island* contestants. Just as I was thinking that the sashes were surprisingly tame for these two, Natalija reached into a large plastic shopping bag behind her and pulled out a balloon saying 'Team Bride' and a giant helium penis with a bow tie around it.

'You pin this to the back of your sash, Kat,' she ordered.

Milo spluttered. 'You have got to be joking!'

'You know we love you, Milo,' Claire said, 'but this is Kat's hen party and you have no say in this.'

At that moment, Luka strolled in. He threw back his head and laughed when he saw the inflatable penis. 'Very classy! Just the thing for my big sister. You know you won't be allowed in any bars in Montenegro with that.'

Kat looked visibly relieved. Laura, dejected, handed around glitzy pink cowboy hats.

Luka grabbed her sides and tickled her. 'You are such a cliché, Laura.'

I was relieved Luka was here. His superpower was to make any atmosphere lighter and he steered Milo into the living room as Maria, Ana, Adelisa and Dijana arrived and began making cocktails in the kitchen. He did pause when he saw Dijana in her short white dress, his eyes widening.

'Now who's being the cliché,' Kat laughed, nudging him out of the kitchen.

Rosa was the last to arrive, dressed demurely in a navy linen shift dress and long silver earrings. Kat had told me that she was thinking of finishing things with Matija, feeling the 'moment had passed', and it was clear that the ice had melted between Luka and Rosa as he was almost back to normal with her. I hoped Luka wasn't behind her change of heart. She deserved some fun.

We ate on Kat and Milo's patio, still warm at nine o'clock at night. Kat had rustled up some appetisers before we left, including gorgeous prawn, lime and avocado tacos, tapenade flatbreads and petit toasts with brie, fig, and thyme. When she brought out the sweet plates, there were gasps of enthusiasm.

'Oh my God, I love these,' Rosa said. 'We must have them in Café Lompar.'

She had made *padobranci*, a Balkan version of mini macaroons, and had filled some with a mango ganache and others with white chocolate and raspberry. I had chosen her *tulumba*, which were like churros and soaked in sweet syrup like baklava.

'How on earth you had time for all this and getting ready for your hen night!' I asked her.

She brushed off our compliments. 'They didn't take long. You're my guinea pigs,' she said.

Luka and Milo came outside, drawn by the laughter and gossiping.

'Go inside, Milo,' Natalija said, 'or we might gatecrash your stag party tomorrow night!'

Kat teased, 'You heard your sister. Have you two eaten the plates I made for you?'

'Of course.' Milo rolled his eyes. 'That greedy brother of yours ate everything within five minutes.'

As we left for the bars, I noticed Kat hadn't finished her champagne. 'I'm trying to pace myself, Mum,' she whispered, and I could appreciate her caution with the reckless twosome in tow.

Tivat at night was transformed. The inky black sky was illuminated with the lights from the hotels, restaurants and clubs, and the atmosphere fizzed and bristled with anticipation. In contrast, the yachts lay as still as statues in the harbour, their ghostly reflections wobbling occasionally in the ebbing water.

We walked along the promenade. Fairy lights had been draped along the palm trees lining the walkway. Men whistled and shouted at the girls as we passed by, shouting '*Lijepo*', meaning beautiful, or 'Sexy.' The young girls lapped it up; Laura, being the youngest, was intoxicated by the compliments and the excitement of the night.

It felt quite natural that Claire, Rosa and I formed our own group at the back while the younger ones surged on ahead, Kat with her closest friends, Ana and Maria.

'Can you believe your little girl is getting married?' Claire said.

'God, it's been so busy I've barely had time to register it.'

'Danilo would have been happy, I think,' Rosa said tentatively. We always danced around the awkwardness of sharing this man, who had made such an impact on our lives and caused so much damage.

'Yes, he would have got on with Milo,' I agreed. 'He looks after Kat and has this responsible and serious side.'

'He has been a good friend to Luka,' Rosa said, twisting her hair behind her ears. 'Luka needed him when Danilo died.'

Claire darted her eyes at me, knowing the conversation was probably making me uncomfortable.

'And what about you, Grace, will you marry again? Will you marry Neil? He is a good-looking man. A steady man.' And in case she had gone too far, Rosa added, 'He is very different to Danilo. You can trust him.'

'I don't know if I'm ready for marriage. It's over two years since Dan died, but I'm still finding my feet. Finding myself.' I shook my head. 'I do love Neil but there's no rush.'

'He is keen to be married, I think,' Rosa said, and I was amazed at her insight. I didn't talk to her about Neil but she had assessed the situation perfectly.

'I barely saw him when he came out and he's back home now. We will have to work at this relationship.'

'He will wait if he is worthy of you,' Rosa said with a small smile. 'And how is Strew?' she asked, turning to Claire.

Claire laughed. 'Stu. Stuart. Feeling extremely sorry for himself. But he's never had it so good. I'm back Monday and the freezer is full of his favourites: chilli con carne, curry and chicken pie. He's a man of simple pleasures! I tried to feed him an artichoke the other day. He told me that he'd never heard of them and they tasted like dogs' bollocks. He's such a prince, my husband.' We laughed and I noticed that hard edge that had been present in Claire's voice when she spoke of Stu had disappeared.

The girls headed into a bar called The Wild West. I could see a bucking bronco to the left of the bar and a pole-dancing pole deeper inside. We could hear Laura squealing with excitement. The bouncers outside, trussed up in their black suits, looked delighted.

'Dear lord, what is this place?' I asked.

'It does not have a good reputation,' Rosa said.

Claire shrugged. 'Come on, us oldies can get a drink and sit in a corner somewhere.'

Kat glanced over her shoulder at me, a look of helpless fear on her face. Once inside, we paid an extortionate amount for a bottle of Prosecco and a topless waiter with a Stetson and cowboy boots brought a tray over to us. At the bar, the girls had lined up Messcher Bombs and JaegerBombs, Jungfraus and Cactus Jacks.

'Jeez, I feel old,' said Claire. 'I've never heard of half these drinks. Remember the good old days when we used to drink Strongbow and Blue Curacao, the height of sophistication? I remember getting drunk on Blue Nun, though.' Claire was having to shout over the strains of Shania Twain's *That Don't Impress Me Much*. 'I feel ancient in this place!'

We lapsed into silence, watching as Natalija swapped her cowboy hat with one of the waiter's and then stroked his chest.

Rosa shook her head. 'Milo would kill her.'

Kat, Maria and Ana were queueing for the bucking bronco. Kat had knocked back a few shots at the bar and was obviously relaxing. Lots of men were congregating around her, her Bride To Be sash sparking several conversations. It was great to see her relaxing. I did worry about her and the responsibility of being a head chef at such a young age, but she loved it. She had gathered her long hair into a bun on top of her head and I could see her familiar look of concentration as she watched a girl on the bucking bronco. As she climbed on, I saw her legs clenched tightly against the horse.

'I don't think I can watch,' I said, swigging my champagne.

'The bucking bronco is a sex position,' Claire told me. 'It used to be one of Stu's favourites.'

'Too much information!' I protested, watching as Kat was flung off the horse in the first ten seconds, Maria and Ana taking photos on their phones.

Rosa nudged me. I looked in the direction she was pointing and saw Laura, Natalija, Adelisa and Dijana gathered around the pole. Laura was rather inelegantly trying to wind her leg around the pole, in a pose reminiscent of a dog lifting his leg against a lamppost.

'Oh, for God's sake, what is she like?' Claire covered her face.

Natalija's attempt was much more successful. She handed her bag to Dijana and twisted her legs high up the pole before slowly winding her body around, drawing cheers and claps from the men nearby.

'It's not the first time she's done that!' Rosa announced.

After a few more drinks at the Wild West, we made our way to a roof terrace. It was nearly midnight and it was quieter here. Kat had refused to go a club, to the chagrin of the younger girls, but they knew better than to protest as it was Kat's night. The terrace gave fantastic views of the harbour, the bright lights of the yachts melting into the Adriatic, and the brooding mountains beyond, maternal and watchful. A cool breeze weaved between the terracotta pots and fairy lights winked along the balustrade.

I ordered a hot chocolate and ignored Claire's glares. Rosa was drinking sparkling water and Claire ordered a Strawberry Daiquiri.

'So, how are things with you and Stuart?' I asked Claire, not worrying if Rosa could hear. She knew everything about us, it seemed.

'I don't feel like murdering him every day. Perhaps every other day now.'

'It'll take time.'

'Besides, he's got to put up with me, too. Not always easy.'

'I'd agree with that,' I laughed, wondering if she'd confessed to him about the night with Mr. Sideburns.

The girls started a noisy game of Truth or Dare. 'I dare you to snog the waiter!' Natalija shouted to Adelisa, followed by hoots of laughter.

'Come on, then,' Claire said, 'what's your truth, Grace?'

'I don't think I want Neil to move in with me yet, but you already know that. I just have to tell him. And yours?' I asked Claire.

'Stu and I are going to couples' therapy. An ultimatum. Either I agree to it or it's divorce.'

'Well, that might not be a bad thing,' I said, wiping the milky foam from my lip.

'And you, Rosa. What is your truth?' Claire asked.

'I've got a breast check up next week and I'm terrified,' she said. 'Truly terrified!'

'Oh, Rosa,' I breathed. That had knocked the wind out of us, and I didn't know what to say.

CHAPTER TWENTY-NINE

❧ Kat ❧

I woke up feeling hot and hungover again. This was becoming a habit. At least last night I actually had been drinking. My face felt matted and crusty, the remnants of last night's poorly removed make-up rough on my skin. A hasty swipe with a make-up wipe clearly hadn't done the job. The blankets on the bed clung to me. I flung them off dramatically with a huff, the noise of which made my head hurt.

The familiar sickly feeling was horrible. I blinked my eyes open again.

This wasn't good. I'd only had a few glasses of champagne last night. I'd been taking slow sips, one sip for every five of Natalija's, tipping some away on the dance floor at that Wild West bar. The memory made me want to hurl. Did I really get on the bucking bronco in front of my mother? No wonder I'd only stayed on a few seconds. My comfy bed was spinning like that bull now.

I wasn't dumb. I knew what the signs meant. Morning sickness. Dizziness. Wanting to pee all the bloody time. The period that never came. I'd been kidding myself it was the Montenegrin heat or the remains of a stomach bug I'd had months ago. I couldn't admit anything else to myself.

I felt like crying, but the clattering downstairs stopped me.

Milo must be in the kitchen. Milo, who I should be confiding in, but I couldn't say the words to myself yet, let alone out loud to him. Then it would be real.

His footsteps sounded on the stairs. A tentative cough. The brush of the door against the carpet as he pushed it open.

'I'm not trying to check up on you, but I couldn't wait to find out how last night went,' he said quietly.

'Don't look at me.' I shielded my face and tried to blink away tears.

'I've seen you hungover and vomiting before,' he laughed. 'I was on that Majorca trip with you last year, remember?'

'Why would you remind me of that now?' I tried to keep it light, force the gravity out of my voice. I didn't want him to know. Not until I knew for sure myself.

'How does coffee and a bacon sarnie sound?' he asked. I loved the Britishisms that came out of his mouth. We were absorbing more and more of each other every day.

'Like I've taught you well,' I smiled, although the thought of food made my stomach churn.

'Back in two minutes,' he whispered, shutting the door gently.

I had two minutes to get myself in a normal state. It was difficult to make it to the bathroom when simply walking in a straight line felt like a challenge on the *Crystal Maze*. I guzzled two glasses of water in the bathroom, retched over the toilet, then got another make-up wipe to finish last night's job. I was nearly done, when a strong wave of nausea came over me, just as I heard Milo pad into our room.

I gripped the edge of the toilet as the little alcohol I'd consumed came out of me. Disgusting.

'Oh dear,' I heard Milo say. 'Maybe the bacon was a mistake.'

'It's okay,' I said. 'I'm starving.' And I suddenly was.

Milo let me curl up next to him as I ate my breakfast in bed.

'So, am I allowed to ask any details about last night?' he grinned. 'Or should this hangover tell me all I need to know.'

I gave him the brief outline of the night, leaving out the spinning bronco and the girls' romp on the pole. I had a feeling I was lucky to have my mother with me or else I'd have been shoved up there to perform. Not that it had bothered Laura much, having Claire as a witness.

'Dare I ask about my sister?' Milo looked to me.

'Let's just say I kept an eye on her,' I told him. 'You'll have to do the same with Luka tonight.'

Milo gave a world-weary sigh. 'Do I have to go to that?'

'Your own stag party? I kind of think you're the required party member.' I pushed him in the side, feeling fortified after my bacon with lashings of tomato sauce. I didn't care what I'd learnt in cooking school, there was nothing better than a good old bacon sarnie.

'I would rather go for a hike or sailing or something. Not a bar crawl and God knows what else Luka has planned.' Milo grimaced.

'That's why you're the perfect man.'

He kissed me gently on the head.

I was grateful I had planned to have today off to recover. I popped out to the pharmacy at lunchtime under the pretext of getting us lunch. The box in my bag felt illicit and unsafe as I smuggled it into the house, slipping it from my handbag to the cupboard under the bathroom sink, then taking it back again as

I realised Milo might look under there for his aftershave when he was getting ready to go out. I didn't want anyone to know about it. This felt like something I had to do by myself.

'Kat, are you sure you don't want to come tonight? Me and Laura are only going to Kotor, not far.' Natalija waggled a manicured hand as an invite later that evening.

'Going out two nights in a row? I can think of nothing worse,' I said.

'Going out once is bad enough,' Milo grumbled from the kitchen where he was waiting for Luka.

'You two are as boring as each other.' Natalija shrugged. 'I'll be back later,' She grabbed her bag. 'Or not,' I heard her mumble over her shoulder.

All of a sudden there was an almighty roar outside our window that shook the glass.

'What the...' I stood up and Milo met me at the window.

'Oh no, is he serious?'

Luka was outside wearing a white suit and helmet. He was riding a pink motorbike complete with side-car adorned in white daisy patterns. He held up a spare helmet, beckoning Milo out.

'Now this I have to see,' I grinned, feeling better than I had all day.

'I'm not getting in that thing.' Milo was as stern as I'd ever seen him.

Luka was finding the whole thing hilarious. 'Come on, man, it's a sweet ride. The others are waiting in town.'

I laughed, surprised at the force of my love for my brother. I'd never met anyone as uplifting or funny or totally ridiculous as him. He'd been my rock for the last year. I suddenly wanted to tell him everything, but instead watched them silently from the doorway.

Milo and Luka jostled back and forth, Milo's protests getting louder. But I knew Luka would work his magic, and indeed it didn't take long before Milo was wearing a matching helmet and folding his giant frame into a tiny side car. They made an insane pair together, and I laughed as I got my phone out to snap pictures.

'Be careful,' I shouted as they rode off, Luka shrieking with glee as Milo looked like he was stuck in a doll-house.

As I shut the door behind me, the bike growling off into the distance, I felt the weight of the world on my shoulders. The house, that had been filled with so much life from Natalija's chattering, now seemed quiet and ominous, as if it was watching me. I had an urge to go out. Forget the whole thing and walk to Mum's or Café Lompar, but knowing what I had to do kept me there.

I tied my hair up, exposing my sweaty neck to the fan in our bedroom and got the packet out from my bag. Montenegrin pregnancy tests had the same ludicrous pictures as British ones, women jumping for joy holding the white stick up in the air or cradling a baby with their partner's arms around them. Where were the pictures of crumbling careers and bulging wedding dresses? That would be my reality, not their cardboard ecstasy.

I read the instructions, but found I couldn't take any of the information in. How hard was it, didn't you just pee on the damn thing? The awkward position I had to stoop in to do the deed reminded me of Ana last night going to the toilet in the street. She must be feeling it today.

It was time to wait. Three minutes. One hundred and eighty seconds.

I just settled myself into our big creamy armchair in the bedroom, when the doorbell rang. I walked down stairs, feeling irritated by the interruption, then saw Mum's dark blonde waves through the glass.

'Mum?' I leaned in to give her a hug.

'Just came to see how you're doing,' she said. 'Are you alright?'

'Getting over the hangover.' I tried to stay breezy. 'Fancy a cuppa?'

'Go on then. I won't stay long though. I promised Rosa I'd help out tonight. That woman needs a break.'

'Come on in.' I worried I sounded formal. 'Tea? Coffee?'

'I'll make it.' She followed me into the kitchen. I glanced up the stairs. It was agonising knowing my fate was up there. My future was drying in the bathroom as we spoke. Should I pop up and look? No. How could I possibly act naturally after that? I was doing a crappy job of that already.

'Biscuit?' I asked.

'Always.' Mum frowned. 'You don't seem right, somehow.'

'I'm fine, I'm fine. The heat.' I busied myself fetching two mugs. 'How's Claire and Laura?'

'Claire's, well, pissed off. Laura stayed out with Natalija, then they tried to bring some Montenegrin men back to the Airbnb. They found them sitting on a yacht in the harbour so they thought they were rich.' Mum stirred the teabags in the liquid, creating brown spirals in the water. 'But it turned out they were just the crew.'

I laughed. 'Still, it doesn't sound like it stopped them.'

'You went home early?' Mum said, turning a statement into a question.

'I told you, I wasn't feeling well. Can't handle my booze these days.' I tried to sound cheerful, but felt tears prick my eyes. Oh God, there was no stopping them.

'Kat?' Mum pulled me towards her, enveloping me in a hug. 'What's brought this on? I knew there was something. A mother always knows.'

'Oh God, Mum,' was all I managed to choke out. Her perfumed shoulder was comforting, but I felt like I would never stop crying. My world was falling apart in front of me.

'Take a breath ... that's it.' She stroked my face tenderly. 'God, everyone's crying at the moment.'

'What?'

'Oh nothing, I just mean, why don't you tell me what's happened? It's not about Ensambla, is it?'

'No, it's...' I couldn't say the words. 'It's better if I show you.'

I went upstairs and grabbed the bundle of toilet roll from the bathroom counter without even looking at it. I knew what it would show, even as I held it in my hand. I knew the two blue lines would be there.

I took it downstairs. I watched her face. I couldn't bear to see her shock but I couldn't look away either.

'Oh, darling.' She put a hand to her chest. Her other hand trembled just like mine as it reached out to take the test from me. Her expression was blank, and yet I could see tears in her eyes. 'You're pregnant.'

'I'm pregnant. Oh!' Just saying it aloud was a whole new surprise. 'I'm pregnant.'

She clutched my hand. 'How do you feel?'

'I … I don't know.' I sat back against the sofa cushions. 'This is the worst timing possible. With everything in Ensambla, the wedding, my whole career, Milo's business. I can't be a full-time Head Chef and have a baby. I can't do it. I won't be able to write the next cookbook. I'll have to turn Café Lompar over to someone else. God, and after all this drama I'll never get another job. I'm screwed, Mum.'

We were silent a moment, holding hands.

'Is this what you felt? When you were pregnant with me? This doom inside? That you'd made a terrible mistake?'

'Darling, it doesn't matter what I felt. This is your pregnancy, your life.'

'My life I've ruined.'

We were quiet again. Mum stroked the back of my hand with her thumb.

'Forget the job. Forget the wedding, everything else for now. How do you really feel?'

I tried to do what she asked, put everything out of my mind. I felt an odd sensation spread in my stomach. There was a baby growing inside there. Another body, another life, other than mine. I'd only focused on my life, but there was another one in the equation. My child. I couldn't ignore it. What was this feeling?

'I think I feel … happy.'

When I looked across at Mum, she had tears in her eyes.

'Oh, please say they're happy tears?' I asked.

'They're wonderful tears. Oh, Kat! Your dad would be so thrilled.' She pulled me to her and we both sobbed. I still felt hugely unsure of the future, but I realised it was okay to be happy.

'I ... can't believe it,' I said as we recovered and started to drink our tea.

There was a loud bang – the door crashing into the wall. I flinched. There was more crashing, then stomping. Mum and I looked at each other in confusion.

'Where is she?' Milo's voice roared from the hallway. 'Where's Natalija?'

'She went out, remember?' I called, wiping my face.

Milo came in to the living room, his face and stance like thunder, as if he was about to tear up the building. I moved to hide the pregnancy test but Mum had already done it.

'I don't believe this. I forgot she was out when I raced back here. Where did that girl go?'

'Milo, what do you want Natalija for?'

In Milo's rage, he didn't see our expressions or feel the atmosphere in the room. 'We need to get her home now!' He pointed at the door, a flare of anger I had never seen before.

'Wow,' Mum said.

'What's happened?'

'What's happened is that my little sister sells her body online to strangers.' He spat the words out in disgust. Oh shit. 'She posts pictures online of herself naked and talks to strangers over the internet. She's on porn websites. It's so disgusting. This is not how we were raised. What is she thinking?' He started pacing from side to side.

'Wait, wait. How do you know this?' I asked.

'The boys were teasing Luka, laughing about something in the bar. I saw the pictures on his phone. *Santa Marija*. Did she tell you about this?'

251

'She told me she modelled...' I tried to sound innocent.

'I'm going to call her and tell her to come home right now. This is unforgivable. She has brought shame on our entire family!'

I looked at Mum and her eyes widened. I needed to sit down. There was too much happening at once. I wondered what would happen when Natalija came back, and whether Milo would still be this angry when I told him about our child. I wanted Milo to be happy about our baby, more than anything I'd ever wanted in my life, but would there ever be a good time to tell him, with all this conflict around us? It felt never-ending.

CHAPTER THIRTY

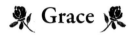 Grace

The sun was warm on my legs as I sat on the balcony. I was due at Café Lompar in an hour and I was enjoying a peaceful moment, gazing at the glorious views of the harbour and the Volujak Mountains behind. Interlacing my fingers through the handle of the mug of coffee, I hugged it close, and I hugged my secret even closer.

Kat's pregnant, I thought, turning the words over in my mind, trying them out and savouring them, hoping they would sink in. I was going to be a grandmother and I was dying to shout it from the roof tops. I knew she thought it wasn't a good time but there's never an ideal time. I remembered when I was pregnant with Kat, I didn't know if I was ready to be a mother or if I'd be a good mother. I didn't have that yearning some women have, as if they are put on this earth with the sole purpose of procreating. Yet, the moment I held her after she was born, I was in love. She was the most perfect thing. Her fingers were folded tightly like the delicate petals of a rose. She had a mop of dark hair, just like Dan, and her long lashes rested on her plump cheeks. I was grinning like a madwoman and was utterly besotted.

'We made her,' Dan said softly.

'She's perfect,' I agreed.

Now my baby was having one of her own and it was momentous. I itched to tell Claire, but Kat had sworn me to secrecy until she had told Milo and they had processed the news.

My phone vibrated on the wrought iron balcony table and I saw Neil's face on the screen. Running my fingers through my hair, I pressed 'Accept'.

He smiled and it gave me a warm, fuzzy feeling. 'Hi, darling. I was hoping to catch you before you went in tonight.'

'Aw, that's nice. I didn't think you had time. Don't you have that golf dinner?'

'Yeh, the Mixed Pairs Open.' He pulled the phone back to show he was in a suit and tie.

'You're looking devilishly handsome,' I said. 'I wish I was there.'

'I wish you were here too. Most of the wives will be there tonight. It would be great not to feel a spare part. There's only Tony and Gus who are single.'

'I'm sorry,' I said. I meant it. Life would be far less complicated if I did stay in one place for longer. I could be one of the 'golf widows', without all these responsibilities and complications. I'd go home and Neil would be in my bed, wrapping his arms around me and kissing me. I felt tears prick my eyes. It had been such an emotional rollercoaster lately, with Claire and Stu, Rosa's anxiety over her scan, and now Kat's pregnancy.

Neil pulled at his collar. 'Well, it's bloody warm tonight and I'm not looking forward to going.'

'Look, it's less than a month to Kat's wedding and then I'll be back for Cass and Mike's wedding and the summer season will be finished. You'll be sick of me then,' I joked.

Neil didn't seem in the mood for humour, though. 'I hate this separation all the time. I don't want to be a single guy and I've met the one I want to spend my life with. Don't you feel the same?' I could hear he was annoyed.

'You know I do, Neil.'

'I'm not sure I do. I'm always the one complaining, feeling that seeing you once in a while is not enough. But sometimes I think you're quite happy with the way things are.'

'I wouldn't say that I'm happy like this. It's just...'

'Grace, I don't want to force your hand, but if we lived together, it would mean we've shown some commitment to each other. I need it, even if you don't.' He paused. 'I wasn't going to do this tonight, but now's as good a time as any. I went ahead with the valuation on my apartment and I'll have a good price for it. We could buy something together. I want to move from the city.'

'So you mean I would sell Willow Cottage?'

'Well, it is a bit small for the two of us. Come on, Gracie, you know this makes sense.'

'I know, but...' I had only owned the cottage just over a year and I loved it just being mine, having my own space.

'I love you. You say you love me,' Neil went on. 'Why are you hesitating?'

'It's just that I love the cottage. It seems perfect for me and I'm not sure I want to move again.' I was aware it sounded pathetic as the words left my mouth.

'Not sure you want to move again or are you just not sure about us?' Neil said bitterly. 'It always seems to be me pushing this. And before you say anything, it's not just because Cass is getting married. I want to take the next step. I do understand that with Kat in Montenegro, you'll be travelling between the two countries, but somehow if we're living together, it won't be so bad. I won't apologise either for wanting to make you my wife.'

'I don't know what to say, Neil. I want to commit, but...'

'You don't need to say anymore. It's patently clear that you don't feel the same way that I do. Have a think about it, Gracie. Do you want this relationship to continue or not? I've been patient enough.' And he put the phone down.

I stared at the blank screen. What was wrong with me? I had this gorgeous man who wanted to marry me and I was hesitating. I was sabotaging my own life.

I did love Neil, but I was scared. I had trusted Dan, given the best years of my life to him, and he had cheated on me for years. Now my life seemed to be slotting into place. I loved the buzz of running a successful restaurant, thinking up new ideas to promote it, and working with Kat as Head Chef was the cherry on the cake. Willow Cottage was my haven, too. Everything in it had been chosen by me. For the first time, I felt I was doing what I wanted to do. And now Kat was pregnant! But when I contemplated a life without Neil, I felt a bit lost. The foundations of my new life seemed on shaky ground. Why was it all so bloody complicated? If only he'd wait a bit longer. But then, did I know what I was waiting for?

I trembled as I slid my black shift dress on and hurried to Café Lompar, my good mood from earlier long gone. I had to focus on the shift ahead, which was going to be a busy one.

Rosa was sorting orders when I arrived just after six. They were hectic in the kitchen and it was all hands on deck. Kat had worked the lunch shift, so Ivan and Bojan were there tonight. I started helping to prep one of the starters: sliced prosciutto ham smoked in the mountains of Njeguski. Montenegrins swear that the air, the location of the village and the way the ham is aired and smoked produce its delicious flavour. We were serving it with herbs, cheese and olives with freshly-baked bread. It was this attention to detail that drew the customers to the restaurant's doors. I also made the Avjar, just as Kat had taught me, a tomato and red pepper dip with lots of garlic and olive oil, served with Montenegrin cheese and rosemary bread sticks. The cheese had a strong and creamy texture and I nibbled on it as I helped plate the appetisers.

'*Santa Marija*! What the hell!'

I turned around to see Luka behind me.

'I thought I was seeing things. Why have they let you loose in the kitchen?'

'Thank you, Luka,' I laughed, 'but I am only plating appetisers and even I can make a dip. You could help too, you know, instead of just eating the food.' He was sitting on a stool, stuffing slices of the Njeguski ham into his mouth.

'I told Mum I'd help her lay some of the tables,' he said, not moving.

'Well, they won't be done with you sitting there,' I teased.

Luka looked furtive and shifted in his seat. He was suddenly serious, which was unlike him.

'I hope you and your mum are getting on better now,' I said. 'I don't want to interfere but she has her own life, Luka.'

He shrugged and speared a gherkin with his fork. I took the plates over to the fridges ready to be served to the first customers.

'Luka, are you okay?' My stomach flipped. He looked very nervous.

'Grace,' he said, 'I have to tell you something. Please don't tell anyone, but I will burst like a balloon if I keep this to myself any longer.'

'Tell me what it is. I'm worried now.'

'You know I came home late from university, after the term had ended?'

I nodded. Kat had told me there must be a girl he was interested in.

'I failed my first-year exams.'

'Is that all?' Relief washed over me.

'It is a disaster. I had to stay on and re-take them. If I fail, that is a whole year wasted. My mother will be ashamed, devastated. I have let her and everyone down.'

I hugged him. 'When will you know if you have passed?'

'My results will come in a day or two.'

'You haven't let anyone down. You are not the first and certainly won't be the last to fail exams. And you might pass these.'

'God, I hope so.' He looked so earnest. 'I have been a fool. I did not work hard enough. There are so many girls at university. It is distracting. I have learned my lesson, though. I am going to avoid women until I finish my degree.'

'Well, I wouldn't make any rash promises,' I smiled.

He nodded. 'You won't tell anyone?'

'Of course not. Let me know when you have the results. Come on, we'd better help with front of house.'

I gazed across the pass to see the restaurant already filling. One of the first things we did in our refurbishment of the restaurant last year was to have the kitchen opened up, so that customers could have a good view of the chefs and how they prepared the meals. It was a good move. Kat was gaining the status of a celebrity with her tv appearances and her cookery books. With her striking good looks, she was recognised in Tivat. When we'd gone to Centinje the other day to see Aunt Sofija, people had been asking for a selfie with Kat.

I wondered how the restaurant would cope when she had her baby. She'd be due early March. Would she be around for next year's summer season? She planned to come back, even if part-time at first, and I agreed to help. I wasn't sure how it was all going to work out, but it would. It had to.

Moving out of the kitchen, I led a young couple to a table near the open windows.

'Will this be okay?' I asked, as I handed them menus. 'Without booking, it's hard to get nearer the window.'

'This is fine,' the young woman said. Her strawberry-blonde hair rested on her sunburned shoulders. 'We're grateful to get in. I told Theo we should have booked.' She nudged his foot with hers.

'Well, I can recommend the *ipsod saka*. It's cooked over hot coals and the meat is so tender that it falls off the bone. Or you could have *cevapi*, which are kebabs with spices and it's served with salad and roasted garlic potatoes. If you want something lighter, there's Café Lompar's speciality, *buzara*, a delicious fish stew, and we have had some fresh tuna and lobster in this morning.' This was a familiar drill to me now. I pointed to the blackboard above the bar. 'The specials' board is over there.' I left the young couple with their menu and greeted the next family queuing at the door.

In a lull later, I stood by Rosa and gazed at the busy restaurant and the darkening sky outside.

'You are good at this, Grace,' she told me, and I smiled at her compliment. Rosa gave praise only occasionally.

'I like to see the place busy like this, as it's meant to be.'

'We were never this full. People come from all over to be here. There was a couple in last week from Danilovgrad. That's nearly two hours away. They'd read about us. I never imagined the place could be so successful.'

'It's brilliant,' I agreed. Then in a pause, it seemed right to ask her, 'When are you seeing a doctor? For your check-up?'

She smiled, but her eyes were serious. 'Two days.'

'You haven't found another lump, have you?' I asked, dreading the answer.

'No,' she said emphatically. 'No. It's just when you've been through something like this, you never relax. It never goes away. I wake up in the morning and it's the first thing I think about.'

'My friend Sylvie had breast cancer. I used to work with her in a charity. She told me eventually a time comes when you stop thinking of it.'

'Yes, I'm sure,' Rosa said.

And I thought of how our happiness and security always seemed to hang by a thread.

CHAPTER THIRTY-ONE

❧ Kat ❧

'All I'm saying is go easy on her,' I said, at the other side of the kitchen island to Milo. 'Natalija's been through a lot – you both have. And I'm sure she wouldn't be doing this if she didn't really want the money.'

'Well, that makes me feel guilty now.' Milo ran a hand through his hair. 'If she needed the money, why didn't she come to me? She didn't need to do these disgusting things. It will be on the internet for the rest of her life.'

'She's a grown woman. I'm sure she knew that before she started. Just don't be too hard on her,' I pleaded. I couldn't bear any more arguments in the house. More drama was the last thing I needed after the thunderstorm of the last two weeks.

Natalija was on her way back. After Milo had found out about the pictures from Luka on his stag-do, he'd been unable to contact his sister as she'd gone to stay in Cetinje for a couple of nights. I was relieved, as it had given Milo time to calm down. He'd been in such a rage that night, eyes bulging, fists balling into his pocket. It was a side of him I'd never seen before. I trusted him, and knew he wouldn't hurt anyone, but angry Milo was not my favourite. He'd gone round pouting for the rest of the night, refusing to go back to his stag do, and stomping around the bedroom like an elephant separated from the pack.

I couldn't tell him about the baby. Not then. Not when he was so annoyed. Mum had winked at me, signalled she would keep my secret until I was ready to tell him, and I was grateful to her. It was torture, though, keeping such a big secret.

Everything I did felt connected to the baby. Every action made me think about our growing child. Even brushing my teeth earlier made me think of future mornings, combing my child's hair and gazing at him or her in the mirror as we got ready side by side.

Milo had come into the bathroom this morning and found me grinning like an idiot. He'd immediately asked what was going on. I couldn't tell him when he was in this heightened state about Natalija and his family. His anger had led him to doubt the reconciliation with his father. His dad had called earlier, asking to arrange a meal out with us in Tivat, and Milo had said no with some sulky excuse.

When I told him about the baby, it had to be the perfect time, not when he was brooding over his sister and father.

I sipped my sparkling water, wondering what Milo would be like as a father. I imagined him walking hand in hand along the harbour with our son or daughter, lifting them up to sit on his broad shoulders. I could imagine him tucking our child in bed at night, reading Montenegrin stories alongside my favourite English books from childhood. And God help our future teenager, I thought, picturing the fiery Milo I knew telling them to stop fooling around and concentrate on school work.

It would be strange that our children would grow up in

Montenegro, a foreign land to me. They would have the same thick Montenegrin accent as Milo, be able to speak the language more fluently than I could by the age of five, and no doubt have curly dark hair and olive skin. Would I look the outcast in my family, pale, with a funny voice, misunderstanding the culture they grew up in? It might feel odd, but I knew we'd make the perfect family unit.

'I thought I was meant to be the one daydreaming?' Milo said as I stood at the kitchen island, gazing into our future.

'What?' I asked. 'Oh, just thinking about ... family.'

He grunted. 'Family. Nothing but trouble.'

I wanted to be annoyed, but I just couldn't. Not when our family was growing under my very own skin.

The front door sounded: Natalija's key turning in the lock.

'*Ciao*, I'm home,' she shouted, completely unaware of the tirade that was about to come her way. She strolled through to the kitchen, wearing denim micro-shorts and a faded band t-shirt that would have looked old and messy on anyone else, but stunning on Natalija. I wondered if she would be quite so eager to stay with us when there was a tiny baby screaming the place down. I had a private smile to myself.

Natalija pulled me for a hug, then looked towards Milo. 'Oh no, what's wrong with you? He's so moody, Kat.' She rolled her eyes.

I gulped, knowing this would wind Milo up even more. If anything, he looked a heck of a lot calmer than he had done previously.

'I think we should have a serious talk,' he said.

'You sound like the Godfather,' she laughed, and we shared a conspiratorial shrug, but she followed him out to sit on the terrace. I loitered, not knowing if I should join them or stay out of the way. Perhaps my presence would keep Milo calm. I sat at the table, under the shelter of the wide umbrella.

'What's up with you then?' Natalija asked, then her phone pinged and she fished it out of her bag, her long fingernails clicking against the screen. Milo's face darkened.

'It's this. You don't take anything seriously.' His voice was weary. 'You've got pictures out there of you naked, for anyone to see, the family, university, everyone, and you don't care. You act like it's nothing.'

This stopped her in her tracks. She looked up at him, her mouth dropping open. Her eyes flickered to me and I looked at the ground.

'How did you...?'

'Luka,' Milo spat. 'He's quite the fan of yours. Don't you care how this looks? How this reflects on our family?' His hands gripped the edge of the table.

'I wasn't really thinking about how it looks. More the money the university keeps demanding and I don't seem to have.' She crossed her arms, and her face was a mixture of anger and shame.

'You could have done anything else. Anything. Don't they have bars in Milan? I'm sure you could have done some waitressing. Anything but this disgusting...' Milo couldn't finish his sentence.

Tears started to roll from her eyes, leaving tracks on her cheeks. 'Well, this pays better. Don't you think I would have done those things instead if I had a choice? And what does it matter to you, Milo? You've got your perfect life here with Kat. I bet you can't remember what life was like before you started your business?'

'I do and I did what I had to do,' Milo answered quickly. 'Something respectful, unlike your pictures. It's pornography.' His lip curled. I stayed silent, unsure of where my loyalties lay. 'Montenegrins are very old fashioned. They will look down on this.'

'I don't know if it's Montenegrins that are old fashioned or just you. This is my life, Milo. Not yours. I'm a big girl now and I can do what I want to,' Natalija said, although she continued to cry. 'You can't make me feel ashamed of myself like this. It's not fair.'

Milo opened his mouth then stopped. He looked at her, his gaze softer now.

'I don't want to make you feel ashamed. I think you are amazing.' He looked to me and I smiled encouragingly.

'You do?' Natalija's wide eyes were child-like.

'Of course I do. I'm the proudest big brother ever.' I didn't know where this was going, but I liked the turn the conversation had taken.

'I can't stand you being mad at me,' Natalija choked. 'But, Milo, I'm making good money, supporting myself. I need to continue.'

'I just...'

'You don't get a say anymore,' she said.

'It's true,' I added.

'I'm a big girl. I won't do anything I don't want to. And the pictures are mine. I control when I put them online.'

'Do you get any pervy messages?' I'd been dying to ask the question since she mentioned her 'underwear' shots to me.

'Some, but I just block them. They are harmless.'

'What if they're not harmless?' Milo asked. 'These men ... they couldn't find out where you live, could they?'

'No, my location is anonymous online, and I have a different name.' She seemed more confident now.

'Well...' Milo sat back. Defeated. 'I don't love it. And I don't love finding out about this from Luka.'

'I should have told you,' Natalija conceded.

'Let's be honest, it's a bit weird telling your brother about your nude photographs, though,' I said, which broke any remaining tension.

'Thank you!' Natalija laughed. 'You don't need to worry about me or protect me anymore, seriously.'

Milo managed a smile, but this quickly turned to a frown. 'Please, I will only worry more. Do you really want to do this forever?'

Natalija sighed then, a weary one. 'I ... I'm not sure. I wish I just had the degree to focus on, nothing but my designing, just like my friends on the course. I would stop this... if I had the money.' She looked at me then. 'Kat, you're so passionate about cooking and Milo, you too. You both get to do what you love.'

'That will be you too one day,' I said, moving to rub her back. We'd all been through a lot in this conversation.

'I know. I worry this will follow me forever though. Ruin my reputation as a designer. You know what the press are like.'

I remembered the media storm we had in Café Lompar after my dad's affair came out. 'Once a photo is out there it's hard to take it back.'

'But I know my sister. You can get through anything. Go after what you want,' Milo spoke.

'If only I didn't need money to do that.' As Natalija talked, my heart went out to her. 'Maybe I could look at something else. Temporary. Just for my final year.'

'The university might be able to help?' I offered. 'If you tell them you're struggling, they can sometimes offer students a bigger loan, or some paid work.'

'Something more glamorous than that,' she said. 'Maybe I could look at selling some of my creations so far.'

'I'm proud of you,' Milo said.

Natalija grinned at him, then stood and made excuses about going to do some work for university. I could see the cogs whirring in her mind. I hoped she would find something. She promised to be back for dinner with us later. Milo watched her walk away but I watched him. There was a glint in his eye and an ease to his movements. I knew at that moment he would be a great father.

'What are you smiling about?' he asked me.

'Oh, it's nothing.' I didn't know if I should tell him now. In my mind I'd imagined a special moment, maybe a restaurant or a private walk along the beach, but was there ever really a perfect moment?

Milo and I had always talked about having children. I think losing his mother at a young age and growing up with a distant father made him yearn to create the family unit he didn't have. I'd been more hesitant. My life was all career. I'd pictured myself with children one day, maybe a girl and a boy, but it had always seemed a long way off. Something I would do when I was an adult or at least felt like an adult. Something we would plan, years down the line, after our marriage.

Life had thrown me another curve ball. My father's death had brought me Rosa, Luka and Montenegro, and I couldn't imagine the path my life would have taken without them. And as careful as I'd been with Milo, I was pregnant. Life would never be the same again.

'Kat?' he asked.

'There's something I need to tell you.'

'I don't know if I can take any more stress,' he said, in mock-frustration, laying his head in his hands, elbows splayed on the table. I hadn't thought about the stress he'd been under, the busy summer season in mid-flow, planning the wedding, his father and Natalija.

'Hopefully this will be stress of a different kind.'

'What do you mean?' He met my eye, the anticipatory twinkle in his chocolate brown gaze making my heart swell with love. Oh, God. Just two words. That's all I needed to say. The most important two words in my life.

'I'm pregnant.'

Nothing moved in Milo's face. He was like stone. For a second, I wondered if he'd heard me. I opened my mouth to speak again.

'You're ... with child?' The old-fashioned Bible phrase made me laugh. It sounded strange. I nodded, waiting for more of a reaction.

'I... What...? I have so many questions.' The slowest smile crept from his mouth, rising until he was beaming. The first true smile I'd seen from him in weeks. 'We're having a baby?'

'We are,' I said, watching tears glisten in his eyes.

'We're having a baby!' This time it wasn't a question. I loved the way he'd taken the news, no hesitation, no instant fear like I'd felt.

He stood and pulled me to my feet, bending and placing both hands on my flat stomach. 'Our baby … is there. Ours?'

I nodded, crying now.

'Do you know how long? How did you find out? Have you taken the test? Why didn't you tell me?' He sounded manic, still holding my sides.

'I haven't felt right for a couple of weeks. I took the test a couple of nights ago, when Mum was here.'

'Why didn't…?'

'You've been so stressed with Natalija. It didn't feel like the right time, somehow.'

'Kat, that thing with Natalija was nothing compared to this. It's the best news I've had in my life.'

He pulled me to him, sweeping me up in a bear hug. My head was close to his chest, and I nestled against it, hearing his heart beating. He was so full of life, and I felt it too. Our baby was literally living inside me, growing every day.

Milo kissed me, deep and slow, a kiss that bonded our family together. As I nestled back in to his chest and he kissed the top of my head, I breathed in his scent, his sweat, his skin. I marvelled at how I could feel like this in a different country with someone I'd only known for a year. Completely and totally at home.

CHAPTER THIRTY-TWO

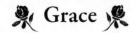 Grace

It was already twenty-three degrees at eleven in the morning as I pored over the figures for the restaurant. Rosa was coming in late after her appointment at the hospital and I was finding it hard to concentrate.

Suddenly, Ana rushed in, flinging her bag on a table. 'Ensambla has a huge board outside. They're advertising wine tasting, party-themed events, ladies' nights.' She was reeling off all she could remember on her fingers.

Dijana spoke to her in Montenegrin, arms flailing, and I caught the odd word – *restoran* and Ensambla.

'What are you all worked up about?' I asked. I had a horrible sense of foreboding. Lovro had been lured over there. How long would Davor stay loyal to us or would he follow his boyfriend? I kicked myself again for not thinking of wine tasting. People love that.

Ana nodded vigorously. 'We will lose customers. We need to do more.'

'Do you really think so? We don't need gimmicks.'

Ana looked puzzled. 'Gimmicks?'

'Tricks,' I elaborated. 'We have simple, beautiful cooked food that people want to eat.' If I said it often enough, I might actually believe it.

'We must do more. Everybody is talking about Ensambla. We must bring more customers in.'

Were Ana and Dijana being dramatic? We were always full and I hadn't been too worried. Still, I started googling: *How to promote your restaurant in ten easy steps.*

When Kat came through to the restaurant later, I didn't mention anything to her. She had enough on her plate, without worrying that Ensambla was trying hard to entice our customers away. Rosa arrived at midday. I tried to catch her eye, but she scurried from the restaurant to the kitchen, greeting customers, taking orders, and helping at the bar.

In a quiet moment, as the girls cleared the tables, I asked Rosa how it went at the hospital.

When she looked at me, I saw the dark rings under her eyes. 'It was fine,' she smiled. 'There's nothing to worry about. It all looks clear. I don't know if I can go through this every time I have a check up,' she said. 'I haven't slept properly for a long time.'

'You need a holiday,' I told her. 'Away from all this stress at the restaurant.'

She nodded. 'Yes, but impossible. It is our busy time.'

She turned her back on me and collected the menus from the tables. The subject was over. I had to admire her strength. She hadn't told Luka about her worries, preferring to shoulder the burden alone. The last thing she needed to worry about now was Luka and his failed exams.

The afternoon was humid and stuffy and the heat radiated from the pavement as I made my way back to the apartment for a few hours respite before dinner. Kat walked back with me.

'Have you told Milo?' I asked as soon as we were alone.

271

'About the baby?' A smile spread across her face. 'Oh, Mum, he's as delighted as I am. I can't believe I'm going to be a mother. My life has changed so much,' she sighed.

'You will be a terrific mother. And your father would have been so proud.'

She slipped her hand in mine for a few seconds. 'I feel I could burst with excitement, but I don't know the first thing about being a mother and I haven't a clue how we'll cope in the restaurant.'

'We'll cope,' I reassured her. 'These things have a way of working out, trust me.' I looped my arm through hers, 'As for being a mother, you will be a natural. Anything you don't know, you'll learn as you go along. I'll be there for you and I'll be over as much as I can.'

'What about Neil?'

'Will you stop worrying?' I scolded her. I'd pushed him to the back of my mind. Kat and my grandchild were the most important things in my life. 'So, can I tell Claire? I'm just bursting to tell her.'

'Yes. Milo is telling Natalija and his father tonight. Things are still strained between them, but perhaps this will bring them together.' Kat crossed her fingers.

'Try and rest now, darling,' I told her as I crossed to my apartment. 'You'll have a busy shift tonight and you'll get more tired as time goes on.'

Kat rolled her eyes. 'That's going to get old really quickly, Mum.'

I skipped up to the stairs of my apartment, passing the irascible Mrs. Jankovic out on her balcony.

'Afternoon, Mrs. Jankovic,' I said breezily. She scowled at me and deigned to nod her head briefly.

Nothing could spoil my mood. I poured myself a cold drink and opened the doors to the balcony. It was far too hot to sit outside. Pulling my feet under me, I fell asleep for twenty minutes on the sofa. The buzz of my mobile phone woke me up.

'Hi, hon.' Claire's face appeared on screen. 'God, you look a mess.'

'Thanks. You look lovely too.'

Claire ignored me. 'I'm at a loose end here and I had to get away from Stu. That's why I'm in the conservatory. Although the bloody rain sounds so noisy on the roof.' She turned the camera around to flash the dismal scene of the water pooling on the patio outside and the sombre grey sky.

'Well, it's too hot here, if that makes you feel better.'

'Hmm, my heart bleeds for you.'

'How is Stu?'

'Not the best patient. Are you surprised? He's a hypochondriac at the best of times, but now he has something really wrong with him. He winces every time he moves. "Would you be so good as to get me a cushion so I can rest my leg, Claire? Claire, my throat is feeling a bit dry, and I could do with a cup of tea. Claire, can you pass my tablets if you've got time?"'

'Poor Stu,' I said.

She grimaced. 'He's living the life of Riley. And he keeps repeating how close he came to death and how it's changed him.'

'You told him about that night?'

Claire nodded. 'He was so angry, so so angry. He wanted me to leave. Thank God Liam and Laura were out. We were up all night. He told me he'll forgive me but never forget it. And I feel so bloody guilty. We're seeing a counsellor next week.'

'It's good you're both trying.'

'Yes, but I'm scared. If a counsellor digs too deep, I might say things I'll regret. Hurtful things. About how suffocated I felt and how close I came to leaving him.'

'Perhaps it's better to clear the air. What have you got to lose?'

'I suppose. I know it's a cliché, but it meant nothing. It was just something I had to get out of my system.' She paused. 'Am I making any sense?'

I nodded, 'Relationships are complicated.' Then to change the subject, I said, 'Well, I've got some news, if you want to take your mind off it.'

Claire smiled. 'Go on.'

'I'm going to be a grandma,' I said.

'Oh, my God, that's amazing!' Claire grinned. 'You must be so chuffed. Congratulations.'

'I am,' I agreed, 'although it does make me feel old.'

'I might have to get you some Tena Lady for your birthday.'

'It's not just grandmas who leak, you know.'

'So, what will you be called? Grandma, Nana, Nanny?'

'There's just nothing cool, is there?' I laughed.

'Are you going to keep going out to Montenegro for the summer and then working from home the rest of the time?'

'I suppose. I'll just have to see. It's all so new. Neil is also a factor.'

'Has he been putting pressure on again?'

'Well, he has had his apartment valued and he wants us to buy somewhere together. He's keen to leave the city.'

'I guess the cottage might be a bit small for the two of you,' Claire said. 'But you *lurve* that cottage.'

'I do. I kind of like my own space.'

'Do you want my advice?' Claire said, suddenly serious. 'You and me, and a lot of women I know, have been with men for most of our adult lives. I was fifteen when I met Stu. Just a kid. You met Danilo when you were in your first year at uni. Sometimes we need to spread our wings. This is the happiest I've seen you. You're super-talented.' She paused. 'I think I'd be straight with Neil, Gracie. Tell him how you feel. If he's not happy to wait for you, he's just not worth it.'

'Maybe.'

'You need to listen to the sage advice of your younger sister. No one else bothers listening to me.'

'Liam and Laura, you mean? I'm sure we were exactly the same as teenagers.'

After Claire rang off, I had a quick shower and made a Sopska salad, which was a creamy and salty cheese, similar to feta. I dressed it with a splash of olive oil and apple cider vinegar, just as we served at Café Lompar. I took it onto the balcony, with an ice-cold Fabrika beer, mulling over what Claire had said, what I should do. It was cooler at five and I watched people walk back from the beach, their steps tired and their shoulders reddened. The tourists were so easy to spot. The locals kept out of the sun during the hottest part of the day whereas the tourists threw caution to the wind, under-estimating how hot Montenegro was in the height of summer.

After I finished eating, I looked at my phone. I had to talk to Neil. Our last conversation had been stilted and awkward. Claire was right. I had to be straight with him. I did see a future with him, but I wanted to wait before we took the next step.

After two rings, Neil picked up the phone. 'Hello, Grace.' I was relieved to see he was smiling.

'I know I usually call later, but I've got some time and I wanted a chat.'

He frowned, 'Okay. There's nothing wrong, is there?'

'No, no, of course not. I just wanted to clear the air about what you said a few days ago.' Neil said nothing, so I went on. 'I'm really happy with you, Neil, and you know I love you. But...'

'I don't like where this is going,' Neil interrupted.

'Hear me out. In a year or two, I don't know, I might be ready to move in, but at the moment, I'm just finding my feet. I don't see that we have to rush things. And there has been a development. Kat is pregnant. I mean, that shouldn't change things between us...'

Why did I sound so apologetic? Had I learned nothing with Danilo? I had to speak up and say what I wanted.

'Congratulations!' he said, but his voice was flat. 'I'm pleased for you, and Kat, of course I am. But this will change things. You're bound to want to spend more time in Montenegro now. Rightly so. Where does it leave us?' He sighed. 'I just think we're in different places at the moment. I love you and want to be with you. And it's more than clear that you don't want to be with me.'

'That's not true...'

'It's not your fault, Gracie. Perhaps you're not ready for a relationship yet. I've been on my own for a few years and I want commitment. I want someone I can come home to, someone who wants to be with me. I want to go the pub and have country walks, travel a bit, perhaps. You want your freedom.'

'I do want those things too, Neil, but I just need a bit more time.'

'I think it's best we have a break and see where we stand. I don't want to be the heavy one, pressuring you all the time. Shall we just see how things go?' He frowned. 'I'm meeting Gus in the pub in half an hour.'

'What about Kat and Milo's wedding?'

'It's over a month away. We'll see then.' He rang off.

I stared at the phone when the call ended. I couldn't breathe. What the hell had I done?

CHAPTER THIRTY-THREE

❧ Kat ❧

The doorbell rang. My pyjama top was riding up over the small undulation of skin that was beginning to take over my abdomen. I tugged the top down as I went to answer the door.

'Delivery for ... Milo and Kat Lompar?'

'Yes, thank you,' I nodded, picking up the brown cardboard parcel on the doormat. I was a closet internet shopper, ordering clothes from my favourite brands in the UK that I couldn't get out in Montenegro, but I wasn't expecting anything. There was no logo and I was surprised at the weight of the parcel.

'Milo, we've got a package,' I called up the stairs, closing the door behind me.

'What are you carrying it for?' He hurried down and rushed to sweep the parcel from me.

'I can carry things.' I frowned at him. 'Our trays of priganice weigh double that.' I wondered how long he'd be fussing over me before the novelty of my pregnancy wore off. If it ever did.

I still felt that something momentous was happening inside me, and kept searching my reflection in the mirror for signs I'd changed. My face still looked like the same old Kat, dimpled smile and laughter creases.

'I'll get the scissors,' I said, wondering if Milo would try to take those off me too. We opened the cardboard to find several packages wrapped in delicate blue pearly tissue paper. Each of them had a tag attached: 'For baby'. We opened them up to find a little brown teddy bear, an old-fashioned rattle, and then a lemon-yellow crocheted blanket.

'Mine when I was younger,' Milo said as we both stroked the soft woven material. He turned it over to show me the embroidered 'M' in white thread.

'It's beautiful,' I sighed, touched. 'Our baby's first ever present. It must be from your father.'

'I slept with this blanket for a good two years more than I should have,' Milo gave a laugh of recognition, mesmerised by the fabric.

Underneath were two more packets, one 'For Milo' and another 'For Kat'.

'You first,' I told him, and he tore the paper off a rectangular photo frame. Milo went quiet as he gazed at it. I peered over his shoulder. The old picture showed a five-year old Milo swinging from the hands of two parents, the whole family grinning at the camera. His dark curls were already beginning to form, and you could see where his eyes came from as his mother's sparkled with joy. If they knew what was ahead, I thought.

'How lovely,' I said, catching the tell-tale shine in Milo's eye as he looked away, placing the frame carefully on top of the blanket.

He swallowed audibly. 'Now you.'

My package was considerably smaller than the others, and I unfolded the paper delicately so as not to rip it. Inside was a purple velvet pouch, and inside that I took out the most beautiful necklace. A simple silver chain held a small pendant, a silver diamond on top of a slightly bigger sapphire.

'Oh my...' You could tell the necklace was old, the chain slightly worn, but still beautiful and eye-catching.

'My mum's,' Milo explained. I looked at the photo, and there you could see her wearing the necklace on top of a plain white shirt. 'She loved that. I think my dad bought it for her.'

'Wouldn't she want Natalija to have it?' I didn't feel worthy of something so valuable. I ran the necklace through my fingers, like stolen treasure.

'Natalija has her wedding ring, plenty of other things too. I guess my dad kept this...' Milo said, his voice breaking.

'I'll keep this forever,' I told him, stretching up to kiss away his tear. 'And give it to our future daughter whenever we have one.'

'It can be your something old ... and blue.' Milo picked me up off my feet, pressing another kiss to me.

'I didn't know Montenegrins had that saying,' I said, realising it was another thing I hadn't even thought about. I had something new, but borrowed? I would have to ask Mum.

Milo placed the necklace around my neck, kissing the back of my neck at the same time. He knew I loved that, the warm feeling spreading from my skin, deeper.

'Milo, this is really nice,' I said, indicating the box. 'Your dad seems so excited to be a grandparent.'

'Mmm,' he agreed.

'This could be the making of him,' I tried.

'I have hoped that before,' he said, but on seeing the crushed expression on my face, he added, 'but this is his chance. Our baby is lucky to have two parents and two grandparents who adore him ... or her. Our baby deserves a grandfather.'

I'd never thought of that, my mum being in the same bracket as Milo's dad, Nik.

'You should call him and tell him that. Invite him round tomorrow,' I told him. 'He can meet my mum, get to know each other.'

'Okay,' Milo said, 'but only because you look so beautiful in that necklace.'

'Even with the pyjamas?' I joked.

'Even more so,' he smiled, giving me one last kiss.

'Right, in the spirit of reconciliation,' I said, rushing to get dressed, 'there's something I need to do.'

I braced myself, feeling oddly nervous, and knocked at the door. The wait for an answer seemed to take forever, and I shifted uncomfortably from one foot to the other. I was trying to wear in a new pair of trainers, but they were proving stubborn, and as I slid my heel slightly out of one of them, I saw red skin where it had been rubbing.

The door opened, and Dav stood there, his hair ruffled, wearing a dressing gown. If I thought I looked like shit answering the door, then at least I wasn't the only one.

'Kat?'

'Hi. Is Lovro in?' I asked, my voice tentative.

'He's upstairs.' Dav was giving me no clue how well I'd be received. I bristled. It wasn't like I'd done anything directly wrong to Lovro. But I still felt nervous.

'Can I speak to him?' I asked, trying to look more confident than I felt.

'Come on in,' he beckoned, and left me to catch the door behind him. I shoved my ankle back into my shoe, feeling my skin shred against the material.

I followed Dav up the stairs. 'I'd offer to take those from you,' he said, gesturing to the flowers I was carrying, 'but I'm guessing they're for him?'

'They are.' I smiled. 'Thanks, though.'

The stairway entered into their open-plan kitchen and lounge, which was as neat and individual as I remembered. I hadn't been for a while, but I knew everything in the kitchen's was Lovro's, from his apron hanging by the door to the cream and green mugs stacked in the corner. The lounge was all Dav, with a bar area, neon sign and industrial-style coffee table.

And there, in the open doorway to the bedroom, was Lovro. I smiled at him, but the confident pep talk I'd given myself on the walk over was fading quickly. He smiled coyly.

'Do you want a drink, Kat?' Dav asked. 'I could do a quick mojito.' He knew they were my favourites.

'Urrgh ... no better not,' I said, thinking that my next mojito was a long way into my future. I felt pleased he'd asked. 'Do you have a diet coke or lemonade or something?' He shrugged and pottered around the kitchen.

'I wanted to come and talk to you,' I said to Lovro.

'Shall we go outside?'

I followed him to the balcony.

'I hope you haven't come to find out inside information on Ensambla,' Lovro said, when we were set-up on the loungers on their little balcony. They had artificial grass on the floor, and I thought how good it would feel to kick off my bloodied trainers and run my toes through the material.

'Would I have brought "I'm sorry" flowers and candles if I was doing that?' I asked, popping the flowers down on their side table.

'Are those candles?' He nodded to the box in my hand.

'Okay, before you see them, I want you to know, Etsy didn't have a lot of options under gifts for gay men so I had to work with what was there.' I presented him the box. I'd bought two sparkly gold candles that were moulded to look like the torsos of some very well-sculpted men. 'They're his and his candles.'

Lovro looked at the gift and gave a little snort of laughter. 'It's about time I put my own stamp on that living room.'

'Lovro, I'm sorry.' I held a hand up to stop him interrupting. 'I need to say this. I was an idiot. A total idiot. From the moment Ensambla set-up next door, to the awful thing I did, like a cartoon villain. It was ridiculous, and I let them come between us. I can understand you wanting to work there because why wouldn't they value such an incredible chef as you? Whatever happens in the future, whether you come back to Café Lompar or not, I want you to know I'm happy for you and I will always think you're a rock star. I'm so sorry I fucked up.'

He smiled, then let out a chuckle. 'I didn't think coming back to Café Lompar was an option. Not after I thought about working at Ensambla.'

I caught what he said. '*Thought about*? Does that mean you're not working for them?'

'Not yet,' Lovro gave me a sheepish smile. 'I haven't given them an answer yet.'

'Thank God! Lovro, we would be more than grateful if you came back. I think Rosa might cry. I would kiss the ground you walk on every day. Mum is prepared to rename the café Lovro's,' I joked but I wanted him to know how sincere I was. 'Would I buy you hot-guy candles if I wasn't serious?'

'Well, I am out of work at the moment.' Lovro sniffed. 'But I'm not sure if I should let you off that easy. I was very shocked by your actions. It takes time to get over something like that.'

I leant back in my lounger. The view at Lovro and Dav's was of the Lovcen Mountains rather than the sea, but was no less spectacular. A plane overhead left a trail of fluffy white clouds in its wake across the brilliant blue. You had the feeling the view hadn't changed for years. Tivat had sprung up but the mountains were permanent.

I thought about Ensambla. Having competition like that brought out a side of myself I really didn't like. I think I feared the closure of Café Lompar because it was something I felt so passionate about, something I'd built my life around. I couldn't bear the thought of it failing. Why did I jump straight to catastrophic thoughts? I should have let Ensambla do their thing, concentrated on Café Lompar.

'I've been an arse. I always hated my old boss for having such an ego, one hint of fame and respect, and it went to his head. I've been the same here. Ensambla is a threat, and I haven't handled it well at all.' I shook my head, embarrassed, then moved to undo my trainers.

'I don't know why you let them get to you so badly? You know Café Lompar is going to do well, no matter how Ensambla are performing.'

'I don't know that.' I said. 'I don't know if I'll ever feel secure as a chef, if I'll ever get over the imposter syndrome.'

'But, Kat, you'd never make it to Head Chef if you weren't up to it,' Lovro said, pulling at my hand. I linked mine through his, pleased to have my friend back.

'Head Chef has been wonderful, the best challenge I've ever done, but it's so much responsibility. And the way I've reacted to competition has not been pretty. I'm no different to the others. I've loved being Head Chef but...'

'Why are you talking in the past?' Lovro frowned.

'I think you should take over now.'

He laughed out loud then stopped. 'What? You can't be serious?'

I'd thought about it for the last few days. It was the perfect option. I was pregnant and soon would need to be off work for a substantial amount of time. Cooking wasn't a family job, especially not the head of the kitchen. We needed someone committed, driven, someone that would be able to work six nights a week. I couldn't do that when I had a baby, neither could Milo with his growing business. If Lovro did it, then I could still help him, still keep an eye on the menu, the kitchen, the staff. And my replacement would be someone from the Café Lompar family. I hadn't told Mum yet but assumed she'd be on board.

I told Lovro everything apart from the impending new member of the family.

'I think you're so exciting as a chef, Lovro. You come up with the best flavour combinations and you're so efficient. Your food presentation is an Instagrammer's dream. I want you to do this job.'

His eyes sparkled with disbelief. 'But I don't get why you have to leave?'

'Not leave, exactly, but take a step back,' I explained. He looked confused. 'I'm...' God, why did this still feel so unnatural to say? 'I'm pregnant.'

'You're pregnant!' Lovro shrieked, then stood up, threw his arms in the air, sat back down, and started to cry. If Milo's reaction was dramatic, then this was a whole new level. 'Oh my God, this is the best day ever,' he said. 'Can I tell Dav?'

'Of course,' I giggled, and I heard mutual shrieking inside. Lovro came back out to the balcony. 'I have new candles and a pregnant best friend.'

'And a job as Head Chef?' I asked, unsure what the answer would be. His face turned suddenly serious.

'Is there such a thing as joint Head Chef?'

'I think you had that role anyway,' I grinned. 'Now come on, I need help in picking the perfect "I'm sorry" present to send to David and Lizzie. If candles can work wonders for you, then imagine what it could do for them.'

'I wouldn't be so sure about that. He's really got it in for you.' Lovro sucked in air between his teeth.

'What do you mean?' I asked.

'I don't know. David seems to be on a mission to compete with Café Lompar, to be better than you. He seems to really hate you.'

'I had that impression too. I just don't know why.'

'Neither do I,' Lovro sighed. 'But I can feel trouble brewing.'

CHAPTER THIRTY-FOUR

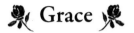 Grace

Time seemed to pass in a whirlwind. Working at Café Lompar was a distraction but I missed Neil all the time. One evening I was walking back to my apartment and I could hear the waves slapping the jetty. In the distance, laughter and music drifted across from a party on one of the large yachts. I realised there was no phone call to look forward to when I got home, no one to call me 'sweetheart' or 'darling'. I told myself to get a grip.

When I got home, I took a cup of tea on to the balcony. I could still hear the party and it made my apartment seem quiet, empty. The universe seemed to be conspiring against me as an older couple passed by, the woman looping her arm in the man's as they walked in step, not speaking, happiness radiating from them. I'd had that with Neil, but I had put on the brakes. I knew the euphemisms: 'space' was a kinder way of saying it was over. And he was the one who'd suggested it.

I hadn't heard from Neil for four days and Claire had told me last night that he'd been seen having lunch with Cathy Shaw in the golf club yesterday. I remembered our first lunch date in The Nineteenth Hole and how attentive he had been. Cathy owned Shaw's Home Accessories in the centre of Bath, where everything was overpriced and pared back, Scandi-style. All the décor was whites and beiges, and even Cathy's hair was beige. Candles cost you at least seventy quid a pop. I found her quite unfriendly, with her cool-blue eyes and thin smile. Claire had called her a snooty cow. 'Thinks she's better than everyone else. I wouldn't read too much into it, Gracie. He does give private lessons and the women request him a lot at the golf club.'

I pulled a cardigan around my shoulders now, feeling the chill. I would go back inside in a few moments, have an early night for a change, read a book.

There was a tap at the door. 'It's only me,' Kat called. She had a key but I had a chain I pulled across at night.

'This is a surprise,' I said, as I let her in and hugged her.

'We cleared everything up early,' said Kat, 'so I thought I'd call in for a cuppa if you're not too tired. I've got my first appointment at the doctor's tomorrow.'

'I've got some PG Tips, but I've just had one. I think I'll have a night cap instead.' I pulled the gin from the cupboard.

'God, I miss alcohol already,' Kat laughed. 'I'm not a big drinker, but a glass of wine with food is lovely and I'll have to avoid Dav's cocktails at the end of the night.'

'How are you feeling with the sickness?' Even though we had both just done a shift at Café Lompar, it was always so hectic that we barely exchanged a few words.

'It's not too bad but it's not just confined to the morning. I feel a bit nauseous throughout the day. When I was preparing those mussels for lunch, I felt really sick. And I'm surrounded by food all day!' She rolled her eyes.

'Aw, it's horrible. I was lucky with you – I didn't have morning sickness but I had lots of cravings. I had a weird addiction to

Angel Delight and ate it every day. Your dad was forever rushing off to a garage to see if they had any Angel Delight left for me.'

'Well, I haven't had any cravings yet but I suppose it's still early days. I'm surprised how much weight I'm putting on already.'

'There's nothing of you,' I insisted.

'Honestly, Mum, my skirts already feel a bit tight.'

'It was lovely to see Rosa and Luka's reaction to your baby news.'

'Luka kept saying he's going to be a cool uncle. He's convinced it will be a boy and he'll teach him how to play football because he says Milo has two left feet. I hope I haven't jinxed things by telling people too early. It's so hard to keep anything a secret here. I've been rushing to the loo too often for people not to get suspicious.'

'Rosa seemed delighted, too,' I said. 'It's funny how much they are part of our family. I'd never have chosen this, but I'm getting used to it.'

I fell into silence for a moment, wondering whether I could really feel Rosa was part of my family. Would there always be this barrier because of her and Dan's relationship? Would I ever forget the hurt and pain I'd felt?

I said, 'Rosa is probably wondering how we'll get a chef like you when you're off. Bojan and Ivan could share Head Chef. I'm not sure either have your creativity but they really are a safe pair of hands.'

'I agree,' Kat said, suddenly very animated. 'They are great but sometimes they don't think outside the box. Bojan is very traditional.' She paused. 'But I've got great news. I went to see Lovro a couple of days ago and he's willing to come back.'

'He's not working for Ensambla? Oh, that's great, Kat.' I knew Kat really rated him and they got on so well.

'I knew you'd understand. Anyway, he's willing to be Head Chef while I'm away and if I go part-time after I have the baby, we could share the role.'

I was speechless. It felt like someone had thrown cold water over me. 'What? Lovro as Head Chef? You've got to be kidding.'

'What do you mean? He has so much potential. What's wrong with him?'

'Well, for a start, what is he, twenty-one? Twenty-two?'

'In London, there are lots of young Head Chefs.'

'Yes, but he's so inexperienced. Up until a year ago, he was just a pastry chef. Granted, he can make great ice cream and desserts, but Head Chef?'

'Mum, you're not a chef. You wouldn't understand.'

'Don't patronise me. I know much more about running a business than you do. Bojan is thirty-four and both Ivan and he have years of experience. Don't you think they'll feel a bit miffed to have Lovro suddenly catapulted to Head Chef? What will Rosa say? God, Kat I can't believe this. How incredibly naïve and stupid of you!'

Kat stood up, brushing her skirt down. She wouldn't look me in the eyes. 'I'm sorry you feel like that, but I know that he would make a great Head Chef. I work with him every day. He's totally committed.'

'So committed, he left Café Lompar to work with Ensambla?'

'He didn't work there, he was only thinking about it, and that was my fault.' Her eyes blazed with indignation. 'Who can blame him? I was an idiot for changing that date. Lovro has principles.'

'Yes, it was idiotic, but this has nothing to do with Lovro's principles. He's just too inexperienced to take on such a role.'

'I've been training him up. We work so well together. He thinks like I do. I totally trust him.'

'Well, Kat, you had no right to offer him the role before asking me first. I have my money invested in this place and I have a say too. And Rosa.'

I noticed Kat blink back tears. I didn't want to upset her but I couldn't believe how she'd acted. First the poster mistake, and now this.

'I was wondering when you'd play that card. I had my reservations from the beginning about working with you. Or is it *for* you? I'm just another worker, after all.'

I felt slapped in the face. Is that what she really thought? Standing up, I began clearing the cups and glasses away.

'This is a partnership, Kat, always has been. It means we both get a say. We don't make decisions without talking to the other first. Especially when you make crap decisions like this.'

'It's too late now,' Kat said. 'I've already told Lovro and he has agreed. He's starting back next week.'

'You'll have to un-tell him then,' I told her. 'Apologise to him. You can't just do these things, Kat. You've got to think about what's right for the business, not just what keeps a friend happy.'

She sighed then. I could tell she was losing her temper.

'Maria told me that I was mad to go into business with my mother and she was right. And do you know what? I think Dad would probably have advised me against it too.' She slammed the door as she left.

I sank back onto the sofa. That last comment was the worst. It just reminded me how close Danilo and Kat were, that she was closer to him than me. I felt the tears spill down my cheeks and I let them fall, too miserable and sorry for myself to brush them away. Perhaps Kat was right and a mother and daughter shouldn't work together, especially run a business together. This was our first real clash. I was fuming with her for making such a rash move without telling me. I liked Lovro but he was in no way ready to run a kitchen. Damn it, Kat was such a pleaser sometimes.

Was I mad to think this could work? Being out in Montenegro for the summer months and running the business from the UK the rest of the time. Was I just arrogant to assume I could do it? I had bitten off more than I could chew. It had cost me Neil, too. Was I having some mid-life crisis, having to prove that I still had something to contribute, that I was still useful? Running Café Lompar was bloody hard work. There was a drama every week with something or other. Shouldn't I be looking at some part-time job serving afternoon teas in a café or working in a dusty bookshop? Going on cruises once a year? I'd always fancied a Fjords cruise. Instead, I was running a restaurant with Dan's bloody mistress. What was I thinking?

Part of me would always be in Montenegro. Kat was having a baby and I would be spending a lot of time in this country, whether I liked it or not. But should I go back home and see Neil, ask him to give us another go and move in together? Or had he already met someone else? I turned things over and over in my mind as I tried to sleep.

The next morning, the light splintered through the gaps in the curtains and I groaned. I couldn't have had more than two or

292

three hours sleep as I remembered looking at the clock at four in the morning. Sunshine filled the bedroom as I opened the curtains, the sea already winking in the weak morning sun. I made myself a strong coffee, deciding I'd go to Café Lompar early this morning. Kat was at the doctors later. Perhaps that was a good thing after last night. I had some big decisions to make.

I wasn't sure I could work at Café Lompar any more. It was probably better if I kept my roles simpler: a mother and grandmother. It hadn't crossed my mind that Kat saw me as her boss, that she felt she owed me something because I had invested money in the business. I'd watched enough episodes of *Hotel Inspector* to know that running a business with family members was a recipe for disaster. I could imagine Alex Polizzi's eyes widening in horror if she heard about our set-up. Running a restaurant with my daughter and my late husband's mistress. Totally fucked-up.

When I walked into Café Lompar at nine o'clock, Rosa was already there.

'You're in early,' I said.

'Hmm.' She was sitting at her laptop, barely glancing up. 'There's lots to do this morning. I want to make sure the orders are in for tomorrow night's tapas event. I could say the same for you.'

'I couldn't sleep.'

'Is everything alright, Grace?' She finally turned to me.

I shook my head. I never usually confided in Rosa, but there was no harm in telling her about Neil. 'I think I am a single woman again,' I said. 'Neil wants me to move in with him.'

'And you don't want to?' Her glasses slipped down her nose. Even glasses made Rosa look sexy.

293

'It's not that I don't want to. It's just I need more time.'

'He's a nice man, Grace, but if he's a good man and if he loves you, he will wait. I, too, am a single woman. I have ended it finally with Matija.'

'Oh, why...?'

She batted away my protestations. 'He was too young. I like watching the sunset; he likes playing video games. I like a nice meal and wine in a restaurant; he wants takeout pizza. I am too old for a motorbike. It's been coming for a while.'

'I thought it might. I bet Luka was pleased,' I grinned. 'Does he know?'

'Everyone knows everything here,' she smiled. 'It was fun for a while, but now I need to act my age. Danilo took my younger years. With Matija, I think I got to live them again, for a little while. But I don't think he could handle these hospital appointments. He's too young. He wants someone his own age, carefree.' She shrugged, 'He'll get over it. There's so much to do in these summer months here, I can barely think of a relationship.'

'Did you know Lovro is back next week?'

Rosa nodded. 'Kat said she was going to see him. They work well together.'

'Kat has asked him to be Head Chef.'

Rosa shook her head, 'He is too inexperienced. No, that can't happen. We will ask Bojan and Ivan to share the role and Lovro as chef. He is a very good pastry chef. Talented. He is no Head Chef. Maybe in the future.'

I was relieved that Rosa felt the same way. I couldn't tell her that we had argued over it. It was too raw.

'Café Lompar will survive while Kat is off, but it won't be the same,' Rosa continued. 'She has built a good reputation. And you, Grace, you have given it new life.'

She seemed to instinctively know I was doubting my place here.

'Luka is coming in to help today,' she said. 'It will be all hands on deck, as you say.'

It was a busy shift and my mind kept wandering to Kat and how her doctor's appointment was going. I hated bad feeling between us. The last time I felt like this was when she had first agreed to stay here and work for Rosa. It seemed a lifetime ago. Once again, though, everything seemed up in the air. It might be better for me to take more of a back seat, become a sleeping partner, keep the money in but leave the management to Rosa and Kat. Life would be less complicated.

Would Neil want me back, though? Was I ready to become a couple again and relinquish my freedom? I felt confused and a bit rudderless. I loved Kat fiercely, but she had her own life. Perhaps it was time I had mine too.

CHAPTER THIRTY-FIVE

❦ Kat ❦

Why did doctors' offices look the same the world over? They always had the same retro material on the sofas and carpet, the coffee table filled with curly-edged magazines, and an overbearing clock with an audible tick, just so you knew exactly how much of your life you were wasting away.

I tried not to watch the clock as the wait stretched on another ten minutes past my appointment time. My leg jittered up and down. I didn't like seeing doctors, not that anyone really does, but since Dad died, and then all those hospital appointments with Rosa, I'd come to associate these waiting rooms with bad news.

Milo laid a comforting hand on my knee. I smiled, reassuring him I was fine. We were only booking in with the midwife to register my pregnancy; it wasn't even a scan or anything remotely clinical.

There was another reason for my unease – the argument with Mum. I knew she would have loved to come with me today. It felt strange that we were arguing. I kept replaying my words to her in my mind. The truth was I loved working with my mother. Yes, we had our differences at times, but she was so understanding and was the opposite of bossy. I hated that I'd said those things to her in the heat of the moment. She was right about Lovro too, I knew that. I was kicking myself for asking him. I had just been so excited to see him.

It was painful that I couldn't share this appointment with her.

'Kat Lompar?'

The man calling my name invited us through, then introduced himself as Locjan, the practice midwife. He was tanned and chiselled, like a character from a Spanish soap opera, and even though I knew better than to stereotype job roles, I was taken aback to find out this hunk of a man was going to be my midwife, helping me through the antenatal period.

'It is lovely to meet you.' He shook both our hands, his English impeccable and spoken with a slight American accent.

We ran through some details: whether this was our first pregnancy, how far along I was, any expectations we held.

'I keep telling her she should rest,' Milo told him, rubbing a hand along his jaw, which was peppered with short stubble. 'My fiancé is a chef and she doesn't stop, always running round, up and down the stairs. It's not good for the baby, right?'

I didn't recognise this chattering Milo. It seemed he had caught my nerves in the waiting room, while I felt relaxed now, sitting back in the leather chair.

'It is perfectly normal.' Locjan gave a practised smile. 'In fact, for first time mothers we recommend carrying on with life as normal for as long as feels right to you. It will help with the transition, and help us monitor how things are going with the pregnancy.'

'Oh,' Milo said, sneaking a glance my way.

It was strange being in this world where we were referred to as Mum and Dad, and everything was centred around the baby. It was a peek into a future I'd never made the decision to have, but I couldn't help the flutter of excitement in my stomach. At least it beat the never-ending, low-grade nausea.

We talked about my family history and any details I knew about my mum's pregnancy with me. The time passed quickly, and I felt my nerves dissipate with each dazzling smile Locjan gave us. We worked out that I was around nine weeks' pregnant, based on my last period, and made an appointment for my first scan in a few weeks' time. I realised that would be a few days before the wedding. I didn't realise I was this far along; I thought maybe I'd be six or seven weeks. My mind whirred: the fact that I'd be getting married in my second trimester; the thought of the nights out I'd had drinking alcohol whilst pregnant. Was I already a bad mother? Disorganised, doomed? Things were going so fast.

'Before I set you free, I just want to get a feel for what support you have around you. Baby's grandparents to start?' Locjan smiled encouragingly.

Milo and I looked to each other, not knowing where to start. Our situation was complicated to say the least.

'Well, my father passed away two years ago, and my mum splits her time between the UK and here,' I started, noticing the micro-movement in Locjan's eyebrow, the tiny flicker of concern.

'My mother is no longer with us,' Milo said, 'and my father ... will be around some of the time.' His face gave nothing away.

'It is important you have lots of support, people to lean on, as it sounds to me that you are both busy people. You will need help when baby arrives.'

There would be plenty of support, with Rosa, Luka and Natalija. But I wondered how difficult things would be when Mum was in the UK? My uneasy feelings resurfaced.

'I will leave you to have those important conversations. Do you have any more questions before we finish today?'

Milo and I shook our heads and before we knew it, we were outside in the sun-drenched car park.

'Oh, I should have asked about my vitamins,' I said, slapping my head.

'Right, we're going back in.' Milo grabbed my hand.

'No.' I pulled free. 'That can wait until the next appointment.'

'Are you sure?' He frowned.

'Yes, stop worrying. You're worse than ... well, everyone I know.'

'I just want our baby to be healthy. And you too.' Milo stroked my arm.

'I don't come first anymore?' I joked.

'You will always come first.' Milo smiled. 'Kat, we're having a baby.'

I didn't know car parks in doctors' offices could be romantic, but as Milo pulled me towards him for a kiss and a tight hold, I felt so unbelievably happy.

'I'm sorry I've got to go out,' Milo said as he got into the car. He'd come in just to change into his work shirt, emblazoned with the business's logo, and I was waving him off.

'Don't worry, you couldn't cancel the Ryknelds.' I smiled, knowing Milo would have cancelled in a heartbeat if I'd let him. 'They're our main source of income at the moment.' The local hotel owner paid extortionate prices to charter Milo's boat for the afternoon. Last week he'd paid my monthly salary to be taken to some fancy dog groomers in Budva.

'I'd love to come in, though,' Milo sighed, 'celebrate with you. We're nine weeks pregnant.'

'I know, that shocked me too.' I kissed his forehead through the open window of the car, and walked to the door. I heard Milo toot the horn and drive away. The sun was baking hot on my neck, the pain of repeated sunburn prickling my skin. I hurried inside to the cool of our house.

It was rare that I had a whole day off from Café Lompar. Most days I worked at least the evening shift, sometimes lunch too. As much as I longed for the time off, I always felt at a loose end, with half of my identity as a chef missing. I had an urge to make balsamic tomatoes on toast, cook something delicious for myself and the new companion growing in my stomach.

There was something I had to do first, though.

I slipped my sandals off and padded up the carpeted stairs to the bedroom. My mind had been unsettled on the car journey home, calculating how far along I'd be at the wedding, feeling the strain of my stomach against my simple linen dress. Although I hadn't got visibly bigger to other people, I could tell there had been a change in my body. It felt as if I was swelling, taking on water, weight and worries.

My fingers fumbled for the familiar silk bag in the back of the wardrobe, the creamy material that had felt so luxurious and special just weeks ago. I hadn't tried on my wedding dress since I'd first seen it in the shop. It fit perfectly then, slim to my skin, but comfortable and with plenty of room. Would I still fit into it?

I slipped the zip down and admired the shimmering material.

'Here we go.' I shook off the maxi dress I was wearing. I would need a whole new wardrobe in a few months, maternity clothes to suit the Montenegrin heat.

The dress still slid up my legs, tightening a little as it got over my bum. It was fine though, and I let out the breath I'd been holding as I was able to pull the material up, settling the straps over my shoulders. I'd forgotten how gorgeous this dress was. I felt like a supermodel wearing it.

My moment of relief didn't last long though. When I turned, I could see the zip in the centre of my back was never going to meet. I could pull it up a few centimetres, but I soon felt it digging a channel in my skin. I was winded with each new centimetre of zip closed. It would never make it to the top. And this was now, let alone after another few weeks.

I shoved the dress down, with less care for the delicate material. I took the thing off and hung it back up, then collapsed on the bed in my bra and pants, too exhausted and frustrated to get dressed again.

I stared at it, as it taunted me from the wardrobe door, the slim fish-tail shape mocking me for ever thinking I'd get to wear it. It was all the parties I'd miss out on, the spontaneous trips away with Milo, the late nights. All a closed door now.

I stayed on the bed for a long time, too tired to move, then decided I needed help.

I texted Mum to invite her over for a coffee and cake. I'd forgotten whether she was working in Café Lompar today, but I wanted to see her.

Be there in 10 x, her reply pinged.

The message was short, to the point, one kiss. It was strange to be getting these sorts of texts from Mum. I didn't know how much to read in to it; sometimes we did send shorter messages. I hadn't seen her since the argument, though, and our communication felt stilted.

I went over the argument again in my mind. Why didn't I think to ask Mum first about Lovro? She joined in every time I waxed lyrical about his talents in the kitchen. He seemed like the natural choice to me. And Café Lompar was such a small family-run affair, I thought Mum and Rosa would automatically be on board. Was I in the wrong? Maybe. It wouldn't be the first time I'd fucked up this year. At least now I could blame pregnancy brain.

I understood why she thought Bojan and Ivan would be better for the position, but now I'd asked Lovro, it would be embarrassing to go back on the offer. Our relationship had taken a knock as it was, and we were in a fragile, post-argument place. I knew he'd understand but I was still reluctant to appoint someone else. It might have been Mum and Rosa's café, but it was my kitchen, surely?

I checked the time and hurriedly pulled my old linen dress on again, grateful that this one at least was roomy enough to move around in. I filled the kettle and plated some brownies I'd made to satisfy my cravings. I plumped cushions, dusted the floor, wanting to make the space nice for her. It was weird to feel this nervous about seeing my mum.

The doorbell rang, and I skipped to answer it, seeing my own tension reflected on her face. Then she smiled and the moment was broken. I reached out to hug her.

'You look beautiful,' she said, following me out to the terrace.

'I don't feel beautiful,' I said. 'I feel big and pregnant.'

'That's ridiculous,' Mum started, but before she could finish, I told her about the dress, the fact that I was nine weeks' pregnant, the impending scan.

'I don't think you're showing at all,' she said in surprise.

'I'm not, but I notice the subtle changes in my body, and that zip was definitely not happy.' I put my face in my hands. 'I was so excited to wear that dress, Mum.'

'It was the perfect dress,' she conceded.

'It was my soulmate. More perfect for me than Milo,' I joked, although the thought of finding a new dress depressed me. It seemed a metaphor for my life now, changing to stretch around the baby.

'Maybe you won't need a new one, the wedding's not that far away now. You won't grow much more in a few weeks. Just watch the cravings.'

'I can't go on a crash diet. It might harm the baby. Are you crazy?' I raised a protective arm to my stomach.

'I didn't mean that,' Mum said, her voice slightly sharp. The tension was still there. I took my elbows off the table. It felt like a no man's land between us.

'I'm sorry,' I said. 'It's just been a big day.'

'I know,' she nodded, the hurt still in her eyes.

'I know it's silly to feel so strongly about the dress – it's just fabric after all – but I was so looking forward to wearing it.' I hoped Mum would understand.

'Mmm.' She didn't say anything else. We both sipped our teas in silence, watching a bird fly overhead, its wings spread out in a show of power and majesty. I envied its freedom, wondering if life was more carefree without arguments, awkwardness and work.

'I've been thinking about Lovro.' I took a deep breath. Mum fixed her eyes on me, brilliant blue beneath her sunglasses. 'I should have come to you first. I realise that now. I thought … well, I suppose I thought the kitchen was my world. My decision to make. But I was wrong, I should have asked you.'

'You should have,' Mum said, tight-lipped. She took a sip of her tea.

'I must say I still think Lovro is the best option.' I needed to be honest, despite her disagreeing. 'I know he's young and not formally trained like the others, but I think he's got the talent.'

'I agree with you he's talented,' Mum sighed. 'He's definitely heading for Head Chef in a few years. He needs a bit of time first, though.'

'I suppose I'd be pretty pissed off if I was Bojan or Ivan and Lovro got the job above me,' I admitted, trying to look at the opposite view.

'True. You don't want a dynamic like that in the kitchen,' Mum agreed.

I nodded, but I was still nervous.

'If you're worried about what to say to Lovro, you can blame it on me, tell him I'd already offered it to the other two. He'll understand.'

I appreciated her offer. 'He will. I can't say it's a conversation I'm looking forward to, but I'll tell him the truth. Covering up a mistake is what's got me in trouble this year.' I still felt the shame of the Ensambla incident.

Mum reached her hand out and took mine across the table. 'I hate it when we fight.'

'Me too.' I squeezed hers. 'I know there were times we didn't exactly see eye to eye when Dad was alive, but we've been so close recently...'

'I love you.' Mum smiled.

'I love you too. I wanted to ask you...' I was excited but I hesitated.

'Yes?'

'Will you walk me down the aisle? Give me away? I've been thinking about it for a while and I want you there with me. It would mean so much.'

The tears in Mum's eyes told me her answer and my eyes filled up in reply.

'I didn't think about it before,' she said. 'Dad would have loved walking you down the aisle.'

'I'll have you both there,' I said, my voice cracking. 'God, I'm an emotional wreck these days. Blame the pregnancy.'

'I've got no excuse,' Mum laughed. 'I would be honoured, Kat. Plus, it will save me from sitting on my own at the wedding.'

'Won't you be with Neil?' I asked, confused.

'We're ... going through a difficult period at the moment. I think he wants to break up with me. In fact, I think we've already broken up.'

'What?' I felt winded all over again. 'What happened? Why didn't you tell me?'

Mum let out a sigh, emotional, exasperated. 'It's been a difficult week. He's been hinting for a while now about us moving in together, me spending more time there with him. I know it sounds ridiculous but I didn't relish the thought of him moving to Meadow Ponsbury. I'm enjoying my own space there. This is new for me.'

'Surely he'd respect that?'

She told me about the argument they'd had the other day, how she felt Neil was giving her an ultimatum. I was shocked. Neil was the perfect man for Mum in so many ways. This seemed so out of character for him.

'This doesn't seem like him. Is there something stressing him out?'

Mum looked thoughtful but eventually said, 'No, this has been going on a while. Maybe it's best that we end it. Maybe it will all be better. Me going back and forth is a bit crazy anyway. I don't need any more distractions; I need to focus on Montenegro.'

'And you're happy about that?'

'Not exactly *happy*,' she said. Mum wouldn't meet my eye now. I could read her misery like a book. The sleepless nights she'd had were written on her face in plain English.

'Look at you, Mum. You're clearly not okay. I've never said this out loud...' I took a deep breath. This was something I'd felt inside but never acknowledged before. 'I knew when you and Dad were together that you didn't have the best relationship.'

She opened her mouth to protest but I carried on. 'Not like you and Neil do. He clearly worships you, Mum. You've been so happy with him. If this is how he feels, and if you can't make it work then fine, that's life, but shouldn't you try?'

'I have tried, I've told him how I feel,' Mum said wretchedly.

'Over the phone and through messages probably, but I think

306

you need to do something to show him how much you care about this. You don't want to move in together, but you do want to be with him. You need to show him that.'

'This isn't some cheesy rom com. I can't just fly back and turn up on his doorstep.'

'Why not? Rosa and I will cover at Café Lompar. Luckily Bojan's back from holiday and Maria said she'd work some shifts while she's back from uni. You could book a flight tomorrow. Today, even! You'll be back in time for the wedding.'

Mum looked up. I couldn't read her expression now, but I hoped she was thinking about it.

'To misquote Miranda in the finale of *Sex and the City:* "Go get our guy."'

With my heart racing, I waved Mum off. I felt excited for her. I knew she was making the right decision going after Neil, and I couldn't wait to hear how it went. It was all so romantic.

I knew exactly what I'd do when they were back together. I'd finalised the table plans for the wedding a few weeks ago, and put Neil and Ollie together on a table with some other Café Lompar staff. He needed to be at the top table, though. Right next to Mum.

It wasn't like Neil was replacing Dad. But he was perfect for Mum, and he needed to be there with her at her daughter's wedding. Firmly a part of the family. I fired off a quick email to my wedding planner at the venue to let her know we needed one more seat at the top table.

Two minutes later my phone was ringing with her number.

'Hello?'

'Kat Lompar? I was pretty surprised to get your email.'

'Oh?'

The wedding planner's voice sounded stiff, uncomfortable. 'I thought the wedding was cancelled.'

'Cancelled?' I could only repeat her words, hearing the absurdity of it as I spoke. I waited for more but nothing came. 'No, it's not cancelled. Why did you think that?'

'Well, your sister told me last week about the fight with Milo, the break-up. We've booked another couple in for that date now.'

'What?!' I practically shouted. Was this some elaborate practical joke?

'I don't have a sister... Milo and I haven't broken up,' I shook my head even though she couldn't see me. 'The wedding isn't cancelled.'

'But your sister came with her husband last week. They said they were cancelling it on your behalf, that you were too upset to let us know yourself.' She sounded calm, certain.

'What?' My head was spinning now, sheer panic creeping in. 'It's a mistake.'

'But we've cancelled everything. The flowers, the band, the...'

I stopped listening. I couldn't process what was happening.

And then it clicked in to place.

'What did this woman look like? The one who said she was my sister?'

'Let me think... blonde, short, curly hair. Her husband was tall. I think I recognised them from somewhere. They work at...'

I finished the sentence for her. 'Ensambla.'

My body turned cold. Lovro was right. Lizzie and David had fought back.

CHAPTER THIRTY-SIX

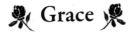 Grace

The flight was booked and I was quickly shoving some clothes into a suitcase when the doorbell rang.

'Luka? Come in,' I said, with as much enthusiasm as I could muster. I had under an hour before the taxi was picking me up. 'Is everything okay?'

'Oh, are you going away?' he asked, seeing some of my clothes strewn on the sofa with the open suitcase beside them.

'I'm popping over to the UK for a few days to see Neil. Kat says that there's enough staff at Café Lompar.'

'Sure,' he smiled, in his typical, easy-going way. Then he flopped down into the armchair.

'If you want tea, do you mind making it yourself?' I said, trying not to sound too rude. 'The taxi will be here soon.'

'I have some good news. I passed my exams!'

'That's amazing, Luka. Well done. Phew, that's a relief.' I exaggerated wiping the sweat from my forehead.

'Yes, it is.' He paused. 'Do you think I should tell my mother? Tell her the truth?'

'I don't think so. Why tell her now? She is none the wiser and perhaps that's better.' I started folding some t-shirts from my wardrobe into the suitcase. 'You carry on,' I shouted from the bedroom as I rifled through some clothes. 'I am listening.'

'*None the wiser?* You English have funny sayings. You see, the thing is I worry that I am not up to this. A law degree. I passed, yes, but by a small margin.'

'I bet lots fail first time,' I said, coming into the living room.

He nodded. 'But it is so hard.'

'Luka?' I paused in the middle of folding some more t-shirts. 'Are you not enjoying your course?'

Luka shrugged, 'Not really. My mother will kill me if I give up, though.'

'I didn't realise you felt like this. If you are unhappy, I'm sure your mother will understand.' I felt for him but, God, I didn't have time for this.

'Do you know what I really want?' he said in a rush. 'I want to become a business man like Milo. I have been looking at courses. I could do a part-time course in Dubrovnik. There is one in Business Management. It would give me more time to help at Café Lompar.'

Rosa wouldn't be too happy with that, I thought, but kept it to myself. 'Look, you mustn't let this one blip put you off.'

'Blip?' he said, puzzled.

'This obstacle, this problem. Don't take it to heart.'

'I have been thinking of this for a while. Don't you think it would suit me better? And Milo has told me he would let me work with him, even consider going into a partnership in time.'

'That's good of him. You are good with customers.'

'Exactly. Perhaps you could mention it to my mother?'

'But, Luka, I will be away for a few days. Don't you think it's better that you tell her? Be a man. I don't mean that exactly...' I could barely concentrate.

310

'Things are still a bit awkward between us. I know that she has ended it with Matija, but she is quiet, withdrawn. Have you noticed?'

I bit my lip, knowing that Rosa had been distracted about her scan. Luka didn't need another excuse to stay at home. It sounded as if he had made up his mind, anyway.

'I'm really sorry. I wish I had more time to chat. You know you can talk to me. But my advice is that you talk to your mother. Tell her the truth. I always find that is the best way.' I thought about how I had prevaricated with Neil and wished I took my own advice more.

Luka stood up. He may have been twenty but he looked like a little boy. 'I am sorry, Grace. I know you have to go and I won't keep you any longer. I will tell her how I feel,' he said, with resolution.

I watched him walk along the promenade, mingling with the tourists, looking as if the world was on his shoulders. He needed his father at a time like this. What would Danilo have said? He was hardly around when he was alive.

That man had shared himself so thinly, never really being there for any of us. It reminded me of when Kat had told him she wanted to go to catering college. He made her feel awful, as if she had let him down. I felt anger surge inside me as I thought of how selfish he'd been. Kat was right, though. Neil made me happy and he loved me. But was that enough? Could we make it work?

Claire was waiting outside in the short stay car park at Bristol Airport in her little, yellow Volkswagen, the daisy bobbing on the dashboard. I'd recognise it anywhere. She gave me a quick hug.

'We'd better get moving sharpish. My time is running out here and it costs a bloody fortune,' she said. 'Ugh, this flipping rain.'

I slung my bags in the boot and hopped in beside Claire. 'Yeah, it is a bit of a shock after Montenegro. It was thirty-five degrees there yesterday.'

'Don't' she said, as she switched on the engine and windscreen wipers. 'Well, this is a surprise visit! So close to the wedding, too.'

'Kat encouraged me. She said I should see Neil face to face. Put my cards on the table. Try and make it work.'

'I'll ignore the fact that I've been telling you the same thing for the last couple of weeks.' Claire pulled out of the airport. 'Look at this arsehole!' She put her middle finger up to the closed window. 'Wanker!'

'I certainly don't miss the city traffic. Or your driving!' I felt shattered after the rush to make the flight.

As we turned on the A4, cars snaked ahead of us and Claire sighed. 'At least it's the tail end of the rush hour. I seem to be permanently on the road these days, dropping Liam off at work and then picking Laura up from the salon. I can't wait until they can drive, although I've got a funny feeling I'll regret those words.'

'Are they still both nagging for a car?'

'They want a car each, which is impossible. They think money grows on trees, that pair.'

I laughed. 'I seem to remember Mum and Dad saying that to us.'

'True.' Claire revved up the engine as we inched forward. 'When are you going to see Neil? Are you calling him first?'

My stomach filled with butterflies. 'I'm going to use the element of surprise and call in tomorrow. He usually starts at lunchtime on Thursdays. I don't quite know what I'm going to say yet. I mean, he might be all loved up with Cathy Shaw for all I know.'

'I wouldn't worry too much about Cathy Shaw. I don't think Neil's her type.'

'I thought he was every woman's type?'

'I heard she's moved in with a woman she met online. It was one of the reasons she split from her ex.'

'Wow, I did not see that coming!' I grinned. 'So, she genuinely wanted to learn to play golf. That's a novelty.' I reached for chewing gum in the glove compartment. 'How's things with Stu?'

'Okay. We're getting there. Having a bit of time apart has helped. I think we were too much in each other's pockets. You know what I mean? I've booked a spa weekend with some of the women from my old school and I need to do more of that.'

'Definitely,' I agreed. 'How did the session go with the counsellor?'

'As awkward as I imagined. Long silences when no one spoke. She's this grandmotherly type, with a grey bun and a knitted cardi. Then she'll come out with the most intimate questions like *Claire, what do you fantasise about when you and Stuart are making love?* It's hilarious and cringeworthy at the same time. We did have a good laugh about it afterwards.'

'That's a good sign.'

Claire nodded. 'It's a shame he won't be able to make Kat's wedding. He would have loved to give her away.'

I smiled. 'She asked me to do it before I left.'

'That's lovely,' Claire said, kissing my cheek, after she stopped the car outside Willow Cottage.

'Coffee?'

Claire laughed. 'You'd be devastated if I said yes. You enjoy a hot bath and a glass of wine. I'll see you tomorrow. Tell me everything after you've seen Neil.'

My stomach churned as I stood on Neil's doorstep, regretting not phoning first. I had a key, but as we hadn't spoken for the last two weeks, it wouldn't have been right to use it. What if he was in bed with another woman? The thought made me feel sick. Before I could change my mind, I rang the bell.

I could hear his bare feet on the floorboards. Then the door was flung open and he was standing before me in the shorts and t-shirt he wore to bed, his hair all tousled. His eyes widened when he saw me, but there was no flicker of a smile. God, this was a mistake.

He opened the door to let me pass. 'Well, this is a surprise. You'd better come in.'

'Not if you don't want me to.'

He smiled. 'Don't be silly, Gracie. Of course, I want you to come in.'

I couldn't stop the smile spreading across my face. Perhaps there was hope for us.

'Coffee?' he said and I followed him into the kitchen. 'How did you manage to get away? Is instant okay?'

I nodded. 'We have enough staff on. It was Kat who encouraged me to come over. Well, I wanted to. I needed to see you.'

I looked around the kitchen and could see the dishes piled in the sink, a loaf on the counter with a knife and butter. A fly buzzed on the window sill. Neil was usually very tidy, a bit of a neat freak. This was so unlike him.

'If I'd known you were coming, I would have tidied up a bit.' He looked sheepish. He handed me a coffee and I sat opposite him at the breakfast bar, feeling nervous. 'So, why did you come over, Grace?'

'Because I've missed you. Because I'm not ready to give up on us.' I felt the tears threaten at the corners of my eyes. 'Because I think we can make things work if we really want, if we really try.' I hadn't meant it to tumble out like this.

He reached over for my hand and laced his fingers through mine. 'I've missed you, too. Missed you desperately. I just thought you didn't want a relationship, that you weren't ready for it.'

'That's not true!' I said quietly. 'Neil, you have to listen to me, really listen.' I took a deep breath.

He sat back and took his hand out of mine. 'Go on. Why don't you explain. Enlighten me. Sorry, I didn't mean that to sound sarcastic.'

'When we met each other just over a year ago, I'm not sure I was ready for love. I wanted to be on my own. Can you imagine what it's like to find your whole life has been a complete lie? The person you loved and that you thought loved you had been involved with someone else for years? The cruelty was breathtaking.' It still hurt when I thought about it and I brushed a tear away.

'I'm not saying all this so that you feel sorry for me,' I went on. 'I don't know if I'll ever get over it completely. My emotions were all over the place. I couldn't grieve properly. I was angry, upset. And then finding this family. It made it all so real. More hurtful. Rosa is beautiful, ten years younger than me. My confidence was at an all-time low. Kat deciding to stay was the last straw, almost, and it took some getting used to. It felt, in a way, as if I was being betrayed again. Pathetic, I know.'

'Not pathetic,' Neil said. 'It's understandable.'

I nodded, not trusting myself to speak.

He sighed. 'And then I came along.'

'Yes, you came along. The attraction was instant.' I smiled.

'It was pretty steamy. I hadn't felt like that about anyone for years.'

'I didn't want to fall in love with you. I tried hard not to. But I couldn't help myself. And I had just bought the cottage in Meadow Ponsbury. It was the first time I had my own place. I met Dan in my first year at uni and all my adult life I was with him. It was only after he died, I could see what was wrong with our relationship.' I paused, sipping my coffee, wondering how much to say. 'I could see clearly how controlling he was, how selfish. I'd been suffocated. Look, I'm not saying I felt anything like that with you, but I just need time to myself. And if it sounds like a bad movie, I'm sorry, but I need to find myself. Do you understand?'

'I do, yes.' He looked into my eyes. 'Where does that leave us?'

'Are you willing to wait for me? Carry on as we are? I love you. It's just that I want my own space, too. Can you accept that? I'd just be going over for the summer months. Although Kat is pregnant, so I will be popping over regularly, but I'd like us both to go. What do you think, Neil?'

316

'You mean I'd be dating a granny?' he laughed. 'Come here, you.' He wrapped his arms around me. 'That's fantastic news. I haven't congratulated you yet.' He kissed my forehead and I felt the relief wash over me.

When we sat back down, Neil became serious. 'Since I've come back, I've had time to think. I've missed you like hell and I realise I've been a complete fool. Part of it was that Cass is getting married. You were right, annoyingly! I wanted to prove I'd moved on. It was an ego thing.' He shrugged. 'Look, I want us to carry on. Having you part of the year is better than not having you at all. This is too good to let it slip through my fingers.'

I realised I was grinning like an idiot.

'I do want to make some changes, though,' he said. 'I want to move out of the city and perhaps cut my hours at the golf club. It would mean I could come over more often with you to Tivat.'

'That would be great.'

He reached for his phone. 'I don't know what you think about this, but there's a house for sale in Meadow Ponsbury. That cul-de-sac of newly-built houses off Honeysuckle Lane.'

The photographs showed a modern house, all open plan with floor to ceiling windows. I grinned when I saw the free-standing, claw-footed bath on a platform in the master bedroom. 'Typical,' I laughed.

'Just imagine.' He winked.

'So, you'd be in Meadow Ponsbury but just half a mile away? Perfect. The best of both worlds.' I kissed him.

I sat on Neil's bed as he showered and we chatted about the wedding.

He emerged from the bathroom, a small towel wrapped around his hips. 'I'm so glad you're staying for a bit and we can fly out for the wedding together. I'm going to ask George about my hours at the club when I'm back and things are more settled,' he said.

'What time do you have to be in work,' I asked, easing the knot from his towel, as we fell onto the bed.

My phone buzzed on Neil's bedside cabinet and I squinted to look at the time. Shit, it was ten past eight. I'd fallen asleep and Neil was snoring next to me. Kat's name lit up the screen.

'Mum, oh Mum' she wailed, as soon as I picked up.

Neil stirred and I tried to quell the panic I felt. 'What is it, love?'

'The wedding's off!' she announced dramatically.

All grogginess I felt on waking had disappeared. 'Have you and Milo argued?'

'No, no,' her voice rose. 'I called the venue this afternoon and everything has been cancelled – the flowers, the food, the ceremony.'

'It has to be a mistake, surely.'

'No, it was David and Lizzie. They did it. She posed as my sister and cancelled everything.'

'The bastards!'

Neil sat up, mouthing *What's happened?*

'I can't believe they'd stoop so low.'

'What can I do?' Kat asked. I put her on speaker phone, her panic filled the room.

'Let me think. We can sort it.' Turning to Neil, I tried to bring him up to speed. 'The wedding venue has been cancelled. Everything. And it's so close now.'

'There must be somewhere else she can have it.' Neil said.

'At such short notice?' I could hear Kat sobbing now. 'Hold it together, Kat. Look, it's not as if you'd planned a big wedding. I'll come back out tomorrow and we can phone around.'

'I'm coming, too,' said Neil. 'I can help.'

I nodded, grateful he looked as distraught as I felt.

'What about Café Lompar?' Neil said. 'Could Kat hold the wedding there? You can't get a better location.'

'At her own restaurant? I don't think that would work and...'

Kat cut me off, 'Neil's right! We could hold it there. We haven't got much time to plan, but I suppose it could be done. I can't think where else we can have it.'

'Tell Rosa,' I said. 'She'll make it work. That woman is a force of nature. We'll be out tomorrow or the day after and we'll all pull together.' I didn't stop to think how odd it was that I saw Rosa, Dan's mistress, as so much part of us now.

Kat had calmed down as I rang off. I kissed Neil a dozen times on his face, laughing. 'You're a genius!'

CHAPTER THIRTY-SEVEN

❧ Kat ❧

The noises coming from the monitor sounded familiar but also surreal, sounds I'd only heard before in movies and medical dramas. My heartbeat, slow and regular, thudded against the gel probe on my stomach. The fetching gown I'd been made to wear was gaping open and my skin shivered in the air-conditioned doctor's office.

Locjan stood to the side, scribbling in my file, while the older, hirsute doctor, with a stethoscope slung around her neck, examined me. She frowned at the screen, moving the probe around and pressing it further into my skin.

Milo noticed and looked to me with concern. I tried to give a little shrug.

Everything was going to plan so far. It was my twelve-week scan. Just two days before the wedding.

The wedding that was hurriedly being put together by Rosa and various other Café Lompar staff members. The wedding being cancelled had felt like the worst possible twist of fate, but as soon as Neil had suggested holding it at the restaurant, I knew everything would work out well. It felt right. Of course we should have it at Café Lompar. Why didn't I think of that all along? I got caught up in the Pinterest dream of a fancy wedding on an island. But a home-spun, last-minute DIY wedding would be perfect.

If we could pull it off, that was.

I tried to drown out any panic by finding something to focus on. The doctor's monobrow did a great job. It was stern, giving nothing away.

Milo squeezed my hand as the doctor muttered something to Locjan in Montenegrin. He was here to translate as our local obstetrician didn't speak English.

Locjan smiled at us reassuringly, then twisted to see the screen when the doctor spoke.

'*Blizanci*,' she said, her eyebrow rising.

'*Blizanci*?' My lovely midwife looked surprised now.

I looked to Milo, who looked about to vomit. My brain struggled to translate. I'd not learnt this word yet, a word that was making everyone act so oddly. Milo said something in Montenegrin and the doctor nodded her head.

'I'll let you tell her, Dad,' Locjan said, a big grin now on his face.

'Kat,' Milo breathed, squeezing my hand tighter in both of his, 'we're having twins.'

I felt my whole world shift. An out of body experience. No. This couldn't be true.

Twins?

I'd never signed up for twins.

'Do they run in the family?' Locjan asked, leaning forwards.

'I ... I suppose they do, my cousins are twins, but...' I stammered.

Milo was staring at me. It was as though neither of us knew

how to react and was waiting for the other to give the cue to the right response. I didn't know if I was going to cry or scream.

I laughed.

Slowly at first, disbelieving, but then it built, as I thought about the shock I'd had that I was pregnant with one child, then that I was about four weeks further along than I thought, and now we were having *twins*.

Milo looked surprised, unsure, but then he joined in too. Tears were streaming down my face.

When two became four...

What would Mum say? Somewhere out there, I felt my dad was looking down on me and laughing too.

'*Izgled*,' the doctor said sternly, and I took Milo's cue to look at the screen. And there they were, our two babies, our two boys or girls, our whole world. Dark fuzzy shapes on a screen that caused an overpowering love to swell in my chest. I was still crying, but definitely not laughing now. I was growing those two innocent, perfect beings inside me, my two babies. Two lives who had never been on a plane or seen the colour of the Adriatic on a summer's day, who'd never sworn or been hungover, never danced or laughed or cried. I loved every single atom of them.

'Do you want to know the sex?' Locjan asked.

Milo and I looked at each other. We'd discussed this before the scan, agreeing that if they could tell this early then we wanted to know. Of course, then we thought there was only one baby waiting for us.

We both nodded vigorously, and Locjan had another hurried conversation with the doctor.

'I'm sorry.' He turned back to us and my heart stopped. 'We cannot tell today. Too soon.'

'That's all right.' My cheeks felt raw and wet from crying.

'At the next scan.' Locjan mimed time passing.

I didn't care. I felt on top of the world, my family unit of four along with me.

I was desperate to speak to Mum and tell her the news, but I wanted to tell her in person and she was coming out tomorrow for the wedding. It could wait until then, although the excitement I felt inside was intense. I had to tell someone. I needed someone to share our joy.

Luka felt like the right person, and Milo and I drove over to Rosa's house, hoping to catch them both before they went in for the shift at Café Lompar. The hairpin bend as you came to their house always made my breath catch. The car suddenly emerged from the trees to a sweep of ocean, brilliant blue, as if the house was on the edge of the world.

Milo pulled the car up outside, then gave my leg a little pat.

'Twins?' he said to me before we got out.

'Twins,' I breathed. It was all we'd been able to say to each other since we'd come from the doctor's.

'Trust us,' he laughed.

'Well, we don't do things by halves.'

I had a funny memory of Dad saying that same phrase to me when I started working in catering college. 'I'm in such awe of you.' I knew catering college wasn't his first choice of career for his daughter, but he learnt that I was made for it. It meant so much to me when he finally said he was proud.

'Come on,' I said to Milo, opening the car door. 'We will need to rely on this pair when we have two children to look after.'

We rang the bell at Rosa's one-storey, whitewashed building, the bougainvillea in full summer bloom framing the door.

Luka answered and beckoned us inside, miming for silence as Rosa talked on the phone.

'In two days' time,' she was saying. She saw us and waved. 'Yes, Café Lompar, in Tivat... Thank you very much.'

'That sounded important,' I said.

'That was a local band. I used to know the lead singer,' Rosa said.

'I don't want to know details,' Luka held up a hand in disgust.

'They've agreed to come to Café Lompar at short notice, ready for the wedding!' Her smile lit up, and I felt I could jump, already on a high from the scan. 'It's all coming together, Kat. Don't you worry about a thing!'

'I feel bad sitting back and letting people do everything for me.'

'You'll be covering Café Lompar this afternoon so don't worry about that,' Luka said.

'Were the reservations okay about the cancellation?' I worried about Café Lompar losing a day's trade and having to cancel bookings.

'We offered a fifty percent discount if they rebook next weekend,' Rosa explained. 'All we need to sort out now is the catering. I'm sure Bojan and Ivan could do it, as well as being guests.'

'I don't want them to have the stress though. They're my friends,' I sighed.

Rosa moved on. 'I'm working on it. Anyway, enough about that. How's the pregnancy?' She touched her hand to my stomach. I was getting used to this new thing where people ignored me and felt they could speak directly to my midriff. From Lovro's singing at me (Britney Spears, of course) to Milo's constant rubbing, I felt I was less interesting than my stomach.

'Well...' I looked to Milo, knowing at least one of us would have to talk. 'We've just had some big news.'

'We're having twins,' Milo said, and I felt the pressure build up again in my head, laughter and tears at the same time. I hoped the emotional incontinence would stop, although seeing the delight on Rosa and Luka's faces was enough to send me over the edge. Milo was wiping his eyes too.

'God, what are we going to be like on our wedding day?' I asked him, shaking my head.

'Twins are a gift,' Rosa said. 'My mother always used to say that twins are very lucky, a blessing.'

'I don't know about that. More a nightmare,' I laughed.

'Kat, I'm going to wind those kids up all the time,' Luka joined in now. 'Come to Uncle Luka!'

'That sounds creepy,' I said.

Rosa laughed, rubbing her side. 'We needed that. It's been a day of revelations.'

'What do you mean?' Milo asked.

'I told Mum this morning. I had to re-sit my exams,' Luka said.

'Oh, Luka,' I soothed, at the same time as Rosa spoke up.

'I wish you'd told me. A mother should know these things.'

He shot her a withering look, one that was almost comical.

'So, what happened with the exams?'

325

'I passed but ... I don't know.' Luka sighed again, leaning his head forward on his chin. 'I think there's a reason I failed the first time. My heart isn't in this course. I've been thinking it for a while. I like law but I can't see myself doing this forever.'

'That's important,' I nodded, remembering how it felt when Dad had encouraged me to do a course I wasn't keen on. He wanted me to be an academic like him, but I knew deep down it wasn't right for me. 'It's important to do something you're passionate about, something you enjoy.'

'Like you and cooking,' Luka agreed. 'I feel I'm letting everyone down, though.'

'That's nonsense,' we all cried.

'If I'd known how you were feeling, I would have told you to do something different a long time ago,' Rosa said.

'I know. It's taken me time to come to terms with it. I always thought Law would be the one.'

'So, what is the one?' I asked.

'I don't know,' Luka admitted. 'This probably sounds crazy but I've been thinking about business. I've always been good with customers...'

'Gift of the gab,' I cut in, then shook my head when I got a confused look for my English phrase.

'And I think I'd be good at it. I'd like to do something like that, I think, start my own company one day.'

'What are you thinking of?'

'Well, there's a business course in Dubrovnik. I could start with that.'

'Or an apprenticeship,' Milo offered. 'You don't really need education to be a businessman. Trust your instincts.'

I smiled at him, knowing that was how Milo had started work. I knew he would have liked a degree or some higher qualification, but he couldn't at the time as he had to look after Natalija.

'That's true,' Luka agreed.

'I could ask one of my cousins,' Rosa started. 'One owns a hotel in Perast. I'm sure he'd be happy for some help and to teach you a few things about running a business.'

'That could be interesting.' Luka smiled.

'Luka, you know we'll be proud of you whatever you do,' I said, wanting to reassure him. 'You don't even need to make a decision now.'

'I've been wanting to expand my boats into the luxury market,' Milo said, tentatively. 'I've started out with some smaller charters, making connections. It's hard to do but it's showing signs of success.'

'It's taking all of your time at the moment, though,' I said, thinking of Milo's late hours and double shifts.

'I wondered about getting some help. Hiring someone to take over that project and help with expansion.'

'Like a business partner?' Luka said, excitedly.

'Not quite,' Milo laughed. 'You're new, but you've worked with me before. Why don't we see how it goes for a while? Have a talk about it tomorrow?'

'OK, partner,' Luka laughed.

'You're brave,' I said to Milo.

'What am I letting myself in for?'

'Finished,' I said to the empty kitchen. The end of a busy shift always felt blissful, and this one was especially so, knowing I was finished now for my wedding. The next time I'd see Café Lompar I'd be wearing a long white dress and carrying a bouquet.

I checked in the fridge, counting the inventory and making sure we had enough for tomorrow's lunch service. A few waitresses were still in the restaurant clearing up.

'Kat?' Ana popped her head through to the kitchen. 'There are people here to see you. Can I send them in?'

I nodded, then waited. I instantly regretted not asking her who was there. Lizzie and David.

'Hello, Kat,' Lizzie said, at least having the decency to look sheepish.

'Don't say you're coming to cancel my wedding a second time. I know it was you.'

I felt an immediate flare in my chest. It shocked me how angry I felt. It made my voice wobble just when I wanted to seem fearless. I wished I had Mum or Milo by my side.

'We came to apologise,' Lizzie said, holding her arms across her body. 'I feel so awful about what we did.'

David shot her a look of warning.

The tables had turned now, but rather than feeling triumphant, I felt incredibly sad.

'Did you really need to do that?' I clutched the edge of the kitchen counter in support. 'I know what I did was stupid, but this is really spiteful. I don't understand it.'

'I know. It's awful,' Lizzie said.

David was looking at me as though he wanted to say something, but he stopped himself.

'Cancelling my wedding? Ruining plans I'd made for months?' David opened and closed his mouth, but I was on a roll now.

'I didn't want to believe it at first. I thought no way could they have ruined the biggest day of my life, just because I...'

'Oh, stop it!' David finally said. I felt as if I'd been slapped in the face. 'You act all innocent, like your life has been ruined, but you've done worse to other people.'

'Worse?' I felt confused now. Lizzie looked as if she wanted the ground to swallow her up.

'You really don't remember me, do you?' David laughed.

'Remember you?'

'I knew you had no idea who I was. It makes sense. Why would Kat Lompar remember the poor little chef she worked with years ago. A chef she had *fired*?'

The second he said it, everything started to click in to place.

'I was so happy to get that apprenticeship. It was changing my life. But you didn't like me, and lo and behold the next day I was packing my bags, not allowed to work in Truffles again.'

I remembered it all. How had I not recognised him before? Back in London, back when I was an overworked, under-paid and unhappy chef in Truffles, David had been one of the people on a chef apprenticeship scheme. I think he was known as Dave then. He had been a good chef, but he was older than the other apprentices, changing career, and seemed to feel he should be treated as senior to the others – he didn't understand the nuances of the kitchen and resented having to clean up after himself and help the team out. I wasn't the only one with concerns, others had talked about it, but it was my job to report back to our Head Chef. I didn't know David was fired after that. We were told he'd had to leave the course.

No wonder he hated me. He thought I did that to him. Was David looking for revenge?

'Marc Douvall told me quite clearly that Kat Lompar had concerns about my cooking. I'd worked so hard to get on that course, but after that no one would have me. I had to move back in with my parents. I felt like I'd lost everything.'

'But you didn't,' I said. I had no idea what I was going to say until I spoke. 'You're an accomplished chef now. You worked past that.'

'It was bloody hard. No one would accept me because I'd been rejected by the *famous* Truffles.'

'But they did, and you proved us wrong,' I said.

David nodded, looking less sure of himself now.

'I didn't get you fired, David. I might have been the straw that broke the camel's back, but there were issues all along. You were late. You didn't listen to others. You wouldn't help out with cleaning. Those things are important, you know.'

He didn't nod but he didn't protest either.

'I'm so sorry if you felt I ruined things for you, but I was just doing my job. I spoke to Marc, but the decision was all his. I didn't even know you were fired.'

'You expect me to believe that?'

'Well, I'm having a hard time believing that you set up a restaurant here just to get revenge on a sous chef you worked with ages ago.'

'That's not why,' David said.

We stood at an impasse. I didn't know what to feel. I was mad at them, but a tiny morsel of me did feel bad for David. I'd been hot-headed back then and, admittedly, I did tend to moan about people rather than nurturing them and helping them get better. I was young and inexperienced. Could I have worked with David rather than complaining? If I'd spoken to him instead of Marc, maybe he would never have lost his job.

'It's true,' Lizzie said after a while. 'David did want to get back at you.'

'By cancelling my wedding?' I said, flaring again.

David sighed now. 'That wasn't the plan. I just got so mad. Things were going so well with Ensambla...'

'To start with,' Lizzie added.

'After the initial rush of business, though, it died down. I thought we couldn't compete with Café Lompar. Then you changed the date on the poster and I just...'

'Got angry,' I finished this time. I could imagine how he felt.

'It was like you were adding salt in the wound. But I know we shouldn't have done anything to your wedding. Well, it was me that convinced Lizzie to do it. I'm impulsive when I'm angry.'

Where had I heard those words before?

'That's how I felt when you were getting so much success.' I recognised my own desperate actions were because I felt we were losing to Ensambla. 'I guess neither of us gets the prize for neighbour of the year.'

David and Lizzie both smiled awkwardly.

'Why did I have to fall in love with a chef?' Lizzie said. 'You're all so competitive and stubborn. I haven't shown my best colours either.'

'Anyway, we can't compete with you,' David shrugged reluctantly.

I had a strange thought. 'Why are we trying to compete? We're both on the same mission here. To cook good food and have successful restaurants? I don't see why we can't both do that.'

David seemed to consider my words. 'Tivat is big enough to have more than one successful fine dining restaurant.'

'Of course, it is,' Lizzie said.

'And wouldn't it be better if we could help each other? Communicate our menus so we don't clash. Send customers over to the other when we're full?' My mind was racing. 'As cheesy as this sounds, we're probably better together than working against each other.' I wondered how different this summer would have been if I'd taken that view when they arrived. But I couldn't change the past.

Lizzie rushed forwards to give me hug. I didn't know if I was ready for this yet, but I let her hug me anyway.

'I feel so bad for what we did. I'm so sorry, Kat. If there's anything we can do to make it up to you, please let me know.'

'Well. We could start working together now?' David said. 'We heard you're getting married here instead. Do you need any help with extra tables? Or staff?'

I considered it. 'Actually, we are still looking for caterers...'

As we started to discuss it, I wondered if I was being foolish to forgive and trust them now. Working with Ensambla made sense, though. Why hold on to petty grievances? Besides, the last few days had been so emotional. I wanted to look to my future: my wedding and my babies. And David could definitely help with one of those.

The screaming alarm confused me in the early morning light filtering through the curtains. Milo was still in bed next to me, which meant it was before six. I reached across to try to turn the noise off, when I realised it was my phone instead. I groped around but only managed to accidentally decline the call. I

332

picked up my phone, groaning miserably as the bright light seared my eyeballs in the darkness.

Two missed calls from Mum. Before I could do anything, it started ringing again.

Oh no, what's wrong...?

'Hello?' My voice sounded croaky and stale. Milo groaned.

'Hi darling, I'm sorry to wake you.'

'Is everything alright?' I felt more alert now. She sounded worried, panicked, but as if she was trying to hide it from me, which made it all the more terrifying.

'We're at the airport now and our flight's been cancelled to Tivat. Some grumble with the airline.' A tannoy sounded in the background and a muffled voice made some announcement.

'Damn, you won't be here for the fitting,' I said. Milo was awake now, watching me as I spoke to Mum. I shuffled up the bed, propping myself on my elbows. 'Well, there must be other flights.'

'That's the thing,' she said. 'There's been some issue with Eastern Europe flights. Just turn on the news.'

I fumbled for the tv remote on my bedside table, switching on the ancient set on top of our chest of drawers. A news camera showed crowded scenes at different airports, then a reporter. A flashing banner rolled across the bottom of the screen. I recognised the words for 'breaking news', but couldn't understand the rest of the Montenegrin. Suddenly the words disappeared and were replaced with English ones.

I had to rub my eyes in disbelief as I read the words 'Chaos in airports: all flights grounded for at least 24 hours.'

Our wedding was tomorrow.

'Shit,' I cursed down the phone at the same time as Mum.

CHAPTER THIRTY-EIGHT

🌹 Grace 🌹

If I heard Jess Glynn's 'Ready for this' one more time, I was going to scream. I was on the phone to Jet2, who we'd booked our flights to Tivat with. There was a momentary pause, when my hopes rose at the thought of actually speaking to a human, before the track started again.

'Oh, for fuck's sake,' I said, turning to Claire and Stuart. Neil was sitting next to me on his own phone, trying to speak to Ryan Air. All flights to the Balkan Peninsula were grounded because of an air traffic controllers' strike over pay, and I wanted to cry with frustration. We were trying to book flights to Italy, hoping to sail across from Bari to Bar in the south of Montenegro, which was about thirty miles from Tivat. It was so close to the wedding, though, we were unlikely to make it in time.

'I'm so sorry,' Neil said. 'If you hadn't come to see me...'

I gave him a reassuring smile, but my stomach was churning. I had to see Kat married tomorrow. She simply had to have one of her parents there.

'Perhaps they'll come to some agreement and the strike will end,' commiserated Stuart, wincing as he moved in his armchair.

'Fingers crossed,' I said, miserably, 'but there'll be a backlog of flights.' I thought of the angry scene on Sky News earlier of an air traffic controller in Croatia, gesticulating wildly and complaining about conditions and pay, and back in Britain the camera panning the crowded terminal at Bristol Airport with bleary-eyed passengers.

'This is eating into our holiday,' one mother had said irritably, surrounded by three small children. 'We've only booked a week and we've already lost the first night.'

'Sail away' by Enya started in my ear.

Claire's phone buzzed on the table. 'It's Kat,' she said, handing her phone to me, and swapping for mine. 'I hate Enya. Not soothing at all!'

'Hi, darling,' I said to Kat on the screen.

'Any luck?'

'Not so far. I can't seem to speak to anyone at the moment. I've been on hold for the last fifty minutes.'

'Look, Mum, don't stress about it. Milo and I have had a chat and we're going to postpone the wedding. I've got to have you here to give me away.'

'No, you will not! I want you to get married. Luka can give you away.'

Neil interrupted, 'Come hell or high water, we're going to get there for your wedding, Kat. Don't you dare postpone it.'

I smiled at him, seeing his determined face.

He went on, 'I've been looking at alternatives. We can get a flight to Italy. Bari. Then we can get a ferry.'

'The crossing is nearly eight hours,' Kat said, looking tearful. 'Let's be realistic, you'll never make it in time. We could postpone...'

'Do nothing now. Carry on planning,' I insisted. 'If we don't make the actual ceremony, we should get there late afternoon, perhaps early evening. The wedding has to go ahead. You've got your honeymoon booked. You're flying to Antigua on Tuesday.'

'I'm not sure... I know it'll be a story we'll laugh about in the future.' Her words rang hollow. 'There's really nothing we can do about it.'

She was right, of course. Everyone's mood was dampened after the phone call. Neil squeezed my hand.

I thought about the rest of the British contingent hoping to come to Kat's wedding: Zoe and Rachel from catering college; Bea from Truffles, one of the sous chefs, and her boyfriend James. Poor Kat had no one on her side apart from Rosa and Luka and the waitresses from Café Lompar, and Lovro and Davor, of course. Aunt Sofija had a chest infection and would be missing the wedding, in any case. My heart ached thinking of her without any of her British family and friends there. I omitted to say real family, even in my head, as Rosa and Luka were part of our messy clan now.

Laura burst in, 'I lurve them! Look, Mum, Auntie Grace. You're going to be well jel!' She dangled her new inch-long talons proudly in front of us and giggled. 'I can't do a thing with them, though. I can't even pick my nose.' She looked around at our glum faces. 'What's up?'

'It looks like that strike is continuing and we won't fly today. We're not likely to get to the wedding in time,' Claire said.

Laura's eyes swivelled to her bridesmaid's dress, hanging on the back of the living-room door. Inside the zipped cover was a dusty-pink, chiffon dress, with a lace bodice I knew she couldn't wait to wear.

'But we must go,' she wailed. 'We can't miss Kat's wedding. That's awful.'

I nodded mutely. Claire handed me a cup of tea, the umpteenth one, as I waited for the phone to be picked up. The living room felt stiflingly hot, a chemical smell lingering in the air, from all Stu's medication. The sofa bed with sheets and blankets folded on top, was propped in the corner of the room, his bed for the last few weeks. It must have been difficult for him, and now he faced the prospect of everyone leaving him for a week as we flew out to Montenegro. Poor Stu, yet here he was trying to console us.

I became aware of Neil reeling off some numbers as he held his credit card in front of him, 'Yes, for six of us,' he was saying into the phone. 'Flight to Bari.' He turned to me, 'There's one going from Manchester. Ten thirty tonight. I'm booking it.'

I looked at the clock. It was three and we'd have to be in Manchester by eight thirty at least. 'Let's get packed!' I ordered. We'll have to leave in an hour!'

Laura looked mortified, 'But I won't be ready.'

'You'll bloody well have to be,' Claire barked.

An hour later, Neil, Ollie and I were negotiating our way through the traffic in Bath. Claire was following behind with Laura and Liam.

'It's a shame Kat's friends won't make it,' I told Neil for the umpteenth time. 'Still, if we make that six o'clock ferry from Bari, we might just get there in time. Kat says that she'll delay the wedding as long as possible.'

I felt so jittery. The last few weeks had been such a rollercoaster of emotions, with Claire and Stu, Rosa and Luka's problems and then Neil and I almost breaking up. Kat's wedding to Milo and the twins were the best news I'd had in such a long time. I couldn't bear not being there for her on the biggest day of her life. It felt like I was really letting her down. Fate seemed to be conspiring against us.

'Do you think we'll make the ferry?' I asked Neil.

'Hmm, it'll be close,' he said, not taking his eyes off the road. 'The flight is just over five hours. Then there's baggage collection, security. We've got to get across to the ferry terminal by taxi. It leaves six o'clock.' He blew out, 'It'll be tight.'

I knew the next ferry wasn't for a couple of hours. If we missed that six o'clock ferry, we'd miss the wedding.

'I certainly don't miss this traffic in Bath,' I told Neil, imagining the air was blue inside Claire's Volkswagen.

Neil was more patient but he said with feeling, 'I can't wait to move out of the city.'

'Got it!' Ollie said from the back seat. 'Sneaky. Nymph. No real vowels. Unless Y counts as a vowel. Five moves.' He was referring to Wordle he'd been playing on the phone.

'It took you twenty minutes,' I teased.

After that, Ollie fell asleep as we left Bath behind us and made our way on the M5.

'I used to fall asleep like that when I was younger,' Neil commented. 'I'm jealous.'

'Me too,' I agreed. 'I'm so grateful for you doing this. Four grand for the plane tickets. Extortionate. We'll pay you back.'

'I'll do all in my power to get you there,' he vowed.

'I know.'

338

The airport was as torturous as it always is, long queues at check-in, the over-priced sandwiches and lukewarm coffees.

'What a palaver!' Claire moaned as she unlaced her trainers as we went through security. 'I've got backache from the car and earache from Laura fretting about missing the wedding and her chance to wear her bridesmaid's dress. What can I do about it? Teenagers, they're so selfish!'

'Do you think Kat is foolish to trust David and Lizzie to cater? I mean, if they're so vicious that they can cancel someone's wedding? I've got a bad feeling about it.'

'Kat's no pushover. They wouldn't try to jeopardise her ceremony now, not something so public.'

'I hope not.'

We all had separate seats on the plane, and the cabin smelled of lingering flatulence and overcooked chicken chasseur. I couldn't stomach anything and had fitful naps rather than a proper sleep. I was sandwiched between a man who kept his light on most of the flight reading his book and calling the attendant to get him another drink, and an eleven-year-old boy who watched 'The Angry Birds Movie 2' and, despite his headphones, kept laughing uproariously, nudging me every time I was about to drift off.

We arrived in Bari at four in the morning. I was so relieved to rejoin Neil, Claire and the others as we left the plane to catch the bus to the terminal. We all looked crumpled and I felt light-headed and groggy as if I'd been drinking.

'Two hours before the ferry. We might just make it,' Neil said optimistically.

Claire nudged me, 'Look at Laura. She's like a meerkat seeing all these Italian men in the airport. Oh, to be seventeen again!'

'No thanks,' I said. 'Let's get to baggage reclaim as quick as we can and then we can get to the ferry. It's a twenty-minute walk there.'

Mercifully, we received our luggage after half an hour of navel-gazing and watching the same battered suitcases on the carousel.

'Now just passport control,' I said ruefully.

Claire nudged me, 'Look at that.' The queue for EU citizens was moving swiftly and purposefully, the staff in their little cubicles urging people on with a cursory glance at their passports. The Non-EU citizens' queue was a mile long snaking in between the retractable barriers.

'Fucking Brexit!' I muttered.

'Well, this should cheer you up,' Claire said, wryly. 'I've just realised I've left my wedding outfit at home. I can see it hanging on my wardrobe. It'll be beach wear for me when we finally get there.'

We emerged from the airport at twenty to six and hopped into two taxis.

'It's only thirteen kilometres,' Neil said.

'I don't think my nerves can stand it!' I said, my heart thumping in my chest.

'Well, the next one's at eight, so we will get to Podgorica.' He didn't articulate what we were all thinking, that we would miss the wedding.

CHAPTER THIRTY-NINE

🌿 Kat 🌿

It was lovely, seeing the glistening in everyone's eyes as I came down the stairs. I'd dreamt of this moment for months and months.

'What do you think?'

'You look gorgeous,' the girls cooed, standing up to give me a hug. Natalija, Maria, and Rosa were getting ready at mine and had been sipping Prosecco since early this morning. It seemed the Montenegrin branch of the bridal party were well oiled at least, as Maria wiped a tear from the corner of her eye.

'Can you tell I'm nearly three months' pregnant?' I don't know why I asked as I didn't believe their cries of protest. 'At least I've managed to cover the disaster of fitting in to the dress.'

'Let's see,' Rosa asked and I spun around. 'I don't see anything.'

I lifted my veil out of the way, revealing the ties and buttons I'd had sewn in by a Montenegrin dressmaker at the last minute. The effect wasn't quite the same, but I didn't mind. My life was changing forever and I was ready to adapt to it. I hadn't been planning on wearing a long veil, it felt a little OTT, but it was the best way to hide the alterations.

'Genius,' Maria laughed.

'You look a million dollars,' Natalija said, 'or a million euros. My brother is going to be over the moon.'

'I hope so,' I smiled, but I felt sick inside. 'I'm so nervous. All those eyes on me walking up the aisle. I don't know if I can do it. I had a dream last night that I tripped on the veil and knocked my teeth out on a church pew.'

'Isn't that meant to be good luck?' Natalija said.

'It didn't feel like good luck,' I grimaced.

'You'll be fine, the wedding will run smoothly. Café Lompar is ready and looks wonderful. I can't wait for you to see it, Kat.' Rosa came over to smooth some of my hair down under my veil.

'Thank you so much, Rosa,' I didn't doubt it. 'I think I'm more nervous about the others making it in time. Mum texted to say she's on the boat now, but it's the later one.'

Everyone shuffled uncomfortably, knowing there was nothing they could say. How could I get married without my family there? Rosa and Luka were so important to me, but they felt as much a part of Milo's family as mine. I needed my mum. Not just to walk me down the aisle, but to hold my hand, to be there for my big day.

'Maybe we could just delay a few hours,' I said, desperately. 'I'll call Mum again.'

It seemed the signal on the boat was patchy at best. 'Hello.... Hello... Kat, we're...'

'I can't hear you,' I said, worried I was making my dress sweaty with the stress of it all. I sighed. This was not how my wedding day was meant to start. It was times like these when I missed the lack of alcohol keenly. Natalija and Maria were infinitely less stressed as they sipped away from their champagne flutes.

'That's it, can you hear me now?'

'Yes.' Finally. 'What time do you think you'll be here?'

'We've just asked the staff. They think about four.'

Perfect. That was only two hours after the wedding was meant to start. If we just delayed, then they would be there. I explained my thoughts to Mum, but was cut off with protests from the whole family.

'No, you have to go ahead with it. You don't want to rush the rest of the day. We arrive into Kotor at four, but it will be later by the time we're there,' Mum said. I could hear the dejection in her voice, although she tried to put on a brave front. 'I'm so sorry we haven't made it, darling.'

'Don't, Mum,' I said, my voice cracking. 'It's not your fault.'

'At least we'll be there for the food and the party.'

'At this rate I'll be wearing a kaftan and a towel on my head,' I heard Aunt Claire say in the background.

'She's forgotten her outfit,' Mum explained. I laughed, relieved to have a distraction for a moment.

'She can borrow something of mine,' Rosa said, listening in to the conversation.

I moved to the next room, shutting the door. I wanted a private moment with Mum. She must have sensed my mood as I could hear the chatter of the others fall away on the other end of the line.

'You must be shattered now, after travelling all night?'

'We're coping. I managed to have a brief snooze on the plane, but poor Neil is running on caffeine alone.'

'Are you sure I can do this, Mum? I've dreamed of you giving me away for months,' I said. 'I can't imagine doing it without you there.'

'It's your wedding, Kat. Today is about you and Milo, not me.

I'm desperate to be there, and don't worry, I will be by the end of the day. The ceremony is just one small part of it. It's not the be all and end all,' she soothed.

'I know,' I sighed. I took a deep breath. 'I know we live far apart for most of the year, and I know we weren't so close when Dad was around, but you're my best friend. More than that, you're the most important person in the world to me.' I heard a sniff at the other end of the line. 'I'm so lucky to have you as my mother.'

'Sweetheart, I feel exactly the same, I'm the luckiest mother in the world,' she said. I smiled to myself. 'We've achieved a lot in the last few years, haven't we? I couldn't have done it without you. You deserve to be happy.'

'And I think the best times are to come. Especially now you're back with Neil and I have these two on the way,' I rested my hand on my swelling stomach.

'And I'll be there for all of it. Even if I'm not there at the ceremony today.'

'Okay,' I smiled, feeling strengthened.

'Plus, this is secretly better. If I'm not the one giving you away to Milo, that means I get to keep you to myself.' We both giggled and said our goodbyes. As I hung up, I heard a male voice in the next room with the girls.

'That had better not be you, Milo Martinovic,' I pushed the door open as I spoke. 'It's bad luck to see the bride… Oh, Nikola.' I recovered quickly, surprised to see Milo's father in the house. 'Thank you for coming today.' I felt a little puzzled to see him before the wedding.

'You look beautiful, Kat. My son is a lucky man, and I am a lucky grandfather.' He kissed me on both cheeks.

I tried to think of a polite way to ask what are you doing here? Nik seemed to read my mind.

'Milo told me about the delays with your family getting here, and how there's no one to walk you down the aisle,' he started. I had assumed I'd walk with Luka instead, although I was a little worried he'd say some dirty joke half way down that would ruin the mood. 'It's your choice but I thought ... maybe I could help?' He offered his arm, as though he was about to walk with me. I took it and stood by his side.

'That's so kind of you, Nikola,' I said. I hadn't thought of him, but now he was here I realised it could work. I was worried about Milo, though. With all the animosity he'd felt towards his father, I didn't know if he'd want him to play such a key role in the wedding. Natalija seemed to share my concern, frowning as she watched us.

'I think Milo wanted you seated at the front,' she said, more diplomatic than I would have expected.

'I asked Milo's permission first, of course,' Nik said. 'He said it was perfect.'

I sighed with relief. Agreeing to have his father walk me down the aisle was a big step for him. Nik had redeemed himself in so many ways recently. Family was important. It was a lesson I'd learnt so many times in Montenegro.

The whole party looked at me expectantly.

'Well. What are we waiting for? We have a wedding to go to!' The others cheered, and I let Nik guide me blindly to my future.

'No, wait, wait!' I shouted.

They all froze.

'Pregnancy bladder. I have to go to the loo!' I ran back up the stairs.

I adjusted my dress after getting out of the taxi. The bridal party drew the eyes of everyone milling about on the street behind Café Lompar. Rosa told me the aisle had been set up through the middle of the restaurant, with the ceremony taking place at the front, facing the sea. This meant I'd need to enter via the kitchen, which felt appropriate.

The hot air in the taxi hadn't done too much damage on my curled hair. I swiped under both eyes, pleased my powder was still in place despite the mid-day sun. I hadn't thought of how difficult it would be to wear so much lace on a hot Montenegrin day. We could hear chatter inside, our guests growing impatient. And Milo was inside. My groom, waiting for his bride to arrive, and the rest of our lives to start.

Music began, with Rosa's cousin playing Montenegrin tunes on an old guitar. We stepped into the kitchen through the back entrance. My stomach churned. I knew it wasn't morning sickness this time but wedding jitters. An entirely new and more pleasant feeling.

The kitchen was filled with wonderful cooking smells already. David smiled as I came past. His Ensambla team had been hard at work since this morning, recreating the menu I'd planned. I knew the food would be delicious, and I was grateful to him for helping. Even if they were responsible for the turmoil of this summer, I had a feeling working side by side was going to be a lot easier from now on. And getting married at Café Lompar was better than any island. I smiled at him and he winked back.

'Let's go.' I nodded and Maria started the procession ahead of me, her blush dress swishing at her feet. Natalija followed her, then Rosa, who was standing in for Laura.

It was our turn. There was no going back now. I felt Nik adjust his arm, stand up straighter. His excitement bolstered me, and I gripped on tight to him. I felt I was five years old again, being led into nursery for my first day away from my parents.

We pushed through the restaurant door, and emerged into a sea of smiling faces. Fairy lights had been strung in a canopy across the Café Lompar ceiling, and a mixture of the Café Lompar and Ensambla chairs formed rows for the spectators, tightly packed in to the space. I had never seen the restaurant looking so beautiful; it was totally surreal.

We drifted towards the front, where a flowered archway had been set up just before the restaurant frontage. Cream and pink roses framed the glittering Adriatic.

And there was Milo.

He turned, his grey suit perfectly tailored and fitted to his body. He looked even more handsome than the first time I'd laid eyes on him. My man, my world, my everything. And the father of my children. I realised I was smiling, grinning from ear to ear, and so was he through his tears.

'You look,' he sighed as we approached, 'the most beautiful sight I've ever seen.'

'You too.' I let out a laugh, a mixture of nerves and relief. Nik gave me one more tearful squeeze then retreated to join Rosa on the front row. Luka stood next to Milo, wearing a matching suit and beaming at me.

'We are gathered here today to celebrate the love between Milo Martinovic and Katherine Lompar...'

The ceremony began. It was a blur, a wonderful, lovely blur of joy and excitement. I couldn't keep my eyes from Milo and his stayed locked on mine throughout, through the readings and the obligatory laugh when a pause was given for any objections.

In the moment's silence, I suddenly heard shuffling sounds, heavy footsteps, and a squeal from the back of the restaurant. Who was that?

Milo and I both turned.

'We made it!' I recognised Aunt Claire and Laura, before Mum and Neil came shuffling in behind them at the back. They were like a mirage. I could see they were ruffled and tired but thrilled to have caught the end of the ceremony. I was so grateful they had made the journey. Mum caught my eye and we beamed at one another.

The officiant cleared their throat and I turned back to my groom, remembering we hadn't actually said our vows yet.

'Milo, I promise to keep you as my favourite person, to love your perfect imperfections, to listen to your endless talk about boats, to bore you with my cooking obsessions, to be the best parent I can be alongside you, and to always be one hundred percent myself around you.' I repeated the vows we'd spent weeks perfecting, our own authentic words.

'Kat, do you take this man to be your husband?'

Just two words, and the rest was history.

'You may now kiss your bride.'

'Yes!' I screamed, once I'd kissed him, and Milo lifted me in the air.

And now finally my family could run towards me. The rest of our guests got to their feet to applaud. Mum got to us first, and Milo and I held her tight, so relieved she was here. Neil pilled in, followed by Ollie, then Luka, and Rosa. Here, in this moment, I felt the happiest I had ever felt in my life.

'Let's party!' Luka shouted.

The clinking of glass interrupted the chat I was having with Rosa, and I turned to see Milo's father Nik stand up. 'It's time for the first dance.' He beamed at us. 'Husband and wife, Mr. and Mrs. Martinovic.'

Milo gave Nik a hug, and then turned to offer a hand to me, reaching out dramatically. I pretended to ponder for a moment before accepting. I felt so much joy, my face ached from smiling.

The restaurant had been arranged into two long tables to accommodate everyone, and we'd all mixed together, Montenegrins and Brits, as we chatted and ate David's delicious appetisers and Buzara main course. The tables were now pushed back to create a dance floor, and our guests spilled out of the front of the restaurant as well, where fairy lights and lanterns twinkled against the backdrop of the inky Adriatic Sea. Our original venue, the island was visible, reminding us of what could have been. I decided I liked this better. Our restaurant team had excelled themselves.

I followed Milo through the crowd to the dance floor, past our Café Lompar tribe. Lovro and Dav were standing in matching blue suits, with Lovro's arms strung around Dav's waist. Maria was clinking her champagne flute against Ana's, and Bojan and Ivan were in a heated discussion about the merits of paprika as a seasoning. Luka trying to chat to Ana, who kept glancing at Maria and subtly turning her shoulder away.

And next to them was my UK family. Mum, Claire, Laura and

Liam, all laughing explosively at Liam goofing around with a straw. Nik and Natalija were listening diligently to Neil and Ollie recount the drama of the journey from Manchester airport. Rosa was draining a glass of Prosecco and looking around for Luka. My heart was laden with love for all of them and the many others that had joined our special day.

Ed Sheeran's voice rose from the speaker, sending a shiver up my arms. It was cheesy but his song *Perfect* was the only choice for our first dance. It had been the song playing as Milo proposed to me. He spun me round and lifted me up in a move worthy of a Strictly professional, something we'd practised for weeks.

'I'm surprised you can still lift me,' I whispered in his ear.

'You lift me up every day,' Milo whispered back.

Everyone cheered and I turned around. 'That's the only routine we've got folks,' I laughed, hoping they weren't expecting more. I moved in to nestle my arms around Milo's neck and we swayed to the music.

I wanted to absolutely savour this moment forever, heaven, until the little surprise we had planned kicked in, and the music changed into the opening strums of *Despacito*.

'Everyone up!' Milo shouted and the dancing begun. Mum came straight over, lacing her arms around us both.

'That was so beautiful,' she said. Milo broke off to twirl her round. Nik was offering his hand to me. I gratefully took it.

'I didn't know you had moves like this,' I said. Nik was a natural. His hips were on fire now the Latin music had started.

'Me and Lucija were quite the dancers,' he chuckled. 'I've still got it.'

'Nik, thank you so much for your help today. I want you to

know that I'm so glad you're here.' I watched him smile. 'I know Milo is too. He may not show it, but he's really happy to have you back in his life.'

'This is all thanks to you. You're a star, Kat, an angel.'

'Excuse me, what are you doing with my wife?' Milo asked, as Nik dipped me towards the floor. We all giggled, and I felt giddy with joy.

As the night went on and I watched people get more and more drunk around me, I started to feel very sober. Luka was performing some kind of one-legged dance move, and he had Milo's tie wrapped around his head. I nearly got trampled by Lovro gyrating around with Dav to Beyonce's *Single Ladies*. This was when being pregnant wasn't so fun. I cast around to see how much cake was left. If I couldn't drink at my own wedding, I could definitely eat, and no one would notice if I had a second slice of David's butterscotch and crunchy toffee cake, I reasoned to myself.

I noticed Mum sitting at a table with Rosa and Claire. Claire was speaking and Mum had her hand over her mouth, her forehead lined and stressed. I stiffened. Something was wrong. Oh God. My heart started to race as I walked over. Claire's eyes looked like they were going to pop out of her head and Rosa had put an arm round her.

'Is everything alright?' I asked as I reached them.

'Oh Kat,' Claire said, noticing me and dabbing her eyes. 'Go on, enjoy your night with your Adonis husband. Ignore us.'

'I need to sit down and this is my wedding. Tell me what's going on?'

Mum gave me a warning look.

'I was just telling these two.' Claire took a breath. 'Well, put it this way, you're not the only one having morning sickness.'

'What!' I asked, my brain struggling to compute. I gasped. 'Laura?!'

'No, thank God,' Claire laughed ironically. 'No, I can't believe it either. But somehow I'm about four weeks' pregnant!'

EPILOGUE – SIX MONTHS LATER

🌹 Grace 🌹

'Ema Lucija, but we'll call her just Ema. Lucija was Milo's mother's name,' Kat explained. 'And Lejla Grace. If we'd had a boy, I would have chosen Danilo.'

'Well, I think they are lovely names and they suit them both perfectly. Not that I can tell them apart yet,' I laughed.

'Ema's nose is upturned just slightly more than Lejla's.' Kat cradled Ema in her arms, and gazed lovingly at her sleeping baby, wrapped in a crocheted blanket, her long, dark lashes resting on her cheeks. Next to the bed, Milo held Lejla, cooing and kissing her, a carbon copy of the twin in her mother's arms. Kat and Milo were both cocooned in the baby bubble, hardly daring to take their eyes from the sleeping infants. Neil had pulled up a chair next to me, seeming right at home amongst us all.

'They both definitely have your nose,' I said, 'and Milo's and Dad's dark hair.'

Kat nodded and closed her eyes for a moment, wincing as she shifted in the hospital bed.

'Stitches?'

'Hmm, but I'm okay,' Kat said. 'They did give us a bit of a fright, coming early as they did.'

Kat's room looked onto the carpark. A fine drizzle was falling.

It was the end of February and a chilly seven degrees. Podgorica, being close to the sea, rarely saw frost but inland the mountains had the remnants of snow.

I thought back to the last time I was in the hospital at Podgorica, when Rosa had that infection, and it felt as if she might not survive. That was when I decided to invest in Café Lompar. It was still incredible to think how much our lives had changed. For the better.

'I just didn't feel right,' said Kat. 'I told Milo I had this pain in my back and he started panicking. You know how he fusses.'

Milo rolled his eyes. 'Was I right to insist that you get yourself checked at the hospital?'

'This time,' Kat conceded. 'Anyway, the pain got worse as we approached the hospital and the staff rushed out with a wheelchair. And, well, it all happened so fast. The little buggers were coming. Milo looked as if he's seen a ghost. I was dilated seven centimetres.'

'She was howling in pain,' Milo said, squeezing her hand.

'You'd be howling if you had twins about to come out from your vagina,' Kat said. She stroked Ema's cheek. 'This little one came first, followed by Lejla, twelve minutes later.'

'She was in distress,' Milo continued. I'd heard the details a few times already but didn't mind hearing them again.

'That's why they used the ventouse. So I had to have stitches. She gave us a fright and now she's being a fusspot taking milk.'

'Do you know when you'll be out?' I asked, as a nurse in light blue scrubs entered the room and spoke in Montenegrin to Milo.

He turned to Kat. 'She wants to take your temperature.'

Kat nodded, 'I did understand that.'

'Open,' the nurse told Kat and placed the thermometer under her tongue. 'It's good,' she said after a couple of minutes. 'Later, midwife come and check stitches.'

'Well, she was quite abrupt,' I said, as she left the room.

'They are lovely,' Kat insisted. 'It's the language thing, I think. I'm hoping to be out in two or three days. They tend to keep mothers and babies longer in hospital than they do in the UK. They want to make sure Lejla takes her milk. My boobs are getting sore and I don't think I'm doing it right. The breast-feeding nurse is coming tomorrow to give me a lesson. I'm hopeless at it and poor Lejla isn't getting enough milk.' Kat was suddenly tearful and I recognised the rollercoaster of emotions most new mothers felt.

'Hush, now. You're doing a great job,' I said, kissing Kat's head. The dark shadows under her eyes were testament to her lack of sleep.

I was pleased she could be so comfortable and open in front of Neil. She could talk about cracked nipples without a trace of self-consciousness.

Suddenly, my phone buzzed on the bedside table. Claire was Facetiming me, her face, rounder than usual, filling the screen.

'Hello, Grandma,' she said. 'Neil, how do you feel about dating a grandmother?'

'Bloody marvellous,' he grinned.

'It's time to wear turtle necks and dust off the SAGA brochures. How's Kat?' Claire asked.

'She's right here. We've invaded her hospital room.' I panned the camera around to take in Kat, lying against her pillows, and Milo and the babies. There was squealing from Claire's phone as

Laura looked over her shoulder. 'Aren't they beautiful?' I said, more of a statement than a question.

'Adorable,' Claire said. 'Oh my God, they look so much like Kat. How are you feeling, Kat?'

I handed the phone over to her. 'I'm fine, Auntie Claire. Well, tired, of course. How are you?'

Claire moved the camera down to show her rounded stomach. 'I'm twenty-six weeks and I already feel like I'm going to burst. They call me a geriatric mother. Can you believe that?'

Laura's lip curled. 'Well, you are old to be pregnant, Mum. It's embarrassing, honestly.'

'I've got news for you, young lady. Your father and I having sex is an expression of our feelings.'

'Ugh, for God's sake. It's disgusting!' Laura put her fingers in her ears.

'I love winding her up,' Claire said. 'It's the best.'

'Congratulations, Laura,' I said, changing the subject. 'Mum told me you had your offer at Nottingham for chemistry. You must be thrilled.'

'I can't believe it,' she said. 'And Liam's just accepted Bristol to do Computer Science, so he won't be too far away.'

'Just as the twins are off your hands, you'll have a little one to take care of,' I told Claire, stating the obvious.

'Tell me about it. Stu and I lie in bed and ask ourselves what the hell we've done.'

'Is Stu back in work?'

Claire nodded. 'He's religiously following the physio's exercises. I think he's scared he won't cope with the baby if he doesn't take care of himself.'

'Are you still ravenous?' I asked Claire.

'Yep. Last night I must have eaten half a pound of Emmental smothered in mango chutney. Stu is forever rushing to the garage to satisfy my latest strange cravings!'

'It was banana and marmite sandwiches for me,' Kat said and everyone laughed.

After Claire rang off, I couldn't resist asking, 'Can I hold one of them?'

Gingerly and slowly, Kat placed Ema in my arms. 'Look, she hasn't stirred,' I said. The weight of her in my arms felt wonderful: warm, comforting and right. I remembered how incredible it felt to hold Kat for the first time. And now I was a grandmother. 'What did you call your grandmother, Milo?' I asked.

'*Baka,* and *Deda* for my grandfather.'

'Have you decided yet?' Kat asked.

I shook my head. 'Perhaps Nana?' I thought it made me sound ancient, but now they were here, I didn't seem to mind so much.

'Kat? Milo?' Rosa's head popped around the door. She entered the room looking glamorous in a grey coat with a fur collar, bringing in the cold air and a cloud of perfume. Behind her came Marko, the man she had been seeing since October. He lived in Tivat and she had known him for years. 'I never thought of him other than a friend,' she'd told us. 'Until that day, on a whim, I called in his gallery and heard him talk about his paintings. The passion he has. It is very attractive.' Marko was over six foot, a great bear of a man, who towered over Rosa's petite frame. Rosa was fiery but Marko was calm. They were Yin and Yang. Even Luka seemed to approve.

Rosa kissed Kat's cheek and hugged her and then Milo. 'How are you, Kat? Oh, aren't they beautiful? Perfect!' It was the first time she had seen the babies, waiting until I arrived from the UK, sensitive enough to make sure I saw them first. Milo handed Lejla over to her and she cooed as she gazed at her.

'Where's Luka? Wasn't he able to come?' Kat looked disappointed.

'Pfft! He is outside talking to a nurse.' We all laughed.

Suddenly, the door opened and Luka came in. 'Well, here I am to rescue poor Milo from all these women.' His smile widened when he saw the twins, one in my arms and the other in his mother's. 'Girls, your Uncle Luka is here to teach you the ways of the world. To protect you from men who will take advantage.'

'I think the life lessons can wait a while' Kat teased, perking up. 'They already have a style guru in their Aunt Natalija.'

'She's coming from Milan next week,' Milo said, proud. 'She managed to get some time off from her new fashion job.'

'Do you want to hold Ema?' I asked Luka.

He looked horrified. 'Should I? Am I allowed?' I handed her over to Luka and he stood there frozen, as if she were an unexploded bomb and the slightest movement might set her off. 'What if I drop her?'

'Stop worrying,' Kat said.

The door suddenly swung open and an officious nurse with a flushed face appeared, her finger to her lips. 'Shh. Visiting is over. Five minutes.'

When she left, we erupted in laughter.

'You lot will be banned from the hospital,' Kat laughed.

Milo stood up, 'Let's have a selfie!' He stood at the end of the bed and we gathered around Kat and the twins. Luka handed Ema back to Kat.

'Say Emmental,' I grinned, making a mental note to ask Milo to send it to me so I could hang the photo on Café Lompar's gallery. Our lovely but crazy, ever-expanding family.

ACKNOWLEDGEMENTS

Writing a book is really hard work, and there are two of us! We have to thank Honno, firstly then, our marvellous publisher, who helped us keep the faith. On behalf of all your authors, we are so grateful for the work you do in supporting Welsh women authors. What would we do without you? For our *Love at Café Lompar* series, though, we would like to thank in particular the lovely Janet Thomas, our editor, who is so thoughtful and sensitive of our feelings. Janet has the superpower of being able to read our minds and sharpen our writing. Thank you for your patience. Thank you, too, to the wonderful Lindsay Ashford, who we actually got to meet in person this year and who rescued our book from the slush pile almost two years ago. Thanks to Yasmin Begum and Simone Greenwood, who have marketed our books and do such a grand job! We were thrilled to be shortlisted for the Katie Fforde Debut Romantic Novelists Award for our first book *Love at Café Lompar* and what a thrill it was to mingle with 'real' authors in London in March.

Closer to home, we are grateful for the continuing support of friend and fellow author, Nadine Riley, our family and friends, and Anna's fiancé, Frazer Conway, (who makes a secret appearance in this, our second book), for cooking, cleaning, and giving much needed support whilst the hard work of writing goes on! Thank you, too, for the support of all those who bought and read our first book and we sincerely hope you like this one, *A Wedding at Café Lompar*. We're keeping everything crossed!

ABOUT HONNO

Honno Welsh Women's Press was set up in 1986 by a group of women who felt strongly that women in Wales needed wider opportunities to see their writing in print and to become involved in the publishing process. Our aim is to develop the writing talents of women in Wales, give them new and exciting opportunities to see their work published and often to give them their first 'break' as a writer. Honno is registered as a community co-operative. Any profit that Honno makes is invested in the publishing programme. Women from Wales and around the world have expressed their support for Honno. Each supporter has a vote at the Annual General Meeting. For more information and to buy our publications, please write to Honno at the address below, or visit our website: www.honno.co.uk

Honno, D41 Hugh Owen Building,
Aberystwyth University, Aberystwyth, SY23 3DY,
Tel. 01970 623150, www.honno.co.uk

Honno Friends
We are very grateful for the support
of all our Honno Friends.